Praise for The Legend of Valentine

"Collins's piercing exploration of faith, sacrifice, and redemption gives this epic love story an intricate depth often missing in similar titles."

— BOOK LIFE by PUBLISHERS WEEKLY

"A complex and ambitious adventure for lovers of ancient historical romance."

— KIRKUS REVIEWS

"An incredible story of Valentine's life—an immersive tale with a surprising twist that shows that true love never dies."

— THE HISTORICAL FICTION COMPANY

"Collins has written a riveting, page-turning story about an elusive historical figure we celebrate every February the fourteenth. In his cinematic account, we get a fascinating look at how he might have lived and loved in Ancient Rome!"

— SAN FRANCISCO BOOK REVIEW

"Collins's creation of a vivid interpretation and exploration of the legend of Saint Valentine deserves widespread acclaim, and will reach a large audience of historical fiction readers."

— MIDWEST BOOK REVIEW

"The Legend of Valentine is an entertaining historical novel about action, love, and what it means to have faith. In time, the storylines intersect via Valentine himself, leading to a final plot twist that befits the preceding spirited adventure and that exceeds expectations, resulting in final satisfaction.

— FOREWORD BOOK REVIEWS

"THE LEGEND OF VALENTINE delivers an arresting fusion of meticulously researched historical fiction, star-crossed romance, and spiritual rebirth."

— INDIE READER

Readers looking for a historical novel full of drama and intriguing characters will enjoy The Legend of Valentine. The narrative is cinematic, with lots of action, conflict, and betrayals. The characters are well-drawn and distinct."

— BLUE INK REVIEW

"The Legend of Valentine is a powerful tale about love's triumph over adversity. Collins melds history and myth, offering readers a unique perspective on a timeless story."

— READERS FAVORITE

THE LEGEND *of* VALENTINE

SHELDON COLLINS

Based on a Screenplay Written by Sheldon Collins & Justin Hogan
Story by Lee Holden Jr., Sheldon Collins & Justin Hogan

ISBN(eBook): 979-8-9913624-4-3
ISBN(Paperback): 979-8-9913624-1-2
ISBN(Hardcover): 979-8-9913624-0-5
ISBN(Audiobook): 979-8-9913624-2-9
ISBN(Special Edition): 979-8-9913624-5-0

Title Production by The BookWhisperer

Cover Design by Tracy Lyn

Map Illustration by Filip Šeršík

Author's Photo Credit: Philip Alderton

Hutchinson & Collins
PUBLISHING LLC

This book is lovingly dedicated to the women who have inspired me the most throughout this journey:

—To my wife, whose unwavering support carried me through countless nights of reading early drafts aloud, always cheering me on.

—To my daughter, who, as a neurodiverse individual thriving in a predominantly neurotypical world, fills me with awe by her courage and determination to take on every challenge she faces.

—To my mother, an artist herself, who has always encouraged my creative passions.

FOREWORD

In 2006, I wrote a screenplay about Saint Valentine, a figure whose legend has captivated me for years. As an acupuncturist, energy worker, and *qigong* healer, I saw clear parallels between Valentine's story and the timeless role of healers throughout history. To me, Valentine was not only a man of love and faith but a healer in his own right.

When I shared this screenplay with my friend Sheldon Collins, I knew it had the potential to become something extraordinary. Collins further developed it, adding historical depth and emotional complexity. Though the film has not yet materialized, Collins's dedication never wavered. His passion for the story led him to conduct extensive research and ultimately adapt the screenplay into this beautifully written novel.

As an award-winning filmmaker, Collins brings a unique storytelling skill set to his writing. His talent for crafting vivid, immersive narratives shines throughout the novel. With keen pacing and deep character development, Collins has written a story that is both historically rich and emotionally resonant.

What strikes me most about *The Legend of Valentine* is how Collins captures the essence of the Valentine legend while grounding it in historical accuracy. He skillfully weaves the world of ancient Rome with themes that resonate today—love, resilience, and courage in the face of adversity.

At its core, *The Legend of Valentine* tells one of history's greatest untold love stories. For centuries, such tales have connected people, and this epic is no exception. Collins has bridged the gap between an ancient world and our modern celebration, reminding us that the enduring power of love transcends time.

It has been a privilege to witness this story evolve, from its early screenplay origins to the remarkable novel it is today. I am honored to have been part of its inception. Collins has crafted a powerful work with *The Legend of Valentine*, one that will captivate readers and stay with them long after the final page.

Prepare to be transported, to be moved, and to witness the enduring power of love through the lens of a man who defied an empire.

Lee Holden

Qigong Master, Energy Healer, TV Personality
Author of *Ready, Set, Slow* and *7 Minutes of Magic*
Founder of Holden Qigong

Introduction

Despite Valentine's celebrated acts of compassion and defiance in the third century, his life remains shrouded in mystery. Over time, different versions of his story have emerged, with some historians even suggesting he may have lived in the fourth century—although this view is less widely accepted. While many revered him as a saint, he was never officially canonized. In 1969, the Catholic Church removed Valentine's Day from the General Roman Calendar, seeking to align the liturgical calendar with historically verified figures. Despite this, Valentine's Day evolved into a global phenomenon, transcending cultural and national boundaries. Today, it is celebrated by over a billion people, dedicated to expressing love in all its forms every February 14.

Yet, the question remains: *was Valentine real or simply a legend?*

ALEMANNI
GOTI
ERULI
Germania Superior
Raetia
Noricum
Pannonia
Gallia
BATTLE WITH GOTHS
AQUILEIA
ALEMANNI ATTACK
MEDIOLANUM
SIEGE OF MEDIOLANUM
RAVENNA
DEODATUS VILLA
GENUA
FLORENTIA
Illyricum
PISAE
ARRETIUM
INTERAMNA
Corsica
ROMA
TIBUR
VILLA HADRIANA
BAIAE
NEAPOLIS
BRUNDISIUM
Sardinia
MARE INTERNUM
IMPERO PERSIANO
Sicilia
SYRACUSAE
CARTHAGO
Africa
NOMADI

PROLOGUE

BEAR & ROSE

"The memory of a first love is a lasting shadow upon the heart."
—OVID

He was just nine years old. She was twelve. They had nicknames for each other: Rose, after the flowers she adored, and Bear, from the time he saved her life—a bond that would never break.

Together, they roamed the woodlands near their home by the foothills of Apenninus Mons, close to the town of Interamna, where dense forests surrounded their village. They moved like untamed spirits, their laughter echoing among the trees as they darted through the undergrowth. She glided through the forest with the ethereal grace of a nymph from ancient myths, her laughter blending with the melody of her movements. At times, her voice lifted in songs of love, sweet and pure. Meanwhile, he dashed from one imagined battle to the next, wielding his wooden sword with the fervor of a seasoned warrior, each swing full of boundless enthusiasm.

"To the river, Bear!" Rose sang out as she ran across a log.

"The hour grows late!" he cautioned, his high-pitched, prepuberty voice rang out.

"The time matters not! A dip in the waters awaits us!" Rose urged, racing ahead, always taking the lead. Other girls stayed at home and dared not escape to play in the woods, but Rose was different.

He grinned at her infectious enthusiasm and followed in her wake, his heart pounding with the thrill of their next adventure. Together, they plunged deeper into the forest as they walked toward the cool embrace of their favorite swimming hole.

Upon reaching the river's edge, they wasted no time shedding their tunics and sandals, leaving only their undergarments, eager to immerse themselves in the water's cool embrace. They leaped into the river with joyful shouts, sending droplets flying in all directions as they splashed and frolicked like carefree spirits. In their youth, they had always done everything together, never questioning whether it was proper to swim half-naked in each other's company. But as they played in the river that late summer day, new feelings quietly began to emerge.

"No splashing," Bear protested with a laugh.

"And who says?" Rose challenged, her spirit undeterred as she sent a cascade of water his way and dove beneath the surface.

As she emerged, his gaze was immediately drawn to her changed form. "Your breasts!" he exclaimed, pointing at her chest.

"What's wrong with them?" she examined them with concern.

"They've grown!" he cried with surprise.

"They have not!" Rose retorted, cheeks flushing with embarrassment.

"Yes…they have!" he insisted, laughing.

"Well, I suppose that is what happens to girls, Bear," Rose replied with a shrug as she escaped the water, squeezing her sandy-blonde hair dry, and began to don her clothing.

"That's strange," he remarked, following her.

They made their way to a nearby log and settled down.

Rose's expression grew somber. All day, she had been dreading the moment when she would have to share the bad news with him, but it had to be done and the sooner the better. "There's something I must tell you, Bear," she began, her voice tinged with sadness.

"What is it?" he asked, his brow furrowing with concern.

"The emperor has summoned my father to take work in Rome—and we are leaving today," Rose revealed.

"Today?!" Bear exclaimed.

"I'm afraid so. My uncle is also unwell, and my father has just received word. We are to stay with him."

"When will you return?" he asked, his heart sinking.

"I don't know, Bear," Rose admitted, her eyes brimming with tears.

His expression darkened as the full weight of their impending separation settled over him.

"You must be happy for me," Rose implored. "With my father's new promotion, he's confident I'll be married off to a noble—or even a celebrated hero!"

With a determined look in his eye, Bear stood tall and declared, "I'll be a celebrated hero one day! I'll save hundreds, perhaps even thousands, of Roman lives."

Rose couldn't help but giggle at his earnest proclamation. The fact that Bear thought first of saving lives rather than taking them only deepened her affection for him. "I'm certain you will be, Bear," she replied softly. "And there is no higher duty than being of service to those in need."

An awkward silence fell between them, the weight of their looming farewell hanging heavy in the air. As they sat side-by-side on the log, the sounds of the river filled the silence, a bittersweet reminder of the fleeting nature of their childhood innocence.

"You could be of service now... if you like," Rose declared, raising an eyebrow flirtatiously.

"What do you mean?"

"If I am married off, I will need to know how to kiss a man," Rose explained, her words carrying a sense of vulnerability.

Bear stared at her in shock. "You cannot be serious," he replied, recoiling from the suggestion.

"Please, Bear. I've never kissed a man before. I must practice now—I've reached the age when society may welcome me," she implored.

"I don't kiss maidens—I'm a soldier!" he declared, attempting to deflect her. In truth, he was still a child, while she had already begun puberty. As with most things in their relationship, she was always one step ahead of him.

Rose peered at him with eyes of daggers. "You disappoint me, Bear."

He sighed deeply, then stood up, resigning himself to this daunting task. "Very well."

She sprang up excitedly. They stood facing each other, Rose towering over Bear, her height and poise only deepening his discomfort. With a deep breath, she leaned down to kiss him, her lips hovering close to his as he awkwardly closed his eyes and puckered. But just as their lips were about to touch, Rose pulled back.

"This isn't right," she exclaimed as she sat back on the log.

"What is it?" he demanded, his heart now racing at the thought of actually kissing her.

"You're at a disadvantage," Rose replied, her gaze lingering on his stature.

"What do you mean?" he asked

"The man I am to wed will likely be taller than me. It makes little sense to practice with somebody of your height," she explained, her voice tinged with defeat.

Bear's frustration was evident, but inspiration quickly lit his eyes. Scanning the riverbed, he announced, "I have an idea." Quickly springing into action, he gathered flat rocks and assembled them into a makeshift platform. With a satisfied grin, he climbed on top, elevating himself slightly above Rose's height. "There. How's this?"

Rose's smile widened at his ingenuity. "Perfect," she replied, her eyes sparkling with amusement as she stood up and approached him.

As her lips neared him, he leaned down awkwardly while balancing on the rocks, his heart pounding in anticipation. Suddenly, their lips met. The sensation sent a surprising shiver down each of their spines. But as they drew closer, Bear's balance betrayed him, and he toppled into the river with a startled shriek.

Emerging from the water, soaked and sputtering, he caught Rose doubled over in laughter. "You must work on your balance, Bear!" she teased, her laughter echoing through the forest.

"I will never do that again!" he declared, his pride wounded.

Rose, still chuckling, offered a playful retort: "Yes, you will!"

"No, I will not!"

Rose turned and ran off through the forest toward a meadow, her laughter trailing behind her as she playfully chanted, "Yes, you will! Yes, you will!"

"Wait for me!" he called, pausing briefly to strap on his sandals before resuming his chase. Suddenly, he halted and hid behind a tree, his gaze fixed on a formidable figure advancing across the meadow on horseback. It was Rose's father—the town's jailer, a man feared by many and someone Bear instinctively knew to avoid.

"Daughter, the hour has come," her father declared as he approached Rose and drew her onto his steed. "And how many times must I remind you not to wander off into the forest without permission?"

"Wait." She hesitated, her gaze darting back toward the forest in search of Bear's familiar figure, but he was nowhere in sight.

"What is it?" her father pressed, his brow furrowed as he followed her gaze.

"It's nothing," Rose replied, lowering her head. She knew better than to reveal her relationship with Bear, wary of her overly protective father's reaction.

With a gentle kick, her father urged the horse forward, and they departed from the forest.

Hardly able to contain his emotions, Bear stepped out from behind a tree and called out to her: "Rose!"

Unheard by her father, she turned in her saddle and gave Bear a small, heartfelt wave in farewell. Bear waved back, feeling a hollow ache begin to settle in his heart. As the horse picked up speed and galloped away, Rose clutched her father and turned her head forward. A tear rolled down Bear's cheek as the truth dawned on him—his feelings for Rose ran deeper than friendship. Silently, he had always imagined them growing old together, a future he had never dared voice to his first and only true love.

CHAPTER 1

PROTECT THE EMPRESS

"Fortune favors the bold."
—VIRGIL

268 AD

In the shadow of the towering, snowcapped Alps, the rhythmic march echoed the relentless pulse of Rome's ambition. A brisk river coursed through the rugged terrain of the northern *Italia* valleys, as a crisp breeze carried the biting chill of the coming winter.

Clad in gleaming armor, each soldier bore the weight of duty with practiced ease, their movements unhindered by the protective metal encasing them. Their rounded helmets, adorned with broad cheek guards, offered a steadfast defense against enemy blows. Long swords rested sheathed in scabbards, and spears were held ready for battle.

An imperial *carruca*, a luxurious covered carriage reserved for the highest of station, commanded attention at the heart of the procession, its four sturdy wheels rolling with purpose over the uneven terrain. Two soldiers expertly guided the powerful quartet of horses, ensuring the carriage's steady advance. Flanking the carriage was an elite unit of the Roman Army, the Praetorian Guard, escorted by additional military forces.

Crafted from fine timber and adorned with meticulous detail, the carriage radiated an air of opulence and authority. Along its sides, the royal purple insignia gleamed.

Valentinus Romanus—known in the annals of history as Valentine—stood at the forefront of a small group of infantrymen, following the stately carriage. At twenty-six, he had matured into a man of imposing yet not overwhelming stature, his Adonis-like presence exuding raw masculinity, as evidenced by the many maidens who put themselves in his path everywhere he went. Now, among the ranks of his comrades, he was a paragon of strength and vigor, his physique sculpted by years of relentless toil and adversity. Muscles rippled beneath his tunic, bearing witness to his unwavering commitment to physical excellence. His rugged features bore the marks of countless battles, and a flattering shadow of sharp stubble adorned his jawline, adding to his hardened visage.

"Keep the pace, men! Who do we fight for?!" Valentine shouted.

"For Rome!" came the unified roar of the legionnaires.

Beside Valentine, slightly younger and shorter, strode Marius, his closest ally—a Christian who typically kept his faith private unless he was around his comrades.

Marius had a rugged, bulldog-like visage paired with a light-hearted and witty disposition, frequently serving as the beacon of morale for the group. With each stride, Marius's massive calves, sculpted by countless miles, propelled him forward with determined purpose.

"We haven't taken respite since summer. You should speak to the centurion—he will listen to you," Marius grumbled, glancing at Valentine.

"If I wish to secure a promotion, I doubt voicing complaints to my superiors will serve me well," Valentine replied.

"I suppose you're right," Marius acknowledged, offering a wry smile.

In Valentine's wake, a cadre of seasoned warriors, his most trusted companions and his chosen family, marched, each marked by the scars of endless conflicts.

Among them was Linus, the resident jokester. Nearby loomed Efebus, a towering colossus whose imposing stature and silent demeanor commanded respect.

Alongside marched Proculo, a warrior whose fierceness in battle was unparalleled, yet he possessed a philosophical depth unusual for a soldier, complemented by a dry wit. "When you are promoted to officer, Valentine, I believe I will desert my post," Proculo interjected.

"And why is that, Proculo?" Valentine asked.

"I fear I may be safer as an outlaw," Proculo jested as the other men in their close circle chuckled. After years of fighting shoulder to shoulder, these men trusted one another deeply, forging bonds only those who have faced death together can form.

Behind Proculo stood Scaro and Albus, brothers whose features belied their contrasting personas. Scaro, the younger brother, often calculated his decisions before acting, yet he had a more laid-back approach to life. In contrast, Albus, the elder and more protective sibling, was notorious for taking action with little consideration of the consequences and was the more hardheaded of the two.

United by duty and valor, these seven brothers-in-arms wove a tapestry of courage and expertise, each contributing their unique prowess to the collective.

"At least our path leads back to Rome. Though I pray we find more righteous company and less sinful debauchery this time," Marius said with a smile, hinting at past mischief.

"I'm certain your Christian God will forgive you, brother. After all, he cannot expect us *all* to walk his righteous path," Valentine quipped.

"Yes, He can!" Marius replied enthusiastically as the rest of the men grinned, appreciating the humor in his seriousness.

"Marius, if your God is so powerful, why must he endure death only to rise again?" Linus asked mischievously.

"Not this again." Marius sighed.

"He makes a point, brother. Would it not be simpler to believe in gods who avert death?" Valentine added.

Marius comically prayed aloud: "Merciful Lord, grant me the

patience to endure the asinine intellects of my pigeon-head companions."

A wave of soft laughter spread among the men.

"Perhaps your God has already shown us mercy, Marius," Valentine remarked.

"And how is this?" Marius inquired.

"Ensuring the safe return of an empress to the Imperial Palace requires far more valor than enduring a boorish general's camp."

"Not all of us seek means to prove our valor, Valentine," Proculo teased.

"Indeed, Proculo. And not every boorish general requires a hundred soldiers to escort them on a diplomatic mission, like this empress we accompany," Marius added.

"Yet boorish generals do not appear as radiant as our empress," Linus added, smirking.

"That she is," Efebus affirmed with a smile.

"I've heard whispers she attracts admirers," Albus blurted out.

"Careful, Albus—the emperor would have your head if he heard you speak of the empress like that. Besides, your tavern maidens hardly qualify as credible sources for rumors," Linus quipped.

"I would wager our empress might find herself quite taken by our Valentine, given the opportunity," Scaro added.

Valentine rolled his eyes—his friends were always trying to push him back toward love and exploits with the fairer sex, much to his annoyance.

"He's not seeking love, Scaro. Isn't that right, Valentine?" Albus interjected, his tone brisk as he cast a meaningful glance at his younger brother.

"The days of falling prey to Cupid's arrows are behind me, brothers," Valentine declared.

"Except for the tavern maiden you had eyes for in Antioch," Marius teased.

"Who assured me she would never leave Carthage," Valentine retorted with a grin.

More laughter rippled through the group.

"You do seem to fancy the unavailable," Marius added.

"Keep your spirits high, Valentine. Cupid's arrow will find its mark again," Scaro reassured him, knowing all too well of Valentine's troubled past with women.

"Thank you, Scaro." Valentine's mind drifted to thoughts of Rose, his childhood love—the truest love he had ever known, though they'd been so young when they met. He wondered how she looked now, as a young maiden, and whether he would even recognize her. Would her beauty and spirit still captivate him? Was she even alive? These questions haunted him. He had once taken a stab at adult love, hoping to forget Rose, but it had ended in heartbreak. Since then, he had given up on the prospect entirely. Instead, he found solace in the camaraderie of his brothers and in the fleshly pleasures of women who couldn't break his heart or bring him unwanted trouble.

As these painful memories receded, Valentine snapped back to the present and said with firm resolve, "Scaro, should you ever catch me extending so much as a gesture of affection toward our empress, drinks shall be on me."

"Oh, we shall hold you to this," Marius said with a hint of playful challenge.

Chuckles echoed through their ranks as they continued to march through the valley, though Valentine's stern visage reflected his true inner sorrow. As the years had passed, Valentine doubted any woman could ever replace the love he had once felt for Rose. Yet, even he could not deny that the empress was, indeed, a beauty—one who fully warranted their overly protective retinue.

From a commanding perch atop the looming mountain, concealed within the cloak of shadows, lurked a menacing threat. A formidable contingent of fifty Alemanni lay in wait, poised to unleash a devastating ambush on the empress's entourage. These Germanic warriors, notorious for their fierce raids into Roman territory, exuded a ferocity that had shaken the empire in recent years. They brandished long, imposing swords with razor-sharp, double-edged blades and curved axes crafted for maximum devastation. Complementing this infantry's armament were stout shields and a cache of bows and arrows. An enduring enemy of Rome, the Germanic tribe stood resolute, eager to strike against the Romans.

Behind the scouts, additional Alemanni were busily soaking large hay bales, bound tightly with rope and soaked in oil. Nearby, small bonfires cast a flickering glow. Positioned adjacent to these fires, units of archers stood motionless, their gazes filled with hatred as they gazed down upon the legionnaires.

Amid this hidden assembly of warriors, an imposing Alemanni forced his way to the forefront. His bald head and untamed beard heralded the onset of the impending conflict.

"Angriff! Für die Ehre der Alamannen!" bellowed the outlander in his native tongue, commanding his men to attack in honor of the Alemanni.

Suddenly, the Alemanni ignited their torches, set the hay bundles ablaze, and unleashed them, letting them tumble down the hillside. The ropes that bound them eventually unraveled as they rolled, transforming them into blazing spheres that scorched the earth. Concurrently, the archers ignited their arrows, releasing a volley that filled the sky, creating a rain of iron.

The Romans, oblivious to the impending danger, continued their march toward the tumultuous river. Suddenly, surging infernos rolled down upon them, followed by the flaming arrows from above. The savage cries of the Alemanni pierced the air, striking a chilling note that seemed to freeze the soul.

"Take cover!" Valentine shouted, his eyes widening at the barrage of arrows and rolling bales of fire hurtling toward them.

Bloodcurdling screams erupted from the Romans as the blazing hay engulfed them, setting aflame the front ranks of soldiers. A deluge of arrows rained down next, finding their marks among the legionnaires. The sight of barbarians, having breached the Alps and now standing on Italia's soil, filled the Romans with a terror as consuming as the flames themselves.

"Protect the empress!" shouted a decurion, a commander of cavalry, his voice ringing out just before an arrow pierced his neck, silencing him instantly. The force of the impact threw him violently from his saddle, his life snuffed away before his body hit the ground, leaving behind the riderless steed.

Valentine whirled around, facing the grim reality of legionnaires falling in droves. The air was thick with the harsh stench of burning hay, charred flesh, and smoldering shrubs. Fire blazed through the underbrush, surging toward him. Behind him, his men braced, preparing for the imminent charge.

"To the river!" Valentine yelled to his men.

Valentine, Marius, and the rest of their infantry hastily discarded their spears before plunging into the tumultuous river—the weight of their armor already threatening to pull them under. The blazing hay bales hurtled over them, narrowly missing their mark.

Struggling against the current, Valentine fought to resurface, gasping for air as he finally emerged. The river's bend guided them toward a shallow bank where the water was waist-deep, allowing them to regain their footing. His gaze immediately locked onto the empress's carriage, now besieged by six Alemanni riding horses, locked in fierce combat with her guards.

The Praetorians fled from the battlefield's inferno. The carriage jolted and careened, its wheels rolling over the searing remains of Roman soldiers.

"The empress!" Linus shouted from the river as the men noticed her carriage race off.

Valentine scaled the riverbank with practiced precision, assisting each of his men as they climbed out of the river. A massive Alemannus charged at him, but Valentine swiftly blocked his ax swing and drove his sword into the enemy's chest. "Form on me!" he commanded his men. Silently, he vowed not to lose any of his friends.

More Alemanni surged forward with the fierce determination of a people intent on capturing Rome's empress, driven by vengeance for the many losses they had suffered at the hands of the legions.

Valentine and his men, their battle-tested unity unwavering, formed an unyielding defense. Swift as a serpent, Proculo engaged an Alemannus in combat, the clash of steel echoing through the air. Next to him, Linus slashed a bloody gash with a lightning stroke across a bearded Alemannus's head. Efebus, with a mighty swing of his sword, nearly decapitated two Alemanni in a single fluid motion.

Meanwhile, Albus was overpowered and pinned to the ground by an Alemannus clad in animal pelts. In a swift response, Scaro sprinted to his older brother's aid and drove his blade into the Alemannus's neck. The lifeless body collapsed, toppling onto Albus, who brushed the enemy aside and offered a quick nod of gratitude toward Scaro before resuming the fight. Suddenly, Valentine noticed the riderless horse navigating the turmoil of battle, its eyes widened with terror, mirroring the horrific scene around it.

"I'm going for the empress!" Valentine shouted at Marius while pointing toward the empress's carriage, swiftly entering the nearby forest.

"Go!" Marius spat as he sliced open an Alemannus's neck.

In a fluid motion, Valentine caught and leaped onto the back of the riderless horse. Gaining mastery over the steed in mere moments, he spurred it forward, accelerating into the thick of the chase.

The empress, usually a picture of elegance and grace, was jostled violently inside the royal carriage, her movements resembling a marionette in a storm. Her woolen *stola* and *palla* tore with each violent jerk, while her lavish jewels scattered like stars in the sky. Struggling to her feet, she staggered to the small window. As she peered outside, a hay barrel slammed into the carriage, shaking the ancient woodwork and causing the structure to groan under the pressure. Flames eagerly licked up the dry timber, quickly consuming it.

"Help!" she screamed, terrified.

The two soldiers driving the carriage resisted the onslaught valiantly, but the Alemanni attack was unyielding. Amid the chaos, one Alemannus chasing the carriage struck a low-hanging branch, unseating him from his horse.

Valentine's chase reached a fever pitch in the forest's shadowy depths. His mare, invigorated by its new rider, cut a swift path through the dense underbrush. Abruptly, two mounted Alemanni converged upon him, their approach silent from the shadows. In a lethal attack, they brandished their axes in unison, aiming for his head. Valentine ducked, deftly evading their deadly arcs and seized the reins from one of the shocked Alemannus, delivering a flurry of punches to his face before maneuvering his foe toward a gnarled tree. A resounding thud that momentarily reverberated through the forest followed.

Heart pounding, Valentine dodged the remaining Alemanni attack, urging his horse toward the beleaguered carriage. An arrow sliced through the air, skimming by his cheek. Behind him, other Alemanni pursued, their savage cries beating in his mind.

The empress's carriage was now a fiery vortex. Arrows continued to hammer its wooden frame. Amid the chaos, a desperate plea shattered the sounds of battle.

"Help! Get me out!" the empress's voice pierced the air.

Abruptly, an arrow struck one of the carriage drivers, piercing his shoulder. He released the reins and toppled beneath the spinning wheels.

As Valentine neared the carriage, he executed a daring leap from his horse. His body slammed into the carriage side, resulting in a desperate struggle for a secure grip. Flames scorched his fingers, threatening to undo his hold. In a heart-stopping moment, his grip faltered, leaving him dangling by one hand. His legs whipped against the ground. Summoning every ounce of his strength, Valentine hoisted himself up until his gaze met the empress's through the carriage's small window.

"Empress, I am here!" he shouted over the roar of flames and chaos.

"Help me, please!" she cried out.

As Valentine struggled to access the carriage's interior, his efforts were interrupted by the sudden onslaught of a sword-wielding Alemannus. In a swift, lethal motion, Valentine deflected the attack and speared the Alemannus in the stomach. The force of the blow stopped the attack cold, and the Alemannus tumbled backward, hitting the ground with a heavy thud.

A remaining driver endeavored to seize control once more to halt the carriage. Although, upon glancing over his shoulder, he met an arrow through his jaw. It struck with brutal efficiency as he collapsed off the carriage.

"Damn this cursed day," Valentine muttered.

The carriage continued to hurtle with reckless abandon toward the precipice of a daunting, rocky cliff, beyond which lay a lake's cold, dark water.

Valentine reached through the carriage opening, his arms

enveloping the empress. With a swift, protective pull, he freed her from the fiery carriage, holding her securely against him as they both gripped the side for support.

"Empress, we must jump!"

"I cannot!" she cried in terror as flames began to singe her hair.

Valentine cast a glance behind him. Realizing the imminent danger, the pursuing Alemanni halted their chase, unwilling to follow them to a certain death.

"We must! Now!" he yelled, yanking the empress into the abyss as the flaming carriage spiraled through the air beside them.

They howled, eyes wide, as they flew off the cliff and plunged into the freezing lake. Their screams were quickly swallowed by the icy water. The cold hit Valentine like a hammer, and the weight of his armor dragged him down. His feet found the lakebed barely in time, and he pushed off, fighting his way back to the surface.

Beside him, the empress flailed, disoriented by the submersion. Valentine reached her, grasping her tightly as he dragged them both toward the shoreline and safety.

As he carried the empress through the lapping waves, he glanced at her but met an alarming sight. Her face was ashen, like sand bleached by the sun, and she was not breathing.

"Empress! Empress!?" he screamed, his face full of panic. They had been charged with protecting the empress. The punishment should she die would be great, but the dishonor worse.

Frantic, Valentine rolled her onto her side, trying to free the water from her body. His frustration mounted with each passing moment—he lacked the skill to save her. In silence, he prayed to every god who might listen, even the one Christians whispered about. He didn't care which god answered, as long as one did.

With a sudden jolt, the empress began to cough up water.

Valentine closed his eyes, exhaling in great relief.

Her eyes met his.

"Where are we?" she inquired.

"Fear not, Empress, you are safe."

"For this, you shall be rewarded," she murmured. She was undeniably beautiful, a detail that had not escaped his notice, though his heart remained unmoved.

"Ensuring your safety is reward enough."

Another fit of coughing seized the empress.

"Please, Empress, rest now. Help will come," he urged gently.

"Your name, soldier?" she managed.

"Valentine—my name is Valentine Romanus."

The empress began to shiver, her voice laced with fear. "This cold may be my death."

"I will keep you warm," he promised, drawing her into his protective embrace. Her hair brushed against his cheek—a touch that should have stirred something within him, but did not.

Valentine's comrades reached the edge of the craggy cliffs above. Concern etched their faces as they observed the tender scene below. Suddenly, their solemn silence was shattered by exuberant cheering as they witnessed the empress—safe, secure, and cradled in Valentine's arms.

Suddenly, Marius shouted, "Drinks are on you!"

CHAPTER 2

RESPITE IN ROME

"Love is a kind of warfare."
—PLAUTUS

The late afternoon light cast a warm glow over Rome, infusing the city with a vibrant energy as its streets remained busy with the day's final activities. Shadows played across the weathered façades of modest buildings, while the sun's waning rays gracefully illuminated the cobblestone pathways, guiding residents and visitors alike as they hurried to complete their errands or enjoy a last stroll before nightfall.

Amid this timeless tapestry, Valentine and his stalwart companions —Marius, Efebus, Proculo, Linus, Scaro, and Albus—strode with purposeful strides, their laughter echoing off the ancient walls of structures that had withstood the test of time. Cloaked in warm mantles over their casual tunics, emblematic of a respite from duty, they walked from a humble eatery heading toward a nearby tavern nestled within the bustling streets beyond the Temple of Castor and Pollux.

As they walked down the Vicus Jugarius toward the Vicus Tuscus, their journey took them past bustling shops, where vendors hawked their wares amid the lively chatter of patrons. Young women cast admiring glances at Valentine—tall, handsome, his features highlighted by the afternoon light—but he remained oblivious to their attention. Instead, his gaze lingered on the Temple of Saturn, where he noticed a couple in love. He wondered how the gods could have granted him a love as radiant as his first, only to have her vanish beyond all his attempts to find her again. It was foolish, he knew, to romanticize a memory from when he was merely nine years old. *How could it have been real love?* And yet, she continued to torment his thoughts all these years later.

"Only three more taverns left to claim, you lavish spender!" Scaro exclaimed, his voice directed at Valentine, who had promised to pick up the tab.

"You fell straight into that wager—three cheers for Valentine!" Marius added, grinning broadly.

The men all cheered, their camaraderie palpable in the cool night air.

"Brothers, she was cold," Valentine responded defensively. "I was merely fulfilling my duties as a soldier."

"And wet—she was very, very wet!" Linus joked as the men erupted into more laughter.

"Merciful Lord, I beg you to forgive these men," Marius prayed playfully.

"'For this, you will be rewarded.' Those were truly her words?" Proculo inquired with a gleam in his eye.

"They truly were," Valentine replied with a smile.

"What transpired next?" Linus inquired, attempting to provoke Valentine. "You were alone with her for quite some time!"

The men grinned as Valentine replied, "Brothers, even if something had transpired—which it did not—a man of virtue does not speak of such matters."

"You are far from a virtuous man!" Albus blurted out jokingly.

"True, yet I am your superior officer now—so mind your tongue, Albus," Valentine retorted playfully. Away from battle, Valentine softened, relishing the camaraderie he shared with these men. Keeping up the ruse of his exploits with women was just another part of the bond.

Albus shook his head and muttered, "It should have been me to have rescued the empress."

Suddenly, with an impulsive flourish, Linus perched himself on the edge of a modest fountain, seizing the moment to command the attention of a small gathering within the area. The fountain's low stone ledge provided just enough height to make Linus feel like a performer onstage. Despite his precarious position, he swayed with deliberate grace—his every movement a testament to his natural showmanship.

"Maidens of Rome, in case you missed the public proclamation at the Forum today," Linus's voice rang out with conviction, "we, soldiers of Rome, have been awarded respite, all thanks to a *hero* among us." His glossy eyes swept across the square, drawing the gaze of curious onlookers.

A few citizens halted in their tracks, their curiosity piqued by the unfolding spectacle.

"Linus, get down from there," Valentine insisted, his tone tinged with embarrassment and amusement. Linus's antics always entertained the men.

"No, sir—I must respectfully decline that order! If you deem it necessary, you may impose military discipline upon me!"

"I may do that!" Valentine replied playfully.

Soft laughter erupted from the others, reveling in the banter as Linus continued his impromptu performance.

"The truth must be told! Citizens, I present the new centurion of the legion II Parthica—Valentine Romanus!"

"It's the one who rescued the empress!" exclaimed an enchanted maiden, her locks as dark as the night sky.

"The very same!" Linus declared, his balance teetering precariously on the edge of the barrel. "And from the treacherous Alemanni!"

The crowd burst into applause, their faces alight with admiration and gratitude for the valiant soldiers. Among them, many maidens cast their eyes toward Valentine, but he dismissed their attention with a casual wave, showing little interest in their adulation.

Meanwhile, Scaro's gaze locked with a curly brown-haired young man of striking beauty lingering at the fringes of the crowd—an exchange laden with recognition and unspoken understanding. Catching the subtle interaction, Albus shot his younger brother a reproachful glare, though Scaro remained indifferent to the unspoken tension.

The enchanted maiden, who had heard of Valentine's heroic tale, approached him with her friend, but Marius quickly intercepted.

"Not so quickly, dear maidens," Marius interjected teasingly. "This soldier is wary of love's grip and still owes us all many more rounds of drinks." His jest elicited soft chuckles, drawing the maidens' attention away, albeit with a tinge of disappointment.

Valentine, less amused, quickly cautioned, "Marius, there is no need to spread such tales."

"Though it is true—is it not?" Marius countered, his playful demeanor tinged with honesty.

"Not everyone shares your confidence in love," Valentine pointed out.

"Indeed, they do not!" Marius concurred, maintaining the light-hearted exchange.

"Linus, you're terrifying the good citizens of Rome!" Albus shouted as he gave him a shove, sending him tumbling into the fountain with a splash.

Laughter rippled through the crowd as Linus emerged, soaked from head to toe. His face contorted first in embarrassment at the amused spectators, then in anger.

"Defend yourself, Albus!" Linus shouted, charging and tackling him to the ground. The two struggled fiercely, rolling into a murky puddle. Before Linus could gain the upper hand, Efebus intervened, effortlessly seizing Linus by the back of his tunic and hoisting him off the ground, which drew more amusement from the growing audience.

Linus's futile fists flailed as Efebus, towering over him, casually ran a hand through his thick red hair, grinning broadly and revealing his darkened, chipped teeth. Nearby, a maiden flashed a coy smile at Efebus, who responded with a playful wink.

"Efebus! Release me!" Linus wheezed amid his struggles.

"Promise to be good?" Efebus taunted him.

"No!"

Without hesitation, Scaro and Proculo moved in to assist with a coordinated intervention. Scaro swiftly tackled Linus to the ground, allowing Efebus to finally break free from his unyielding grip. Together, they flipped Linus onto his back like a helpless turtle. Albus then seized the moment to playfully smack him across the face, adding to the lighthearted chaos. "Enough, enough!" Linus yielded as the men eased up.

Marius turned to Valentine with a grin. "As I suspected, nothing of interest here. I'll take my next drink now, bar maiden!" he quipped, playfully gesturing toward the nearby *taberna*.

"I fear my coin pouch will be empty before the night is through," Valentine remarked, eager to avoid the shenanigans.

"Ah, how fortunate for you that your new promotion affords you a higher wage! Onwards!" Marius teased, gesturing toward the tavern once more.

Valentine smiled warmly. "Where would I be without a brother like you?"

"Suffering, I would imagine!"

"Onward," Valentine urged, giving Marius a playful nudge as the last light of the day faded.

Suddenly, his smile vanished, and his heart skipped a beat as his eyes locked on a striking figure—a young woman with raven-black hair intricately braided and secured with delicate pins, accentuating the graceful curve of her neck. She was draped in a deep crimson stola of fine wool, the rich fabric perfectly suited to the cool evening air. A matching palla was wrapped around her shoulders, offering warmth and a touch of dignity. Beside her stood an older, wealthy man, portly and dressed in a lavish toga that exuded opulence and authority.

Their laughter drifted above the din of the street, drawing Valentine's attention to the luxurious carriage they had just arrived in. Drawn by a team of exotic slaves, it gleamed in the light of freshly lit torches, illuminating the entrance to a grand villa, where a private evening gathering was underway.

The portly man ascended the marble steps leading to the villa, trailed by a captivating woman. She paused briefly to adjust her stola, and in that moment, her eyes met Valentine's across the distance. Time seemed to halt as their gazes locked.

Valentine raised his hand in a tentative wave, but her response was a mere fleeting smile and a polite nod before she turned to ascend the steps. The flickering torchlight illuminated her figure as she disappeared into the warmth and luxury of the evening's festivities.

Valentine stood transfixed, as if he had just seen a figure from another world.

"Wasn't that...?" Marius's voice trailed off, sensing Valentine's pain.

"Lucia," Valentine whispered, her presence stirring the memory of his only serious—and ultimately futile—attempt at love since Rose.

"Give her no mind, Valentine. She is of no concern to you anymore." But Marius's words fell on deaf ears as he stared at the grand villa.

Forever imprinted in his memory, the day Valentine sought Lucia's hand raced through his mind. It was in the perfect embrace of summer, with golden sunlight filtering through the olive groves of Lucia's father's rustic villa. Valentine had meticulously planned every detail, but her harrowing revelation shattered the idyllic moment.

"What do you mean he has paired you with a man of nobility?" Valentine had asked Lucia, his youthful words tinged with disbelief and desperation.

"You know my father, Valentine. His will is resolute. I am to marry Firmus. There is little I can do to sway him," Lucia revealed.

"Then let us leave! We can start anew—far from your father's reach!" Valentine pleaded.

"I will not betray my family, Valentine."

"And what of us—our love, our plans?"

"I'm sorry, Valentine. My decision is made." Lucia caressed Valentine's face, a single tear betraying her resolve. She then turned and walked back to her father's villa.

"Lucia—wait!" he called after her.

But she did not turn back.

Slumping against the stable door, Valentine's eyes softened. Lucia had been his first adult heartbreak, yet the pain still paled in comparison to losing Rose. What stung most in that moment was the realization that no woman might ever replace Rose, leaving him cursed to love only a memory from the past—of a girl he would likely never encounter again. This truth made Lucia's betrayal all the more devastating, as if her saying yes to his proposal could have cured his almost constant longing for Rose.

"Hello!" Marius waved his hand in front of Valentine's face. "Lucia's day of reckoning will come."

Valentine blinked, snapping back to the present.

"I did not expect to see her here. I thought she was still living in Interamna," he remarked, his vitality seemingly drawn from him.

"The Christian God preaches forgiveness as a balm for a wounded heart," Marius offered gently.

"They appear happy. Her father must be pleased," Valentine retorted bitterly.

"Come, the warmth of a drink may help fade your memory and find forgiveness."

"Not now, Marius," Valentine declined, shaking his head as he walked away.

"Where are you off to?!" Marius called after him.

"Leave me!" Valentine shot back, disappearing down a dark alley.

Marius sighed, shaking his head gently. It had been a while since he had witnessed Valentine in such a state.

Linus, Efebus, Scaro, and Proculo approached.

"Where is he off to?" Linus asked.

"To mask a broken heart," Marius shared.

"What?!" Linus replied as the others looked at Marius in disbelief.

"He saw Lucia," Marius added.

The men sighed in quiet recognition, the story of Valentine and Lucia was still fresh in their memories.

"He still owes us another round!" Linus slurred, breaking the tension.

"We'll manage—onward!" Efebus ordered as he embraced the men and marched them toward the tavern.

"Gladly!" Marius replied as they began singing a song known in the legion.

As Valentine wandered through the vibrant streets of Rome, the moonlight danced upon the ancient cobblestones. After spotting Lucia earlier that evening, he had ducked into a tavern, desperate to drink away his memories in solitude. The wineskin he now carried had originally been hanging as a decoration behind the bar—a dusty *uter* the owner kept for show. But Valentine had insisted on buying it, paying well for the privilege of leaving with it slung over his shoulder, filled with wine, as he staggered through the night, determined to drown his sorrows.

The uter hung heavy in his grip, its leather worn and stained as he drained the last drops of wine, the bitter warmth sliding down his throat. Around him, the city had settled into the stillness of night, broken only by the distant murmurs of late revelers and the muffled laughter spilling from tavern doors. The solitude of the hour pressed in on him, the once-familiar streets now twisting and turning with the shadows, guiding him through the labyrinth of his thoughts.

He stumbled on, the wine's warmth stirring a simmering anger as memories of Lucia's betrayal flooded his mind. Lost in the swirl of emotions, he walked with a sense of defiance down the dim street, oblivious to the approaching carriage behind him.

The sound of hooves slowed as a noble lady returning from a feast ordered her driver to halt. "Soldier, it is late—where are you headed at this hour?' she inquired, her tone a mix of curiosity and subtle concern. Her gaze lingered on Valentine's tall, muscular frame, his build and age leading her to assume he was a legionary.

Valentine dropped his uter and turned to meet the gaze of the noble lady. At thirty years old, she possessed an ageless beauty, her features striking and refined. Her brown hair was elegantly swept up into an intricate style, revealing the graceful curve of her neck and framing eyes that seemed to pierce through him with their intensity.

"I am not certain, my lady," Valentine said, swaying slightly.

Despite his imposing stature, in that moment, he seemed more like prey to her than a soldier. The noble lady cast a discerning eye over him, her gaze lingering on his features longer than she intended, though she sought to mask any sign of interest.

"It appears you are empty," the noble lady observed, gesturing toward his uter on the road.

Valentine's eyes flickered down to the uter, and with a slight slur, he replied with a grin, "That… is an understatement."

She smiled and, with a slow, deliberate motion, opened her carriage door, saying, "Care to join?" Her voice was as smooth as her invitation. Her eyes sparkled with intrigue as she gently lifted the hem of her stola, revealing the delicate curve of her legs. The soft fabric brushed against her skin, offering just a glimpse of her graceful form—a subtle yet tantalizing gesture that spoke of both elegance and desire.

Deep within the noble lady's elaborate chamber, nestled upon the Caelian Hill, the intensity of their union grew, each moment punctuated by the sultry moans that filled the room. Serena's brown locks, once meticulously styled, had now tumbled freely down her back, a stark contrast to the composed woman he had first encountered. A few stray strands fell over her shoulders, framing her voluptuous breasts, which caught the warm, flickering light of the oil lamps, accentuating the sensuality of the moment.

She was an ethereal beauty, straddling Valentine with a commanding presence, her movements fluid and graceful as she took control, dominating him in every way. Their heat mingled as she rode him, her hips moving with a relentless rhythm, driving him deeper into her with each thrust. Her breath hitched as she felt him fill her completely, her hands gripping his muscular shoulders for support as her movements grew more frenzied. The bed creaked beneath them, adding to the symphony of passion that filled the room—a reckless dance of two lost souls seeking solace in the raw, unbridled act of sex.

Valentine's frame tensed beneath her, his own breaths coming in ragged gasps as he matched her fervor, his hands gripping her hips, guiding her rhythm as they both chased the same elusive high. The room was thick with the scent of sweat and sex, their bodies slick with exertion, their mingled cries the only sound in the otherwise still night.

When the climax finally came, it was like a tidal wave crashing over them.

"Yes, yes!" she cried out, her voice a mixture of ecstasy and desperation, as her eyes rolled back, her pupils dilating until they were nearly swallowed by the shadows. Her body quivered as she reached the pinnacle of pleasure, her voice rising in a final, shuddering moan as she felt Valentine's powerful release inside her. She collapsed against him, trembling from the aftershocks of their lovemaking, her skin flushed and damp with sweat.

"That was excellent," she commented, as though he had been a fine meal.

The flickering light of oil lamps cast a warm glow over Valentine's naked form, highlighting his impressive build and well-defined physique. His broad shoulders and sculpted chest glistened with a sheen of sweat, while his chiseled jawline and strong, angular features softened in the aftermath of their passion. Exhaustion was evident in his deep-set eyes, half-lidded and adrift in the lingering haze of the evening's indulgences.

Serena draped her leg over his, ogling and touching him. "Venus was in a good mood when she fashioned you."

"Thank you," Valentine replied humbly, his thoughts briefly drifting back to how swiftly the pain of his encounter with Lucia that evening had faded.

Suddenly, Serena rolled over, her mind preoccupied with her own concerns. "If only my husband could please me so."

Valentine's eyes widened in shock as he propped himself up on one elbow. "You're married?"

Serena smiled mischievously. "If one could call it that. Stay calm, soldier—my husband favors men, which is undoubtedly where he is now."

"I must go, my lady. This is not right." Valentine began to rise, realizing what a grave mistake he had made.

"Wait!" Serena grasped his arm. "There's no need for alarm—and please, call me Serena." She knew all too well that, as a soldier, Valentine was in grave danger if her husband ever caught them in the act. Even though her husband preferred the company of men, he could legally demand Valentine's life or use his authority to ruin him.

Valentine stood, his face tightening with vexation. *How could I have been so foolish? he thought.* This wasn't just a lapse in judgment—it was a betrayal of something deeper. He had been chasing shadows ever since losing his childhood love, always searching, never finding. Lucia had been another failed attempt, leaving him for a nobleman without a second thought.

Now, he found himself entangled with yet another noblewoman, only to discover he was nothing more than a distraction. It wasn't love; it wasn't even close. It was a hollow echo, a reminder of how far he had drifted from what he'd once held dear. The weight of his folly pressed down on him, filling him with a deep sense of frustration and shame.

"Where are you going? I'm not finished!" she protested like a child.

"I am," Valentine replied sharply.

Suddenly, Serena stripped a gold ring from her finger. "Then I shall pay for you to stay," she said as she tossed it toward him.

Snatching it skillfully from the air, Valentine scrutinized the golden ring. It was worth nearly a week's pay, a tempting bribe indeed. He shook his head, reflecting bitterly before muttering, "Perhaps love can be bought."

Serena's lips curled into a hopeful smile, her body unabashedly enticing him once again. But before her seduction could take hold, a deep, loud voice boomed through the residence: "Serena!"

Valentine and Serena froze.

"It's Tullus!" Serena whispered loudly.

"Who's Tullus?" Valentine asked.

"My husband!"

The revelation of Tullus's identity intensified with sudden, urgent pounding at Serena's bedroom door. Valentine's gaze quickly swept across the opulent chamber, his features sharply outlined by the dim light of the room's few flickering lamps.

Serena quickly slipped into her deep crimson stola, cinched at the waist with a slender belt woven with gold thread. The rich fabric shimmered in the light, a stark contrast to the ominous threat on the other side of the door.

"Serena! Are you there?!" Tullus's voice thundered from the hallway.

"You told me he was away!" Valentine snapped in a hushed tone, his eyes flashing with betrayal and panic.

"He was!" Serena's voice was a trembling whisper. "He'll have your head if he finds you here! The terrace, quickly!"

The pounding on the door continued relentlessly, each knock echoing through the room, counting down the moments they had left in safety.

Valentine darted toward his escape route. The brisk winter breeze wafting through the chamber promised a brief respite from the imminent threat.

Serena's voice, filled with desperation, called after him, "Soldier, tell me your name!"

Valentine paused and turned back at her. "So you may report me to your husband?"

"By Jupiter, I swear not to tell anyone of you."

Valentine, poised on the precipice of departure, hesitated, casting a long look at the woman who'd so thoroughly ensnared him—their brief interlude marked by passion and betrayal.

"Tell me, or I will scream!" Serena insisted.

"Valentine. My name is Valentine," he declared before disappearing into the darkness.

"Serena! What are you doing in there?!" Tullus's voice grew more insistent, almost shrill in its intensity.

Steadying herself, Serena moved with swift grace to unbolt the heavy door she had insisted on installing—for her protection, or so she had claimed to her husband.

As the door swung open, Tullus entered, a mid-forty-year-old man contrasting Valentine in every way. His shorter stature and balding crown seemed incongruous amid the grandeur of their surroundings.

"Why must you always lock this door?!" Tullus asked as he bustled toward his garments.

Adorned with her crimson stola, Serena elegantly reclined on a regal chair that appeared more like a throne, offering up the vision of her divine form as a distraction.

"Husband, we have discussed this matter. In the dead of night, what if a prowler were to rob me of my beauty?"

"Unlikely," Tullus replied as he hurried around.

"I thought you to be away?" she inquired.

Amid the turmoil, Valentine carefully descended from Serena's three-story villa, using the intricate architecture of Rome's opulent residences to steady himself. With each cautious step, he lowered himself from the second floor and leaped to the ground below. As he landed, he noticed a distant neighbor, just as the man was closing his shutters. Valentine offered a wave of acknowledgment, only to receive a cold stare in return; the man's scrutiny bore down on him like a hawk's piercing gaze before closing his shutter with a deliberate finality.

In Serena's chamber, Tullus continued to pace about. "I was on my way out of the city when I heard a rumor that General Claudius may have summoned the 2nd Parthica Legion without Caesar's approval."

"Soldiers departing Rome?" Serena exclaimed, her concern thinly veiled over a more personal dread of solitude. Pivoting swiftly, she asked, "What of our city's protection? When is this to occur?"

"I've yet to catch wind of the specifics, yet certain senators will find this information valuable. Therefore, I have decided to attend Senator Junius's grand banquet after all, and I require suitable attire."

"So you say," Serena replied, her tone laced with feigned interest.

"One must nurture connections with the Senate and people close to the emperor if ambitions are to be realized," Tullus replied defensively.

Ignoring his attempt at justification, she pressed, "When will General Claudius return? We might extend another invitation. Your last encounter seemed to amuse him. Perhaps he'll be inclined to assist with your transition to senator one day."

Tullus, clad in an extravagant wig, lavender tunic, and equally loud boots, responded, "My dear, do you truly believe I would be privy to the comings and goings of Rome's most esteemed general?"

Taking a moment to digest Tullus's outlandish appearance, Serena responded.

"No, husband—I suppose not," she stated bluntly.

"Then, perhaps you'll allow me to focus on my concerns without further ado."

"Gladly," she retorted, her lack of interest palpable.

"Splendid."

With that, Tullus departed swiftly, a picture of satisfaction, leaving Serena in their expansive chambers and familiar solitude. Yet, instead of pursuing rest, she found herself irresistibly compelled toward the terrace.

Stepping outside, Serena noticed Valentine's silhouette disappear among the greenery of Caelian Hill. Although she had clandestinely welcomed numerous senators and even gladiators into her chamber before, none had made such an impression as Valentine.

Her gaze shifted downward, and an unassuming object caught her attention—the gold glint of the ring she had offered him. It sat confidently on the terrace wall, a silent testament to the evening's events and a reminder of Valentine's reluctance to be beholden to her heart. Holding its heft in her hand, she smiled, reassured in knowing that integrity still thrived in some men.

CHAPTER 3

GENERAL CLAUDIUS

"Let them hate me, so long as they fear me."
—Caligula

Amid the rolling hills and rugged terrain near the northeastern border of the Italian peninsula, just outside the strategic city of Aquileia, one of Caesar's advisers rode briskly along a narrow path that wound through the rocky slopes. The once fertile plains were now scarred by recent skirmishes, with remnants of broken weapons and makeshift barricades scattered across the landscape. The adviser, known for his slight build and thoughtful demeanor, navigated the unforgiving terrain with a small retinue of Praetorian Guards for protection. Clad in a wide-sleeved *dalmatica* adorned with wooden decorations and draped in a fine mantle befitting his station as the bearer of the emperor's missive, he carried the weight of his mission with solemn determination. Behind him, the distant peaks of the Alps loomed, casting long shadows over the bloodstained land.

The terrain, marked by sparse vegetation and patches of snow and ice, offered little respite from the biting chill of winter. As the riders pressed forward, they encountered the aftermath of a recent clash. Strewn across the frozen ground were the remains of fallen soldiers, their bodies bearing witness to the brutal realities of border warfare. Rounding a bend, they came upon a grim display of two crucified Roman soldiers. Though not officially banned, crucifixion had fallen out of favor in the empire, with other forms of punishment now preferred. The adviser shuddered at the sight, the grisly image of the soldiers nailed to the crosses sending a chill through him deeper than the winter cold.

Beyond the ancient forest, a beacon of civilization revealed itself—the dimly lit camp of the Eastern Legion. Its glow gradually emerged before the adviser, reflecting the resilience and determination of those who guarded the empire's frontier. The adviser and his Praetorian Guards slowed their pace as they approached the camp's entrance. The perimeter guards, recognizing their authority, saluted and swiftly granted them passage.

A pungent odor from the distant pyres greeted all who entered the camp, a grim reminder of the inevitable toll of war. Outside the camp, the fires consumed the fallen soldiers, their ashes left to the winds. Inside, a makeshift infirmary of tents housed the wounded, where men withered in pain—some barely clinging to life, others receiving what care could be offered. Countless small fires flickered against the darkening sky. The sounds of moans and wails echoed through the disciplined rows of tents, with larger ones marking the quarters of higher-ranking officers. As the adviser continued his ride, the winds shifted, carrying the acrid scent of burning and the lingering stench of death.

The *principia*, the heart of the encampment, sprawled across the largest expanse of land. Constructed from sturdy timber and locally sourced stone, it housed the administrative offices alongside the *aedes*, where the legionary standards, altars, and statues of the gods were kept. As the adviser and his escorts approached, the clamor of activity reverberated from within its walls. With a sense of apprehension, the adviser dismounted and moved toward the entrance.

Within its fortified walls, a roaring fire and bronze braziers cast a flickering glow across a spacious chamber. Here, General Claudius and his staff gathered, poring over intricate battle maps that adorned a sizable wooden table, illuminated by the dancing flames.

Claudius commanded the room with an aura of absolute authority. His cropped silver hair framed his stone-gray eyes, illuminating his sculpted features—etched with the marks of a life dedicated to discipline and leadership. A prominent scar above his brow added a fierce edge to his appearance—a relic of a childhood injury and a reminder of the battles he had faced long before taking up arms. At fifty-four years of age, he moved with the vigor of a man half his years, exuding power and confidence. A red *sagum* draped over his broad shoulders, complementing the worn yet regal after-battle attire he still wore, further adding to his imposing figure.

At his side stood seasoned *praefecti legions*, the highest-ranking officers of his legions, each dressed in simpler military garb suited for command, though none as adorned or imposing as their general. Among them moved the *praepositi vexillationis* of the cavalry.

"And what of the *cataphracti*? Are they prepared to lead the charge?" Claudius's voice boomed across the room.

"We lack the men to relocate while maintaining our positions, General," replied a short officer. His tone spoke of deeper issues.

"How many were lost today?" Claudius inquired, his glare piercing.

"At least a quarter, General. Including…" He paused, reluctant to deliver the news. "Including many from the sixth cohort."

"My nephew?" Claudius's eyes boiled with fury.

General Aurelian, keen and unwavering, stepped forward with the assurance of a battle-hardened commander. Though he shared the rank of general with Claudius, Aurelian held less influence, serving as Claudius's most trusted ally.

"I'm afraid he perished in battle as well, General," Aurelian replied respectfully.

The wind picked up at that moment, bringing its chill through the room.

"Curse that fool of an emperor! Where is my legion?" Claudius lashed out, slamming his fist down. "I sent for them weeks ago!"

A heavy silence descended upon the room, freezing the most seasoned officers.

"I raised that boy as if he were my own," Claudius muttered to Aurelian, his voice laden with sorrow. His thoughts briefly turned to his younger brother, Quintillus, and the sacred oath he had sworn to safeguard his son. The weight of this news would strike him like a legionary's blow.

"The men spoke highly of your nephew's bravery, General," Aurelian interjected softly, attempting to offer solace.

The officers discreetly averted their gazes, seeking refuge in tasks elsewhere as Aurelian sought to soothe Claudius's anguish.

Suddenly, the adviser burst into the room, momentarily obstructed by Claudius's vigilant guards.

"General Claudius, greetings. I bear an urgent message from Emperor Gallienus," the adviser announced.

"Come forward," Claudius commanded.

The adviser approached, greeted respectfully, and unfurled the intricately designed scroll.

Claudius snatched it from the adviser's grasp and read it aloud:

"General Claudius, I desire that those who serve under the banner of Rome, regardless of their religious convictions, shall find solace and acceptance among their comrades...."

Claudius continued to read the message silently as his expression twisted with anger.

Suddenly, he lowered the scroll and looked at the adviser for answers. "Soldiers are perishing in battle, and Caesar sends me this? Where are my legions?!"

The adviser, visibly uneasy, responded in a formal tone.

"General Claudius, I am the emperor's religious adviser and the emperor has dispatched me to address the treatment of Christian soldiers within our ranks."

"I do not require a religious adviser—I require my legion!" Claudius replied firmly.

"General, if I may, I have been sent by the emperor himself due to rumors of persecutions still being conducted within our ranks. On my ride in, I witnessed two—"

Claudius's hand lunged forward, grasping the adviser's throat. In a tone steeped in steely resolve, he proclaimed, "Romulus and Remus laid the foundations of Rome, not the whims of superstition. I will not ask again—where is my legion?"

"I...don't..." the adviser gasped, his complexion shifting to a desperate purple, eyes wide with distress.

Finally, seemingly at the last possible second, Claudius released him, sending the adviser sprawling to the ground, gasping for breath. Claudius crossed to the table of maps while not a soul dared move.

"Send our new adviser to the front lines. Perhaps then he will show us the power of the Christian God over Rome's gods," Claudius declared.

"Yes, General!" came the swift response.

Clutching his injured throat, the adviser pleaded, "Please, General, I am not a soldier—have mercy!"

His protests echoed through the room as he struggled against the guards who had seized him. His worn shoes, leather *calcei*, scraped against the ground, the sounds of his resistance filling the tent. The others watched in silence, knowing he was being sent to the most perilous position in any Roman battle formation.

"Aurelian, stay. The rest of you—leave us," Claudius ordered.

Swiftly and with relief, the entire staff cleared the area.

"Condemning Caesar's adviser is dangerous," Aurelian cautioned.

"No less than angering Rome's gods," Claudius countered. "Dispatch a message to the emperor, informing him of the tragic demise of his esteemed religious adviser at the hands of marauding Goths. Express our profound condolences, and pledge swift retribution in return. Tell him that the body could not be recovered, and insert the usual formalities."

"Perhaps it would be better to present a body bearing the scars of barbarian weapons, minus his head. Such a ruse could divert any suspicions the emperor may harbor," Aurelian suggested.

Claudius paused and then remarked, "A wise strategy. Gallienus will undoubtedly be upset upon discovering I summoned the Second Legion back without his approval."

"Are you certain that was wise?" Aurelian questioned.

"If I were to wait for Caesar's approval for every tactical order I make, we would most certainly lose every battle."

"Understood."

"And, Aurelian, see to the adviser's guards—leave no loose ends."

Aurelian nodded and departed. Stepping outside the command center, he took a deep breath, drawing comfort from the crisp air. His gaze quickly captured the shadowed outline of the legionnaire camp as he pondered Claudius's harsh rebuke toward the emperor's adviser. Charged merely with delivering the emperor's message of compassion, the recollection was a stark warning of the dangers. *Nobody must know,* he silently resolved.

Clutching his fur cloak for warmth, he delicately retrieved a small fish emblem from a concealed pocket in his tunic. The smooth surface of the carved symbol, a gift from his mother years ago, was worn down from his secret devotion. After ensuring he was alone, he placed the emblem carefully amid the underbrush, a solemn act of departure from a piece of himself he dared not reclaim. As he walked away, he felt the weight of his decision bearing down on him.

CHAPTER 4

IF FATE WILL HAVE IT

Rome hummed with the energy of daily life. Laborers hurried to and fro, loading and unloading various goods. Tethered to carts reinforced with iron, oxen trudged along the cobblestone roads. The air was redolent with the scent of the city, mingling with the cries of merchants and the clatter of commerce.

Amid the lively scene stood a modest stone basin, a simple yet elegant testament to Roman craftsmanship, dedicated to Venus, the goddess of love. At its center, a finely carved statue, fashioned from exquisitely polished and painted Luna marble, captured her ethereal beauty with understated grace. Water gently cascaded from the basin, infusing the air with a refreshing coolness. Nearby, children played, their laughter mingling with the soft murmur of the crowd as the city basked in the warmth of the day.

As the sun reached its zenith, signaling the onset of noon, the recently promoted centurion lay fast asleep in the shadowy confines of a textile merchant's shop. The night before, after his encounter with Serena, Valentine had noticed the shop's wooden sliding door left unlocked—the merchant, in his haste to close for the night, had neglected to secure it. Exhausted and still slightly inebriated, Valentine had slipped inside, seeking refuge from the biting winter air. Wrapped in a woolen cloth taken from the merchant's stock, he found much-needed warmth.

Now, as the sun's rays pierced the dim interior, they stirred his dreams, carrying him back to the day when he'd first met Rose. He remembered their home near the foothills of the Apenninus Mons, where dense forests surrounded their village. As a young boy, Valentine often wandered the forest alone, his bow slung over his shoulder for protection—a concession from his father, who had deemed him too young to carry a steel sword. Instead, he wielded a wooden one, a cherished gift that symbolized the man he would one day become.

On one of these solitary walks, he first spotted a young girl on an early spring day, moving with quiet determination along a well-worn path through the ancient forest. She carried a basket of flower petals and a single rose. Her clear, pure voice rose in song, the lyrics of her own making:

> *In the woods where roses bloom,*
> *My heart delights in love's sweet tune.*
> *With every petal, love's light shows,*
> *In nature's arms, my spirit glows.*

Suddenly, as she turned a corner, young Valentine watched her come to an abrupt halt. The single rose slipped from her grasp, its delicate petals trembling as it floated gently to the forest floor.

Before her stood a chilling sight: two bodies, clad in humble village tunics, gruesomely nailed to towering wooden crosses. Horror washed over her as she recognized the men—local farmers known for their unwavering devotion to spreading the Christian faith. She gazed upon the lifeless forms of the once-zealous missionaries, frozen in shock.

Young Valentine continued to observe her from a distance. She was slightly older and taller than him, and the thought of making his presence known to her made him feel shy. Suddenly, amid this gruesome spectacle, a pack of wolves, drawn by the scent of blood, emerged from the shadows of the forest.

Startled by their sudden appearance, the girl recoiled, staggering backward. As she did, her foot became caught on a hidden root, causing her to lose balance and tumble to the forest floor. Her basket tumbled beside her, scattering rose petals across the path as she gasped.

Shock and fear surged through young Valentine as he watched the scene unfold in front of him. Instinctively, he propelled himself toward her, uncertain how he would fend off the pack of wolves on his own.

With primal instinct, the wolves quickly fixed their gaze on the girl, their eyes gleaming with hunger as she found herself at eye level with them.

In the tense silence of the forest, she instinctively cried out, "Father!"

With savage determination, the beasts lunged forward.

Scrambling to her feet, she dashed toward a tree, desperate to climb it, but its thick trunk defied her every attempt. Tears streamed down her cheeks as she glanced back, terror flooding her heart as she realized there was no escape. Overwhelmed, she backed against the tree, clasping her hands together in a desperate prayer, her voice trembling as the wolf was now only a few strides away from lunging at her. "Please, God, please..."

Suddenly, an arrow sliced through the air with a menacing hiss, narrowly missing the wolf's eye by a hair's breadth. The dominant beast, startled by the sudden threat, skidded to a halt, its gaze snapping away from its intended prey to fixate on a new challenger: young Valentine.

He stood atop a nearby boulder, his young figure silhouetted against the forest's shadowed backdrop. His hands trembled as he fumbled for another arrow, realizing he had missed his mark entirely.

The girl's eyes flickered toward him, her fate hanging in the balance of his next move.

Sensing the predator's growing aggression, young Valentine solidified his resolve. With a primal roar that echoed through the forest, he brandished his wooden sword high above his head. He then charged toward the wolf with reckless abandon, attacking the wild animal with the fierce courage of a Roman legionary, his youthful voice cutting through the tension like a blade.

For a fleeting moment, the wolf hesitated, uncertainty flickering in its amber eyes. Then, with a low growl rumbling from its throat, the predator turned and fled to the safety of the forest, followed by its pack as young Valentine continued to charge after it.

However, in his final step, he stumbled over the gnarled roots of the oak, tumbling to the forest floor with an undignified thud directly next to the girl, who was curled up in a ball, terrified by the entire scene.

"Dear maiden, are you well?" he asked from the forest floor.

"I am," she replied, her gaze still sweeping the surroundings for predators.

"Is it gone?" he asked.

"I think so," she replied.

Valentine sheathed his wooden sword, sprang to his feet, and extended his hand. "Fear not, dear maiden. They will do you no harm. I will protect you."

His voice, though higher pitched than hers, was a balm to the girl's frazzled nerves as she retrieved her basket and stood.

"Thank you," she drew a deep breath and stood up, now towering over him.

Valentine picked up a rose she had missed and handed it to her.

"Silly boy," she replied with a smile.

"I'm not silly," he firmly declared. "I'm as brave as a bear!"

"Yes, you are," she replied with a chuckle. "And I shall call you my Bear."

Valentine smiled, reveling in someone finally acknowledging his bravery. "What should I call you?"

"My father nearly executed the last boy who addressed me by my name—so, why don't you just call me Rose instead?"

"Like the flowers?" he asked.

"My favorite," she responded warmly. Then, in a sudden burst of playfulness, she tossed her basket of rose petals into the air, sending them fluttering down around them in a colorful cascade, catching the dappled light of the forest. With a soft giggle, she skipped off.

"Wait! Your flowers and petals shall not gather themselves," he yelled after her.

"Leave them, little Bear—come play!" she exclaimed, spinning around with youthful jubilation.

"It's Bear—not Little Bear!"

"Bear it is!" she shouted back.

NESTLED among the rolls of fabric and hanging textiles of the market stall, Valentine smiled as he continued to dream about his first encounter with Rose.

Upon arriving at his stall late to work for the day, the merchant nearly stumbled upon Valentine sleeping on the ground with his wares and sighed in frustration. "What have we here?"

Yet, before the merchant could voice his discontent, Marius stepped forward, holding a *situla*, a small water bucket, in his grasp.

"Leave this to me, sir."

With a mischievous grin, Marius dowsed Valentine's head with the bucket of water.

The abrupt torrent startled Valentine into consciousness, eliciting a sharp "Ahh!" from him as confusion quickly replaced his initial shock, surveying his unexpected locale.

"Good morning!" Marius exclaimed, standing over him.

"What is the meaning of this?!" Valentine sputtered.

"I should ask the same of you," Marius retorted. "The men and I have scoured Rome high and low for you—yet, here you lie. In this merchant's stall."

"There are inns right down the street," the merchant added, some-what miffed.

"Which is where *we* all slept. Remember?" Marius added jokingly, relishing the moment.

Valentine glanced around the stall as the events of the previous evening swept over him like a cold wave: the encounter with Serena, the exhaustion that had seeped into his very bones, and the crushing weight of shame for having defiled the sanctity of love.

He had been too disheartened to return to the inn. A part of him recoiled at the thought of facing his comrades and confessing the truth of what had transpired. Instead, he had sought the solace of the streets, finally collapsing in this vendor's stall and repurposing it as a makeshift bed.

Marius helped him to his feet. "We're headed beyond the city walls today, to the temporary encampment in the *Suburbium*. The tribune has given us just one more day's leave to enjoy the Lupercalia festival. And, of course, we couldn't possibly celebrate without our level-headed centurion," he teased.

Embarrassment flushed Valentine's cheeks, but he quickly sought to mend fences. Dipping into his coin bag, he extended a small offering toward the merchant.

"Apologies, sir," Valentine said sincerely.

"Very well," the merchant replied, his annoyance assuaged by the gesture as the men exited the stall.

Across from the stall, Valentine washed and drank from Venus's fountain as Marius grinned beside him.

"So, you have been here throughout the night?" Marius probed.

"Not exactly," Valentine replied unenthusiastically. The hint of an untold story colored his voice as he inhaled water and dried himself with his tunic.

"Well, it sounds like somebody has a tale to tell," Marius said, his curiosity piqued. "Hungry?" His voice dripped with sarcasm.

"I could eat an entire ox," Valentine admitted.

"Good," Marius grinned. "Then I know just the place."

VALENTINE AND MARIUS sat down at a *popina*, a modest tavern tucked into a corner overlooking a bustling intersection in the ancient city. The lively traffic of citizens and vendors passing by offered a constant reminder of the vibrant city life. The men's small, roughly hewn table wobbled on the uneven stone floor, and the legs of the stools creaked beneath them. Before them lay a simple fare of cheese, coarse bread, a bowl of vegetable soup, and a jug of watered-down wine.

Valentine's hunger engulfed him as Marius pondered in amazement the story of the previous night's events that Valentine had just recounted.

"Let me be sure I grasp your entire tale: It has been five years since Lucia left you for a nobleman. Then, you reencountered her, fled the scene, and attempted to drown your bitterness in wine. Subsequently, as if fate had a hand in it, you found yourself coerced and seduced by a striking noblewoman, who insisted you join her in bed not just once but repeatedly."

"More or less," Valentine grumbled while sipping his soup.

"And what *exactly* about the evening did not sit well with you?"

"You neglected to mention that she was married and offered to compensate me to service her in bed," Valentine added sharply.

"True." Marius paused for theatrics. "Still, it was an enjoyable night, was it not?"

Valentine finished his soup before responding, "Hardly."

Marius looked perplexed. "Allow me to pose a question," he began thoughtfully. "Why do you think you are drawn to women of this nature?"

Valentine paused to consider, then replied, "I don't know. Though, I do seem to attract women who are out of reach."

"That's precisely it!" Marius couldn't help but shout.

"I'm not certain I follow," Valentine leaned back in his chair, enjoying some live performers that had just begun playing a light melody from across the street.

"The teachings of my God suggest—"

"Let us not speak of your God right now," Valentine interrupted him, glancing around to ensure nobody was in earshot.

Marius, noticing his caution, lowered his voice. "I'm not forsaking Rome's gods."

"Marius, it's not about a single god. Christians reject Roman traditions and refuse to honor the gods that protect the empire. How can they preach love for all humanity while turning their backs on the very gods that safeguard us?"

Marius leaned in earnestly. "Have I told you of the teachings of Paul, the apostle?"

"No, though I am not certain I am in the mood for a religious lesson right now. Besides, I'd prefer not to be seen discussing such things openly."

Marius, unfazed by Valentine's concern, pressed on. "Very well, then I will tell you a short tale instead. There was once an apostle who wrote to the Galatians, speaking of a teaching from the Christian God —'man reaps what he sows.' That thought lingers in my mind, Valentine...when I think of you."

"How so?" Valentine inquired, his confusion evident.

"The apostle was not merely speaking about the acts we perform but the essence of our being," Marius replied excitedly.

Valentine scoffed lightly, swirling some water around his jug. "So, the Christian God teaches that we attract what we are, not what we want?"

"Yes, very much so," Marius nodded. "Our innermost being, our spirit, shapes the world around us. If we cultivate love within ourselves, we will attract love into our lives. It's not a guarantee of a life without hardship; rather, our light will draw others who share that same light."

Valentine reflected upon this message. "I fear all I have loved has been lost, my friend."

"You speak of Lucia," Marius replied quietly.

"I speak of Lucia and...others. My father from battle. My mother and brother, at the hands of bandits." Valentine hesitated as he recalled the childhood memory of witnessing his mother's and brother's deaths, evoking an emotion he did not wish to reflect on any further.

Marius remained still, acknowledging the gravity of the moment. He had known about Valentine's family being taken from him and could see his suffering.

Fighting back his emotions, Valentine asked, "Do you truly believe this? That by nurturing our virtues, we change ourselves and the world around us?"

Marius responded with unwavering conviction, "I do. The apostle journeyed far and wide, braving countless dangers to spread this message. He believed that the transformation within each of us could ripple outward, changing the world one heart at a time."

As Valentine sat in the late morning light, the faint warmth of the sun enveloping him, he wrestled with the weight of Marius's words and the memories of his past. The teachings of the Christian God, once distant and foreign to him, resonated on some level.

"Perhaps there's some merit to your beliefs after all."

"Fearing love will not help you find it, brother," Marius said earnestly.

"When did you become so insightful?" Valentine jested.

"It's far easier to spot *your* flaws than mine," Marius replied light-heartedly. "With that in mind, perhaps we should let fate decide your destiny tomorrow."

"How do you mean?"

"Lupercalia is tomorrow, and, oddly enough, there's a smaller celebration in the Suburbium, just off the Via Flaminia, not far from our encampment—one that mirrors the grand event on the Palatine Hill."

"And why would we bother going there?"

"For one, it's near our camp. More intriguingly, they have a game designed to bring couples together—something not found in the traditional celebration."

"You must be jesting," Valentine replied.

"Not at all. Apparently, one of the town's magistrates has a countryside villa in the Suburbium, and each year he resorts to this drastic measure, hoping to marry off his less-than-desirable daughter," Marius said, amusement flickering in his voice.

Valentine shot him a skeptical look. "What is this strange fascination you have with traditions that are not Roman?"

"Let us call it 'new Roman,'" Marius smirked.

"Very well, what does this 'new Roman' festival and game have to do with me?" Valentine asked, still unconvinced.

"This could be your chance to take part—to embrace love openly rather than from afar!" Marius added, his excitement unshaken.

Valentine chuckled. "I doubt such a festival will ever lead me to love. Even so, I will attend, if only to witness the absurdity of it all," Valentine replied, knowing Marius would be relentless otherwise.

"Excellent!" Marius cheered, rising to his feet, unfazed by Valentine's lackluster response. "And I'll handle this," Marius added, jumping up to pay the proprietor. "Try not to get in any more trouble while I am away."

"I'll try," Valentine replied with a smirk.

As Marius stepped away, Valentine's attention drifted across the paved street, drawn to the enchanting melody that had underscored their conversation. A troupe of local performers, *musici*, stood in front of a pottery shop, captivating a modest crowd with the harmonious sounds of flutes, citharae, and lyres.

A young maiden, close in age to Valentine, let her brown hair, streaked with faint blonde locks, fall freely around her face. Hiding behind its soft waves, she still exuded a wholesome beauty as her voice carried the sweetness of a nightingale. Singing as part of a small group of *cantores*, their voices wove together in perfect harmony. Though her eyes remained tilted toward the ground, her voice alone captivated the citizens who paused to listen, entranced by the choir's ethereal sound.

> *In the woods where helleborus bloom,*
> *My heart delights in love's sweet tune.*
> *With every petal, love's light shows,*
> *In nature's arms, my spirit glows.*

Valentine seemed utterly absorbed by the scene before him.

"All is settled," Marius declared, indicating that he had paid.

"That voice," Valentine remarked, not having even heard Marius's words.

Marius followed Valentine's gaze. "Indeed lovely, and a beauty to match."

"Do you recall that maiden?" Valentine asked, unable to tear his eyes away.

"I would have remembered her," Marius jested.

The melody crescendoed into a lovely finish.

The small gathering crowd erupted in applause.

The maiden appeared frozen before nodding uncertainly.

Valentine and Marius joined the cheers, applauding as citizens began to disperse, with some entering the pottery shop where the performers had been stationed.

The shopkeeper distributed coins to the ensemble of performers, marking the end of their engagement. The maiden accepted her payment and promptly retrieved a walking staff. She stood motionless at an unusual angle as the other performers gathered their earnings and exchanged parting words. Her demeanor suggested she was waiting.

"Shall we make haste, Centurion?" Marius asked sarcastically as Valentine sat still.

"A moment," Valentine replied.

"When we spoke earlier about opening your heart, I did not mean at this very instant," Marius jested.

Valentine seemed enraptured, oblivious to his surroundings, completely captivated by the maiden. Unlike the others with their hair pinned up, hers cascaded freely down her back, striking him like an arrow to the heart. On rare occasions, her gaze lifted, and her sea-blue eyes cut through him, leaving a lasting imprint. She radiated a beauty that seemed to emanate from within, captivating him completely.

"Perhaps more wine, then?" Marius suggested as he noticed their cups were nearly empty. Realizing that no one was attending to them, he got up and made his way across the popina, searching for the owner to request more wine.

Valentine nodded, hardly comprehending what Marius had asked, as he struggled to recall where he had heard the maiden's voice before now.

At that moment, he watched her let out a faint sigh, then cross the road with deliberate steps, her walking staff guiding her. As she reached the midpoint, an accidental encounter with three boys playing tag sent her staff clattering to the ground. Valentine perched up in his stool as he witnessed this. Unperturbed, she stooped, her fingers searching the ground with practiced ease to retrieve her staff.

Abruptly, the maiden's head turned toward the rhythmic thunder of hooves clattering against the cobblestones from a distance as riders galloped through the city. Citizens began to part the road as Praetorians heading toward the palace shouted, "Make way!" Their relentless gallop threatened to trample any obstacle in their path.

The maiden attempted to spring to her feet; however, the strap from her ankle boot snagged on a dislodged stone, causing her to stumble and fall to the ground.

Valentine jumped up and yelled at the maiden, "Take heed!" With the agility of a seasoned warrior, he overturned the table, darted beneath an ox, narrowly missed colliding with a flower merchant—sending petals swirling into the air—and swiftly pulled the maiden toward him. In a fluid motion, they rolled together, their surroundings blurring into a whirlwind as they tumbled, culminating in their landing mere inches apart in a close embrace, safely away from what would have been a fatal conclusion.

Finding himself atop the maiden, Valentine paused to catch his breath while petals showered around them. Her heart pounded as she sought to calm its frantic pace.

"Fear not, dear maiden," he gasped.

"Unhand me, sir!" she roared.

Having witnessed this scene, Marius shook his head and muttered, "Incurable."

Valentine peeled himself away from the maiden just as a figure with fiery red hair and youthful energy dashed toward them.

"Agatha!" cried the young woman as she quickly helped her sister.

"I'm fine, sister," the maiden assured as she began to brush herself.

Valentine extended his hand. "Please, allow me."

The maiden rose to her feet on her own. "I am quite capable, sir."

Approaching them, Marius held the walking staff, his face adorned with a knowing smirk that conveyed many unspoken thoughts.

"Valentine," Marius began, "Who are your new friends?"

Without a word, the redhead swiftly took the walking staff and handed it to her sister, but not before gazing admiringly at Valentine who tried to regain his dignity. "My apologies, those horses were—"

"Are you in the habit of attacking people, sir?" Agatha chastised him, her gaze locked toward the ground.

Valentine, startled, hastened to explain, "Dear maiden, perhaps you are unaware or blind, yet that rider nearly ran you down! You scarcely budged."

"Indeed, I am blind, sir!" Agatha snapped as she lifted her beautiful yet unfocused eyes toward him. "Though, it was not merely one horseman; there were three. And from the sound of their hooves and the rhythm of their gallop, they were mounted on Numidian horses, which suggests the lead rider was an imperial messenger with Praetorian escorts. As for my lack of movement, my shoe was trapped by a poorly laid stone, undoubtedly the work of a careless worker who left the stone higher than its neighbors."

Valentine's heart sank. "My deepest apologies, dear maiden. I did not know you were..."

"Blind? And how could you? You entered from across the way and nearly trampled over that poor flower merchant who was already walking with a limp before you tackled me to the ground. So, I thank you, but we must make haste now," she said before reaching for her sister. "Come, Porcia."

"Yes, sister." Porcia attempted to make eye contact with Valentine, who paid her no heed.

Unaccustomed to being addressed with such candor, Valentine was completely taken aback. He marveled at the maiden's astuteness; her insight surpassed anyone he had ever encountered, transcending both gender and the constraints of her lack of vision.

"Wait! Might I ask where you live or perhaps if you plan to attend the games at the circus or a show at the theater?" Valentine asked, his voice tinged with desperation, not wanting their encounter, however odd it had been, to end.

"No, thank you," the maiden sharply replied.

Porcia asked Marius, "Did you say his name was Valentine—the soldier who rescued the empress?"

"Indeed, and I am Marius, also at the empress's service...and you are?" Marius asked.

"Porcia! And this is my older sister, Agatha." Porcia leaned close to her sister's ear and whispered with a giggle. "It's him—the one all the maidens speak of."

Agatha nodded, unimpressed. "I see. It appears rescuing maidens in distress is your familiar art form?"

"Uh, yes, I mean…" Valentine fumbled his words nervously as Agatha's straightforward and insightful remark caught him off guard. "My lady, I was hoping to—that is, might you be inclined to—"

"Thank you, yet we're not the type to tarry. Come, Porcia. Father will be home soon. We must prepare the meal." Agatha began to walk off.

"Wait!" Valentine reached out and grabbed her by the arm. "May I—"

In a swift movement, she pivoted and delivered a sharp rap to Valentine's shin with her walking staff.

"Ah!" Valentine screeched, grabbing his shin.

"Do not touch me without my consent, sir!" Her voice sliced through the air.

"Apologies, I only wanted to—"

"Thank you, but we must go. Come, Porcia." Agatha led the way with her staff.

Porcia threw a playful smile over her shoulder.

Valentine watched her walk off in awe while massaging his shin, while Marius appeared quite amused.

"Throughout our acquaintance, brother, I have never witnessed you falter so miserably with the fairer sex. Perhaps your beauty is lost on those who cannot behold you?" Marius quipped with a smirk.

"She's remarkable," Valentine said, still gazing after her.

"Yes, very much so—and blind—and excellent at beating you with her stick." Marius grinned, then slapped Valentine on his back.

"Not what I meant," Valentine replied, still mesmerized by the unexpected encounter.

CHAPTER 5

A GIANT OF A MAN

"Justice is the foundation of lawful authority."
—CICERO

In the early days of spring, the Suburbium along the Via Flaminia, located on the northern outskirts of Rome, buzzed with life. This area, a harmonious blend of farmland and communal spaces, was home to both farmers and those seeking respite from the chaos of the city, forming a vibrant community just a short distance from the capital. Distinguishing this peaceful suburb was a temporary military encampment, strategically established by the emperor due to growing concerns over northern threats. A vexillation of the *Legio II Parthica*, typically stationed at the fortress in *Castra Albana*, twenty miles south of Rome along the Via Appia, had been relocated to the Suburbium to bolster defenses. The presence of these troops, though uncommon, underscored the area's strategic importance and brought an unusual dynamism to local life. While soldiers were generally separate from civilian life, here they became an occasional but notable presence within the community.

As evening approached, a slender stream of smoke ascended gracefully from a hole in the roof of an abode in the Suburbium. It was a modest two-story structure, where the rustic charm of terra-cotta tiles met the enduring solidity of fired bricks. The residence was nestled between a gentle hill and a secluded grove of ancient oak trees, offering a serene retreat from the bustle of the nearby city. In the forefront, a small garden was beginning to come to life, with early blooms shyly opening and young shoots stretching toward the fading light. Along one side of the house, an ancient grapevine, meticulously cultivated over generations, wound its way up the wall, its thick, woody tendrils supported by a sturdy wooden trellis.

As daylight waned, a powerful black horse trotted along the muddy path toward the dwelling. Mounted on the imposing steed was a figure known to all—Bruttius, Rome's *Triumvir Capitalis*. Traditionally tasked with maintaining public order, overseeing the city's prisons, and executing sentences, Bruttius was far from an ordinary official. His unparalleled expertise in administering torture and executions set him apart, and he took a personal interest in ensuring that justice—or his interpretation of it—was fully executed.

Where others in his rank might delegate such grim tasks to slaves or freedmen, Bruttius relished the opportunity to assume the role himself, particularly when the emperor requested it or whenever the mood struck him. His performances at executions were legendary, inciting the crowd to a frenzied fervor and earning him the infamous title of Executioner Triumvir—or simply "The Executioner." His presence was commanding, with his bald head gleaming like a polished helm atop broad shoulders and powerful arms. The dark stains on his tunic told silent stories of his ruthless craft.

Bruttius had little in common with his predecessors, preferring the solitude of life outside the city. The distance offered him a rare solace, allowing him to leave his grisly work behind and focus on his family. Arriving at the rough-hewn wooden stockade, Bruttius dismounted with deliberate, measured grace. He unstrapped an enormous, custom-forged executioner's sword from the handmade leather sheath hanging beside his horse. This was no ordinary weapon but a tool of precise terror, with a broad, heavy blade designed to deliver a single, devastating strike. The hilt, wrapped in dark leather worn smooth from countless executions, bore a crossguard shaped like the outstretched wings of a predatory bird.

As he guided his horse to the stall, a figure emerged from the shadows—Tiber, a trusted slave, with Thracian origins, who lived in a small abode Bruttius had built for him, neighboring their animal stalls, and who helped tend to the livestock as well as watch over his daughters. He was a middle-aged man Bruttius had bought for his experience in combat as well as his ability to tend the horses. His strong, weathered build spoke of years of labor. His voice was calm as he greeted his master.

"*Dominus*, welcome back," Tiber greeted him.

Bruttius nodded as he handed Tiber the horse. "Thank you, Tiber. Everything in order?"

"Yes, Dominus. Your daughters are preparing supper," Tiber replied as he guided his horse into the stall.

Bruttius turned toward the entrance of his home. The stout wooden door awaited him, both inviting and formidable, much like the man who lived within. Inside, the weight of his duties would continue, but for now, his mind was at ease—his daughters were safe, and his trusted slave would see to the rest.

Upon entering, Bruttius carefully set his sword onto its wooden rack and proceeded to a nearby side table. There, he washed his hands —hands that had both taken and nurtured life—in a simple basin of water mixed with a pinch of ashes, which helped scrub away the grime of the day.

"Greetings," he declared, his voice resonating through the room.

In the rustic kitchen, filled with the rich aromas of an imminent feast, Agatha and Porcia worked seamlessly together. Agatha chopped vegetables, her knife moving rhythmically against the wooden table, while Porcia carefully stirred a pot of lentil soup simmering over oak embers in a low hearth. The steady heat from the embers allowed the soup to cook slowly and evenly. As her father approached, Porcia extended a cloth for him to dry his hands.

"Hello, Father, how was your day?" she asked.

"Two executions. Both deserted their ranks," Bruttius replied unfazed.

"Did they suffer?" Porcia inquired, her voice tinged with concern.

"Only one. My metal dulled on him," Bruttius murmured.

Porcia's gaze shifted away, a wave of discomfort washing over her features. She loathed the thought of anyone being tortured, the mere idea sending a shiver down her spine.

Bruttius walked toward Agatha, who stood by the stove. Sensing his presence, she offered her cheek, ready to receive his kiss that marked their reunion.

"Each night you return unharmed is a blessing, Father," Agatha said.

"Thank you, my dear," Bruttius replied, his voice warm.

He wandered into the living room and settled into his beloved oak chair, a masterpiece of intricate carvings at the head of the family's dining table. In a small niche in the wall, an oil lamp with a subtle engraving of a fish—the quiet symbol of their Christian faith—cast a soft, flickering glow over the room.

Porcia served her father a steaming bowl of soup and poured deep red wine from a clay jug into his cup. The wine caught the soft glow of the oil lamp.

With deliberate steps, Agatha carried over a dish of cabbage, freshly picked from their garden. They settled into their accustomed places around the oak table, ready to share the evening meal.

Bruttius closed his eyes and bowed his head, a gesture mirrored by Agatha and Porcia. "Lord, we are thankful for the food and fellowship we share. Keep Camilla's spirit under Your watch. Amen."

Porcia gently kicked her father under the table, hinting at an oversight.

"Also, Lord, forgive me for severing the heads of the soldiers who deserted their post. Though my *duty* demands such actions, I pray their souls to find Your peace," he added, somewhat reluctantly.

"Amen," echoed Agatha and Porcia.

"Thank you, Father," Porcia said with a hint of pride, acknowledging the completion of their ritual.

As they began to eat, it wasn't long before Agatha sparked the conversation. "Father, what if those men had a legitimate reason to abandon their post? Perhaps they were urgently needed at home."

"We have discussed this, Agatha. Their punishment is a matter of justice, and you should not concern yourself with state affairs."

"A woman's voice may be silenced in our courts, yet I would still like mine heard at this table," she retorted sharply.

"You *do* encourage us to speak our mind, Father," Porcia added, siding with her older sister.

"Daughters, I have no interest in revisiting this old debate. All citizens must abide by Roman law. The soldiers I executed today violated those laws, and the emperor himself called upon my services. It is not our place to judge," he stated decisively.

"But our God teaches us to forgive—even Jupiter advocates tolerance," Agatha argued while sipping her stew.

"Jupiter himself would recognize the necessity for order and the consequences of actions," Bruttius countered.

"What would Mother say of all of this, were she alive today?"

"That's enough, Agatha," he commanded, his tone firm. He hated to think what a Rome without order would mean for Agatha. It was his duty to ensure her world remained safe.

"As you wish, Father," she replied, having detected the rising frustration in his voice.

Bruttius's gaze softened as he watched her at the table. Her likeness to Camilla, his late wife and their mother, was undeniable. Each glance at Agatha brought back the memory of when he'd first laid eyes on Camilla. Lost in thought, he allowed himself to drift into those cherished memories, recalling that moment as vividly as if it were yesterday.

He had begun courting Camilla soon after starting his career as a jailer in their Tuscan hometown. Surrounded by criminals at his work, Bruttius was relieved to return home to her—a beacon of light, filling his heart with joy. Their love grew quickly, and soon they welcomed two daughters: Agatha, who inherited her mother's resolve and adventurous spirit, and Porcia, who was playful like her mother.

Camilla introduced Bruttius to her Christian faith, challenging his pagan beliefs. Together, they discussed love, forgiveness, and salvation, with Camilla guiding her family down this spiritual path. Their home became a center of faith, filled with discussions and readings from scrolls. However, in a cruel twist of fate, a thief ended Camilla's life soon after they settled in the Suburbium. Agatha and Porcia, still young, were left in Bruttius's care, burdening him with the loss and the task of raising his daughters alone. Every corner of their home, every mention of Camilla's name, stirred a deep sense of helplessness for not having protected her.

Her death hung over him like an inescapable shadow. Ashamed that he hadn't been there to protect her, Bruttius wrestled with the thought that his turn to Christianity had angered Rome's deities. Seeing traces of Camilla in his daughters, he opened their home to Christian gatherings despite the risks. Though the emperor showed tolerance, safety was never certain—one wrong word to the wrong person could bring hostility, betrayal, or worse.

These gatherings became a thread that kept Camilla's memory alive. While Bruttius didn't fully convert to Christianity after her death, he honored it as the faith of their household, preserving it as a precious link between his daughters and their mother. Beneath it all, he remained a man adrift in his grief, anchored not by faith, but by loss.

"You grow more like her with each passing day," Bruttius murmured as the focus shifted back to the table. Though he intended his words as praise, Agatha's demeanor resurrected Camilla's memory, a bittersweet torment. Having lost one dear to him, he vowed that he would never allow it to happen again.

"How so, Father?" Agatha inquired.

"She, too, questioned our laws and religion."

"As Mother should have," Agatha replied firmly, reminding him once again of her.

Bruttius cast an endearing glance toward her, a gesture not missed by Porcia, whose gaze lingered on Agatha brushing a faint blonde streak of her otherwise brown hair behind her ear. Agatha had inherited Camilla's beautiful hair color, something Porcia had always envied, though she would never admit it. Eager to steer the conversation toward herself, and notorious for spilling secrets, she interjected with a mischievous smile, "Agatha and I met a soldier today."

"Porcia, you promised you wouldn't!" Agatha replied, attempting to take command as the elder.

"A soldier?" Bruttius inquired with uncertainty.

"Sister, Father should know," Porcia teased the tale. "He was an off-duty officer, Father—a strong and handsome man—who rescued the empress and Agatha thought familiar."

"Porcia, why do you bother Father with trivial encounters with insignificant men?" Agatha questioned, visibly annoyed.

The air tensed once again.

Bruttius ventured to ask, "What is this man's name?"

"Porcia, hold your tongue!" Agatha snapped, her patience wearing thin. She was embarrassed yet felt strangely drawn to the man who, without regard for his own safety, had protected her.

But Porcia, her emotions running high, shot back, "Why should I? You don't see the way they all look at you—I do!" She stormed up the stairs, then slammed her door before retreating into her room, leaving a heavy silence in her wake.

"Porcia!" Bruttius called after her, his voice blending concern and reprimand. He then turned to Agatha, seeking understanding. "Agatha, what is your sister referring to?"

Agatha confessed, "The soldier—he paid me more heed than her."

His voice, gentle yet probing, asked, "Is that all?"

"Yes, Father," Agatha replied.

Bruttius let out a soft laugh.

"Tease all you want, Father—we both understand no suitor will ever meet your standards."

"That's not what I—" he started.

But Agatha quickly interrupted him, "Nor will one love me due to my lack of sight."

As he absorbed her words, he was struck by the painful truth they held. The chances of Agatha ever marrying were slim, and her survival and safety as she grew older was his paramount concern. He had always vowed to provide her with unwavering protection and support, a promise he intended to uphold until his last breath—a duty he expected Porcia to inherit one day, as he was convinced no man would want to assume the duty of caring for a blind woman, despite her stunning beauty. Nonetheless, he sought to offer comfort, carefully addressing her concerns.

"With time, my dear. Until then, I will tolerate no heartache for my daughters, especially not over a *soldier*."

"Those thoughts are furthest from my mind," Agatha declared firmly, and indeed, they were.

The protective fortress Bruttius had erected around her heart left no entry for potential suitors, a stronghold he was determined to guard zealously.

Bruttius sighed. "Good—then let us eat and leave your sister to sulk."

"As you wish, Father."

CHAPTER 6

BLIND LOVE

*"Accept the things to which fate binds you,
and love the people with whom fate brings you together,
but do so with all your heart."*
—MARCUS AURELIUS

A stone's throw from Bruttius's dwelling, farmers and Romans seeking respite from the bustling capital reveled in the outdoor festivities of Lupercalia. Held annually on February 15, this exuberant celebration traced its origins nearly a thousand years earlier. It wove together a myriad of practices aimed at fertility and purification, honoring the god Faunus and commemorating the legendary tale of Romulus and Remus—Rome's founders said to have been nurtured by a she-wolf in the sacred Lupercal cave.

Amid towering cypresses and olive trees stood a *Luperci*, his bare chest smeared with the blood of the sacrificed goat. He marked the foreheads of young men with the same blood, a sacred act believed to endow them with virility. Fueled by wine, the men raced along a trail that weaved through the woods, bypassing a crowd feasting under the early spring rays. Music and laughter floated through the air as expectant maidens and pregnant women awaited, their hearts filled with hope, to be lightly touched by the bloodied hides in the men's hands, believed to impart the blessing of fertility and an easy birthing.

The festival reached its pinnacle with the introduction of a game devised by one of the local magistrates of Rome, a middle-aged man with silver hair who resided in the area. Clad in a tunic, he approached the stage, exchanging greetings with many familiar faces along the way, clearly pleased with himself for creating this novel way for couples in the community to meet. As he neared the platform, his daughter Vibia wove her way through the crowd. Her dark, thick hair was styled in an intricate arrangement of braids and coils, a mark of her noble lineage. With a robust figure, Vibia commanded attention more through her father's esteemed status in Rome than any charm of her own. Her hazelnut eyes were sharp, though they lacked the warmth that might have softened her otherwise stern features. Upon reaching her father, she wrapped him in a warm, familiar embrace and whispered into his ear.

"Father, remember what we discussed," she implored, her eyes holding a spark of mischief.

"I'll do what I can, Vibia—no promises," he gently countered, then continued toward the platform.

Arriving onstage, the magistrate gestured for the gathering crowd's attention, his hand cutting through the chatter like a keel through water. A hush fell as his rich and authoritative voice resonated above the din.

"Esteemed citizens, we invoke the gods for health, prosperity, and the continuation of our lineage, for it is through fertility that our empire endures. Therefore, let the matchmaking game begin!"

His words were the spark that set the main event in motion. The crowd erupted in cheers, some amused by the magistrate's relentless efforts to find a husband for his daughter. Musicians struck up a lively tune as couples began to dance in the open space before the platform—an act openly encouraged by the magistrate, eager to stir excitement. Meanwhile, eager young men and women sat at benches arranged for the occasion, waiting in anticipation for their names to be drawn from two clay urns.

The magistrate moved gracefully toward the urns on a small table on the stage. His hand reached into their depths to select a name from each, uniting a young man and woman in the tapestry of love and destiny. As he was about to proclaim the first pairing, Linus made his way forward, offering a last-minute entry as he handed the magistrate a slender strip of papyrus.

"Another bachelor for you, sir," Linus announced.

"Very well," the magistrate responded, taking the paper as Linus withdrew with a playful grin. Instead of depositing the strip into the bachelor urn, the magistrate paused, his attention caught by the name written on it. A smile unfurled on his lips as he gazed over at his daughter.

Meanwhile, at the festival's fringe, Valentine and his companions were huddled around a table, immersed in the joy of wine and camaraderie, oblivious to the subtle dramas unfolding on the stage.

Albus twirled a wine cup absentmindedly, voicing his hopes: "I wish for a beautiful maiden—with simple morals, a generous dowry, and large breasts."

"Mother would have scolded you for such words, brother," Scaro teased. Despite their sibling rivalry, he held his brother dear.

"Very well, then only large breasts will do," Albus retorted.

The men smirked and joined in the banter.

"I yearn for a maiden of sturdy build," Efebus declared boldly.

"Not surprisingly," Valentine chimed in smoothly.

"She should be akin to a mighty oak," Proculo quipped.

Efebus grinned, eliciting laughter.

"Let us hope that none are as unsightly as Proculo's past she-wolf," Marius teased.

"I paid ten sesterces for her!" Proculo exclaimed.

"We know! If only the Greeks had known of this tragedy," Marius mused, sparking more laughter.

The magistrate's voice suddenly captured the moment's merriment: "Our inaugural match: Marius Copius and Porcia Tertia."

A wave of cheers rose from the men as Marius leaped to his feet and scanned the jubilant crowd. "We have met!" he exclaimed, acknowledging Porcia with a wave, her smile bridging the distance between them.

"Poor girl," Valentine quipped, the jest sparking chuckles.

"Valentine, it's the maidens we met in Rome!" Marius added as he advanced toward Porcia.

Across from the dancing crowd, Valentine's eyes locked onto them. Porcia was engaging with other maidens, though keeping a careful eye on her sister. Agatha seemed lost in the music, her fingers tapping in time. Despite the revelry around them, Valentine was immediately captivated by Agatha.

The magistrate announced more names, "Valentinus Romanus and Vibia Aemilia."

Valentine's world halted as he heard his name cry out. He looked toward Vibia, the magistrate's daughter, who stood and acknowledged him with a playful wave.

"I did not submit my name," Valentine said, confused.

"Perhaps your destiny requires a helping hand," Linus remarked mischievously.

"Linus!" Valentine exclaimed. "I did not ask for this!"

"Marius suggested it!" Linus confessed as laughter erupted from the group.

"She's quite the beauty, Valentine!" Efebus exclaimed sarcastically.

"Oh, indeed," echoed Proculo jokingly.

"Onward, Valentine," Scaro urged as a chorus of "Val-en-tine!" rose from their circle, pushing him toward his fate.

Valentine surveyed the crowd, the weight of their gaze pressing heavily upon him. There was no backing out now without embarrassing the young lady. He took a deep breath and marched forward toward Vibia. Yet, as he approached, a sense of unease crept in. This setup felt foreign to him—this contrived ritual had little to do with the ancient traditions of Lupercalia. He preferred to trust in fate to guide the course of his life, especially when it came to matters of the heart.

Vibia stood encircled by her companions at the maidens' table, where murmurs of Valentine's strikingly handsome features floated in the air.

"You're the most fortunate maiden here, Vibia," said a freckled companion.

"It must be fate," Vibia quipped with a twinkle in her eye, knowing all too well that was not the case.

Valentine approached and offered a respectful nod, determined to treat this encounter as he would any other duty. With the favor of the gods, he hoped it would be over soon enough. "Greetings, Vibia. Would you care to join me?"

"With pleasure, Valentine," she replied, a glimmer of excitement in her eyes.

They moved together into the open space, joining the lively and informal dance of the festival, where the music played on and laughter filled the air. As they danced to the cheerful melody, Vibia leaned in to spark conversation.

"I've heard of your daring rescue of the empress," she remarked.

"Thank you. Yet, it was a collective effort," Valentine responded modestly as she sensed his unease around her.

"Such courage speaks volumes of your character."

"Thank you," he replied awkwardly as she smiled flirtatiously.

"You must have every maiden in Rome vying for your attention," Vibia continued, her tone laced with playful flattery.

Valentine paused, carefully weighing his words. He had deliberately steered clear of this dating game, seeking to evade the complexities of intimate conversations with a woman, fearing they would leave him vulnerable to heartache once more. Yet, as he instinctively swayed to the music's rhythm, his thoughts drifted to Agatha. An undeniable sense of familiarity tugged at him, drawing him closer, as if destiny itself were leading him in her direction. Finally, he could wait no longer.

"My sincerest apologies, Vibia," Valentine said, halting their dance abruptly.

"Have I said something to offend you?" she asked, her brow furrowed as he stepped back.

"Not at all," he replied warmly. "However, there is someone I must speak to urgently. May I escort you back to your companions?"

"As you wish," she replied, her gaze downcast.

Valentine knew he had disappointed her. As they reached her friends, he paused and said sincerely, "Vibia, you shine like a gem in the sands—thank you for the dance." With that, he departed, leaving Vibia with a satisfied smile while her friends exchanged knowing glances.

As he approached Agatha, a mix of anticipation and unease flickered through his chest.

"Pardon me, dear maiden. I believe we met yesterday in Rome," he ventured.

Agatha smiled, "You *are* persistent, Valentine."

"You recognize my voice?"

"Your voice, your walk, your fragrance," she softly retorted.

Valentine self-consciously sniffed at himself.

Laughing softly, she assured him, "Your scent is pleasant."

He smiled. "Why do you not play this dating game?"

"Last year, I was paired with a drunken fool who nearly guided me into a table. Though I may be insightful, I am still blind."

"Do you enjoy dancing?"

"I am fond of music, and if I did not fear faltering, I'm certain I would enjoy it."

"Would you dance with me—if we danced slowly, away from the dangers of the crowd?" he proposed, a hint of hope in his voice.

Under normal circumstances, her response would have been a firm no—after all, dancing too closely with men was frowned upon, not to mention straying from the crowd. Yet something about Valentine sparked a sense of security, prompting a soft "Very well," from her lips.

Brightened by her agreement, Valentine asked, "May I offer my arm?" mindful of the importance of her consent this time.

"You may," she affirmed, rising with her staff.

Their moment, however, was quickly interrupted by Marius and Porcia's arrival.

"Where are you going with my sister?" Porcia asked, a protective edge to her inquiry.

"It's all right, Porcia. I am in the company of a Roman *hero* who will protect me from any two- or four-legged beasts—is that not so, Valentine?" Agatha jested.

Valentine's laughter mingled with his affirmation: "I suppose it is."

Agatha smiled.

"Stay within sight, then," Porcia warned Valentine, glancing toward Tiber, who sat nearby, keeping a watchful eye on them.

"We won't stray far," Valentine assured her.

"If Father discovers that you drifted too far away—"

"Porcia, that's enough. Please assure Tiber all is well," Agatha stated firmly.

"As you wish, sister," Porcia replied as she watched them walk away and then gestured to Tiber that it was all right.

"Your sister could not be safer," Marius reassured her.

"I hope so, for his sake," she conceded, her gaze lingering on them.

Marius guided Porcia into the lively dance, joining a group of thirty revelers who were enchanted by the blend of flutes, harps, and singers.

"You're quite the dancer!" Porcia exclaimed, her tone playfully incredulous.

"Surprised?" Marius responded with a smile.

"Indeed," Porcia replied playfully. "I expected you to be more clumsy."

Marius let out a chuckle, then, in a humorous display of self-deprecation, he deliberately stumbled over his own feet and collapsed to the ground with exaggerated theatrics.

"Like this," Marius jested from the ground.

Porcia's laughter rang out as she delighted in his whimsical antics.

AWAY FROM THE CROWD, Valentine and Agatha shared their slow dance in a serene meadow. Words seemed elusive to him as he slowly danced with her to the distant melody.

"Father has warned me of your type," Agatha broke the quiet.

"And what type is that?" he asked with a hint of relief.

"Soldiers...men."

"Sadly, I am both," he replied lightheartedly.

"My father believes men chase the elusive, only to wander once a maiden is within their grasp."

"He's wrong—it's your kind we fear," Valentine countered.

She stopped dancing, "What could *you* possibly fear from a woman?"

"A broken heart, for one," he admitted, his tone growing tender.

A soft laugh escaped her. "Truly?" she probed.

"That amuses you?" he inquired, a touch of surprise in his voice.

"Yes, it does—have you ever found love?"

Valentine hesitated. "Once, though we were far too young. And later, when I thought it was love, until she chose a nobleman over me."

"I'm sorry," Agatha replied, sensing his pain as they continued dancing to the light melody from afar. She sensed the undercurrent of his emotions, an openness, and a vulnerability that drew her in. "Shall we stroll?" she proposed. "There's a nearby brook where I delight in the stream's natural melody and the fragrance of the flowers."

"As you wish," he consented as he noticed the nearby brook not far away.

"I regret the pain you've endured in your past. A broken heart need not be caused only by an arrow's pierce," she remarked.

He found her insightfulness captivating. It seemed she could peer directly into his thoughts, a poignant irony considering she could not see. His usual apprehensions about intimate conversations—and even his thoughts of Rose—dissolved in her presence.

"I fear my heart is safer on the battlefield. Under the protection of our gods."

"The Christian God teaches forgiveness. Have you forgiven your past lovers?" she inquired, her boldness cutting through the air.

"The first was a twist of fate, so yes, forgiveness came easily. The latter, however, betrayed my trust, making forgiveness far more elusive."

Her keen perception picked up on the subtle shifts in his tone.

"Your pain does not go unnoticed. I am sorry for it."

"Thank you." He appreciated her sincerity. "So, you are a Christian?" he queried, curiosity piqued.

"Would you disapprove?" she countered, her voice laced with gentle defiance.

"Most soldiers honor the gods of Rome, though I am not one to judge," he confessed.

"The Christian God brings me strength in times of need," she shared, her voice trailing off as she revisited memories. "I learned of a missionary from Antioch whose conviction was so strong that, even imprisoned, his prayers led to a miraculous escape during an earthquake."

"Do you truly believe in such miracles?" Valentine asked, wanting to get to know the woman who was quickly capturing his heart.

"I do, though I have yet to witness one," she replied.

"Where did you hear of this tale?" Valentine's intrigue deepened.

"In my youth, my mother welcomed Christian farmers to our home for prayer. I would sit quietly, watching and listening to their stories, even as some of them met a martyr's fate," she reminisced, a shadow of sadness in her tone.

"You could *see* as a child?"

She hesitated. "Yes, I was not always blind."

Valentine hesitated, wondering if he should inquire but then gently asked, "What happened to your sight then?"

Agatha's voice faltered as the unsettling, guttural growl of a caged wolf in a nearby cart drew her attention. Her face paled and she tightened her grip on Valentine's arm, her body stiffening in panic.

"It's only a caged wolf. Likely en route to the Coliseum," Valentine assured her. "Are you well?"

"Yes, you must forgive me. The sound of that wolf reminded me of a childhood memory."

Regaining her composure, they approached a picturesque stone bridge arching over a murmuring brook. The faint aroma of flowers drifted on the breeze.

"As does the scent of those hellebores," Agatha remarked, her smile blooming.

"Their scent evades me," Valentine admitted.

"Your sense of smell is not as keen as mine," she replied proudly.

Valentine smiled, ever impressed by her. "Would you share this childhood memory of yours with me?"

"It's a bit silly, though when I was a child, a wolf nearly attacked and killed me. A brave boy saved me by firing his..."

Valentine stopped, realization flickering in his eyes, "Bow and arrow at the wolves!" he exclaimed, finishing her sentence.

A profound silence enveloped them, laden with the weight of this astonishing revelation.

Agatha's voice filled with wonder. "Could it truly be?"

Their voices overlapped in recognition.

"I knew you seemed familiar! Fear not, dear—"

"Dear maiden! It *is* you!" she completed his sentence.

"Yes, it is I—the silly boy...your Bear!" Valentine exclaimed.

"And I, your Rose." Her smile illuminated the world around them.

"Your hair... it's darkened to brown, and your face—it's no longer pudgy; rather, it's elongated."

"I did not have a pudgy face!" she protested.

"Did so!" he replied as if the moment had transported him back to childhood.

Laughter erupted from them. In that instant, it felt like they had roamed the forest only yesterday. She turned toward him, her gaze as intent as if her vision had returned. Her voice softened.

"Oh, Bear, I prayed our paths would cross again."

"You were my first love, my only real love," he confessed.

"Your first heartbreak—that was me?" her voice laced with emotion.

With emotion, he nodded and murmured, "Yes."

"Oh, Bear," she said, wrapping him in an embrace that bridged the gap of years. "I am truly sorry for leaving you."

He had found her—the one who had drifted away—and at that moment, in her tender embrace, he vowed silently never to lose her again.

"You still owe me for an unfinished kiss that day by the brook," he said jokingly, brushing away his tears.

The memory of their first kiss brought a burst of laughter, warm and unrestrained.

"May I?" she asked, inching her fingers toward his face in an intimate gesture.

"And what if I were to say, 'You may not?'" he quipped, the twinkle in his eye matching the lightness of his tone.

"I'd imagine it would not make much difference," she admitted, her hands already mapping the landscape of his face, appreciating his sculpted features. "They say you're quite handsome."

"People say many silly things," he demurred.

"Is it true, then?" she asked, her hands retreating.

"I would not claim to be unsightly," he quipped, eliciting more laughter.

Agatha paused as a silence filled the air.

"And me? Do you find me attractive—despite my being blind?" she asked earnestly, looking downward.

His voice softened as he instinctively caressed her cheek. "Indeed, very much so."

"That's curious," she mused.

"Why do you say that?"

"Porcia tells me I catch many an eye, yet I've no desire for hollow admiration."

"How do you mean?" he inquired, confused.

"Why would I want to be with a man who would see me only as a blind woman?"

Her response pierced his heart. "You doubt a man's ability to see the real you?"

"Indeed, I do."

"Would you like to know who I see?" he replied, drawing his hand from where he'd caressed her cheek to under her chin.

His touch caused a warmth to radiate through her, raising her hopes. "Only if you wish to tell me."

Valentine gently lifted her chin and gazed into her eyes. "I see a courageous and beautiful maiden before me—one who has never turned her back on adversity—not now, nor when we were children. The one I have always loved and still do."

A smile escaped her, tinged with emotion as her eyes brimmed with unshed tears.

"You do not see a blind maiden?"

"I do, yet so much more," he whispered.

The warmth of his breath brushed against hers as she muttered, "I am ashamed to be the one at a disadvantage now."

His lips hovered near hers. "Agatha, you have never been, nor will you ever be—at a disadvantage," he affirmed.

Her body melted into his as he kissed her. Their lips searched and deepened with an unhurried rhythm. Slowly, they moved to the passion that had been denied years earlier but was now found. He held her tightly to him, and she felt his strong embrace awaken her senses. Emotions swirled through each of them but none as strong as the indescribable love they felt for each other at that very moment.

Suddenly, from afar, Porcia's call sliced through their intimate moment: "Agatha!"

Startled, Agatha and Valentine sprang apart as if someone had discovered their innocent mischief.

"Oh no, not now," Agatha murmured, hearing Porcia's approach.

Breathless, Porcia, with Marius by her side, marched to them with astonishment and disapproval. Tiber trailed them, several strides behind.

"Are you mad?" Porcia spat. "I leave you alone for one second, and you do *this*!"

"Incurable," Marius quipped with exaggerated seriousness.

"What is this urgency, Porcia?" Agatha inquired calmly.

"The men are to leave urgently—and you promised not to stray from my sight!"

"Porcia, Agatha, all is well?" Tiber shouted out.

Porcia turned. "Yes, Tiber, thank you." Porcia turned back to Agatha. "Now you've done it, Agatha. Father will hear all about this."

"It's all right, Porcia. I will speak to Father," Agatha assured her.

Marius interjected, "Valentine, I'm afraid it's true. General Claudius has summoned the Second Legion back to the front, and we must leave tonight."

The distant sound of soldiers rallying to their call filled the air: "Second Legion, to the camp! Second Legion!"

Valentine sighed, then faced Agatha, whose expression mirrored the sudden change in their fortunes and his own emotion.

"You're being called away?" she asked, her voice a whisper of hope fading. "How can it be that we're being torn apart once again?"

In that moment Valentine cursed his choice to become a soldier, but he could not throw away his duty to Rome and his troops. "I am afraid it is so, my dearest," he said sadly, the weight of the moment pressing upon them.

Agatha's eyes welled with tears. After all these years, having finally found each other only to be divided again. *It can't be,* she thought, refusing to believe it.

Marius and Porcia stepped back to allow them a moment to express their farewells privately.

"Promise me you'll return," she implored steadily.

"Upon my honor, I will return to you, Agatha," he assured her, quickly removing his wool scarf and handing it to her. "Keep this—it will remind you of me."

Marius, noticing the other men calling for them, shouted out jokingly, "Cupid, hurry along—we need to return to the encampment."

"Farewell, my dear Rose," Valentine proclaimed, gently pressing a kiss on Agatha's cheek before hastening away. "Guard her well, Porcia," he entrusted, his words trailing behind him as he rushed past her, and then Tiber, who offered only a disapproving glance but remained silent as Valentine continued swiftly on his way.

"Silly Bear!" Agatha called out with affection and sadness.

Valentine spun around and shouted playfully, "I am not silly!"

Chapter 7

The Senate

"The rule of the people is close to freedom,
but the domination of the few is closer to the lust of kings."
—Tacitus

In Rome, the Senate assembled in the Curia Julia, an imposing structure boasting towering doors and lofty walls made of marble-faced concrete. Its exterior was graced with sophisticated columns, supporting an expansive interior where hundreds of senators gathered in a semi-circular arrangement around a speaker.

At fifty-one years of age, Emperor Gallienus stood tall and formidable, commanding attention across the assembly. The senators, once the powerhouse of Roman politics, now spoke with voices that echoed faintly in contrast to his. The intricate folds of their togas seemed to weigh heavily upon them, as if bearing the weight of the emperor's overarching authority. Gallienus's voice boomed as he addressed them.

"Esteemed senators, our illustrious empire faces unyielding threats on all fronts. Along the Danube, there are relentless raids. In Germania, the Alemanni test our borders. In the east, the Heruli sack our cities. Yet, under my steadfast rule, Rome remains the capital of the world."

The senators stomped their feet, a sign of approval for what was being said and a practice designed not to interrupt the speaker.

The highest-ranking senator, and also *princeps senatus*, was Senator Paternus. As the leader of the Senate, he held the authority to guide debates and speak first in major matters. Additionally, he served as consul, one of the two most senior elected officials, holding significant sway over the Senate. He stood with dignified resolve. "Rome owes you a debt of gratitude, Caesar. Like your father, you have served us with unwavering dedication. How may we aid you in this hour of need?" he inquired before retaking his seat, eliciting subtle nods of acknowledgment from the chamber.

Emperor Gallienus continued to address the assembly: "Senators, today's agenda surpasses the usual discussions on external dangers or economic challenges. Today, I urge you to create policies and channels to illuminate adversaries hidden within our society's weave. Usurpers such as Regalianus, Ingenuus, and now, the notably formidable Postumus call for our unwavering resolve and decisive action."

At the mention of Postumus, the atmosphere in the Senate shifted palpably. The senators were all too aware of the personal tragedy Gallienus had suffered at the hands of the man who had declared himself emperor of the western provinces. Postumus had not only rebelled but had also ordered the execution of Gallienus's son, Saloninus, after besieging him in Cologne. The murder of the emperor's heir loomed large over the chamber, adding a layer of silent intensity to the proceedings.

Senator Paternus, recognizing the unspoken tension, rose with dignified resolve. "We stand by your side, Caesar," he said, his voice steady.

The chamber erupted in the sound of stomping feet.

Gallienus seized the momentum, his voice rising: "Senators, I refuse to echo the oversights of my predecessors. Together, we will root out any internal threats in their infancy and feed these traitors to the lions!"

The Senate roared in approval as Senator Paternus began to rise again. However, before Senator Paternus could reach his feet, young Senator Junius, with brown curly hair and hazel eyes that echoed his ambitious nature, quickly stood and interjected.

"Caesar, if I may, given your father's tragic demise at the hands of the Sassanids, would it not be wise for us to also deliberate on the looming threat to our eastern borders, in addition to any internal..."

Gallienus retorted sharply, "Senator Junius, should King Shapur dare march upon us from the east, rest assured that my legions will crush his forces with the precision of an eagle striking a field mouse!"

Laughter filled the room as Senator Junius recoiled to his senate with mocking glances directed at him.

Undeterred, Emperor Gallienus continued scolding him: "And, Senator Junius, this matter better not be the cause prompting your incessant requests for a *private* audience with me."

The laughter abruptly ceased, replaced by stern glares directed at Senator Junius, whose overly ambitious nature had evoked a mixed response from his colleagues.

Senator Fabius, another youthful senator of average stature and an ally of Senator Junius, locked eyes with him and subtly shook his head in disbelief.

Emperor Gallienus continued addressing the assembly: "Senators, let us maintain our focus. Rest assured, under my rule, our military continues its onslaught against our external enemies, and usurpers like Postumus will eventually meet their grim fate. However, let us deliberate on policies to strengthen our resolve moving forward."

Caesar recognized Senator Didius with a nod. He was his second consul and one of the highest-ranking members of the Senate. His distinguished white hair, paired with a philosopher's beard that bore two distinct curls parting at the chin, lent him an air of wisdom and authority reminiscent of the great Marcus Aurelius.

Senator Didius rose. "Caesar speaks the undeniable truth. We must be responsible for crafting policies that will stabilize and shield Rome from all her threats. Let us take a moment to engage in meaningful discourse on this crucial matter."

Emperor Gallienus observed the senators' animated discussions with a vigilant eye. Despite his outward calm, an underlying current of unease was evident. As he watched the senators debate, memories of his father, the previous emperor of Rome, weighed heavily on his mind. He vividly remembered the day when the imperial messenger brought news of his father's capture by the Persians, who humiliated him as a human footstool before his execution. The haunting image of his father's skin, treated and showcased in a Persian temple as a war trophy, haunted him.

Suddenly, General Aureolus, Caesar's most trusted military adviser, approached Emperor Gallienus discreetly. "Caesar, the entirety of the Second Legion is en route to the northeastern frontier, near Aquileia."

Emperor Gallienus appeared momentarily stunned.

"General, as I confront treachery among the Senate, it seems betrayal materializes before me," he admonished. "I authorized the deployment of a *vexillatio* of cavalry, not the entire legion!"

The murmur in the chamber subsided as Emperor Gallienus seethed with frustration.

"My apologies, Caesar; by some means, General Claudius managed to mobilize *all* the men," General Aureolus reported shamefully.

Sensing the tension, Senator Paternus asked optimistically, "Favorable news from the front, sire?"

Caesar's gaze fixed intently. "No, Senator Paternus. I fear the tidings are far from favorable." In a rare moment of openness, Emperor Gallienus divulged to the assembly, "Contrary to my explicit orders, I have just received word that one of my generals has deployed an entire legion to the battlefield contrary to my directive. This failure in our lines of communication will be investigated and addressed," he concluded, his eyes narrowing on General Aureolus, who backed deeper into a dark corner.

Senator Junius took notice of the general's admonishing, momentarily relieved that the assembly had shifted their eyes elsewhere.

Emperor Gallienus stood and continued to address the next matter at hand. "Senators, as we navigate our internal challenges, we must remember what has always made Rome strong: our ability to adapt and assimilate what is different into the fabric of our empire. It is crucial that we prevent the formation of isolated groups that lie beyond the reach of our state. Despite my decree of tolerance, I have received troubling reports of continued hostility, violence, and persecution of Christians. We must address these divisions and bring them into the fold if we are to strengthen Rome."

The assembly responded with more approval as Senator Paternus shifted uneasily in his seat before rising to address the Emperor. "Caesar, your enlightened edict has nurtured increased harmony across our empire, making instances of such hostility quite scarce."

"Regrettably, Senator Paternus, my spies report the contrary. I recently dispatched my religious adviser to the front to address our generals on this matter, only to receive his headless body in return, allegedly at the hands of our enemies. I entrust this Senate to enforce our tolerance decree with vigilance, ensuring every citizen's protection. A more secure Rome is a more formidable Rome."

General Aureolus reached a silent breaking point and exited the room as the senators stomped their feet in acknowledgment, though mixed reactions were evident.

As discussions unfolded, Senator Junius and Senator Fabius exchanged another meaningful glance. Despite Senator Fabius's silent shake of disapproval, Senator Junius ignored the warning, stood up again, and addressed the emperor directly.

"Caesar, if I may, while I empathize with the tragic loss of your religious adviser, I must caution against attributing our discord to the persecution of Christians alone. Our empire faces multifaceted challenges. Perhaps it is prudent to explore the grievances of *all* our citizens, not just those of the Christian faith."

Emperor Gallienus looked at him scornfully. "Senator Junius, the logic behind my father's choice to elevate you to the Senate remains a mystery to me, regardless of any contributions your *mother* might have made to this end. Now, it appears you have failed to observe that our Christian populace has surged in recent generations, encompassing even those within our legions. Your comments, much like your senatorial appointment, are *ill-considered*. My decision remains unchanged."

Once again, Senator Junius took his seat, eliciting another wave of light laughter from the assembly as Senator Fabius buried his face in his hands.

Emperor Gallienus concluded the assembly: "Senators, we stand at a pivotal juncture; unity must prevail. With that, I bring this assembly to a close."

The emperor greeted his consuls, Senators Paternus and Didius, who promptly moved to his side, expressing their admiration and steadfast allegiance as they escorted him away.

Meanwhile, in a nearby corner, Senator Fabius found Senator Junius visibly simmering with anger over Caesar's sharp reprimand.

"You've become quite skilled at navigating our political landscape," Senator Fabius joked.

"Silence, Fabius. I can tolerate Caesar's insults, but not yours," Senator Junius asserted sternly.

"My jests are but playful, my love," Senator Fabius replied as he affectionately and discreetly reached for Senator Junius's hand.

Senator Junius quickly recoiled and replied, "Caesar is gravely mistaken in attempting to silence me. Christian tolerance alone cannot shield our empire from barbarian threats and cultural upheaval."

"Be cautious, Junius," Senator Fabius warned.

"I will endure no more humiliation. My intellect is wasted on an emperor lacking common sense and straying from our traditional beliefs."

"Junius, Caesar is fearful of usurpers and rightfully so, perhaps in time—"

"No, the time is now, Fabius. Senator Paternus has lost his influence, and Senator Didius lacks strategic vision. I will ascend to the highest seat in the Senate—if not under this Caesar, then under the next."

"What do you propose?" Senator Fabius whispered as Senator Junius paced in the hall.

Engulfed in contemplation, Senator Junius's bruised ego and simmering fury ignited a storm of thoughts. He refused to stand idly by as Caesar threatened to unravel the empire he cherished. His mind drifted back to his childhood, raised by devout Roman parents who had introduced him to daily rituals and offerings at the household shrine, honoring the Lares and Penates, the protective spirits of the home and family. He recalled his teachers, who had instilled in him the sacred stories of deities like Minerva, goddess of wisdom, and Mars, god of war, whose tales of valor and strategy had shaped his courage and intellect. Now, he pondered how his hesitation to act might displease the gods, endangering not only the fate of Rome but also his standing in their divine eyes.

"It's time I convened with like-minded generals," he concluded with unwavering resolve.

"What?! Have you lost your senses?" Senator Fabius exclaimed in disbelief, glancing around nervously to check if anyone was listening. "Were you not listening when Caesar threatened to throw traitors and usurpers to the lions?"

"I am well aware of the risks, Fabius."

"Are you? And which generals do you intend to approach?"

"Aureolus and Claudius," Junius replied resolutely.

"Only the most dangerous men in our empire—responsible for the deaths of thousands," Fabius replied.

"Exactly—yet both are staunch Romans and openly disagree with Caesar's directives."

"You're proposing a coup," Fabius whispered. "And within the sacred hall of the Curia Julia, no less!"

Senator Junius paused, letting the weight of the moment sink in. "I suppose I am."

Fabius glanced around nervously, leaning in closer. "Who do you think you are, Julius Caesar? You know how his story ended."

Junius smirked. "My dear Fabius, it is not how our stories end that matter, rather how they begin. Now, if you'll excuse me, I have work to do."

With that, Senator Junius strode away, his steps heavy with the confidence of an emperor.

"Junius, wait!" Fabius whispered urgently, his voice almost swallowed by the vastness of the hall, before hurrying after his colleague—and deranged lover.

Chapter 8

Farewell

The morning light filtered through the wooden shutters, casting a soft glow across the modest kitchen. Agatha stood by the kitchen table, her fingers nimbly identifying the ingredients laid out before her. The fragrance of freshly baked bread and aromatic herbs wafted through the air, mingling with the morning songs of the birds outside.

Porcia moved about with effortless grace, her knife rhythmically chopping vegetables, while Agatha felt for the apples, pears, and nuts. A soft melody hummed from her lips, filling the room with a sense of tranquility.

"You appear in good spirits this morning, sister," Porcia remarked, her tone gently prodding.

Agatha smiled. "And why should I not be?" she asked, fully aware of her younger sister's insatiable curiosity. "I did not hear Father depart this morning," she remarked, attempting to steer the conversation elsewhere.

"His first execution was moved earlier today. He left at dawn," Porcia replied.

"I see," Agatha said as they moved toward the table.

"Will you be joining me in town today, or will you be working in the garden?"

Agatha paused, "I would like you to take me to see Valentine today."

Porcia stiffened. "To the encampment?"

"Where else?" Agatha replied.

"It took us nearly the entire walk home to convince Tiber not to mention our encounter with the men to Father. Do you truly think he would now agree to accompany us to their military encampment? Father would never allow it. Besides, I'm quite certain they have already departed," she remarked.

Agatha's face remained resolute. "Porcia, I'm not sure they have, and we needn't trouble Father with our every action. We've snuck out without Tiber noticing before, haven't we?" Before Porcia could respond, Agatha added, "Besides, are there not matters of the heart that only sisters should share?"

Porcia sighed reluctantly. "It's dangerous, Agatha."

"Which is why you'll accompany me and we will travel during daylight only," Agatha countered.

Porcia knew there was little point in trying to dissuade her sister once her mind was set. "Very well," she relented as she thought of perhaps seeing Marius as well. "Though we must be swift. Tiber will notice if we're gone for too long, and the encampment is no place for maidens."

Agatha nodded. "As you wish."

Porcia sipped her water, then added, "You did not share much after Lupercalia."

A slight smile escaped Agatha's lips as she thought of her encounter with Valentine.

"Are you in love with him?" Porcia finally asked, stunned that Agatha could be so taken by a man she had met only twice.

Agatha blushed as she reached for a piece of bread. "If it is not love, then I may not know what love is."

Porcia leaned in closer. "Come, sister, you mustn't hold back. I would very much like to know every detail. What else did Valentine say to you?"

Agatha sighed, a dreamy expression softening her features. "It is not what he said, as much as it was how I felt in his presence. There is a familiarity when I am around him. I feel safe with him."

Porcia nibbled at her food, her thoughts racing. She had never considered the idea of her sister running off with another man. The notion was completely foreign to her, even unsettling. She had always envisioned herself by Agatha's side.

"He kissed you," Porcia blurted, unable to contain herself any longer. "I saw you."

"Porcia!" Agatha replied, blushing deeply.

"What? I am your sister. I deserve to know these things."

Agatha chuckled. "You certainly do not, though if you must know, yes, he did."

"And?" Porcia pressed for more.

"And what?" Agatha replied. "It is not the first time we have kissed."

"What?!" Porcia gasped, her eyes widening in shock.

"I kissed him when we were children, if you must know."

Porcia sat back, stunned. "You didn't think *this* was important enough to share with me?"

"We've only just rediscovered our connection. Besides, you were far too young to understand any of this back then."

"What other secrets are you hiding from me? You chose not to discuss your feelings on our way home from Lupercalia—and now this!" Porcia asserted, her eyes wide with feelings of betrayal.

Agatha smiled. "I was still coming to terms with my emotions, Porcia," she replied softly. "Do not take this so personally."

"And now?" Porcia probed further.

"And now, there is more I wish to say to Valentine."

Porcia sighed, unsure of where this conversation was leading. This was far more serious than she had anticipated.

Agatha added, "I promise to share more with you after I speak with him today."

A silence hung in the air, the weight of Agatha's request sinking in.

Porcia hesitated, torn between her sister's plea and their father's stern warnings. "You know how Father feels about us courting a soldier."

"I do. Though, if it were up to Father, we would never court at all," Agatha replied. "And what of you and Marius? You spoke fondly of him after Lupercalia."

"He was a bit silly for my liking, though entertaining. In any case, they are all deploying today, and I will not have my heart broken over a *soldier*, nor should you."

"I am aware of the risks, Porcia." Agatha placed her other hand over Porcia's. "Please, take me to Valentine today, and do not share any of this with Father. After all, we must have secrets that remain between us."

Porcia gazed into her sister's eyes. She could feel the love her sister had for Valentine but grappled with the concern she had for her sister's well-being. Nonetheless, she succumbed to Agatha's plea. "Very well, I shall take you."

THEY WALKED along a dusty road toward the encampment. Porcia led the way, while Agatha walked beside her, using her arm for guidance.

"There are so many soldiers and tents ahead. How will we ever find them? We certainly cannot enter the encampment on our own," Porcia said, her voice filled with worry as she realized this was probably a pointless trip.

"Guide us around the perimeter. We will find a way," Agatha replied with calm certainty.

As they approached the *castrum*, the sounds of military life grew louder: the clang of swords being sharpened, orders being shouted, and the rhythmic tramp of soldiers' boots. Tents were neatly arranged in rows, with soldiers moving purposefully among them, preparing their gear and tending to their mounts.

Porcia guided Agatha carefully around the perimeter of the

castrum, taking in the lively scene and avoiding the more crowded areas. "We must find them quickly," she murmured. "It looks like they're preparing to depart."

Agatha nodded, her senses heightened by the unfamiliar surroundings. She could hear the murmur of voices, the neighing of horses, and the occasional laughter of comrades-in-arms. Each sound painted a vivid picture in her mind, helping her piece together a vision of the bustling camp.

Porcia's eyes darted from face to face, searching for the familiar features of Valentine and Marius.

"You must take us into the encampment," Agatha urged.

"It's too dangerous, Agatha. Private citizens aren't allowed, let alone women."

"Just ask one of the soldiers if they know of Valentine or Marius and where they're camped," Agatha pressed.

Porcia hesitated, then pulled her hood lower, concealing much of her face before adjusting Agatha's cloak. They moved forward, slipping past two guards who were too engrossed in conversation to notice them. The temporary encampment, hastily thrown together, lacked the strict watchfulness of a permanent castrum, granting them a narrow window to proceed.

Linked by the arm, Porcia guided Agatha through the camp. Soldiers glanced their way, but Porcia kept her gaze forward, nodding briefly when necessary. Around them, some men polished armor, others warmed themselves by fires, and a few spoke in hushed tones. Each step stretched time as they continued their search.

"That's far enough; they must have left," Porcia commented as her arm tightened on Agatha's grip, her anxiety palpable.

"Do not fret, Porcia. The soldiers are here to protect us, not harm us. We'll find them," Agatha reassured her, squeezing her sister's arm gently.

"I think we should leave," Porcia stated, noticing a few inappropriate glances from some of the soldiers. It began to dawn on her that they might be mistaken for the same kind of women who followed men from the taverns.

Just then, Agatha's keen ears picked up a familiar voice amid the din. Her heart leapt as she turned her head toward the sound. "There, Porcia, over there," she said, pointing in the direction of Valentine's voice.

Porcia followed Agatha's gesture and spotted Valentine, his tall figure unmistakable even in the crowd. He stood with Marius, Efebus, and Proculo, deep in conversation as they adjusted their gear.

"You're right! It's them!" Porcia exclaimed, her relief evident.

Without hesitation, they made their way toward the men. Valentine glanced up, his eyes widening in surprise and joy as he saw Agatha and Porcia approaching. He nudged Marius, who turned and broke into a broad grin.

"Agatha! Porcia!" Valentine called out, closing the distance between them with quick strides.

Agatha's face lit up with a radiant smile as she reached out, her fingers brushing against Valentine's arm. "I knew we would find you," she said, her voice filled with confident affection.

Valentine took her hands in his, his expression tender. "I'm so grateful you came. Where is Tiber? It's not safe for the two of you to be traveling alone, especially here."

"I told her this much, yet she would not listen to me," Porcia replied in her defense.

"I've been thinking of you since our last encounter," Agatha admitted, her voice low.

"And I, you," he replied warmly.

Marius stepped forward, his eyes twinkling as he greeted Porcia. "It seems fate has brought us together as well," he said, his tone light and playful.

Porcia smiled and replied jokingly, "Are you still tripping over your feet?"

"He's good at that, even on the march!" Efebus chimed in from the background.

"Hey!" Marius replied with laughter.

Valentine turned to Agatha, his gaze unwavering. "Will you walk with me?"

Agatha nodded. "Of course, let us find a quieter spot."

"Do not leave me here for long," Porcia ordered.

"Rest assured, you're in good company," Marius replied. "Besides, our centurion should hasten unless he wishes to incur the wrath of his superior," he added with a playful smirk, as Valentine waved him off.

He led Agatha away from the camp's commotion, navigating through the structured chaos in search of a private corner. Once they found a quiet spot, away from prying eyes and ears, Valentine turned to her, his expression grave.

"I wish we had more time," he said softly, brushing a strand of hair from her face.

Agatha caressed Valentine's hand. "I wanted to see you again, to wish you farewell and to express how much it means to have found you after all these years."

He gently squeezed her hand. "The thought of our reunion kept me awake last night—my heart too restless for sleep. You cannot imagine how long I have searched for you, Agatha."

Her voice was tender, "I wanted to tell you that I believe in you, Valentine. I trust you will return."

His eyes softened as he sensed her subtle doubt. Her words, though filled with conviction, revealed a layer of vulnerability. He offered a reassuring touch and said, "Do you remember when we were children and you told me to wait for you at the forest's edge?"

She smiled, reflecting fondly on their childhood. "How could I forget?"

"Did I ever fail you then?" he asked.

"No, you were always there."

Valentine gently lifted Agatha's chin. "Then, know this: as before, no matter what stands in my way—I shall return to you. If you will await me."

"I will," she replied. Her voice cracked as she uttered, "I suppose I only needed to hear you say it."

Valentine leaned down, his breath mingling with hers before his lips met hers in a gentle kiss. The world around them seemed to blur, leaving only the two of them in sharp focus, bound by their unspoken vows and his promise to return. Though he offered reassurance, deep down he knew that only the gods could foresee what the future held.

CHAPTER 9

CRIES OF BATTLE

"We make war so that we may live in peace."
—ARISTOTLE

General Claudius's legion stood poised at the war front, bolstered by the additional troops he had summoned, ready to unleash a coordinated assault against the Goths. Thousands of soldiers, draped in furs and cloaks over their scale armor, presented a disciplined force on the field. Small fires dotted the landscape, providing warmth in the early morning spring air. Mist and smoke curled around their weaponry—spears and swords for the infantry, bows and arrows for the auxiliary units.

Amid the infantry, Valentine meticulously inspected his cohort. As he traversed among his men, his esteemed title of centurion resonated in their salutations, and his attire denoted him as a symbol of authority. In particular, his new sword, a masterpiece of craftsmanship, shimmered with lethal sharpness. Approaching two young newcomers within his cohort, he imparted words of encouragement.

"Luca, your swiftness will catch them off guard. Harbor no doubts."

"Gratitude, Centurion—I will not falter," Luca responded with determination.

"Remmius, your strength is our advantage. Ensure it lasts," Valentine reassured him.

"Understood, Centurion," Remmius affirmed.

The formidable Gothic warriors emerged from the shadowy depths of the dense woodland across the semi-frozen field. Their armor, less refined than the Romans', bore a blend of looted Roman equipment and traditionally crafted leather and scale armor, with some chainmail still in use. Crude yet effective swords and axes glinted menacingly in the dawn light, casting flashes across the landscape. The warriors advanced with less discipline but with a menacing unity, their gaze fixed firmly upon the legionnaires. Suddenly, the air reverberated with the thunderous beat of drums, the haunting blast of horns, and the fierce war cries of the Goths, unleashing a palpable surge of restless energy that sent shivers down the spines of all who heard it.

Valentine focused intently on his enemy, his eagerness for the upcoming battle unmistakable. Surrounding him, the clash of armor signaled the soldiers' rallying. As he passed one of his men, he overheard a whispered prayer to Mithras, the eastern god revered by many legionnaires. The moment brought Agatha's words to mind, her gentle guidance echoing in his thoughts: *"The Christian God gives me strength in times of need."*

Valentine had always approached religion as a civic duty, having been raised to honor the gods and uphold the rituals passed down through generations. For him, offerings to Jupiter and Mars were not performed out of personal conviction but rather out of necessity—to keep the gods appeased and ensure their favor for the empire. Questions of life, death, and fate belonged to the realm of philosophers—the Stoics, Epicureans, and others who wrestled with such mysteries.

But now, standing on the threshold of battle with death looming before him, a deep unease gnawed at his soul. His admiration for Marius and his love for Agatha had introduced him to a new kind of faith—one unbound by ritual, rooted instead in something deeper, something personal.

As he approached Marius, his steps faltered. Marius knelt in quiet prayer, shielded from view by Efebus, Linus, Proculo, Albus, and Scaro, all standing guard as the chaos of the camp surged around them. The serene devotion on Marius's face stood in stark contrast to the turmoil raging in Valentine's heart, deepening the sense of uncertainty that had begun to consume him.

Unable to resist the pull any longer, Valentine knelt beside Marius.

"I will join you in Christian prayer," he said, his voice steady despite his uncertainty.

Marius, taken aback, nodded, "Very well."

Valentine looked up at Linus, Proculo, Scaro, and Efebus and nodded, signaling for them to join as an act of unity.

In a calm tone, Efebus asked, "Are you certain this is wise?"

"We will require the strength of all our gods today, Efebus," Valentine firmly responded.

"Very well—kneel!" shouted Efebus.

In response to Efebus's commanding voice, the rest of the cohort, except for Albus, swiftly knelt. Albus, standing firm, expressed his reluctance, "I would prefer not to be staked to a cross, Valentine."

"As you wish, brother," Valentine replied.

Scaro, visibly disappointed, looked up at his brother. "Show respect, Albus!"

Turning his head away, Albus ignored his younger brother's plea, then shook his head in dismay, embarrassed by how easily swayed his younger brother could be.

"Let him be, Scaro," Valentine intervened and nodded at Marius, who took his position facing the group and planted his sword tip into the ground, the cross-shaped hilt raised high.

Marius's voice carried across the immediate vicinity as he prayed aloud: "Lord, we seek Your strength as we stand together. Let Your love, which knows no bounds, guide us. Help us unite in our shared purpose to defend our homeland, drawing on our courage and resolve. Amen."

"For Rome!" Valentine's voice rang out.

"For Rome!" echoed the men around him, their spirits ignited.

The serene moment was abruptly shattered by the sound of hooves hammering against the stony terrain, signaling the arrival of General Claudius and Aurelian, flanked by a procession of officers and guards.

The men instantly stood erect, falling into a respectful hush.

"Centurion!" General Claudius thundered.

"Yes, General!" Valentine snapped to attention.

"Name and rank!" the general demanded.

"Valentine Romanus, Centurion for the 3rd Cohort!"

"The officer recently promoted by the emperor?" Claudius scrutinized him closely.

"Yes, General!" Valentine confirmed, standing firm and attentive.

Claudius leaned forward in his saddle, his voice carrying a hint of challenge, "If memory serves, isn't it customary for generals to confer such honors?"

His words hung heavily between them.

"The emperor's benevolence was greatly appreciated, General," Valentine replied while meeting General Claudius's piercing gaze.

"I'm certain it was," Claudius replied, his voice dripping with disdain. "An officer, yet you allow your men to disregard Rome's gods?"

Valentine held his ground. "I only wished to strengthen morale, General."

Claudius quickly countered, "The gods of Rome demand loyalty, and those who spurn their rites endanger us all. Superstitions like this undermine the very order of our empire."

Albus shook his head, watching anxiously. Rumors of Claudius's brutal treatment of Christians had reached them all. He knew it had been a reckless choice to worship openly on the battlefield, and now he feared for his brother's safety.

The general's gaze swept over the nearby light infantry unit who would initiate the skirmishes, younger and less seasoned soldiers with little armor.

"You soldiers, come forward," Claudius commanded. "Strip the armor from these Christians and prove yourself worthy. Let us see how their God protects them now."

At his behest, the young men of the light infantry moved forward. Valentine, angered by Claudius's unnecessary cruelty, knew there was no room for dissent. He nodded to his men and they relinquished their armor to the less experienced warriors.

Leaning closer, Claudius warned in a low, menacing tone, "If the gods do not favor us in battle, I will see you all crucified!"

Valentine acknowledged the gravity of the situation with a nod, recognizing the risk he had invited upon himself and his brothers-in-arms. He felt a deep pang of guilt for exposing his men to such danger, knowing they would face the battle with only their faith and valor as their shield. The sight of the young soldiers donning their armor filled him with dread; he had failed his men by stripping them of their protection.

"General, I am not a Christian," Albus hastily claimed.

"Excellent, then perhaps your Christian comrades have not angered the gods after all," Claudius retorted while signaling for the light infantry soldiers to confiscate Albus's armor as well.

With an authoritative call, Claudius and his entourage departed swiftly.

"What right does he have to choose which gods we worship?" Marius said bitterly.

"Be grateful that he spared your life...Christian," Albus spat.

"Enough, Albus!" Scaro intervened, seizing his brother with a determined grip.

"Perhaps you should listen more closely to your older brother, little twit!" Albus challenged, the childhood taunt reigniting old grievances.

Scaro, infuriated by the demeaning nickname, tensed to retaliate, but Albus—angered by his younger brother's defiance—struck first, delivering a swift punch across Scaro's face. Valentine quickly intervened to halt the growing conflict.

"I despise you!" Scaro shouted at Albus.

"Enough! Both of you, stand down! That's an order!" Valentine's voice boomed with authority. "The general might strip us of our armor, yet he will not divide us! Together we fight, together we live!" he shouted at them. "Back to your positions, now!" The clamor of impending battle surrounded them, but Valentine's focus remained sharp. He could not afford to have his brothers-in-arms, friends he had trusted through countless campaigns, divided in the face of the enemy.

Scaro moved toward his brother to embrace him, but Albus took a step back, his eyes cold with unresolved anger. Forgiveness would not come easily. Scaro sighed, knowing this storm between brothers would eventually settle. Since their childhood, Albus had always been slow to forgive.

The soldiers lined up as ordered.

"On my signal," Valentine commanded, positioning himself at the forefront of their formation.

Suddenly, the blaring of Roman trumpets and the deep thrum of war drums filled the air, mingling with battle cries, clashing weapons, and chanting, creating a deafening symphony that signaled the start of combat. Arrows streaked across the sky like falling stars, raining down on the advancing Goths. The relentless hail struck their front lines, breaking their charge with brutal precision.

Above the chaos, the Roman standard, the golden eagle, gleamed in the sunlight.

Valentine raised his sword high. "Who do we fight for?" he bellowed.

"For Rome!" came the thunderous reply.

Valentine signaled the younger infantry to charge, their feet pounding the earth as they sprinted forward to close the gap and evade the deadly hail of arrows. The Goths, caught off guard by the sudden rush, hesitated. Without missing a beat, Valentine surged ahead, leading his seasoned men with relentless determination. His heart pounded as his men thundered behind him, war cries ripping through the air.

As Valentine witnessed the oncoming charge of the Goths', time seemed to halt. He peered into the enemy's face and saw the best and worst in humanity. For a moment, he did not see soldiers but rather a sea of men all fighting for what they cherished most. The battlefield became a crucible of raw emotion, igniting a terror within their human souls. And, in that brief instant, he felt the presence of a divine force. Yet, as swiftly as the revelation came, it vanished, replaced by the stark reality of a Goth wielding his sword in the direction of his skull.

Overlooking the battlefield, General Claudius sat tall on his horse, its steady breath audible amid the distant cries of battle. Beside him, General Aurelian scanned the horizon, taking in the advancing enemy forces. The rhythmic beat of war drums echoed across the field, signaling orders to the troops.

"Send word to the southern archers," Aurelian commanded the standard bearer.

With a nod, the standard bearer raised a flag in the air, while the musicians' horns blared in response. Another river of arrows soared through the sky, descending upon the enemy with deadly precision.

Amid the chaos, General Claudius, reflecting on the earlier escapade with Valentine, turned to Aurelian with a grave warning. "Mark my words, Aurelian, should we fail to curb this Christian tide, it will spell the end of Rome as we know it."

"The Goths are our enemy today, General. One battle at a time," Aurelian replied.

"An enemy you cannot see is always your enemy," Claudius retorted, turning his gaze back to the battlefield.

"Why do you despise the Christians so?"

Claudius sighed, his eyes reflecting the bloodshed before him. "I grew up on a modest farm in Pannonia. My father often sent me to deliver crops to a wealthier neighbor's villa. They were Christians, though they concealed it well. Their son, older and filled with bitterness, mocked me whenever he could, ridiculing me for worshiping our gods. My younger brother, Quintillus, was too small to make the journey, so I handled the deliveries alone."

Aurelian glanced at Claudius, noting the eerie calm with which the general recounted the memory, even as the battlefield erupted before them.

"One day, the boy's taunts turned to violence. As I rode away, he hurled a jagged stone at me. It struck my forehead, and I tumbled from my horse. When I returned home, my father saw the wound and demanded justice. The Christians, however, denied everything, swearing loyalty to Rome, insisting their son could do no wrong. They went so far to accuse me of lying, saying I likely fell from my horse through my own clumsiness. My father believed the Christians and whipped *me* for bringing dishonor to our family.

Claudius turned his gaze to Aurelian, then touched the scar on his face. "This reminds me of their deceit. That Centurion earlier, worshiping a false god on my battlefield—it was as if I was staring at that same boy who left me with this mark."

Aurelian's expression tightened briefly before he gave a solemn nod, acknowledging the weight of Claudius's words. Together, their eyes returned to the horizon. Aurelian knew it was rare for Claudius to share such a tale, yet he also understood that the battlefield often disarmed even the most hardened of men. Despite their division in faith, in this moment, with their gazes fixed on a common enemy, they stood united in purpose.

The release of more arrows cast a darkened glow, their shadows dancing across the chaos below. Romans and Goths clashed violently at the center, a whirlwind of destruction and death. The air was filled with the sounds of metal on metal, the cries of the fallen, and the relentless march of chaos.

Valentine displayed his battlefield prowess amid the turmoil. With a quick thrust, he impaled a Goth warrior, following up with a lethal cut to another's neck. Marius skillfully blocked an ax attack at his side and countered with a dagger strike.

"They're flanking us! Stay close!" Valentine bellowed.

Efebus, exerting his might, cleaved through an enemy warrior, his strength unmistakable. Nearby, Proculo grimaced as a sword slash left a deep wound on his shoulder, his lack of armor a clear disadvantage. Yet, he retaliated, crippling his attacker with a swift cut to the leg before burying his sword in his foe's head.

Amid the fierce battle, Valentine spotted Linus and Scaro engaging two Goths not far off, their swords clashing with the enemy's. However, in a fleeting moment, a tragic slip on a slick ax head sent Scaro to the ground. Seizing the opportunity, a Goth thrust his blade into Scaro's unprotected torso.

Scaro screamed as the blade went through him.

Linus rushed to Scaro's aid, but it was too late.

"Scaro!" Linus's cry filled the air.

Valentine sprinted to their side, only to meet Scaro's lifeless gaze.

"No!" Valentine's cry pierced the air. His friend couldn't be gone—it couldn't be true. His heart plummeted as a torrent of guilt, anger, regret, and grief crashed over him, each emotion sharper than the last, distorting the very fabric of his reality. The world around him seemed to blur, as if time itself faltered under the weight of his despair. But the brutal truth of war clawed its way back into his mind, forcing him to choke down his anguish. With a steely resolve, he pushed the pain aside and snapped back into action.

Albus spotted them and rushed to his fallen brother, collapsing beside him in despair. "Scaro! No!" he cried, his voice raw with grief.

Valentine watched as Albus cradled his lifeless brother, fully grasping the depth of his loss. He knew this would tear Albus apart—despite their differences, Scaro was everything to him.

Linus and Valentine continued to fend off further assaults. "Defend yourself, Albus!" Valentine ordered, but Albus was paralyzed by grief as enemies closed.

With a mighty slash, Valentine severed a Goth's arm while Linus speared another. A third Goth swung a deadly blow at Valentine, but Efebus, in a quick motion, grabbed an ax off the ground and hurled it, striking the Goth squarely in the forehead. He crumpled to the ground, dead instantly.

The Goths pressed their attack with renewed ferocity. Marius battled his way to Valentine, Linus, and Efebus, forming a protective circle around Albus, who knelt beside Scaro's lifeless body. Even amidst the chaos, Albus's grief was palpable.

"Jupiter, take me instead—take me," he murmured, his voice laced with sorrow and feelings of guilt for not embracing his brother before battle.

Atop the strategic hill, where the clamor of fighting was a distant echo, General Aurelian observed a critical weakness near where Valentine and his men bravely fought.

"We're outnumbered on the northeast hill. Shall I send more infantry?" General Aurelian asked Claudius, who was shielding his eyes from the dawn's glare.

"Which cohort is there?" Claudius queried.

"The third."

"Command the archers," Claudius ordered.

Aurelian hesitated. "We cannot; the archers will strike our own."

"The Christians have strayed from their formation. Proceed with the archers," Claudius insisted, his gaze brooking no argument.

With a resigned expression, General Aurelian conveyed the order to the signal officer. "Target the northeast hill with archers," he reluctantly commanded.

Soldiers swiftly hoisted flags, relaying the command across the tumultuous field.

Amid the chaos of battle, Valentine fought with courage, but fatigue was setting in. His brothers, surrounding him, bore a more visible toll of the blood-soaked battle.

"Stand firm!" Valentine rallied, trying to buoy the spirits of his men.

Suddenly, a piercing hiss resonated through the air. Valentine looked up in disbelief, his features sharply contorting as he saw the incoming volley of arrows from their lines.

"Shields!" he screamed, but it was too late. One arrow struck him with devastating force, piercing his chest near his heart. Grasping the shaft, he felt an unbearable pain surge through him, while blood oozed from his armor-less body. His strength failed, and the great warrior fell. As he gazed skyward, the image of arrows blurred, transforming into iron petals showering over him as his mind slipped away into unconsciousness.

Marius reacted instinctively, fear and urgency propelling him forward. He grabbed a shield and darted over to provide cover against the deadly rain from above.

"It's friendly fire!" Marius roared in disbelief, then commanded the others to seek cover and raise their shields.

Albus, still overwhelmed by grief, cried out as an arrow struck his leg, the sharp pain momentarily eclipsing his sorrow. Around them, Roman and Goth soldiers fell victim to the indiscriminate barrage of arrows. A decurion, hit squarely by one in the throat, slumped life-lessly from his horse, leaving the steed riderless and panicked.

In the chaos, Marius hastily tended to Valentine's side, snapping the shaft of the arrow lodged in him. With one hand grabbing his shield, he defended them from the continuing rain of arrows, shouting for others to help.

"Is he alive?" Efebus's concern was palpable.

Marius leaned down, his heart heavy with the fear of losing his closest friend. With a surge of hope, he realized Valentine was still breathing. "Not yet gone," he murmured, pressing his wool scarf against the wound to stem the bleeding. As he worked, Efebus fended off an attacking Goth, his sword clashing violently as the battle raged around them.

"Secure that horse!" Marius barked to Linus, his voice cutting through the chaos as the volley of arrows slowed the Goths' advance. "And help me with him!"

Linus quickly seized the riderless horse, while Efebus and Marius hoisted Valentine up onto the steed, their movements swift and precise despite the turmoil. Marius mounted behind him, holding his friend securely as they prepared for a swift retreat.

"There's medical aid beyond the hill!" Linus suggested.

"We're not heading back there," Marius replied, then turned his horse. He knew the only reason the archers had been ordered to fire upon them was because Claudius, deep down, wanted them dead.

"Where to then?" Linus inquired.

"To allies," Marius replied with resolve. "I'll return when I can!"

With a sharp cry of "Ya!" he spurred the horse into a frantic retreat, leaving the battlefield and its carnage behind, while only one question clouded his thoughts: *Will Valentine survive?*

CHAPTER 10

BUNDLE OF DECEIT

"It is a society of beasts:
with the difference that among them
they are peaceful and do not bite their own kind,
whereas men only wish to tear each other apart."
—SENECA

The midmorning light of spring glowed gently over the rolling hills of Rome's Suburbium, where a small villa lay nestled amid the forest. Its modest exterior blended harmoniously with the natural landscape, while gardens filled with herbs and blooming flowers lent an air of quiet charm. Simple statuettes adorned the grounds, reflecting traditional Roman aesthetics.

Senator Junius approached the villa, wrapped in a simple, unadorned cloak. General Aurelian, armed and stationed at the entrance, observed Junius's approach with the scrutiny of a scholar poring over a scroll.

"The roads can be treacherous for a lone traveler. Yet here you stand, Senator Junius. Alone, I presume?" Aurelian inquired, his gaze sharp with scrutiny.

"Indeed, as agreed," Junius confirmed. "Is General Claudius within?"

Aurelian paused, casting a final suspicious glance before replying, "He is."

Suddenly, General Claudius emerged from the shadowed doorway, his elegant toga catching the morning light.

"What pressing matter brings you here, Senator? Is this the emperor's doing?" Claudius sneered.

"Thank you for agreeing to meet me at a discreet location, General. I can assure you Emperor Gallienus played no part in my presence today. I am here solely for the good of Rome," Junius declared. He then glanced briefly at Aurelian before returning his focus to Claudius. "Might we discuss this matter alone?"

"General Aurelian is my trusted confidant."

Junius nodded. "I assure you this is not a conspiracy of any kind but rather the joining of a shared purpose," he affirmed, his gaze shifting between the two men.

"What purpose?" Claudius inquired suspiciously.

"I am here to propose an alliance," Junius stated firmly, his voice unwavering. "Not driven by personal gain but forged from the necessity to safeguard the future of our beloved empire."

"If you speak the truth, let us discuss further inside," Claudius replied.

"Thank you, General."

The trio entered the villa, the door closing quietly behind them. As they entered the atrium, Claudius subtly signaled to Aurelian, who acted swiftly. Seizing Junius, he pinned him against a nearby wall and drew his dagger, positioning its razor-sharp tip menacingly close to Junius's throat.

"What's this?" Junius exclaimed, his back pressed against the wall.

"A measure of your truth, Senator," Claudius declared, his gaze piercing. "Convince me this is not a ploy, as your life depends on it."

"By the eternal light of Vesta, I swear, there is no deceit in my words." Junius's voice trembled. "My loyalty is not to a single emperor but to Rome and the gods who watch over her! Please, General, you must hear me!"

"How can I be sure you're not just a weapon in someone else's hand—a sacrifice sent to test my loyalty?" Claudius growled, his tone sharp with suspicion.

"I know we share the same *traditional* beliefs, General! This emperor does not! Please, hear me," Junius pleaded earnestly.

Aurelian's blade gently sliced the side of Junius's neck, drawing a trickle of blood. "Ahhhh!"

"On your command, General," Aurelian stated.

Tears formed in Junius's eyes. "My motives are pure! I swear it by Jupiter!"

A silence hung in the air, sweat beading on Junius's brow.

"Your desperation is palpable, Senator," Claudius replied, his voice cold. "How can you prove your loyalty?"

"Give me an order, General! I stand ready to serve you faithfully," Junius begged.

"Sit," Claudius ordered, gesturing toward a nearby bench as if addressing a canine. Junius nervously took a seat, his relief palpable as he straightened his tunic.

Claudius sat across from him, his demeanor commanding.

"Speak," Claudius ordered again, his voice firm and authoritative, leaving no room for hesitation.

Junius nervously began: "Caesar's tolerance toward Christians and mismanagement of military mobilization has left great distaste amid the Senate. Many of us believe it is time for a transformation in power —somebody who can restore Rome to its true glory. I believe that somebody is you, General. The Senate and people will rally for your ascent."

"And what is it that you seek in return, Senator?" Claudius asked, his eyes narrowing.

"I seek only to serve as your princeps senatus, a steadying force under your rule," Junius replied. The title, the highest honor a senator could receive, would grant him not just rank but the respect he craved. He would stand as a trusted adviser, sharing the burden of decisions and guiding the state alongside Claudius. For Junius, it was about more than mere status—it was power, honor, and the dignity he had been denied for far too long.

As Claudius listened intently, his expression remained unreadable as he mulled over Junius's words. His thoughts drifted to recent events, recalling how the emperor's reluctance to dispatch the requested legion had resulted in the needless deaths of his loyal soldiers—men undeserving of such a fate. He recalled having just returned from encountering Valentine on the battlefield, the *emperor's* newly appointed officer, and how he had permitted Christian prayers. Despite their differences, they harbored the same belief: *Caesar must be stopped.*

"Suppose I agree with you, Senator. What course of action do you propose?" Claudius inquired.

Junius's eyes lit up as he began to lay out his plan. "With a skilled military leader like yourself guiding Rome, the empire would not overextend its legions but rather defend our dominion," Junius began to rise as if addressing the Senate, but Aurelian intervened, keeping him seated.

"Senator, you are treading the path of treason. Any misstep on your part and we could all face the consequences," Aurelian warned, his tone firm and cautionary.

Senator Junius ignored Aurelian, turning again toward Claudius with conviction. "I will not falter, General. You will take the reins of power if you trust me to guide your ascent."

A rare grin broke through Claudius's stoic façade. "I remain torn between killing you and embracing you as an ally, young man."

Aurelian allowed himself a brief smile.

"Do not mistake my youth for ignorance, General—though I may not wield a sword as you, my words cut equally deep," Junius asserted confidently.

Claudius leaned in, his demeanor intense. "How do you propose to gain Rome's favor for me?"

"General, envision the streets of Rome bathed in the celebration of an ovation; the populace's admiration for you is already abundant. Such a spectacle would also warm even the coldest hearts within the

Senate. They would witness, firsthand, the full extent of your strength and leadership." An ovation had not been granted since the first century, but Junius knew it was a more palatable request for the emperor.

"A parade?" Claudius replied with disdain, his tone sharp with skepticism. Unlike most of his peers, he was one of the few generals who had little interest in public adoration, caring more for power than empty displays of glory.

"Indeed, General. It would serve as the perfect beginning to your ascent," Junius responded, his smile tinged with a hint of nervousness.

Aurelian's eyes moved back and forth between Junius and Claudius, unspoken thoughts swirling behind his stern expression.

"What will Caesar think of honoring me so?" Claudius inquired, his tone tinged with skepticism.

"I will ensure he sees this for *his* benefit."

"What of General Aureolus? He is also loyal to Caesar," Aurelian warned.

"Not as loyal as one would presume," Junius retorted. "I will ensure General Aureolus is not a threat."

The room fell silent as Claudius considered the senator's proposal. It was risky, but so was allowing the current emperor to remain on the throne.

"If I were to agree to this, I would need your assurance that you will throw yourself on your sword if you should falter. Otherwise, rest assured, you will be hunted and tortured so severely by me that even the gods will recoil from such brutality. Agreed?" Claudius asked firmly, his gaze unwavering.

"Yes… agreed," Junius replied nervously, his voice betraying a hint of apprehension.

"Furthermore, when I take command, the Senate must be ready to serve under my directive only."

"They will welcome the change, General," Junius responded with a hint of excitement. "And those who do not we will eradicate like weeds from a flourishing garden."

Claudius offered a wry smile. "We shall see the reach of your influence, Senator. For now, that will be all."

"As you wish, General," Junius nodded respectfully and swiftly departed—silently reveling in the reception of his plan.

Claudius and Aurelian watched Junius's departure in silence, their thoughts lingering in the air like a ship navigating through foggy waters.

"Your thoughts, General?" Aurelian broke the stillness.

"Uncertainty and ambition go hand in hand," Claudius replied, his voice a low rumble.

"Do you believe the emperor sent him to test our loyalty?" Aurelian inquired.

"No. If he were a spy, he would have faltered on your dagger."

"And Caesar? He will not relinquish the throne without a fight."

"Nor would I," Claudius agreed.

"You will need an empress," Aurelian added, breaking the tension.

Claudius's expression lightened. "I may have one in mind."

The next evening, in the opulent chamber of Serena's villa, Iset, her most trusted slave—a woman in her mid-thirties of Egyptian descent—moved with quiet precision, lighting oil lamps as the last rays of sunlight filtered through the room. At the same time, Serena held a polished bronze hand mirror, her gaze focused intently as her fingers traced over her breasts. Sensing their heightened sensitivity, she realized that she had not bled for weeks. The early morning bouts of vomiting, once dismissed as illness, now pointed unmistakably to the firm belief growing within her: she was with child.

She pondered the only plausible explanation and arrived at a single answer—Valentine. There had been no other intimacy since, certainly not with her husband, who often returned home in the early hours after sharing a bed with another man. Perhaps this was a divine sign, she mused—a child, blessed with Valentine's valor and beauty, would soon grace her life. Though she had longed for such a blessing, she had resigned herself to the belief that the gods would not allow it. Yet now, the tides seemed to have turned. There was only one issue that remained: her husband. Tullus would never allow a child not born of his bloodline. The embarrassment and shame it would bring upon him would be immense. Such a betrayal could even cost him his chance at becoming a senator one day. As her mind raced with mixed emotions, Iset approached and gently put her arms around Serena.

"Are you certain?" Iset asked in a hushed voice.

Serena nodded as she touched her belly, which was not yet showing.

"Tullus will call for our physician to remove it the moment he notices I am with child," Serena replied, fully aware of the grave danger that awaited her.

"When he returns from Rome, beg your husband to bed you. When the child is born, he will take it as his own," Iset responded with a strategy born from years of serving the Roman elite.

"He has not bed me in years, Iset. I do not presume begging will sway him now."

Their conversation was interrupted by another servant whose demeanor radiated urgency.

"Excuse me, my lady. General Claudius has arrived."

Serena draped her gown over herself, considering a different approach. "Perhaps there is another way. Escort the general to my chamber," she ordered Iset with a knowing smile.

"As you wish, my lady," Iset replied, returning the smile.

Moments later, Iset greeted the general, who waited in the entry-way, dressed in a military tunic and appearing more groomed than usual.

"My lady has asked me to escort you to her chamber, as she is still preparing herself. Would you follow me, General?" Iset requested, and Claudius obliged.

As they entered Serena's chamber, the heavy wooden door swung open, and Iset announced the general before closing the door behind them.

Across the room, Serena brushed her brown locks in the flickering light of oil lamps. Claudius smiled as he approached her, navigating the sturdy wooden bed that lay between them, its frame adorned with intricate carvings.

"My husband believes you may help him ascend to senator one day," Serena began. "He enjoyed meeting you immensely at our last engagement…as did I," she added, hinting at their previous encounter with a seductive smile.

"Where is Tullus?" Claudius's voice dripped with disdain.

Serena stood, weaving around him like a temptress, dressed only in her silky robe.

"Away," Serena replied playfully.

"Will he be joining us this evening?" Claudius inquired, his eyes filled with lust as he peered at Serena.

"I'm afraid not," Serena replied sarcastically as she slithered up next to him while running her fingers down the front of his tunic. "Your timing is impeccable, General. I was delighted to receive your message."

In a swift motion, he grabbed her, pulling her close, but she resisted, pushing him away with every ounce of her spirit.

"Wait," she cried, her voice laced with defiance. "What if I told you I grow tired of our infrequent encounters—that I desire a real man by my side—one who does not favor men nor beds me as if I were his mistress?"

Claudius, erect and mesmerized by her, reflected upon his political ambitions before replying, "Then, I would say we have much to discuss."

"Discourse is overrated, wouldn't you agree?" she replied swiftly, then gazed at him innocently. "What would you do to win my honor, General?" her voice softened as she seductively inched back toward her bed.

Uncertain of her implication yet intrigued, Claudius shuffled forward and replied, "I would do what is required."

"Would you?" she replied rhetorically, then began to slip away.

Suddenly, Claudius's patience thinned as he pulled her to him and passionately kissed her. Yet, as his arousal grew, he suddenly released her, his mind preoccupied with a message he had received from one of his officers, whom he had tasked with spying on her.

"What is it?" she asked, surprised by his abrupt change in demeanor.

"I would do what is required if I were the only one," he stated, looking at her suspiciously.

"What do you mean?" she asked innocently and worried that, despite there being no possible way for him to know, he had somehow sensed that she was with child.

"Do not deceive me, Serena. I have eyes far and wide," he glared at her, his tone laced with warning.

A defiant laugh bubbled from her throat.

"You waste your money on bad spies. For a general, I would expect more."

"Would you?" his hand stretched out and grabbed her by the throat while pressing her against the nearby wall. A couple of months ago, there was a man who escaped in the middle of the night from your terrace. Who was he?!" he demanded, then loosened his grip, allowing her to speak.

Serena gasped, her voice trembling with fear as she quickly responded. "He was a slave! I sold him to a family in Baiae! I have only been with you since our last encounter," she lied.

With a swift movement, he slapped her. The sound echoed throughout her chamber as she tumbled to the ground, holding her cheek in shock.

"With my power and your nobility, we could rule Rome," he spat at her. "He was a *soldier*—now, who was he?"

A heavy silence settled over the room.

Her secret was out, though not entirely.

Serena raised her hand, signaling for a moment's pause as she climbed into a nearby chair, pulling herself together while she collected her thoughts and silently weighed her options. She knew disclosing Valentine's identity to the general would provoke jealousy and endanger his life. The thought of her unborn child growing up without knowing their true father was overwhelming. Conversely, withholding this information might result in the general abandoning her, leaving her at the mercy of Tullus, who could order their physician to surgically remove the child from her—a procedure as perilous as any abortive herb, which she would never consider. The risks, both to her life and her child's, were simply too great.

"Very well," Claudius proclaimed as he began to exit.

"Wait!"

Claudius stopped, then slowly turned.

Desperation tinged her voice as she spoke, indicating the terror that gripped her. "If I reveal his name, will you promise no harm will come to him?"

Claudius's gaze hardened. "The past will only hurt us if there is deceit in your truth."

The walls seemed to hold their breath as she confessed: "Valentine. His name is Valentine. I saw him once, this past winter—nothing more. I swear it."

Claudius froze, his eyes widening with rank fury. The very air seemed to vibrate as his anger erupted. "Valentine?! The one who rescued the empress?"

"You know of him?" she asked, shock evident in her voice.

Rage twisted Claudius's features as he stepped closer, his voice a dangerous growl. "Valentine Romanus—the centurion who I caught worshiping the Christian God on my battlefield?"

"I can assure you, nothing came of our encounter!" Serena insisted, clinging to her lie.

Claudius waved her words away with a sneer. "It matters little now. My officers reported that he deserted his ranks, fleeing with a wound near his heart. If he ever resurfaces, I can assure you, I will order his execution without hesitation."

Serena gasped. "What?! You promised no harm would come to him if I told you his name!"

Claudius's voice turned cold. "Your Christian lover fled my battle-field as quickly as he fled your terrace. Are you proposing we should be merciful to deserters?"

"No—of course not," she replied, her voice faltering as the gravity of her situation sunk in.

"Good. Then we are in agreement," Claudius said, his gaze drifting to her breasts. "Now, where were we?"

Her hand rose, a silent plea for restraint, but Claudius paid it no heed. With deliberate motions, he removed her robe, leaving her naked and more vulnerable than ever. Backing her against the wall, he reached between her legs and began touching her while Serena's thoughts drifted to her unborn child. "Wait..." she muttered softly, yet her words and hesitation only aroused him further.

He swiftly removed his tunic, then draped her face down over her bed and inserted himself inside her to make her forget about Valentine once and for all. As she clenched the sheets, she surrendered to his violent thrusts from behind her as a whirlwind of emotions ran through her mind—yet amid them all, one stood out to her: *he must believe the unborn child is his own.*

Chapter 11

Soulmates

"We suffer more often in imagination than in reality."
—SENECA

Valentine lay weak in a villa nestled in the woodlands of Arretium. Nearby, a separate building had been transformed into an infirmary—an unusual and extraordinary feature for the time, much like the proprietors themselves. The infirmary was a solid structure, crafted from a blend of stone and timber. Soft light from oil lamps enveloped the room, casting a warm glow over the rows of beds where patients sought solace and recovery. Beside Valentine, Marius sat, his hands clasped in prayer, hoping for his friend's recovery from a severe injury that had left him drifting in and out of consciousness.

Deodatus, the physician and proprietor of the villa, moved about caring for other patients with a blend of wisdom and gentility befitting his middle age. A beacon of medical expertise and empathy, his tall, handsome figure and traditional Roman features radiated a profound knowledge. Approaching Valentine's bedside, he began to cut away at the old bandages with practiced ease, his forceps deftly removing them altogether. His presence brought skill and a comforting assurance to the healing process.

"Are there any signs of improvement?" Marius asked, his voice trembling with hope and fear for his friend.

"Let us see," responded Deodatus as his thoughts drifted back to Valentine's surgery. Removing the entirety of the arrow's shaft had been challenging for him, requiring the utmost precision and skill to avoid exacerbating the injury. Yet, as he surveyed the wound, a sense of apprehension gnawed at him. The surrounding tissue appeared alarmingly red and swollen, extending outward like a menacing tide. Pus oozed from the wound, tainting the air with its foul odor. Deodatus couldn't shake the nagging doubt that he might have missed something crucial—a hidden abscess or remnants of the arrow inadvertently left behind. These unsettling thoughts weighed heavily on him as he meticulously cleansed the wound with vinegar and water.

"I'm afraid his injury persists," Deodatus remarked somberly.

Marius, his face etched with worry, lowered his head in disheartenment. Despite weeks of clinging to hope for Valentine's recovery, the outlook only seemed to worsen, casting a shadow of despair over his heart. If Valentine passed, it would fall to Marius to inform Agatha—a thought that filled him with dread.

Amid this tense atmosphere, a youthful and vibrant voice belonging to Regalus, a twelve-year-old with dark hair and eyes reflecting his Indian heritage, broke the silence. Adopted by Deodatus and his wife, he briskly approached, his steps filled with purpose as he began collecting the soiled bandages, efficiently placing them in a small pail.

"Thank you, Regalus," Deodatus said.

"Mother has prepared the herbal remedies, Father," Regalus announced.

With Regalus's announcement, Charu, his mother, entered the room. At forty-seven years of age, she carried herself with the depth and serenity of an old soul. Her dark hair and eyes, complemented by her earth-brown skin, exuded a quiet strength. With poise, she approached Valentine's bedside, each step purposeful and urgent.

Deodatus yielded his place to her.

"He's in your hands, my love," Deodatus murmured, his voice filled with affection as his eyes met his wife's. The unspoken understanding between them reflected the shared journey of healing and hope they had walked together.

She held a paste made of turmeric and applied it to Valentine's wound. Her healing knowledge drew upon a rich tapestry passed down through generations, rooted in the mystic traditions of India. Her father, a respected healer from an ashram near Ujjain, had imparted to her the ancient wisdom of Ayurveda. This ancient and revered medical system was a legacy that she embraced with pride.

After Charu had applied the herbal paste to alleviate the pain, Regalus and Marius observed silently as she tenderly held Valentine's wrist, closed her eyes, and focused on his pulse. Moments later, her eyes fluttered open, revealing a deeper understanding of his condition.

"What do you sense?" Marius asked, hopeful his friend would recover despite Deodatus's concern.

"His body is frail," Charu declared, her confidence wavering as she doubted the poultice's effectiveness against such a severe and persistent injury.

Valentine groaned, his discomfort palpable.

"He's in pain," Charu remarked, swiftly moving to retrieve the opium, a remedy she knew well. She handed the clay bowl to her son. "Regalus, my dear, hold this steady for him," she instructed. Regalus, his young face set with determination, carefully took the bowl, a sense of compassion inherited from his parents.

Charu then lit the opium in the small clay bowl and positioned it over an oil lamp to produce smoke. "Slowly, now," she said as she guided her son's hands, ensuring the smoke wafted gently toward Valentine. She skillfully held the bowl near his nose, allowing the soothing vapors to provide relief.

Valentine stirred on his bed, inhaling the comforting essence of the opium.

"Will you use your qi on him now, Mother?" Regalus asked, his young voice filled with curiosity. He had always been fascinated by his mother's proficiency in qigong energy healing, a skill she had acquired from a Chinese healer who had often visited her father's ashram in India.

"Yes, my dear, I will," Charu replied with a gentle smile, setting aside the opium. She began to attune herself to the subtle energies surrounding Valentine, moving her hands in deliberate, measured sweeps above his body. Each motion seemed to dissolve energetic blockages and enhance the flow of qi, her slow, relaxed movements perfectly in sync with her breath.

Regalus watched in awe as his mother's hands seemed to pull on invisible threads of energy with a mystical force. Even in his youthful state, he could sense a shift in the room, as if the very air had thickened, like a mist settling into a mountain valley.

Suddenly, Valentine's body jerked, and beads of sweat glistened on his forehead as he let out a pained groan. Marius rose quickly, moving closer to the bed, his concern etched deeply upon his features. Charu paused, withdrawing her hands momentarily from their position above Valentine's wound.

Deodatus approached, concern in his eyes as he met Charu's gaze.

"He's in God's hands now," Charu uttered, her voice tinged with solemn acceptance as if sensing Valentine was teetering on the precipice between life and death.

"Let us pray," he suggested as he initiated a prayer for recovery or peace in his passing to the Christian God.

Valentine's eyes fluttered, briefly capturing the sight of a simple wooden ichthys, the Christian fish, hanging subtly behind Deodatus. Suddenly, the carved symbol merged seamlessly with a hazy memory. From his perspective, Valentine could see himself galloping on a horse through the forest with Marius behind him shortly after the arrow's fateful strike. The trees on each side of them blurred into a whirlwind of motion, creating a tunnel of radiant light. Through this dreamlike state, Marius's voice resonated, distant yet unmistakable, imploring, "Stay with me, Valentine—stay with me!"

Suddenly, everything turned to pure white, and a serene stillness enveloped him. In the next instant, Valentine experienced a sensation of detachment from his physical form, as if his spirit were delicately lifting away. A serene tranquility enveloped him like the river water of his childhood.

As he gazed down upon his body from an elevated vantage point, he observed Deodatus praying. He could see Charu, her eyes closed, hands poised above his chest, radiating light that streamed from within her and into him. Marius and Regalus stood in prayer alongside them, their expressions blending hope and concern. In this moment, suspended between worlds, Valentine felt an indescribable sense of love and divine presence, a peace beyond words.

As his spirit drifted on the verge of surrendering to the afterlife, a woman's voice suddenly pierced the ethereal silence, calling him back just as he teetered on the brink of letting go.

"Valentine, Valentine," her voice resonated, tugging at his soul with a force that tested his readiness to depart. Suddenly, the scene below him shifted, and he could vaguely see Agatha asleep in her bed, a vision calling out to him. Their bond transcended time as if their souls intertwined across lifetimes. In that fleeting moment, he made his silent decision, and the world around him stilled and faded into darkness.

Around Valentine's bedside, Deodatus, Charu, and Regalus all peered down at his body, their expressions reflecting the shared uncertainty of his fate. Regalus watched as his mother scrambled for Valentine's wrist, checking for signs of life in his still form.

In a suspended moment, they all held their breath in anticipation. The fading light passed slowly across the walls marking time as night approached.

After what seemed like hours, relief washed over them as Charu's demeanor softened, her eyes opening to share the news they'd hoped to hear.

"He's alive," she announced, piercing the heavy silence.

"Amen," Deodatus murmured.

Marius released a deep, grateful exhale. His friend was still with him.

Agatha worked in her vegetable garden at the entrance of her home, delicately harvesting cabbage and kale for dinner. With a cloth and spade, she expertly removed thorny weeds, protecting her hands from their sharp barbs. While humming to herself, her mind drifted to Valentine's kiss and the lingering warmth it had left in her heart. Pausing, she adjusted the wool scarf he had bestowed upon her, a simple yet cherished token that bridged the gap of his absence with its silent presence.

The distant sound of horse hooves suddenly captured her attention, their rhythmic beat igniting a flicker of hope for Valentine's return. As the sound grew nearer, however, her sharp ear recognized the familiar cadence—it was Porcia's horse, accompanied by Tiber. Their father had insisted she learn to ride, an uncommon skill for women, but necessary for their safety and independence.

Porcia dismounted and handed her horse to Tiber, who took the reins and tended to the animals. She then approached Agatha with a satchel of goods from her shopping excursion.

"The garden looks lovely today," Porcia remarked, glancing around.

Agatha reached for her spade in the soil before responding, "If you say so," her tone tinged with melancholy. She brushed the dirt from her tunic before attempting to rise.

Sensing Agatha's mood, Porcia gently inquired, "Sister, what troubles you? Are you thinking of *him* again?"

Agatha bristled at the inquiry, her insecurities flaring. "Father would have me confined here forever, tending to his needs, neglecting my own life. Is that your wish for me as well?" she retorted, tears welling up as she grabbed her walking staff and hastily gathered her basket of vegetables, brushing past Porcia.

"Agatha! That's not my wish for you at all," Porcia responded, her voice cracking as she hurried after her sister.

Agatha slowed, Porcia's gentle touch anchoring her. "Sister, the right man will come along one day—whether it's Valentine or someone else," Porcia reassured her.

Wiping her tears, Agatha murmured, "I did not mean to let my emotions overcome me."

Seeking to lift her spirits, Porcia retrieved a scroll from her basket and, with a playful tone, remarked, "I have something here that's sure to brighten your mood."

"What is it?" Agatha inquired, a slight smile gracing her lips.

"A scroll from a Christian friend, someone I hope you'll have the chance to meet someday. Would you like me to read it to you?"

With a dreamy sigh, Agatha implored, "Only if it is a tale of love, not war."

A tender smile graced Porcia's lips as she replied, "Those are my favorite kind too."

Inside their home, Agatha and Porcia made themselves comfortable on a *lectus*, a low, cushioned couch with ornate wooden legs and intricately carved details. The intimacy of their bond enveloped Agatha in a reassuring warmth. Yet, before Porcia could start reading from the scroll, Agatha confessed, "I do think about him far too often."

"Valentine?" Porcia inquired, setting the scroll aside.

With a heavy sigh, Agatha confirmed with a nod.

"It has been some time, sister," Porcia gently reminded her.

"I know," Agatha whispered. "Is it foolish to still hope that he may one day return?"

"What does your heart tell you?"

Agatha hesitated briefly before admitting, "It tells me he's alive. I sense his presence. Just last night, I dreamed I was calling out to him; he was in danger, and somehow, he heard me."

With a soothing gesture, Porcia reached out, clasping her sister's hands.

"You and Valentine were always off adventuring in the forest when we were younger," Porcia reminisced uneasily.

"He was my closest friend," Agatha affirmed softly.

"I thought I was your closest friend," Porcia teased lightly.

"You're my sister. That's different."

"I would have enjoyed exploring the forest with you," Porcia confessed, a hint of old hurt coloring her voice.

"Oh, Porcia, you were so young then," Agatha responded, though Porcia appeared restless with the explanation.

With a resigned nod, Porcia acquiesced, "As usual, you're right, sister."

Agatha settled back into the lectus, allowing a tranquil calm to envelop the room.

Porcia sighed deeply. "How long will you allow the memory of Valentine to torment you? I cannot bear to see you with a broken heart. What if Valentine perished in battle, or perhaps his affections now lie elsewhere? You cannot spend the rest of your days dwelling in the past."

"I cannot bring myself to entertain such dreadful possibilities, Porcia. And I will continue to hold Valentine in my thoughts for as long as I deem fit. After all, I do owe him my life," Agatha countered softly, her thoughts drifting back to the harrowing moment of survival against the wolves.

"Sister, the men from Valentine's legion have returned to Rome. Most of the maidens have received messages from the wounded. If Valentine were alive, why hasn't he sent word to you?" Porcia probed, mindful of the heartache her question might evoke.

Tears welled up in Agatha's eyes once again.

"I don't know," she whispered.

Porcia embraced her, determined to keep Agatha close. After all, she was her sister's unwavering protector.

CHAPTER 12

THE ART OF PERSUASION

"No sacred alliance,
no loyalty exists in the kingdom."
—ENNIUS

I n the heart of Rome, the Forum thrummed with life. Among this crowded expanse moved Junius, whose keen and observant eyes locked onto a figure of military might—General Aureolus. Draped in the regalia of his rank, the general walked with the confidence of one who commanded legions. As Junius navigated closer, the *Rostra* loomed ahead. It was a stage of power where words had shaped history, where Cicero once thundered, and Caesar charmed. Here, in the shadow of these titans, Junius planned his subtle game.

With a cleverly crafted pretense of clumsiness, Junius artfully orchestrated a misstep, brushing against the general as if by accident. "Oh! My apologies, General, this crowd can be quite unforgiving," he exclaimed, his voice carrying a well-practiced tone of contrition.

General Aureolus, momentarily startled, turned to face his unintended assailant. "Senator Junius," he replied, his voice a mix of caution and curiosity, "Yes, the Forum is a world unto itself."

"Our paths seem aligned. May I walk with you?" Junius ventured, seizing the opportunity to engage the general in a private conversation.

"As you wish," Aureolus responded, gesturing for Junius to join him.

With a casual smile, Junius spoke first of lighter topics. "General, have you seen the latest races at the Circus Maximus? The rivalry between the Blues and Greens is truly something this season."

General Aureolus chuckled. "Yes, it's quite the spectacle. Those charioteers indeed know how to please the crowd."

"I find their strategies almost as thrilling as the races themselves," Junius added, hinting at a deeper understanding.

"Indeed, it mirrors the complexities of military tactics in many ways," Aureolus noted, appreciating the analogy.

As they reached the more secluded corridors of the Forum, Junius steered the conversation into deeper waters. "General," he began, his voice barely above the whisper of the history around them. "Your early departure from the Senate meeting a few months back did not escape my notice. I trust the emperor's recent decrees have not weighed too heavily upon you."

General Aureolus, his voice equally subdued, mirrored the inquiry: "I might ask you the same, Senator."

Junius allowed a wry smile, an unspoken acknowledgment of their discomfort with Emperor Gallienus's recent policy changes. "The emperor certainly does not shy away from expressing his convictions with striking candor. One could argue that such unreserved expression contributes to his unique allure. Yet, I'm curious, General, how do you perceive his ongoing proclamation advocating for Christian tolerance?"

A momentary pause followed as Aureolus turned to face Junius directly. His eyes held a flicker of introspection. "Are we speaking in confidence?" he asked, his tone indicating the gravity of what would follow.

"Of course, General," Junius replied, his assurance evident in his calm demeanor.

"I find his tolerance of these foreign beliefs...difficult to digest."

Junius nodded, his eyes never leaving the general's face. He searched for the subtleties of truth in Aureolus's guarded demeanor before responding, "As do I." With a discreet gesture, he then encouraged the general to resume their walk.

"And the eastern front? Am I mistaken in believing the Sassanid threat seems gravely underestimated? Not to mention the turmoil we're facing with the Palmyrene and Gallic breakaways?"

"You are indeed perceptive, Senator," Aureolus acknowledged, his voice carrying a grave undertone. The empire's reach is overextended. The Sassanids present a ceaseless threat, and the ascent of the Palmyrene empire further strains our dominion. Your inquiries are intriguing, yet where do they lead, Senator?"

Junius slowed and drew closer while lowering his voice: "Do you believe in a Rome where new leadership, one with a keen eye on these turbulent waters, may navigate more adeptly through the challenges from the east and the internal schisms we witness?"

"Such thoughts had not crossed my mind," he confessed.

"You know of Postumus. Might that have been the motivation for his secession, in carving out the Gallic empire?" Junius asked, his words delicately wrapped in the guise of casual speculation.

"It's conceivable, though I cannot be certain. My familiarity with Postumus is quite limited," Aureolus replied thoughtfully.

A light chuckle escaped Senator Junius, drawing a puzzled look from him.

"What amuses you?" Aureolus inquired.

"It is fortunate for us that Postumus lacks a commanding general such as yourself," Junius commented with a hint of seriousness.

"Why do you say that?" Aureolus pressed, intrigued by the senator's perspective.

Junius offered a thoughtful gaze before responding, "Because, General, with a leader of your strategic insight and prowess at his side, Postumus could present a formidable challenge to the stability of our empire. Your leadership ensures our legions remain unmatched—a pillar that upholds and protects the fabric of Rome."

"I'm uncertain of your point, Senator," General Aureolus responded, baffled by the implication that Junius may be nudging him to defect.

Junius gestured dismissively, effortlessly lightening the mood. "Come, General, let us not dwell on hypotheticals. We serve at the pleasure of this emperor, with all his virtues and flaws. I do not wish to burden your thoughts with such tantalizing, yet unattainable, visions. May the strength of Mars be with you in battle. Now, I must take my leave. Good day, General."

"And to you, Senator," General Aureolus replied, his voice now colored with contemplation as he reflected upon the seed Junius had planted and the intriguing possibilities.

AT SERENA'S VILLA, the air was thick with anticipation within the intricately designed walls of her noble residence. The triclinium, the grand dining hall where Roman elites reclined to feast, embodied the wealth and prestige of its owners. Its U-shaped arrangement of beds, called *klinai*, allowed diners to lounge in luxury while being served, fostering conversation and alliances. Mosaics of mighty gods and legendary battles adorned its floors, a perpetual reminder of Rome's indomitable spirit and influence.

Wearing a wig that appeared comedic to everyone except the wearer himself, Tullus lounged upon a bed so expansive it could have held an emperor's dreams. The deep shades of royal purple, embroidered with gold accents, stood in stark contrast to his pale skin, making him seem almost like a living sculpture, frozen in a moment of indulgence. Each time he gulped his wine, it was as if he drank the very essence of Roman decadence.

General Claudius reclined nearby on a cushioned *lectus*, adorned with carved lions at its feet and golden laurel motifs, giving it an almost regal appearance. Unlike Tullus, the general had an air of restraint about him. Dressed in his military tunic, he sipped his wine and listened to Tullus ramble tales of politics and the history of his noble family.

Amid this display of power and opulence, enslaved men moved with purpose, their muscles honed from relentless labor. A few still bore faint bruises around their necks, reminders of the collars they had once been forced to wear. Tullus, his eyes glazed with indulgence, let his gaze linger lustfully on one of them before redirecting his attention back to Claudius, who remained impassive, his face betraying no sign of the thoughts stirring behind his calm demeanor.

"You pay us homage, General. Visiting as you do with so many of your brave soldiers. How fares the battle in the north?" Tullus asked nonchalantly.

Claudius's eyes responded with an intensity that filled the room. "Our enemies are relentless, as am I."

Tullus leaned forward slightly, a wry smile forming on his lips. Raising his wine in a silent toast, he slurred, "You make Rome proud, General—and thank you for the wine. You were too kind to bring it."

Claudius toasted Tullus in return. "Not at all, Tullus."

The massive wooden doors slowly swayed open as the wine cascaded down Tullus's throat. Sunlight filtered through the open windows, casting a soft glow on the richly adorned room. Through the gentle haze of burning incense, Serena entered, her presence like the soft rustling of leaves—quiet, yet impossible to ignore. She was draped in a traditional Roman stola, which flowed gracefully around her, the fabric catching the warm light. Iset followed closely behind, ever loyal and a constant source of strength.

Tullus's eyes gleamed with mischief as he spotted Serena across the room. "Ah! There she is—'The Queen,'" he jeered, a sardonic smile playing on his lips. "She doesn't lift a finger—yet parades as if she were the empress."

Serena met his gaze with a wry glint in her eye. "Greetings, husband. It's good to see you too," she replied dryly. Then, with a nod of acknowledgment, she added, "General."

Claudius politely nodded back. "Serena."

"Husband, I'm taking the *litter* to the Via Sacra and will need all the slaves," Serena declared.

Taken aback, Tullus inquired, "What? Why all of them?"

Serena teased with the faintest hint of a smirk. "I believe somebody's birthday is approaching. I require aid with your gift if you must know."

"Ha! It must be as big as the Colossus of Rhodes. And if I should need my men?"

"I'm sure Rome's finest general will tend to all your needs," she replied swiftly.

Tullus sighed, shaking his head in mock exasperation. "You see what I endure, General." After a thoughtful beat, he waved dismissively at her and her servants. "Go. All of you—protect the Queen—farewell!" he ordered, then chuckled as more wine spilled onto his robe. Gazing at Claudius, he muttered, "Women—just a staple of society."

Claudius smirked in return and took another sip of his wine as he observed Serena and her entourage gracefully exit the room.

"Come, Tullus—let us retire to the terrace and enjoy the afternoon breeze," he suggested.

Appearing slightly annoyed at the move, Tullus replied, "Are you certain? It is far more comfortable here."

"I am," Claudius replied resolutely.

"Oh, very well," Tullus relented with a soft chuckle. "You generals can be quite particular," he teased as he rolled off his couch. "Then, you must hear a favor of mine!"

"Certainly," Claudius replied as he stepped outside.

Unlike the richly frescoed interiors, the terrace offered a breathtaking panorama. Laid out beneath them was the vast landscape of Rome, gleaming with its architectural masterpieces. Their elevated vantage point provided a stunning view, including the vision of the Flavian Amphitheater in the background.

"Quite the sight, wouldn't you say, General?" Tullus boasted.

"You've been fortunate to inherit such a home," Claudius replied. "I hail from humble origins and had to earn or take all that I now possess."

"Indeed—I have been fortunate!" Tullus agreed heartily, his voice carrying a light jest. He then shifted his tone, becoming slightly more serious. "All right then, General. Here is the favor I would like to ask of you, old friend."

Claudius turned, facing Tullus. "I'm listening."

Choosing his words carefully, Tullus inquired, "You are close with Caesar and respected by many members of the Senate, are you not?"

"I suppose," Claudius replied, his voice tinged with the weariness of a man currently at odds with Caesar and who held little regard for most politicians.

Pausing to gauge Claudius's reaction, Tullus carefully remarked, "My wife had a rare moment of clarity. She suggested that a man of your influence might help secure my ascent to the senatorial rank."

Claudius grinned as his gaze dropped momentarily to the world below, watching Serena's litter, a small dot amid the bustling street, being carried away from the residence. The air hummed with the distant sounds of Rome—faint echoes of merchants haggling in the markets, the occasional rumble of a chariot's wheels on cobblestones mixed with the distant roar of the crowd from the Flavian Amphitheater.

Tullus, fueled by wine and ambition, pressed on, "I speak in earnest, Claudius."

Without warning, Claudius reached for a gleaming dagger, drawing it forth with deliberate precision.

Caught off guard, Tullus, teetering between intoxication and clarity, slurred, "Oh, what a lovely dagger. What are you doing?"

"With you, old friend—I would shed blood." Claudius intoned, his voice thick with emotion. He drew the blade along the periphery of his forearm, letting the blood flow, painting a vivid picture. The bold, raw gesture echoed ancient rituals where blood sealed oaths and allegiances—or did it?

Bearing witness to this deeply personal act, Tullus could hardly contain his horror. "General, you go too far!" he exclaimed, the sheer intensity of the moment breaking through his drunkenness. "I already know your loyalty—you need not scar yourself to prove such valor."

Claudius rubbed the knife over the fresh wound, smearing it with blood, then wiped it along his tunic and coolly responded, "Then, how would I explain fighting off your assassin?"

Time seemed to halt, the grandeur of the Capital's backdrop contrasting with the chilling realization dawning upon Tullus. The sounds of the empire faded into the background, replaced by the thundering of Tullus's heart. Confusion transformed into stark terror.

"Wait!" he bellowed, his eyes wide with horror.

Mercilessly, Claudius thrust his dagger deep into Tullus's belly, the motion fluid from years of practice. The blade found its mark with cruel precision, eliciting a profound sense of betrayal from Tullus—a soft, guttural cry escaped his lips.

"And taking your wife as my own," Claudius added, his voice dripping with venom and triumph. As the words flowed, he viciously twisted the dagger and curved upward, slicing Tullus's stomach open beneath his robe. The sharp, cold metal forced Tullus's knees to surrender beneath him. He slumped onto the edge.

"Please…" Tullus rasped.

The weight of Roman politicking seemed to overcome him as Claudius nudged Tullus's obese body over the terrace's edge.

As he plummeted to the ground, time appeared to stretch out; each passing moment elongated as he stared up at Claudius in utter shock.

With a resounding thud, Tullus's body struck the marble entrance below. A moment later, a solitary drop of blood followed, landing on his forehead like a tragic crown.

Above, Claudius surveyed his handiwork. For a fleeting moment, regret gnawed at him. Slaying a fellow Roman was not his customary way, but necessity often demanded harsh choices, he reasoned. The gods would certainly understand his motives, recognizing the righteousness in his ruthless decisions. After all, Rome deserved a worthy empress, and Tullus was simply a wretched obstacle that had to be removed for the greater good to prevail.

Methodically, Claudius wiped away the bloodstains, erasing any evidence of his transgression as quickly as he wiped away any lingering regret. The murder weapon slid back into its sheath with an eerie calmness as he whispered, "Sleep well, old friend."

CHAPTER 13

DIVERGING ROADS

"Fate leads the willing and drags along the reluctant."
—SENECA

Valentine twisted restlessly under layers of blankets, while twin braziers flickered fiercely at either end of the infirmary. He was abruptly awakened by a patient's moan, sitting up with a start, his eyes scanning the room as if seeing it for the first time. Nearby, Deodatus gently closed an older man's eyes, then glanced up at the small wooden Christian fish on the wall, his gaze lingering for a moment. With a soft exhale, he murmured a quiet prayer.

As he concluded, a woman covered the man's corpse with a sheet. Deodatus somberly turned to depart, but Valentine's voice halted him.

"What was your prayer about?" Valentine inquired.

Deodatus paused, turning back to meet Valentine's gaze. "I asked God to receive his soul into His love and care."

"When you prayed for me, was it the same?"

"It was," Deodatus affirmed. "Why do you ask?"

Valentine felt the urge to share more—about the divine presence he had sensed, the out-of-body experience, and visions of Agatha—but something held him back. He wasn't sure how Deodatus might respond. Visions weren't unheard of, especially in moments of healing; in fact, many believed the gods sent guidance during such times. Yet, what unsettled Valentine wasn't the vision itself but the question of who had sent it. Amid the chaos, a sense of peace had washed over him—a peace unlike anything the Roman gods could offer. The light he saw wasn't harsh or commanding but warm, pure, and filled with love. Agatha's voice, gentle yet urgent, called him back—not with the force of authority, but with love.

The realization settled within him: he had been touched by the Christian God, not Rome's indifferent pantheon. Yet, even with Deodatus being a Christian, Valentine wasn't ready to speak those words aloud. He had heard Deodatus speak of faith with confidence, but he wasn't there—not yet. The revelation was too new, too fragile. *How could he explain something he hadn't fully accepted in his own heart?* To say it aloud would make it real, exposing his uncertainty and vulnerability—something he wasn't ready to confront.

So instead, he held back and replied simply, "No reason."

"How are you feeling?" Deodatus asked, gently steering the conversation.

"Alive, thanks to both you and Charu. Though I am uncertain how I'll ever repay your kindness."

"You'll find a way," Deodatus replied warmly. "Though it wasn't all our doing. If Marius hadn't found help and a carriage along the way, I doubt you would have survived the long journey. You have a good friend in him."

"This much I know," Valentine agreed, gratitude filling his voice.

"And another one up there," Deodatus added, glancing upward.

Valentine nodded, still grappling with the disbelief that he had survived. His gaze shifted to Charu, who was applying her qi to a patient. "I don't recall ever seeing a place quite like this. The work you and Charu do is extraordinary, especially considering the constant presence of suffering."

Deodatus, locking eyes with Valentine, responded, "Where there is suffering, there too resides compassion."

Valentine nodded, touched by the depth of Deodatus's insight. "I believe it's time for me to depart," he declared.

"Your recovery is still in its early stages. You're welcome to stay longer," Deodatus said.

"I am thankful, yet there is a maiden I must return to."

"Then we shall wish you well on your journey," Deodatus replied, sensing Valentine's determination. "Marius took the letter you wanted delivered to this maiden."

"Did he? That's a relief," Valentine replied, appreciating the news. The thought of Agatha hearing of the soldiers' return without word from him troubled him deeply. He feared she might lose hope.

THE NEXT DAY, Valentine embarked on his journey, wrapped in a cloak over a tunic and carrying a satchel with coins, provisions, and a few personal items. With a walking stick, he planned to follow a series of dirt paths winding through the hills of Tuscia, leading him toward the Via Cassia. From there, he would follow the well-traveled route south to Rome. Longer hair and a burgeoning beard now obscured his once pristine military visage. Approaching the forest's brink, he halted to look back at Deodatus and Charu's villa. A smile briefly lit his face as he reflected on their kindness.

As he ventured into the forest, sunlight filtered through the trees, wrapping the surroundings in a warm glow. His steps were resolute, but it wasn't long before fatigue set in, his breaths becoming labored. The months of inactivity had taken a greater toll on his physical stamina than anticipated. As he leaned against the trunk of an age-old tree, his thoughts drifted to Agatha, pondering if perhaps the Christian God had offered him a new opportunity at romance. This peaceful contemplation was abruptly interrupted as Decimus, a thief infamous throughout the valley, emerged from the shadows of the trees, sword in hand.

"Hand over the bag and any coins," Decimus demanded.

"Leave me be," Valentine warned, his voice steady.

"Or else?" Decimus taunted. "I see the blood on your tunic. Grant me what I desire, or you will depart this world swiftly."

Valentine's eyes dropped to his tunic, realizing for the first time that his injury had reopened. Standing tall, he met Decimus's gaze with a steely one of his own, his hand gripping the walking stick as though it were a weapon.

"I warned you," Valentine stated, unwavering.

"So be it," sighed Decimus, disappointment in his tone. With a swift lunge, he aimed his sword at Valentine, who, with quick reflexes, dodged his barrage of attacks. Utilizing his staff, Valentine delivered a sharp jab to Decimus's abdomen, leaving him gasping for air and crumpling to the forest floor.

Just as Valentine sensed triumph, the quiet of the forest was broken by the approach of two more figures: Spurius, hardened by the legacy of his Roman centurion father, now turned to a life of banditry, and Felix, the fiery and eager recruit to their rogue ensemble.

"You're outnumbered," Spurius announced, stepping forward with a menacing calm, his gaze fixed on Valentine. "And the man whimpering at your feet is my cousin."

Valentine swiftly claimed Decimus's fallen sword.

"I have no quarrel with either of you," Valentine replied. "I seek only safe passage."

"Hand over your bag, and you will be spared," Felix blurted out.

"The bag stays with me," Valentine asserted, fully aware that his survival depended on it.

"Have it your way," Spurius retorted, raising his weapon and charging forward. The forest echoed with the clash of metal as Valentine deftly deflected the attack. Seizing the opening, Valentine countered with a precise strike of his sword's hilt to Spurius's forehead, rendering him unconscious as he crumpled to the forest floor.

"My turn," Felix declared with misplaced confidence, diving into the battle. The young bandit, quick and keen to make his mark, unleashed a flurry of attacks. Valentine found himself pressed hard, maneuvering to evade the strikes with diminishing strength until he was backed against a tree, fighting for his life with dwindling vigor.

Just when his demise seemed inevitable, the quiet of the forest was pierced by the whistle of an arrow, slicing narrowly past Felix's head and embedding itself in a nearby tree. The sudden threat caused Felix to pause and glance toward the arrow's origin, granting Valentine a critical moment as he delivered a swift slice to Felix's leg, halting his assault.

"Ahhh!" Felix exclaimed, his hand flying to his leg as pain seared through him. Losing his balance, he tripped over an unseen stone and crashed into the forest ground. Valentine advanced, his sword poised at Felix's throat.

"Please, sir. I have a wife and child!" he begged, his young voice tinted with desperation and fear.

Valentine gazed into his eyes, recognizing a plea he might once have coldly dismissed. Yet, at this moment, he remembered the compassion recently bestowed upon him and replied simply, "Run."

Felix wasted no time. He scrambled to his feet and helped Decimus, who was just regaining consciousness. Together, they vanished into the shelter of the forest.

As Valentine watched them fade into the distance, his strength waned, and dizziness overtook him. Collapsing to the ground, the forest seemed to blur around him. A young voice echoed, "Valentine...Valentine," but darkness soon claimed him, drawing him unconscious.

Later that night, in the quiet of the infirmary, Valentine lay back in his bed once again, still unconscious. Deodatus, with Regalus's assistance, replaced his soiled bandages.

"Will he recover, Father?" Regalus asked, his voice overflowing with concern.

"Yes, my son," Deodatus responded with confidence. "His heart is strong."

Just then, Charu passed, her presence calming. "Now it's time for our brave son to assist with supper," she said softly, coaxing Regalus to join her.

"But I want to help Father," Regalus protested.

Charu, guiding him away, replied, "One lesson at a time."

"I will join you both shortly." Deodatus's voice trailed after them.

Suddenly, Valentine's stillness gave way to motion as his eyes fluttered open.

"Welcome back," Deodatus greeted, dabbing the sweat from his brow with a cloth.

"Where am I?" Valentine responded, defying his weakened state.

"You were found in the forest by Regalus, who, against our rules, went hunting alone. It seems his disobedience served you well."

Valentine's memory slowly came back. "He fired the arrow."

"Indeed, and consider yourself fortunate it did not find a more lethal mark—Regalus's archery leaves much to be desired," Deodatus quipped.

"It appears I am now in debt to your entire family," Valentine acknowledged.

"God guided you to us for a reason, Valentine," Deodatus said, securing the last bandages.

"I do not know your God," Valentine replied, though the words felt hollow. Something had shifted in him, more than he cared to admit.

"He seems to know you," Deodatus assured confidently. "Now, try to rest," he suggested, turning to leave.

Valentine reached out, gripping Deodatus's arm. "Wait. There is more I need to understand," he finally admitted, prompting Deodatus to halt. "When I was unconscious, I experienced visions...and heard a voice I didn't recognize at first."

"Whose voice?" Deodatus inquired.

"Agatha," Valentine replied. "She is familiar to me. Yet it wasn't just her voice that struck me. There was something more—something I couldn't explain. It felt...divine. I realize how strange this must sound."

Deodatus met Valentine's gaze with a knowing smile. "You stared death in the eyes, Valentine. Most men wouldn't have survived your wound. God has given you a second chance at life—perhaps at love as well."

When Valentine heard these words, he knew them to be true. The realization settled within him like the stillness of dawn. "I am uncertain where to start. Like my father before me, fighting for Rome is all I've ever known."

"Rome still needs men willing to fight for a greater cause,"

Deodatus said, his voice full of encouragement. "If you choose to stay, we will help you find your path."

Valentine's thoughts drifted. "I must return to Agatha once I am healed."

Deodatus nodded. "And you will—this time, perhaps, with a deeper sense of purpose."

ALONG THE MARBLE surfaces of the Curia Julia, where power and peril danced an intricate duet, a profound silence welcomed Emperor Gallienus. Cloaked in the authority of his office, he addressed Rome's senators.

"Today offers another occasion for celebration, Senators. Through my strategic guidance, our legions have successfully pushed back the Goths' defenses and confined them within their lair."

Senator Paternus rose to his feet with the dignity befitting his role as consul. His voice resonated through the chamber as he declared, "No force in Rome's arsenal can overshadow the magnificence of your leadership, Emperor. It is in your wisdom that we place our trust. How may the Senate be of service to you today?"

But before the last note of his homage could settle, an urgent figure disrupted the reverie. A military messenger, adorned with the urgency of war, approached the emperor. He presented a scroll to Caesar.

Gallienus carefully read it, and a chilling transformation took over. His complexion paled, and a dark omen shadowed his regal expression. "Betrayal!" he thundered, his outcry reverberating ominously. "General Aureolus has aligned with Postumus the Usurper! The very fabric of our empire is under assault!"

Pandemonium descended upon the Senate, shattering the tranquil decorum that had once reigned supreme. Senators, their composure shattered by the gravity of the betrayal, grappled with the magnitude of the unfolding crisis.

"By the gods, how could this happen?" cried one senator.

"Surely this cannot be true! Aureolus was one of us!" another exclaimed.

"Our legions, the tactics—Aureolus knows them all!" a third added, his voice laced with disbelief.

Senator Didius rose to his feet, embodying staunch loyalty and righteous fury. "We must rally our forces, Emperor! Let no traitor find refuge under your reign!"

"No, Senator Didius, to rush into war invites only ruin!" Senator Paternus interjected, his voice strained in the chaos. "Rome's strength is not boundless; we must safeguard her with wisdom, not squander her in haste!"

Voices collided in fear and uncertainty, "Are we no longer safe within these walls?" one senator queried anxiously. "Who can we trust when corruption so easily taints Rome's heart?" another lamented. "Our enemies grow stronger as we fracture from within!" echoed a third.

In the chaos, the emperor's commanding gaze swept across the Senate. "Silence!" he thundered, and the chamber immediately hushed. "This betrayal may wound us deeply, though it will not bring about our downfall. Rome has stood firm for countless generations, and she will not fall to the schemes of a lone traitor! We will stand united and crush this rebellion with unyielding resolve!"

The senators, their faces drawn with the looming threat of civil strife, nodded in solemn agreement. Caesar's decree was absolute, and they would follow it, even if it led them into the uncertain abyss ahead.

With deliberate poise, Senator Junius rose to address the emperor. "Caesar, if I may," he began without waiting for permission. "Throughout our history, over-celebrated generals have often mistaken themselves for the hand that guides the tiller of Rome. Under your rule, generals like Aureolus, Claudius, and Aurelian have been kept from dangerous pedestals. We must continue to silence these generals, as you have so wisely done."

The chamber buzzed with the silent acknowledgment of Junius's point, the senators acutely aware of the precarious balance between honoring and over-empowering Rome's military champions.

Perched upon his elevated seat, Emperor Gallienus cast a discerning eye upon Junius, contemplating his words with his usual and anticipated skepticism. "Senator Junius," he responded, his voice carrying the weight of authority, "while your counsel demonstrates shrewdness, it overlooks the broader perspective I must consider. In times when threats such as Aureolus cast a shadow over our legacy, these moments demand we fortify the ties with my generals, granting them the honors they have rightfully earned."

Junius rose swiftly, forestalling any interjection from the consuls or fellow senators. "Caesar, are you suggesting that we should now honor generals like Claudius and Aurelian with a triumph or ovation, thereby fostering loyalty within our ranks?"

"That is exactly my intention, Junius!" Gallienus responded firmly, making the idea his own. "I hereby decree that the Senate take immediate action. The ancient ceremony of ovation shall be held to commemorate my recent victory against the Goths, celebrating the valor of generals like Claudius and Aurelian upon their return to Rome. Let this serve as a reminder to all: Rome does not forget the loyalty and service of her faithful sons!"

"Your wisdom in matters of statecraft shines brightly, Caesar. If it pleases you, I humbly offer my services in overseeing the ovation that befits your grand vision."

Gallienus pondered Junius's offer for a fleeting moment as the other senators' murmurs provided a backdrop of uncertainty. Finally, he issued his command: "Very well, Senator Junius. See to it that the execution is flawless, yet let it not outshine the modesty befitting an ovation. We are concluded here." With his final words spoken, Gallienus stood, leaving the hall with the authority of one whose word was law.

The Senate rose as one body, a wave of respect rippling through the chamber in silent homage to the emperor's commanding presence. Senators Paternus and Didius stood together, watching as Junius slipped into the Senate hallway. Paternus let out a mocking chuckle. "Junius, ever the impatient youth—speaking when he should listen. Now Caesar has him arranging the very ovation he so subtly tried to discourage."

Didius's laughter was a low rumble. "Let him toil with parades and festivities; it will temper his brash ambition."

Concealed within the secluded confines of a shadowy alcove,

shielded from the scrutiny of the Senate, Senator Junius met Senator Fabius, his voice a whisper of conspiracy. "They presume weakness where none exists, Fabius," he confided, a sly smirk playing upon his lips.

In the flickering torchlight, Fabius's gaze shimmered with pride. "You orchestrated today's affairs with masterful precision, Junius—you commanded the stage."

A genuine smile, a rarity amid Junius's usually calculated demeanor, graced his features. "Thank you, my love," he murmured. "My alliance with Claudius is now secure," he whispered proudly.

"And your path to princeps senatus begins to materialize! Truly magnificent," Fabius added, his smile reflecting genuine admiration.

WITH HER CLEAR and ethereal voice rising above the cobblestone streets of Rome, Agatha stood in front of her favored pottery shop. Surrounded by her fellow musicians, her harmonies gracefully traversed the air, captivating both bystanders and her assembled choir. With the conclusion of a particularly poignant melody, applause erupted spontaneously.

Among the gathered onlookers, a slender young man named Novius, distinctive with his quirky countenance and leaning on a crutch, was especially animated, his applause fervent, his calls for "Encore, encore!" ringing out in eager anticipation.

Porcia, a choir member herself, quickly spotted Novius in the crowd. With a welcoming wave, she beckoned him to join them as she approached Agatha. Admiration filled the air as citizens gathered around, their faces lit with appreciation for Agatha's skillful singing. Nearby, Tiber kept a protective watch, while the merchant, who had hired the musicians to attract patrons to her stall of fine textiles, greeted new customers with a smile.

"Sister, your voice was especially captivating today," Porcia observed, gently drawing her away from the fanfare.

"Thank you, Porcia. You were wonderful as well," Agatha

responded. "Let's stop by the market. I would like to pick up some pork meat and bread."

At that moment, Novius approached them with a noticeable limp, his enthusiasm barely contained.

"Greetings, Porcia. Both of you possess such beautiful voices—particularly yours, Agatha," Novius said, a hint of awkwardness in his voice.

"Thank you, kind sir. Have we met?" Agatha asked.

"Agatha, this is Novius, the gentleman I've mentioned," Porcia began to whisper, "the one who's been lending us the scrolls."

"Oh, it's a pleasure, sir. My sister has praised your generosity, and your tales about our Lord have deeply moved us," Agatha said warmly.

"Please, just Novius," he insisted, steadying himself on his crutch, his gaze lingering on Agatha with admiration.

"Agatha, Novius lives just beyond our doorstep, and with the break of dawn, he's already working at his father's fish stall in the *macellum*," Porcia added.

"That would explain the distinct aroma," Agatha quipped with a playful smile.

"I'd be glad to share some of our catch with *you*," Novius offered fondly.

Agatha paused, noting his directness, but Porcia eagerly interjected, "What a splendid idea, Novius! You could be our guest for dinner. It'd be a lovely opportunity for you and Agatha to become better acquainted." Porcia turned to her sister, "Agatha, Novius also lacks ability. He had a terrible accident as a child when his father's carriage mistakenly ran over his leg—he's had to walk with a limp ever since. You two have much in common!"

Agatha's attention suddenly turned to Porcia, a storm of unspoken frustration stirring behind her sightless eyes. The boldness of Porcia's unannounced matchmaking efforts, coupled with the insinuation that her only suitors were now men with disabilities, ignited a spark of indignation. Struggling to contain her desire to confront Porcia directly, Agatha responded with restrained calm: "That's quite the tale, Porcia."

"Isn't it just?" Porcia responded, oblivious to Agatha's irritation, her face alight with enthusiasm.

Turning to Novius, Agatha replied resolutely, "I'm sorry, Novius, I'm afraid fish stew will not work."

Confusion and disappointment filled Novius's face. "Maybe some other time?" he managed, his gaze shifting between the sisters in search of clarity, only to meet Porcia's equally puzzled look.

"I'm afraid not. Thank you and goodbye, Novius," Agatha stated firmly. "Come, Porcia; come, Tiber," she added, pulling her sister away from Novius, her staff clicking against the cobblestones for guidance.

"Apologies, Novius—goodbye," Porcia called back as they left Novius, who gave a farewell wave before returning to his fish stall.

"Agatha, why are you doing this? Novius is fond of you and lives nearby. He would make a perfect husband for you, and we could all live close," Porcia pressed, bewildered by her sister's rejection.

"Porcia, I will promptly advise you the day I appoint you as my magistrate of Suitor Affairs. Until then, I will not tolerate you surprising me with stray men, especially those who reek of fish! Understood?!"

CHAPTER 14

THE OVATION

"If you want peace, prepare for war."
—*VEGETIUS*

Rome's ancient streets buzzed with anticipation as families and citizens from all walks of life gathered along the cobblestones, eager to witness the historic ovation for General Claudius and Aurelian. The air resonated with the soft melodies of flutes, setting a solemn yet festive tone. Amid this scene, children perched atop shoulders for a better view, their eyes wide with curiosity. Vendors skillfully navigated the crowd, offering figs wrapped in leaves, clay figurines of the gods, and honeyed cakes.

General Claudius and Aurelian marched at the head of the esteemed procession, their bearing exuding the grandeur of the event. Clad in military tunics with purple accents and crowned with myrtle wreaths, they embodied the martial pride of Rome. The crowd's cheers echoed through the streets as the two generals paraded before the emperor like gleaming trophies.

"Your victories have indeed served you well, General. Caesar has, at last, honored you." Aurelian commented.

"The time for honor was on the battlefield long ago," Claudius replied tersely, continuing his march while acknowledging the crowd with a wave.

"Nevertheless, the recognition is appreciated, is it not?" Aurelian countered.

"If Caesar truly aimed to recognize, he would have awarded us a triumph, not this diminished shadow of one. At least then, we would have approached by chariot rather than marching like prisoners to this monotonous sound of flutes."

Aurelian grinned and then remarked, "Well, I find the gesture impressive, given Caesar's usual restraint in authorizing such celebrations."

"What I find impressive is how that cunning little toad, Junius, swayed the emperor into mandating this ovation—an act that perhaps only Jupiter himself could fathom. Our young senator may prove useful after all."

Aurelian remained silent, ambivalent about Junius and his growing influence over the emperor and Claudius.

As the procession neared the Forum, the anticipation among the crowd reached its peak. The Curia Julia loomed on one side, the Senate's meeting place, while the rostra, adorned with the rams of conquered naval ships, stood as a proud symbol of Roman victories. Senators, dressed in their distinctive togas, and other dignitaries had gathered, ready to offer their formal welcomes and begin the ceremonial speeches.

In a discreet corner of the Forum, Senators Didius and Paternus engaged in a low, earnest dialogue. Senator Junius approached them eagerly, his steps filled with anticipation.

"A successful gathering, wouldn't you say, Senators?" Junius inquired, probing the consuls for praise.

"Less dreadful than anticipated, Junius. I imagine Caesar will deem it adequate," Paternus replied, his comment laced with his characteristic indirect praise, aiming to temper Junius's excessive enthusiasm.

Unfazed, Junius continued, "While overseeing the ovation, I

conversed with our generals. General Claudius, in particular, shared an intriguing perspective on the Senate," Junius remarked, subtly inviting further discussion.

"Claudius's valor is unquestionable. Yet, how do his military insights translate to Senate politics?" Didius inquired.

"Oh, Claudius holds the Senate's role in high esteem," Junius asserted.

"Does he?" Paternus interjected, skeptical.

"Without question. His insights on enhancing the Senate's influence in governance were quite illuminating."

"He spoke of this?" Didius inquired, his curiosity visibly piqued.

"In a manner of speaking, yes."

Taken aback, Paternus commented, "That's quite a refreshing viewpoint, one that our current emperor certainly does not share."

"The general emphasized that strengthening the Senate's influence could bolster imperial governance. He deeply admires this caesar, yet he also appeared earnestly committed to preserving our traditional values," Junius shared.

Didius and Paternus exchanged glances, silently questioning if the other was contemplating the same thought. Though steeped in deceit, Claudius's admission of his respect for the Senate stirred memories of governance reminiscent of the great emperors like Trajan and Marcus Aurelius. In those days, the Senate had wielded considerable influence, acting as a true partner in governance. However, Claudius's recognition was a stark deviation from recent norms, reviving hopes for a rekindled alliance between the Senate and emperor. Junius's snare had been expertly laid, with Didius and Paternus unwittingly stepping directly into it.

"Claudius's favor among the legions and the people is indisputable," Didius noted.

"And having a military leader of his stature advocating for the Senate could prove quite advantageous for us all one day," Paternus added.

"My thoughts were the same," responded Senator Junius. "The general even expressed his eagerness to discuss these matters further with both of you."

"He has?" Paternus inquired, clearly surprised.

"Yes, Senator, in fact, the general holds a deep reverence for seasoned wisdom," Junius remarked, flattering his fellow senators.

"Let us not embellish, Junius," Paternus interjected, eyeing him skeptically.

"By Jupiter, I speak the truth," Junius assured.

Didius glanced at Paternus, uncertain. "Tonight's banquet might be an opportune moment to delve deeper into this with the general himself."

Junius remained silent, awaiting Paternus's decision.

Reflecting on the potential outcomes, Paternus turned to Junius. "Arrange a suitable time for us to converse with the general at the banquet," he directed.

"I shall attend to it, Senator Paternus," Junius assured him, nodding respectfully.

"You have done well, Junius—and allow me once again to commend you on a flawless organization of this ovation," Paternus declared with less restraint, then added, "Rest assured, I shall personally communicate my high regard for your efforts to Caesar himself."

"Thank you, Consul. Your words humble me," Junius replied graciously.

Nearby, perched upon their majestic thrones and elevated above the congregation of senators and nobles, Emperor Gallienus and Empress Salonina, adorned in their royal attire, graciously acknowledged their subjects with waves as the generals approached the rostrum.

"Parades fill me with such joy," Salonina remarked while Gallienus surveyed his senators and guests skeptically.

"Conversing and conspiring—it's a complex task to discern loyalty," Gallienus pondered aloud.

"Dearest, do not burden yourself with such thoughts."

"I remind you that my father, our former emperor, was captured and tortured at the hands of our foes," Gallienus countered, his voice revealing the root of his deep-seated fears.

"A fate you will not share," she reassured him confidently. "Let us revel in the celebrations. After all, the glory is all yours."

A sense of unease emerged as Gallienus watched General Claudius and Aurelian ascend the Rostra, surrounded by senators welcoming them with cheers and praise. He questioned his decision as he recalled Claudius's unilateral military action earlier that year. "I ought to be stripping Claudius of rank and medal for past insubordination rather than seeking to gain his loyalty," he vented to his wife.

"Enough of this, my love. Your capacity for forgiveness distinguishes you. Do not allow General Aureolus's betrayal to cast a shadow over the loyalty of others. Choosing to honor the generals today was an act of great insight. They will return to the battlefield, bearing your name as a banner of inspiration against our enemies."

Gallienus gazed at Salonina admiringly while gently squeezing her hand. "As ever, *you* are my most trusted counsel, my dearest."

Empress Salonina gave him an adoring smile. "Show Rome who is truly being honored today, my love."

Beneath their elevated viewpoint, Claudius and Aurelian halted. Gradually, the area brimmed with as many participants of the ovation as it could accommodate, transforming it into a sea of military might and celebratory fervor.

As Emperor Gallienus rose, the sound of horns signaled his approach. Escorted by the Praetorian Guards, he made his way to greet his generals personally. The guests stood in acknowledgment, admiration clear in their eyes, as the crowd parted, revealing a path where slaves scattered flower petals before him.

Claudius whispered to Aurelian, "Behold, the suckling pig that feeds off the nourishment of our victories approaches."

Aurelian's smirk quickly faded as the emperor approached, giving a nod to one of his Praetorian Guards.

"Kneel before Caesar!" the Praetorian boomed.

Claudius and Aurelian exchanged uncertain glances before dropping to one knee.

Gallienus stood over the kneeling generals, fully in command, his voice booming through the assembly. "Behold, my distinguished generals have arrived!" The crowd, puzzled by the unexpected formality, watched with amusement as Gallienus relished the moment.

Claudius, misjudging the situation, began to rise, but with a hand on his shoulder, Gallienus pressed him firmly back down. "Honor the crown first, General," the emperor ordered, his words cutting through the assembly. "I will tell you when to stand." Suppressed laughter rippled through the crowd as Gallienus, in a calculated display of dominance, extended his hand toward Claudius. The gesture, heavy with expectation, was an unprecedented assertion of power, catching even his closest advisers off guard.

The light glinted off the emperor's ornate ring. Though unaccustomed to such an act, Claudius bent forward and pressed his lips to it, masking his inner turmoil beneath a façade of calm. The crowd, momentarily stunned by the rare and calculated show of authority, watched intently.

Until now, the thought of dethroning Gallienus had seemed beneath Claudius—more suited for Aurelian or another trusted subordinate. But as Gallienus held him in this forced submission, his disdainful gaze heavy upon him, Claudius's resolve solidified: the assassination would be his alone—a day he now eagerly anticipated.

With a patronizing pat on Claudius's head, Gallienus said, "Now you may rise, General."

Gallienus nodded to the Praetorian Guard, whose voice boomed, "Long live Caesar!"

The crowd's response followed—a thunderous wave of confusion and heartfelt acclaim, as they struggled to interpret the emperor's uncommon display.

LATER THAT EVENING, nestled within the sprawling confines of the grand palace, a magnificent feast was underway in a cavernous banquet hall lined with towering columns. Countless flickering oil lamps bathed the room, casting enigmatic shadows upon the frescoes of Roman gods and heroes that graced the walls.

The festive air was alive with the sound of music as musicians masterfully played lyres and flutes. Their melodies harmonized, accompanying dancers whose graceful movements enchanted onlookers. Moving effortlessly across the marble floor, these performers, draped in silk, showcased the rich cultural tapestry of Rome. Their attire sparkled, mirroring the exotic elegance and splendor of the emperor's court.

A boisterous crowd gathered, comprised of the elite and privileged. Many reclined on dining couches, indulging in roasted meats, fresh fruits, and flowing wine. Adorned in luxurious togas, stolas, and tunics, the guests immersed themselves in the opulence of the banquet.

In the distance, away from the epicenter of the revelry, General Aurelian passed by Senator Junius, who was conversing with Senators Didius and Paternus.

"Good evening, Aurelian," Junius greeted, his voice tinged with the warmth of wine, "And when, pray tell, may we expect General Claudius to grace himself with our presence?"

"As you can see, Senator, General Claudius is holding court with Caesar."

"Correct you are, Aurelian. And, might I say, you do a splendid job attending to all the general's needs," Junius remarked playfully. "One wonders where he would be without your wits," he added as the wine began to affect his demeanor.

Senators Paternus and Didius exchanged smug glances, their amusement growing as they observed Aurelian's mounting frustration in response to Junius's playful banter.

Before Aurelian could formulate a response, Junius persisted in his verbal onslaught. "Come now, General," he teased. "You gaze upon me as though I am a rogue ambushing you in a backwater tavern. Where are my manners? Allow me to present the esteemed consuls, Senators Paternus and Didius."

"Senators," Aurelian acknowledged with a firm handshake.

"Please acquaint yourselves while I attend to our general," Junius proclaimed, his movements carrying an air of grace as he headed toward General Claudius and Caesar.

Aurelian cast an annoyed glance at Junius, his distaste deepening as Junius's influence grew. Turning to the senators, he masked his disapproval with a thin veil of civility. "The young senator certainly has a flair for the dramatic."

Emperor Gallienus and Empress Salonina reclined on their *lecti*, the elegant couches reserved for banquets, while General Claudius, the guest of honor, sat by their side. The poised and regal trio reflected the grandeur and significance of the celebration.

An older senator, wearing a toga bordered with a thick purple strip, approached Gallienus. With a respectful nod, he said, "Congratulations on your victories, Caesar."

"Your benevolence is appreciated, Senator."

The senator added, "Your father would have been proud."

Gallienus nodded, his eyes briefly clouded with remembrance, before turning to Claudius. "I wonder what Emperor Valerian would have done with you, Claudius?"

Caught off guard, General Claudius managed a tentative, "Caesar?"

Gallienus replied with a chilling voice, "Would my father have praised you for your triumphs in the north or reprimanded you for your insubordination?"

"You are undoubtedly referring to my decision to mobilize the Fifth Legion."

"And let us not overlook the unfortunate death of my religious adviser," Gallienus pointed out.

"Both were indeed regrettable occurrences," Claudius conceded.

The emperor's glare intensified as he addressed Claudius. "While you may not adhere to Christian beliefs, remember, there's a nuanced art to engaging the people without pandering to them," he advised sternly. He leaned in closer, emphasizing his point: "My empire must grow from within as it grows from without."

Sensing the moment's weight, Claudius replied, his tone reflective and conceding: "My apologies, Caesar. Perhaps some of my actions may not have been as sound as they should have been."

"Indeed," Gallienus responded, his voice edged with gravity. "Let me be clear, General, I will not tolerate insubordination again."

"Understood, Caesar," Claudius responded reverently, though a storm of emotions brewed beneath his composed exterior. He possessed countless justifications for deploying the legion as he had— each decision carefully considered and calculated.

Yet, at this moment, the actual conflict was not about strategy but a battle of egos—an arena in which he knew it wise not to challenge the emperor directly.

Gallienus's eyes drifted to a huddle of figures by one of the many columns. In the middle, he observed Aurelian holding court with Paternus and Didius.

"Intriguing, is it not, General?"

"Caesar?" Claudius replied.

Gallienus's voice became contemplative: "How when a dog bites, it does not always bare its teeth." Claudius followed the emperor's gaze to where Aurelian stood. Gallienus then redirected the conversation. "What news from Mediolanum, Claudius?"

"The men are camped outside the city."

"The Gallic rebels have not surrendered?" Gallienus probed further.

"They await my command. I am certain this siege will be etched in history, and I will not shy away from leading my men to victory," Claudius declared, his voice resonant with determination and a palpable sense of pride.

Gallienus arched an eyebrow. "*Your* men? Surely, you mean *my* men —perhaps I should lead my army to this glorious victory if it is indeed one that history will remember?"

Claudius carefully noted, "I am certain Caesar has more pressing political matters to attend to."

Gallienus turned sharply. "Did I not conquer the Alamanni in one of Rome's greatest victories?" His words were not so much a question as a forceful reminder of his accomplishments. The room's murmur gently faded as those present felt the swell of Caesar's emphatic energy.

"You did, Caesar," Claudius responded with feigned respect.

"And what of Aureolus? Do you suppose that traitor will present himself on the battlefield?" Gallienus spat.

"It is likely," Claudius replied.

"Then you must bring me his head, and I shall have it sent to Postumus," Gallienus continued, his voice edged with cruelty. "Let him see what fate befalls those who dare to defy me."

"As you wish, Caesar."

"We must reclaim Mediolanum, Claudius."

"And I will," Claudius declared.

Gallienus, eyeing Claudius's calm demeanor, felt a surge of anger. The general's unwavering composure stoked the emperor's fury. Seeking to reassert his dominance, Gallienus responded with iron resolve. "Send word to the men that their caesar will lead them to victory," he commanded, his gaze sharp and unyielding.

Claudius paused for a moment, seemingly taken aback by the decision. He then replied, "They shall be inspired to hear this news, Caesar, as am I," his voice steady and respectful.

"Excellent," Gallienus acknowledged before greeting the young senator. "Senator Junius, your timing is impeccable."

"A magnificent festivity, Caesar," Junius replied. "In time for what though?"

"To end half-hearted efforts and empty political promises," Gallienus declared, punctuating his words with a hearty sip of wine.

Junius glanced at Claudius with concern, but the general remained stone-faced. "I'm not certain I follow."

"Your caesar is going to lead the siege of Mediolanum, and General Claudius assures me that Rome will herald it as one of its greatest victories!" Gallienus proclaimed.

Following his bold declaration, Empress Salonina cast a worried glance. "Husband, might I suggest entrusting the general with coordinating your visit to the battlefield, to ensure your safety? The attack on me last winter by the Alemanni tribe was peril enough for us to endure, would you not agree?"

"Indeed," Gallienus affirmed, turning to Claudius. "See that a messenger is dispatched only when the victory is assured."

"As you command, Caesar," Claudius replied.

Junius, brimming with enthusiasm, proclaimed, "We shall honor your coming victory with another ovation, Caesar—one to eclipse even this!"

Gallienus let out a dismissive scoff. "An ovation? Those are for generals, not emperors. When I am honored, it will be with a triumph!" His tone was resolute, intentionally belittling Claudius's moment of recognition. "Nonetheless, I commend your initiative,

Junius. Perhaps, when the time comes, I will entrust you with the planning of that triumph."

"With honor, Caesar," Junius replied humbly.

"Now, Empress," Gallienus said, his voice softening, "let us withdraw."

Empress Salonina gracefully accepted her husband's hand. The assembly stood aside in respectful acknowledgment as the imperial couple made their exit.

Junius then turned to Claudius, who now reclined content at his place of honor, overlooking the gathering of elites and senators.

"I have delivered on my promises, General," Junius proclaimed proudly.

"Far beyond my expectations, Junius," Claudius acknowledged with a nod.

"The senators are eager to meet you. While General Aurelian may momentarily hold their interest, it is indeed your voice they most ardently await."

"How did you anticipate Caesar would succumb to the snare?" Claudius inquired in a hushed voice, his gaze focused on Junius.

"Pride often leads to one's undoing," Junius remarked with a knowing grin.

"You may prove to be a valuable princeps senatus, after all," Claudius replied, a hint of approval in his voice, before descending to join the senators.

Junius watched him go, his eyes gleaming with excited anticipation.

CHAPTER 15

LOVE LETTERS

"Love is a thing full of anxious fears."
–OVID

Porcia navigated the capital's narrow cobblestone streets with Tiber close behind, her arms carefully cradling a cloth-covered basket. She exchanged warm greetings and light banter with familiar faces along the way. As she rounded a corner, she unexpectedly collided with Marius, his features partly hidden by a thick beard. The impact startled them both, causing Porcia's basket to slip from her grasp, spilling its contents and revealing a scroll.

"Oh!" Porcia exclaimed as she knelt to gather her scattered belongings.

Tiber sprang into action, shoving Marius against a wall to protect Porcia.

"Pardon me, dear maiden," Marius offered, still not fully aware of whom he had collided with. "I meant the lady no harm," he assured Tiber.

"It's all right, Tiber," Porcia commanded, giving him a meaningful look. Tiber released Marius, who immediately dropped to the ground to assist her.

As Porcia reached for the scroll, her fingers barely grazed the parchment before Marius snatched it away, a mischievous glint in his eyes. He held it just out of her reach and teased, "And what might this be?"

"Hand that to me at once!" Porcia commanded. "My father holds power over life and death—he oversees the executions in Rome. Do not play with me!"

Tiber was about to intervene, but Marius gestured for him to wait, then asked Porcia, "Have we not met?"

"I think not," Porcia replied, reaching out again for the scroll.

"If memory serves, Valentine and I—"

"Valentine?" Porcia interrupted, her face a mixture of confusion and realization.

"Yes!" Marius's face lit up with recognition. "At Lupercalia earlier this year, we were matched!"

"Marius!" Porcia exclaimed, blushing as she now recognized him.

"Indeed—you remember!" he smiled. "Your scroll," he said, politely returning it.

"Oh, how silly of me." She laughed lightly, accepting the scroll. "I did not recognize you with your beard! Thank you," Porcia took back the scroll and tucked it into her basket.

Tiber stepped back, giving them space to converse.

"That's quite all right, I was—"

"Where is Valentine?" Porcia interjected, urgency coloring her tone.

Marius hesitated briefly, choosing his words. "I am afraid he was badly wounded."

Porcia's eyes widened. "Oh no, will he survive?"

"His condition was grave when I saw him last," Marius replied. "I fear for him, but I could not stay by his side without risking a charge of desertion. As it is, I had to fabricate a tale of being captured by the Goths just to avoid punishment from the legion."

"I understand," Porcia replied. "He's alive, though," she murmured, recalling the countless times she had consoled Agatha, attempting to convince her that Valentine was gone forever.

"I hope he is," Marius replied, his tone somber. "He often spoke fondly of your sister." His expression brightened momentarily. "He entrusted me with a letter to deliver to Agatha. I must see her. Is she here?"

"She's at home. Do you have the letter? I can give it to her." Porcia quickly offered.

"He requested that I deliver it directly to her. However, his directions to your residence were unclear. I could not find it."

"Either way, I will have to read it to her. So, you might as well give it to me now," Porcia pressed. "Moreover, my father forbids us from bringing men by the house while he is away."

"Ah, I understand. I am being redeployed to the front lines tomorrow. I will not be able to deliver the letter until I return."

"Where is the letter?"

"I left it at my cousin's residence, who lives close by. If you would like to accompany me there, I could give it to you, and perhaps we could share a meal after?" Marius suggested warmly. "Under Tiber's protective watch, of course," Marius added, while offering a smile toward him.

Porcia hesitated, mindful of the time and errands she needed to do.

"I know a delightful eatery where we could enjoy wine and perhaps exchange tales of the Christian God?" Marius suggested, his gaze lingering on her basket, where she hid the scroll.

Porcia's eyes widened in surprise. "How did you know?"

"Most women do not carry concealed scrolls. I, too, have served as a messenger," he replied with a soft grin.

As a squad of praetorians marched past, Porcia lowered her voice. "We should not discuss this here. I will come with you to retrieve Agatha's letter, though I must return this scroll to my friend before midday."

"Then, you'll certainly need a strong Christian soldier to escort you," Marius suggested, grinning and offering his arm playfully. Porcia couldn't help but smile as she accepted.

Under the golden embrace of the afternoon sun, the rooftops of Rome glowed warmly, providing an idyllic setting for Marius and Porcia as they enjoyed the lingering moments of their meal. Tucked away in a cozy corner of a *popina*, a lively Roman tavern where patrons gathered for simple meals and abundant wine, they were surrounded by the vibrant life of the city square, with a magnificent view stretching toward the Capitoline Hill. The air was filled with the murmur of conversation and the clink of cups as locals indulged in the day's offerings. Tiber sat a few tables away, out of earshot but keeping a careful watch over Porcia.

The table was strewn with the remains of a modest yet richly satisfying feast. Fresh loaves of bread, their crust firm, had been dipped into olive oil, fragrant with a medley of herbs. A variety of cheeses accompanied the meal, their flavors ranging from sharp and tangy to creamy and rich. The centerpiece had been a sumptuous dish of pork, braised in wine and oil, seasoned with *garum*, each bite filling them with warmth. Generous servings of red wine rounded off the meal, their deep flavors providing a perfect counterpoint to the savory dishes.

"This day has been lovely, Marius—the meal, the wine, the vista," Porcia remarked.

"Let us not forget my captivating tales!" Marius chimed in jestingly.

Porcia laughed softly. "Indeed, how could I? And speaking of memorable encounters, how did you meet Valentine?"

"My first duty with the legions was on the arid expanses of the Syrian frontier, during the turmoils that followed the infamous battle at Edessa. My hands were more familiar with farming tools than the grip of a *spatha*. Yet, it was there, amid the dust storms and battle cries, where I met him."

Porcia leaned forward, captivated by the tale.

"During a fierce engagement against the Sassanid forces, I found myself stranded, without my shield, exposed to attack. Valentine came to my aid, shield raised, standing back-to-back with me against an endless wave of adversaries. His courage that day spared my life."

"Remarkable," Porcia reflected, her voice filled with admiration for Valentine's valor. "And to find such friendship amid the horror of war is a blessing indeed."

Marius nodded while reflecting momentarily on their friendship.

"He's akin to a brother. His valor and loyalty are unparalleled—he ever watches over us. For this, the men hold him in high esteem."

Porcia drank her wine, subtly masking her admiration for Valentine.

"And his affection for Agatha. I have not witnessed him display such fondness toward a woman—" he paused, gathering his thoughts "—in quite some time."

"He speaks of her often?" Porcia inquired, her voice tinged with mixed emotions.

"Endlessly. He adores Agatha," Marius affirmed warmly.

Setting her cup aside, Porcia fixed Marius with a firm look. "It's a great responsibility to care for somebody like my sister," she declared, her eyes conveying the weight of her commitment. "Agatha lives in a world of darkness, and I...I am her eyes. It's a duty I have wholeheartedly embraced—often at the expense of my own ambitions."

Marius felt the profound significance of her words. "Your devotion to Agatha is the living embodiment of the Christian God's teachings— yet He also spoke of the importance of community. Even those who give so much should receive care in return."

Porcia paused, contemplating his words as she reached for her wine, her feelings about Marius and his counsel swirling uncertainly.

"Perhaps there is space in your life for balance—a place where you can find joy and companionship alongside your duties to your sister," Marius suggested gently.

"You speak of a life that feels unattainable to me. I know no other duty than this one," Porcia confessed, her voice tinged with a mixture of resignation and longing.

Marius leaned in, his voice soft yet resolute. "When I return from battle, I would like to show you that a life beyond duty is possible—if you'll allow it?"

Porcia hesitated, clearly grasping the implication of his offer. "I'm not sure I can."

"Is it something I said?" he asked.

"No, not at all."

"I admire your strength and compassion," Marius added, reaching for her hand.

Hope and anticipation stirred within Porcia as his hand clasped hers. Yet, duty anchored her heart. She rose suddenly, her smile warm but tinged with the melancholy of her predicament.

"I must return home," she said, her voice steady though it conveyed subtle contemplation. "Thank you for this meal and your kind words, Marius. I will reflect on them."

Marius smiled. "As you wish."

LATER THAT AFTERNOON, Porcia guided her horse at a leisurely pace along the familiar path toward home. Tiber followed at a respectful distance, giving her space to reflect on the day. Bathed in the warm summer rays and still slightly buoyed by the wine she had shared with Marius, she savored the unhurried ride. With an hour of daylight remaining and her father occupied with overseeing a late execution, she felt no urgency to rush.

As she rode, Marius's parting words echoed in her mind. The thought of someone else taking over as Agatha's caretaker unsettled her. *What if somebody mistreated her? What if a suitor like Valentine grew weary of the responsibility? How could anyone care for Agatha as well as I?* These troubling thoughts, intensified by too much wine, influenced her next actions.

Valentine's letter, sealed and rolled tightly in her hands, felt like the key to her lingering questions. Ordinarily, she would have waited until she was with Agatha to open any letter addressed to her sister. Yet, she reasoned, *what difference did it make when I open it?* Agatha couldn't read it herself. *What if it contains distressing news?* Surely, it would be wiser to read it first, to better present the contents to Agatha, sparing her further distress.

With that thought, she broke the seal, unfolded the letter, and began to read:

My Beloved Agatha,

As I lie here, my body weakened by an arrow's cruel blow, my thoughts are consumed by you, filling me with the will to endure. Though the distance between us is great, your presence is ever near, a beacon of light in these darkest of days. When I saw you again, I was struck by your beauty, as timeless as the stars. The memory of our past sustains me, fueling my belief that they are not the final chapters of our tale.

I vow to return to you. When that day comes, let us leave behind the turmoil of war and the clamor of the city. Imagine us, hand in hand, wandering the familiar woods of our youth, forging a life of peace, bound by love.

Forever yours, in heart and soul,

Valentine

A tear trickled down Porcia's cheek as she felt overwhelmed by a tumultuous wave of emotions. On the one hand, she felt joy that a man could see beyond Agatha's disability and love her so deeply. On the other hand, a pang of envy surfaced, knowing she had never received a love letter herself. Yet, as she pored over the letter, another feeling emerged, distinct from envy or joy. The phrases *leave behind* and *wandering the woods of our youth* leaped at her, stirring memories. She envisioned a young Agatha running across their meadow toward the forest to meet a young Valentine, while she remained alone at the doorstep of their home, shivering as a cold wind swept over her. As this image took hold, tears streamed down her cheeks as she internalized one emotion above all—fear of abandonment.

She rolled the scroll back up, tucked it deep into her satchel, and kicked her horse forward, grappling whether to deliver Valentine's love letter to Agatha or not.

As she approached the stalls, Porcia spotted Agatha finishing up with the chickens in a nearby pen. She dismounted and handed her horse to Tiber, who led the animals to their stalls. With her satchel slung over her shoulder, Porcia walked over to join Agatha.

"Hello, sister," she greeted warmly.

"Hello, Porcia, how was your day?" Agatha asked, wiping chicken feed from her hands with a cloth and picking up her walking staff to return to the house.

"It was lovely. I returned the scroll we read to Novius. He still asks about you," she remarked while gently guiding Agatha by the arm.

"And as I have told you and Novius, I am still uninterested," Agatha replied firmly.

"Yes, you made that quite clear to both of us upon our last encounter."

"Then, my feelings should not come as a surprise to either of you," Agatha added, slightly annoyed. She paused and tilted her head to capture the fleeting warmth of the sun and the familiar farm sounds grounding her in the moment. With a reflective exhale, she lowered her head, momentarily drawn away from the sensory comforts of her surroundings.

Porcia asked softly, "What is it, sister?"

"The warmth of the sun is magnificent. I only wish to see all it illuminates."

"And if that day should come—who would you like to see first?" Porcia playfully asked.

Agatha pondered, then responded with heartfelt passion: "Valentine."

Porcia came to an abrupt halt, a knot tightening in her stomach. Inside, she screamed, *How could she wish to see him before me?* This burning question, coupled with the lingering effects of the wine, the emotions Marius had stirred, and the memory of Agatha's dismissive treatment of their friend Novius, ignited a fire within her.

Agatha sensed Porcia halting abruptly but couldn't see the anger that flashed across her face. "I know you do not care to hear me speak of Valentine, though his memory fails to escape me."

Porcia reached her breaking point. Realizing that Marius was leaving for war the next day and that the return of either him or Valentine was uncertain, she did the unthinkable.

"I must tell you, sister. I have heard news of Valentine," Porcia blurted out.

Agatha's head snapped toward her. "What?! Why haven't you mentioned this before?!"

"I thought your memory of him had faded," Porcia retorted.

Agatha's patience wore thin, her tone urgent. "Porcia! What news?!"

"I'm afraid he was...taken in battle," Porcia stated solemnly.

A guttural gasp escaped Agatha's lips as her knees wobbled. Time seemed to freeze as Porcia observed her sister's normally serene expression contort with pain. For a fleeting moment, she considered retracting her words, witnessing the depth of Agatha's anguish.

"Who told you of this? Surely, you jest," Agatha whispered, her voice tinged with desperation as she clung to a sliver of hope.

Porcia's guilt deepened. "I'm sorry, sister. I'm afraid it's true." Then, pressing on, she shamelessly covered her tracks. "A soldier friend of mine swore it so."

Tears, thick and unrestrained, flowed freely down Agatha's cheeks as she uttered, "No...please, God, no."

Porcia reached out, gently taking Agatha's trembling hands into her own, drawing her close as if she were the only solace in her life. "Sister, please do not be upset," she pleaded. "There will be other men better suited for us."

But it was too late. The words had struck Agatha like a sword, piercing her heart more deeply than any arrow ever could. With a heartbreaking cry, she collapsed into Porcia's embrace, clinging to her like a widow to a coffin.

Entangled in her web of emotions, Porcia held Agatha upright, her touch gentle as she patted her back. "Fear not, sister. I am here," she murmured soothingly, the shadow of her deceit enveloping them like the darkness of dusk.

NESTLED in her luxurious villa in Baiae, Serena radiated serene fulfillment, far removed from the complexities of Rome. Her terrace, a peaceful sanctuary, overlooked the shimmering Gulf of Naples, where she enjoyed the gentle warmth of the late-summer breeze. Draped in a light tunica that elegantly accommodated her growing pregnancy, she embodied refined grace. Attentive slaves fanned her in a steady, rhythmic motion as she sipped honey-sweetened water and savored the rich, briny taste of fresh olives.

Seated across from her, Iset remained ever watchful—not merely a servant but Serena's trusted confidante. Beside Iset sat Zeno, a young Greek scribe who had been referred to Serena by a prominent local Roman family. Renowned for his sharp intellect and polished skills, Zeno had mastered reading and writing in both Greek and Latin, having studied under some of the finest tutors in Athens. Now, with quill poised over the parchment, he prepared to capture every word as Serena began to dictate a letter.

"Scribe, begin the letter with…"

"Sorry…" Zeno interrupted.

"We've only just begun," Serena replied, raising an eyebrow.

"Yes, my lady. However, my name is Zeno—not Scribe."

Iset rolled her eyes, gesturing for him to do as he was told.

"Very well… Zeno. Write this: 'To my beloved Claudius, I must apologize for my hasty departure from Rome without prior notice following Tullus's… unfortunate incident,'" Serena began, sharing a knowing glance with Iset. "Regretfully, I received distressing news that one of my cousins in Baiae was gravely ill, and I hastened to her side."

Iset interjected, "My lady, it may be more convincing to tell him that it was your *mother* who fell ill—such news would surely justify your urgent journey to Baiae."

"You're right, Iset. Scribe—Zeno—change it to my mother's illness," Serena instructed as Zeno glanced at her curiously, then swiftly adjusted the narrative, his quill racing across the parchment to keep up with her fabrications.

"What should I say next?" Serena pondered aloud.

"Perhaps, since this is a love letter, you might consider praising your suitor's virtues or notable qualities," Zeno suggested.

Serena paused, reflecting briefly before responding unapologetically, "It's not that kind of a love letter, Zeno."

Iset waved Zeno off dismissively and interjected, "My lady, you could frame the narrative around your passionate encounter, which has brought us to where we are today," her gaze briefly dropping to Serena's prominently swollen belly.

"Excellent suggestion, Iset," Serena agreed, gently massaging her belly. "Write this: 'I am reminiscing on an evening we shared several months ago, an encounter so passionate that even Venus might look on with envy—wherein you declared your undying love for me. I am lying here now, longing for the day when you shall swiftly return, and we can relive such moments together.'"

"Exquisitely articulated. I am certain such a provocative opening will resonate deeply with him," Zeno complimented.

Iset interjected, "It may also be prudent to allude to the divine hand in your departed husband's regrettable misfortune and the new life you now bear." She and Serena exchanged a meaningful glance, their eyes reflecting the shared secret about Tullus.

"Precisely, Iset," Serena remarked as her fingers delicately traced the silver rim of her water cup. "Zeno, transcribe the following: 'From our divine union, the gods have seen fit to grace us with a precious gift, despite Tullus' misfortune. I bear within me the flame of life, our child, conceived from the depths of our boundless love—a herald of the future we shall share.'"

"Excellent, my lady," Iset commended.

Zeno paused and asked, "My lady, forgive my interruption, but I fail to understand—after your husband's death in Rome, you now carry the child of your new suitor... from this Claudius?"

Iset promptly smacked the back of Zeno's head. "Mind your place, Scribe! Your role is to inscribe the domina's words, not to pry into matters beyond your station."

Zeno was stunned, not only because a slave had dared to lay hands upon him, but because it had come from a woman. "My lady, I demand—"

Before he could finish, Serena raised a finger, silencing him at once. She shook her head slowly, her gaze sharp and unyielding, leaving no room for further protest.

Quickly recognizing that he was not being held in favor, he offered a hasty apology, "My sincerest apologies, my lady. I meant no offense."

Serena peered at Zeno and gently nodded toward Iset.

"And... Iset, of course," Zeno added begrudgingly, swiftly

returning his focus to the parchment. Serena allowed a brief smile to escape, acknowledging Iset's unwavering loyalty.

As she massaged her pregnant belly, Serena imparted her closing sentiment: "Though I yearn for the day when we may reunite in Rome, I deem it wise for our child's well-being to be born amid the mild climate of Naples and the support of my family here." She paused momentarily, casting a glance in Iset's direction. "Anything else, Iset?"

Zeno shook his head in disbelief that the opinion of a slave was now being favored over his own, but he bit his lip and remained silent.

"Tell him you shall journey to his side once your child draws breath."

"Indeed. Add that," Serena directed, then paused, pondering aloud, "What signature befits this letter?"

Before Zeno could utter a word, his thoughts veering toward *Insincerely yours*, Iset interjected, "'Loyally yours,'" her smile radiating approval.

"Excellent, Iset. It's a wonder I even bother hiring scribes when I have you by my side. Write that, Zeno, then bring it here," Serena instructed gracefully.

He presented the letter to Serena, who carefully examined it.

"Seal it," she instructed, her tone carrying an air of finality.

Zeno returned to the table, letting the wax drip onto the edge of the scroll. He pressed down with Serena's signet ring, which bore the emblem of her house—a serpent entwined around a crescent moon— sealing the letter with her authority. "All finished, my lady."

"Thank you. Collect your payment from my *procurator* on your way out," Serena replied dismissively.

"As you wish, my lady," Zeno said, quickly departing and placing the scroll on the table as he exited.

As he left, Ballavan, an imposing thirty-eight-year-old figure clad in traditional Maharashtrian attire, approached the terrace. Serena had acquired both Iset and Ballavan from slave traders—Ballavan, with his origins in India, was valued for his formidable and unique presence. Serena had paid a high price for Ballavan, desiring him for her household due to the rarity of such exotic slaves in Rome. Over time, Ballavan's mastery of the ancient martial art of malla-yuddha proved invaluable, elevating him to the position of Serena's most trusted guard. As Ballavan drew closer, Iset watched him, her expression softening as his sandals quietly shuffled across the villa's mosaic tiles.

"Greetings, Ballavan," Iset greeted with a smile.

"Greetings, Iset and my lady, you summoned me?" Ballavan asked.

"We did, Ballavan. You are to deliver this scroll to General Claudius, who encamps with his legion outside Mediolanum. It is an urgent and confidential message. You must ensure it reaches the general untouched by any hand other than his own. Understood?" Iset explained.

Ballavan nodded, the seriousness of Iset's instructions momentarily rooting him to the spot. "I will guard it with my life."

Serena added, "Ballavan, take the local roads north to Rome and then follow the Via Flaminia; it provides the quickest route toward Mediolanum. Avoid the main legion paths and try to travel with a mercantile convoy for added discretion. They often transport dispatches and can provide camouflage. Disguise yourself as a Roman as best as you can to attract minimal attention."

"As you wish, my lady," Ballavan replied, ready to execute her commands.

Concealing the love letter within his tunic, Ballavan bowed deeply to both women.

"I look forward to your return, Ballavan," Iset said, her smile warm and affectionate.

Ballavan returned a faint smile, then turned on his heel and exited the villa. Serena and Iset watched as he walked away, his stride purposeful and steady, until he disappeared into the villa's embrace.

"He's a good match for you, Iset," Serena remarked, noting their affection toward each other.

"I agree," Iset responded as they shared a playful smile. Her gaze then shifted toward Serena's swelling belly. "It won't be long now, my lady. Do you ever reminisce about Valentine?"

Serena paused for a moment, her expression softening as she considered her child's true father. Then, she replied firmly, "That is a name we mustn't ever repeat."

"Understood, my lady."

Serena reclined onto her mattress and closed her eyes, relaxing as her slaves gently fanned her. She had done what she must to survive and murmured contentedly, "Ah, Naples in the summer is truly a delight."

CHAPTER 16

HIGHER CALLING

"We are not born for ourselves alone;
a part of us is claimed by our nation,
another part by our friends."
—CICERO

Valentine gazed out his bedroom window at the valley near Arretium, where the verdant landscape, bathed in the golden hue of a late-summer dawn, stretched out to the edges of the secluded forest. After relocating to the residence near the infirmary, he reveled in the luxury of Deodatus and Charu's Tuscan villa.

Each morning, Valentine embarked on a journey of tranquility. The villa's open courtyards and stone archways framed views of the expansive gardens. It was a sharp contrast to the rigid discipline of military camps and the chill of steel armor. Here, he felt the stirrings of a new life filled with peace and serenity. The garden was a lush tapestry of life, each plant and herb resonating with an energy that Charu understood deeply. Under her guidance, Valentine began to learn qigong, joining her in the garden most mornings while she mentored him in this ancient art form.

"Qigong is not just about movement, Valentine," Charu explained. "It's about achieving harmony between our life force and the world around us. By observing nature all around us, you begin to understand yourself and your place in this world. Move as nature moves, with ease, without force, with effortless power."

Mirroring Charu's slow, deliberate movements, Valentine strove to attune to the subtle qi she described.

"Look at the trees; notice the movement through the branches and leaves. Is the tree moving?" Charu asked.

"It is," Valentine replied.

"The tree only moves when the wind touches it. It may seem as if the tree itself is moving, yet it is merely following an unseen power—the wind. Your body is like the tree. Qi is the invisible force that moves through you. It is the breath in your lungs, the beats of your heart, and the light in your mind. You must learn to flow with this energy, to let it move freely through you, much like a sail capturing the wind. This is how you cultivate your qi."

Valentine listened intently, pondering whether he might one day apply Charu's teachings to aid others as she did. The art required patience, a calm mind, and a profound sensitivity to the natural forces that enveloped them. Under Charu's vigilant guidance, Valentine began to feel this power stirring within himself.

ON ANOTHER DAY, as the late summer sun cast long shadows across the garden, Valentine stumbled over a stone. He extended his arm to steady himself, but a sharp pain flared in his chest, a reminder of his wound. Charu seized the moment to teach, closing her eyes and cupping her hands as if to channel qi toward the source of Valentine's pain.

"Healing is an exchange of trust," she murmured softly. "You must trust me, yes, but even more, you must trust the power of your own body to heal. Close your eyes now, and tell me what you feel."

"I sense warmth," Valentine admitted as he sensed Charu's qi.

"Where does the pain come from?"

"From my fall," Valentine replied, trying to make sense of the discomfort.

"Search deeper; where do your thoughts lead?" she urged, encouraging him to explore more deeply within.

Valentine focused, his mind drifting back to the battlefield, to the harrowing moment the arrow nearly pierced his heart.

"Tell me what you see?" Charu asked, sensing his discomfort, her hands shifting and hovering above his chest's center.

"I see the arrow piercing through me."

"And how do you feel?"

"Helpless...as if my breath is slipping away," he muttered, his voice quivering.

"Stay with this moment," Charu guided. "Embrace the arrow with your whole heart. Let it become a part of you. Surround it with peace, with love. And if your mind wanders, gently bring it back to this place of love."

Valentine took in her words, adhering to her instructions. They remained in silent meditation, the minutes stretching long yet fleeting swiftly. Charu focused her qi, guiding the energy, while Valentine worked on dissolving his mental barriers, fostering a pure, free-flowing connection between his mind and body.

"Now, slowly open your eyes and tell me how you feel," Charu gently prompted.

Valentine smiled, his eyes flickering open. "The pain has vanished," he declared, astonished. "How did you achieve this?"

Charu smiled. "Sometimes, the body tricks the mind into holding on to pain, even after the pain is gone. If left untreated, it can cause more harm than the injury itself."

Valentine was taken aback by this insight. It challenged his instincts as a soldier, revealing a vulnerability he had rarely allowed himself to see. In that moment, he understood a new kind of strength—not of muscle but of spirit and inner power.

His lessons with Charu expanded from the tranquil garden into the villa's infirmary, where shelves held jars of dried herbs and vials of potent potions. Charu guided him through each item, her voice a soft cadence rich with the wisdom of Ayurvedic medicine.

"This one is to reduce the swelling," she explained, handing him a small jar. "It's made from willow bark, known to ease pain and help soothe the body." She then gestured toward a cluster of delicate purple flowers. "And this—lavender—to calm the mind and aid your sleep."

"Could you teach me how to prepare these myself?" Valentine replied eagerly.

"Certainly," Charu responded, impressed by Valentine's enthusiasm for learning.

By the soft glow of an oil lamp, he meticulously inscribed his notes onto a parchment scroll, detailing sketches and observations on the properties and uses of each herb. In the solitude of the night, he revisited every lesson, his stylus carefully tracing each word. Though uncertain of where this knowledge would lead, something deep within compelled him to grasp the full depth of his recovery.

The infirmary had become more than just a place of healing for Valentine; it was his training ground. He spent countless hours observing Deodatus and Charu as they expertly treated patients. Though his medical knowledge was far from Deodatus's depth, he eagerly absorbed the basic principles and procedures for managing common ailments. He assisted Deodatus and Regalus in caring for patients, sometimes taking an active role and, at other times, simply providing comfort and reassurance.

Prior to Valentine's arrival, Regalus had lingered in his parents' shadows. As time passed, however, Regalus grew fond of Valentine, following him everywhere and learning from his every move, just as Valentine was learning from them. Deodatus and Charu had welcomed Valentine into their family with open arms. Their home, once strictly defined by routine, now thrived with the energy of their new guest. Regalus, with his quiet curiosity, became akin to the younger brother Valentine never had.

One day, a woodcutter's son entered the clinic, his arm marred by a deep gash from an unforgiving blade. After Deodatus examined and cleaned the wound, he stepped back, folded his arms, and instructed

Valentine to stitch it up. Feeling the weight of Deodatus's expectations, Valentine took up the needle and thread. His hands were steady, guided by the knowledge and confidence he had gained under Deodatus's tutelage. Regalus, ever happy to be at Valentine's side to help, assisted.

"Excellent work, Valentine; you are learning," Deodatus murmured behind him, his voice calm and reassuring. As Valentine finished stitching the wound, a wave of satisfaction washed over him, and he smiled at Regalus to thank him for his aid.

The woodcutter's son looked up at him with a grateful smile. "Thank you, sir."

"You're welcome," Valentine replied warmly.

As he rinsed the blood from his hands in a nearby basin, he reflected on the wounds he had inflicted throughout his life. A series of haunting images—adversaries perishing in agony—flashed through his mind. These memories often stirred him from sleep as the lingering guilt of his past deeds clashed with who he was becoming.

He found solace in the prayerhouse Deodatus and Charu had built. From the outside, the structure resembled a barn. Deodatus had intentionally designed it this way to avoid attracting the attention of traditionally minded locals and Roman soldiers. Constructed of timber, it appeared unassuming. However, upon entering, visitors were welcomed by rows of handcrafted benches and a wooden fish hanging behind a beautiful altar. Small openings punctuated the walls, allowing shafts of light to mingle with glowing oil lamps, creating a serene ambience that fostered reflection and peace. This quiet place became a sanctuary for Valentine, a space to contemplate his new path.

After numerous theological discussions with Deodatus, Valentine decided to convert to Christianity. His prior exposure to the faith had been limited to Marius's occasional prayers and lectures, along with a brief conversation with Agatha. However, the more he learned and pondered, the stronger his inclination grew toward conversion. Guided by subtle and unmistakable signs and the prospect of a fresh start, his path became clear.

On the day of his baptism, Valentine stood in the prayerhouse, bathed in its soft light, surrounded by the local congregation he had come to know. With no bishop to perform the rites, Deodatus, devout and trusted by the community, stepped forward. He carefully recited the vows, mindful of the sacred tradition he upheld, ensuring Valentine's initiation into the faith was both solemn and true to their beliefs.

Deodatus raised his hand and made the sign of the cross on Valentine's forehead, marking him as a servant of Christ. Holding a vessel of holy water, Deodatus began the baptism with a prayer, his voice gently filling the tranquil sanctuary: "Lord, as we baptize this servant in Your name, may this water represent his rebirth into Your grace. Cleanse his past and lead him into a new life of faith and devotion."

The congregation watched in respectful silence, deeply engaged.

As Deodatus poured the water over Valentine's head, memories of his turbulent past surfaced—the haunting memories of battlefields where he had taken lives, the acute pain of surviving his family, and the relentless yearning for redemption that had driven him to this very place—flooded his mind. Yet, each drop of water seemed to wash away his old self. For the first time, he felt resolute in his belief, accepting the Christian God as the one and only deity. The thought filled him with a profound sense of relief, as if a great weight had been lifted from his shoulders. The confusion that had once clouded his heart dissipated, replaced by a newfound clarity and peace. Valentine felt more alive than ever, his spirit rejuvenated by the divine presence he now fully embraced.

Whispering, "Forgive me, Lord," he addressed not Deodatus but the divine presence enveloping him, feeling a deep connection to the God he had chosen to follow.

As the ceremony ended, Valentine opened his eyes to the gentle smiles of the congregation. Their warm and welcoming faces now symbolized not just fellow believers but a community that had accepted him, flaws and all. He wished Agatha were among them, but he knew in his heart that their paths would cross again at the right time.

Deodatus placed his hand on Valentine's shoulder and said softly, "You are reborn, Valentine," his voice easing as the formality of the ceremony transitioned to a moment of heartfelt connection. "Walk in the light of the Christian God, and let His love guide you."

"Thank you," he said, his voice thick with emotion. "I will."

He remained in reflective silence as the congregation began to disperse, their murmurs of encouragement weaving through the air.

In the tranquil early hours of the following day, Valentine sat down to write a new letter to Agatha, his thoughts entwined with the profound experiences of his baptism.

Dearest Agatha,

With each new dawn, I embrace words lit by a recent awakening—my acceptance of the Christian God, a path you've already walked with such grace. My baptism was not just a washing away of the old but a step closer to where you've always been, spiritually one step ahead, guiding me, even unknowingly.

These unspoken words carry the weight of a promise from a man transformed, eagerly anticipating the day I can fully share this journey with you. Know that my love, now deepened by faith, grows stronger each day, inspired by your example.

Forever yours,

Valentine

He paused, the weight of his confession settling deeply within him. Though he couldn't send the letter just yet—lacking a suitable courier —he hoped she would appreciate his words when they were finally reunited. Writing these letters awakened something profound within him. Taking a deep breath, he carefully rolled up the letter and placed it with the others he had written to Agatha, each tucked away securely under his bed. Each unsent message marked a step closer to the man he aspired to be upon their reunion.

WITHIN THE STRATEGIC confines of his command tent, General Claudius surveyed the Roman encampment outside Mediolanum, now held by the forces of Aureolus, a general no longer loyal to Rome. The city, a vital hub in northern Italia, had fallen under his control as he sought to expand his influence. Rumors of an alliance with the breakaway usurper, Emperor Postumus, added a layer of complexity to the rebellion, though the extent of that support remained unclear. Flanked by his senior officers, Claudius studied the detailed map spread across the tactical table, marking the points where his legions had attempted to breach the defenses.

"How many rebels are within the city walls?" Claudius asked, lifting his gaze from the map.

"It's difficult to estimate, General. The rebels entered from the north, and there's a chance they've swayed some of our own," an officer reported.

"Have we severed their access to food and water?" Claudius queried another officer.

"Yes, General. However, Aureolus likely anticipated our siege tactics and has stockpiled enough provisions to withstand a winter blockade."

"And the battering rams at the main gate?" Claudius pressed.

General Aurelian interjected, "They met fierce resistance. As soon as we moved the rams into position, the rebels launched arrows, stones, and boiling water from the walls. They hold the high ground, General. We lost an entire cohort yesterday."

Claudius nodded gravely, absorbing the grim details. "By Jupiter, what game does Aureolus play? We have the city surrounded—it's only a matter of time before they must yield."

"Perhaps he aims to weaken us as winter approaches," Aurelian mused.

"And then?"

"Dispatch reinforcements?" Aurelian speculated, casting a significant glance.

Claudius shook his head sharply. "Postumus won't risk his forces for Aureolus, alliance or not."

Aurelian hesitated. "It's unlikely, but we can't rule it out."

Claudius turned to one of his officers. "Do we have scouts positioned to intercept messengers and lookouts prepared for ambushes?"

The officers exchanged uneasy glances before one bravely spoke. "Not yet, General. Our focus has been on breaching their walls."

Claudius slammed his fist on the table, scattering maps and markers. "Fools, the lot of you! Aureolus once commanded Rome's finest cavalry and safeguarded this entire peninsula—he's two steps ahead of all of you! Assume he's already called for reinforcements. Station guards at every entry point, day and night. If it comes to it, we'll starve them into submission."

The officers all responded in the affirmative and waited for any other orders.

"Disperse!" Claudius screamed at them as they scattered away like flies startled from rest. Claudius's tone softened slightly. "Aurelian, stay behind."

An officer suddenly stepped into the tent. "General, a private courier has arrived with a message intended solely for your eyes."

"Bring him here," Claudius commanded.

The officer departed to fetch the courier, while Claudius addressed Aurelian. "It's time to send word to Gallienus to visit us at the front."

"Are you certain?" Aurelian gently challenged.

"Quite."

The officer returned, ushering Ballavan into the tent, whose Indian origin immediately sparked curiosity.

"This is him, General," the officer reported.

"General, I carry a message from Lady Serena," Ballavan announced, presenting the sealed letter.

"You're a long way from home," Claudius remarked, eyeing Ballavan as he took the scroll. He quickly broke the seal and scanned the contents. As he finished reading, he looked up, meeting Ballavan's gaze. "This cannot be," he muttered, visibly shocked. "She's truly with child?"

"Yes, General, very much so," Ballavan confirmed.

Aurelian, standing aside, seemed equally stunned by the revelation.

"When will we know if it's a boy?" Claudius inquired.

"Soon, General," Ballavan replied, subtly hinting at the child's imminent birth.

Turning to Aurelian, Claudius remarked, "It appears my encounter with Serena bore more fruits than merely securing an empress."

As the news sank in, Claudius's mind drifted to thoughts of his upbringing. Raised with an iron fist, he now had an opportunity his father never had—a chance to elevate his family's status from mere survival to enduring greatness. He envisioned a future where his name would be immortalized, carried on by his offspring, transforming from rags to riches, from powerless to the most powerful. This child, this legacy, would be his mark on history.

"Rest assured, it will be a boy, General," Aurelian asserted confidently, snapping Claudius back to the moment.

"Inform Lady Serena that upon the birth of my son, I expect her immediate return to Rome for our union. I will not have my child raised by a widow mistress," Claudius ordered. "And use the military courier to notify me the moment she returns."

"As you wish, General. Anything else for Lady Serena?" Ballavan inquired.

"Tell her, upon my return, we shall have a discreet wedding. The boy shall carry my name—and may the gods grant her a swift birth," Claudius added firmly.

"Certainly," Ballavan replied before departing.

Aurelian, pausing briefly, ventured, "It seems congratulations are in order."

"Not quite," Claudius replied tersely. "Send word to Gallienus— victory is in sight."

With a nod, Aurelian left to carry out the command.

CHAPTER 17

CROWNING AMID CHAOS

"They can because they think they can."
—*VIRGIL*

In the weeks following his baptism, as autumn unfurled its colors at Deodatus and Charu's villa, Valentine's bond with Deodatus and Charu's son, Regalus, continued to deepen. Having another mentor besides his father, Regalus enjoyed Valentine accompanying him on hunting excursions in the forest and sparring sessions with wooden swords. With youthful zeal, Regalus soaked up every lesson Valentine imparted. Initially centered on basic sword techniques, their training gradually morphed into meaningful dialogues.

"Strength," Valentine instructed while demonstrating a precise swipe of his wooden sword, "lies equally in the power of your swing as it does in knowing when not to draw your sword."

Regalus listened intensely, his eyes wide, as Valentine shared stories of introspective moments that had driven him to seek a different path. These sessions became a key part of Valentine's recovery. Each day, he felt his physical strength return, his thoughts more apparent, and his spirit lighter. In Regalus's innocence and eagerness, Valentine saw his transformation mirrored.

After an energetic training session one brisk morning, Regalus looked up at Valentine as they paused to catch their breath. "Do you miss being a soldier, Valentine?"

Valentine stood gazing over the villa before turning to Regalus. "I miss the camaraderie," he confessed, his voice filled with a hint of nostalgia. "Yet, I've found a new brotherhood here—and a different kind of courage."

Regalus's eyes sparkled with youthful enthusiasm. "Perhaps I will be a brave soldier one day like you!" he said playfully.

Valentine chuckled softly. "My father once told me, 'True valor comes from within, not from the donning of armor,'" he said, his voice thoughtful as Regalus mulled over the words. As he spoke, Valentine found himself reflecting on the moment his father imparted this wisdom long ago.

He had been nine years old then, his days filled with pretend battles and heroic feats. With a wooden sword clutched tightly, he gallivanted across their farmstead on the outskirts of Interamna, lost in his world of grand adventures. However, on this day, his idyllic play was abruptly interrupted by the commanding voice of his older brother, Rufus, whose authoritative tone brooked no argument.

"Valentine, your chores!" Rufus ordered from across the farmyard.

Reluctantly, young Valentine complied with his brother's demands, his spirit resisting the mundane tasks ahead. Groaning to himself, he shuffled toward the animal stalls.

"There you go, dung head," Rufus teased, unable to resist provoking his younger brother.

"I'm not a dung head!" Valentine shot back defiantly, his temper flaring.

"Oh, yes, you are," Rufus said with a smug grin, taunting him further.

Valentine's anger boiled. He raised his wooden sword and charged at his older brother. "No, I'm not!"

Rufus, noticeably taller and bearing the slight edge of early adolescence, armed himself with a hoe and towered over young Valentine.

With ease, he deflected each of his younger brother's blows, all while continuing his taunts. "Not bad, dung head," he jeered with a smirk.

"Stop calling me that!" Valentine shouted.

With a swift maneuver, Rufus deftly struck Valentine's leg, causing him to stumble backward into a stack of hay.

"Some soldier you'll make! You fight like a chicken!" Rufus taunted.

"I do not—I am as brave as a bear!" Valentine's patience wore thin, his youthful rage rising like a storm unleashed. With sudden determination, he charged at his brother with reckless abandon. Caught off guard, Rufus stepped backward and tripped over a shovel behind him.

Seizing the moment, Valentine pounced on his brother, landing a firm punch on his nose. Blood spattered from the impact. But before he could deliver another blow, their father, clad in the tunic and armor of a Roman legionnaire, intervened, pulling Valentine away from his brother.

"Enough!" their father bellowed, his voice commanding attention. "Valentine, I told you to tend to your chores!"

"I don't want to do my chores! I want to fight for Rome—with you!" Valentine protested, then retrieved his wooden sword from the ground, his resolve clear.

"Perhaps Rome needs you to clean the stables," Rufus quipped, gingerly touching his injured nose as he regained his footing.

"Die, savage barbarian!" Valentine cried out, pointing his wooden sword menacingly at his older brother.

"Enough—both of you!" their father thundered. "Rufus, when I depart, you shall be in charge, and I expect you to help your brother! And Valentine, you must obey Rufus's orders!"

"I don't want you to leave, Father!" Valentine confessed, his voice trembling with fear and uncertainty.

Moved by his son's display of vulnerability, Valentine's father knelt beside him, his heart heavy with the burden of his impending departure. "I know, son," he murmured, his voice soft yet resolute. "Remember, Valentine, true valor comes from within, not from the donning of armor. While I am away, our home must be guarded. Will you take on this duty?"

He reluctantly nodded, his eyes glossing over with emotion.

"VALENTINE!" Regalus's voice cut through the memory, pulling him back to the present.

"Sorry, Regalus. My mind was elsewhere," Valentine replied, shaking off the lingering emotions of his recollection.

"I asked you if you ever regret having been a soldier?"

Valentine shook his head. "No, not at all. I gained much from the experience. Yet, I've come to realize that there is still more to learn and much to contribute."

Regalus nodded thoughtfully, taking in the depth of Valentine's wisdom.

With a comforting arm around Regalus's shoulders, Valentine guided him forward with paternal warmth. "Come, it's time for us to return to our duties." They walked back to the villa, their steps aligned in the silent communion of their conversation.

As AUTUMN LEAVES commenced their graceful descent, the prayerhouse radiated in the gentle dawn light, welcoming the sacred vows of a young couple. Deodatus, with Valentine at his side, presided over the marriage ceremony. The couple's eyes sparkled with future promises as they listened intently. At the crucial moment of blessing, Deodatus gave Valentine a nod. Stepping forward, Valentine spoke from the heart: "May your union be blessed with the strength of faith, the warmth of love, and the light of hope. May you walk together in God's grace today and throughout your lives."

As the couple sealed their vows, a profound joy surged through Valentine. For the first time since childhood, he felt an inner lightness —a sense of love and purpose that reached far beyond the shadows of the battlefield. The thought of uniting couples in their sacred unions rekindled his spirit, lifting the weight of his past. In that moment, he realized that there was a higher cause to fight for—a divine calling that brought healing, unity, and a new sense of life.

Once they were outside, Valentine wasted no time in seeking out

Deodatus. As he approached, his voice was clear and filled with renewed purpose. "Deodatus, today has revealed my path."

"And what path is that?" Deodatus inquired, his curiosity sparked by Valentine's determined tone.

"Uniting those in love is how I will serve," Valentine replied with conviction, a newfound joy lighting his words.

"If you are to become a priest, you must be ordained, and you may be required to lead a life of celibacy," Deodatus advised.

"How is it that you live with Charu then?" Valentine asked confused.

"I am not an ordained priest. I cared for a bishop who lived in Arretium, and before his death, he taught me the rituals of the church. Since his passing, we have been awaiting a new bishop to be appointed in the valley, but many years have passed without one. In the meantime, I have been conducting the services for our community."

"I would like to continue assisting you in marrying couples, if you will allow it," Valentine remarked.

Deodatus responded encouragingly, placing a warm hand on Valentine's shoulder. "Your faith has indeed guided you well. In the coming weeks, we will witness more unions, and you may continue to assist me."

"I would be most grateful," Valentine replied earnestly. "After which, I must return to Rome and retrieve Agatha. I wish to invite her here to establish a home together and contribute to this community," he explained, then added with a grin, "if they will have us, that is."

"The community will welcome you both with open hearts and even aid you in building a home," Deodatus assured him.

"I am grateful."

"Come, while you may not be an ordained priest, there is still much we can discuss about helping others wed before you return to Rome," Deodatus added with a knowing smile.

Weary from his travels yet eager to lead his soldiers to victory, Emperor Gallienus had established a formidable command post outside Mediolanum. Nestled within the protective embrace of the Roman legions, his tent stood out—prominent and guarded, an opulent island amid the orderly chaos of the military encampment. The night air, cold and mist-laden, carried only the faintest flicker of light from the smoldering braziers scattered around.

Two Praetorian Guards, positioned diligently at the entrance of the emperor's quarters, shattered the sudden silence of the night when arrows—deadly shadows—swiftly silenced them, finding their marks.

Inside, the disturbance snapped Gallienus from a troubled sleep. Fumbling in the dark, his hands found and lit a small lantern, its feeble light casting long, ominous shadows across the lavish interior. As he called out to his guards, his voice echoed with a mixture of urgency and fear, only to be met with silence. Before he could secure his defenses, the tent flap rustled quietly, and General Claudius emerged into the dim circle of light.

Relief and anxiety surged through Gallienus as he recognized his general. "By Jupiter, you startled me, Claudius!" he exclaimed, a nervous laugh betraying his unease. His eyes flickered toward the still-open tent flap. "Where are my guards?" he demanded, suspicion creeping into his voice.

Claudius's expression was grave. "I apologize for the disruption, sire—however, an urgent matter requires my attention."

Gallienus felt his pulse quicken. "What matters? Speak plainly, Claudius."

"I am afraid your assassination has been ordered."

Disbelief and anger swept across Gallienus's face, his voice thick with emotion. "What?! By whom?"

Meeting the emperor's gaze, Claudius whispered the chilling revelation: "By me."

Gallienus's eyes bubbled as he lunged for his sword, but Claudius had already drawn his blade and swung it with lightning precision, severing the emperor's head in a single, clean blow.

The tent, now a somber chamber of secrets, was eerily silent. The glow from the oil lamp cast a haunting light on the decapitated head of Emperor Gallienus, whose expression was forever fixed in a shocked grimace by the flickering shadows. Claudius kneeled and clutched the hair of the severed head, addressing it as though it could still hear: "I hear no praise from senators or Christians now."

Aurelian entered, the soft thud of his boots on the tent floor breaking the heavy stillness. He carried one of the bows, the same weapon that had silenced one of the guards outside, their bodies now mere shadows beneath the canopy. His gaze locked with that of Claudius, who stood before him holding the emperor's decapitated head by its hair. Kneeling partly out of habit rather than reverence, he watched Claudius hoist the head, proudly showcasing his prey while declaring simply, "It's done."

Aurelian lowered his head, absorbing the gravity of the moment and the looming transfer of power. His mind raced with countless thoughts. "Shall I summon a messenger to dispatch news to the Senate?"

Claudius responded decisively: "No, I will dispatch a messenger to Junius, who may inform and prepare the Senate. It's time to put the young senator to work." Then, with a calm gesture that belied the gravity of his actions, he casually dropped Gallienus's head onto the ground.

"Stage the tent to appear as if one of Aureolus's Gallic rebels struck it, and prepare his body for transport. Station two guards outside with strict orders not to enter or allow anyone in. We shall address the troops at dawn."

"As you wish."

As Claudius began to walk away, he paused, turning back to face Aurelian with a piercing gaze. "It's time to return Rome to its glory."

Aurelian nodded, his expression a mask of resolute agreement.

Claudius patted his loyal conspirator on the shoulder before turning to depart.

Alone now, Aurelian stood amid the grim aftermath, his gaze fixed on the emperor's lifeless body and the severed head beside it. The bloodshot eyes of the emperor seemed to stare back at him, accusing, as if they could see into the depths of his conflicted soul. In the chilling silence, he mumbled, "May God forgive me."

The Roman encampment stirred as dawn's first light painted the horizon. The air was brisk, thick with anticipation as soldiers assembled before the imperial tent, awaiting the day's command.

Standing before them, Aurelian's presence alone demanded silence. "Soldiers of Rome," he began, his voice resonating with a grim authority, "this dawn brings grave news. Our emperor has been taken from us—assassinated by Gallic infiltrators under the cover of night."

A murmur of disbelief and shock swept through the assembled ranks.

Aurelian raised his hand, commanding silence once more. "In these times of uncertainty, Rome looks to her sons to defend her honor and her people. We stand on the precipice of change, a moment that will define the future of our great empire," he proclaimed, his gaze sweeping over the assembled troops.

As the sun broke over the horizon, its rays illuminated Claudius, who approached, standing by Aurelian's side. His armor gleamed, almost ethereal in the dawn light, marking him as more than just a general among them. "Here stands your leader, tested in battle, unwavering in loyalty," Aurelian declared. "General Claudius will lead us forward to avenge our fallen emperor."

The soldiers gazed upon Claudius, awaiting his words with eager anticipation.

"Soldiers of Rome," Claudius's voice carried powerfully across the field. "The loss of our emperor shakes the very foundations upon which Rome stands." His steps were measured as he moved before them, his gaze meeting theirs directly—not as a distant leader but as a comrade in arms. "Our borders are under siege, threatened by barbarians who envy the light of our civilization. Yet, what is Rome if not the sovereign of adversity?"

Inspiration sparked within the ranks. "We stand with you, General!" a young soldier called out, his voice igniting a chorus of support.

Claudius continued, fanning the flames of their collective resolve. "Now is the time to embrace the customs of our ancestors, to the strengths that have forged Rome into the *domina* of the world. Our unity, our valor, and our devotion to the gods who guard us—these are the arms we bear against those who would see us fall!"

The rallying cry grew fiercer as cheers thundered from the soldiers.

"Imagine a Rome unburdened by division, an empire where our ancestral beliefs and traditions unite us all!" Claudius proclaimed, his conviction intensifying. "A Rome where honor, duty, and allegiance stand pure, unsullied by alien creeds. Devotees of a morbid cult despise our values, forsaking the virtues that have erected our empire. Their insurrection demands the wrath of the gods!"

"Ave, General Claudius!" shouted a loyal commander from the heart of the crowd.

Sensing the shift in the air, Claudius pressed on. "The path ahead is fraught with peril, yet it is a journey we embark upon as one. Under my leadership, we will not merely survive; we will thrive, expanding our borders, enriching our people, and securing Rome's glory forever!"

The murmurs of agreement grew louder, the initial shock of Gallienus's assassination giving way to a burgeoning sense of purpose.

"As we stand together at the dawn of this new era, let us pledge to uphold Rome's timeless ideals. With your swords and courage, remember your families, your honor, your Rome—and together, we will carve a future worthy of our ancestors!"

Thoroughly captivated, the assembly echoed with shouts of assent. Looking out over the men, Claudius saw the reflection of his ambition in their eyes. He had sown the seeds of loyalty and vision, crafting his message to ignite their passion.

Stepping back to let his words resonate, he allowed General Aurelian to take the foreground. Aurelian advanced with a presence that captured every eye.

In his hands, he held the purple *paludamentum* of Gallienus—a commander's cloak symbolizing power and martial prowess.

"Soldiers of Rome," boomed Aurelian, his voice echoing across the assembly. "Today marks the dawn of a new era for our empire. The challenges before us demand a leader of unmatched valor, vision, and dedication to Rome's glory—a leader who will restore us as the unrivaled sovereign of the world."

Each man held his breath, anticipating the momentous occasion unfolding before them.

"In recognition of his unwavering loyalty to Rome, his proven leadership on the battlefield, and his vision for our empire's future," Aurelian proclaimed, his gaze intently fixed on Claudius. "I hereby proclaim General Claudius—Emperor Claudius!" With a sense of solemn ceremony, Aurelian placed Emperor Gallienus's purple cloak over Claudius's shoulders. As the cloak settled, the cheers of the men affirmed the legitimacy of this transfer of power.

Aurelian then bellowed, "Ave Imperator!"

The soldiers' response was instantaneous and electrifying. "Ave Imperator!" they echoed, a thunderous chorus that signaled the dawn of Claudius's reign.

As voices surged around him, Claudius felt a rush of emotions. He stood tall, his heart swelling with pride and accomplishment. From his humble beginnings, he had clawed his way to the pinnacle of power, now recognized and revered by the military, his men. And soon, he would have a son who would also look up to him.

In this moment, Claudius felt more than just an emperor; he was the embodiment of ambition and determination, showing what any Roman could achieve with unyielding resolve. The echoes of "Ave Imperator!" ignited his spirit, each cry reinforcing his newfound authority and the overwhelming love he held for his loyal soldiers. The future of Rome was now in his hands, and he vowed to lead it to unprecedented glory, his way.

Chapter 18

Act of War

"In times of war, the law falls silent."
—Cicero

Emerging from a stately carriage drawn by two white horses at a quieter side of the Roman Forum, Claudius stepped onto the cobblestones, beginning his solemn walk toward the Curia Julia. Flanked by Senator Junius and trailed by the loyal General Aurelian, he moved along a less frequented route, subtly shielded by a cordon of Praetorian Guards who cleared a path, offering him a rare moment of privacy amid the anticipation of his impending proclamation. The distant murmur of the crowds waiting at the main entrance lingered in the background, adding to his growing anxiety about the momentous event ahead. With a hint of impatience, Claudius turned to Junius.

"Is the Senate all gathered?" he asked sharply.

"Yes, Caesar," Junius responded.

"Very well. I expect them all to conform to my directives or face replacement," Claudius asserted, his voice unwavering.

"Precisely—and to that end, I have identified those who will resist your policies," Junius replied, presenting Claudius a parchment listing five senators.

Claudius examined the list briefly, "What would you have me do with them?"

"At the right moment, I propose you expel these senators for treason or incompetence, as they will impede your endeavors," Junius suggested cautiously.

Claudius concealed the parchment within his toga and redirected the conversation: "What more should I be apprised of today?"

"Caesar, this is only a day to celebrate your valor and officially proclaim you emperor of Rome. As one of your consuls and the new appointed princeps senatus, I will introduce you, followed by your recount of military triumphs. Prominent senators will then express their support. Subsequently, the Senate will pledge their loyalty, confirming your ascension. We will, of course, observe all necessary legal and religious rites, concluding with public accolades and your declaration before the people," Junius elaborated.

"Celebrations and speeches, yet the front waits on edge," Claudius commented, his tone laced with impatience.

Junius grinned. "Indeed, Caesar—politics is a meticulous affair. Nonetheless, I am confident today will proceed without hindrance. There shall be no room for debate or discord. Today is about acknowledging your claim as Caesar and ensuring the Senate and populace's endorsement."

As they neared the Curia Julia, Claudius muttered: "I will give them a reason to acknowledge me."

Upon entering, Junius's voice resonated through the hall, "Senators of Rome, I present to you General Claudius, commander of our legions, the vanquisher of the Goths!"

The Senate erupted into robust applause, eager to hear Claudius's vision for governance and the new balance of power that Junius had advocated.

"Senators of Rome," Junius continued, his voice echoing in the grand chamber as he stepped forward to take center stage, where Senators Paternus and Didius had previously stood as consuls. "With due respect for his valor and the legions under his command, General Claudius asserts his rightful claim to the imperial throne. I stand here today to convey his will to the Senate," Junius declared, his voice firm, though the tension in the room was palpable.

The senators exchanged wary glances, their whispered unease barely suppressed. Paternus and Didius responded with only slight, hesitant nods, their restrained gestures betraying the shared understanding that resistance was futile and submission to Claudius's authority inevitable.

Junius hesitated, awaiting any further reaction, but Claudius silenced him with a single gesture, commanding him to sit before another word could be uttered.

"Senators," Claudius thundered, commanding the entire chamber as Junius resumed his seat. "I am a man of action, not one for drawn-out speeches or grandiose ceremonies. The legions have proclaimed me emperor, and Rome requires a leader capable of protecting her and restoring her grandeur. My military achievements speak for themselves, undisputed and clear. Out of respect for you and for the traditions of Rome, I have stepped away from the battlefield to declare my intention to lead our empire from this day forward. Those prepared to carry out my commands without hesitation may stay. Those who object may leave."

Claudius's declaration resonated with the directness of a general addressing his troops rather than a politician speaking to his peers. He paused, allowing his ultimatum to resonate as senators looked on in dismay. This was not the conciliatory inauguration they had anticipated, nor the one Junius had assured them.

An annoyed Senator Piso, seated next to Senator Didius, quickly rose to his stalky and aged feet despite Senator Didius attempting to hold him down, breaking the tense silence. "General Claudius, when we last spoke, you promised a governance that would include balanced Senate involvement in legislative debates and even in matters of national defense."

"Senator Piso, is it?" Claudius inquired.

"Indeed, General," Senator Piso confirmed proudly. "We met after your ovation."

"Remain standing, please," Claudius commanded as he pulled out the list Junius had provided him earlier. "When I announce your names, my Praetorians will escort you out, and you will face charges of treason."

A palpable wave of shock rippled through the chamber as Claudius, with a stern demeanor, began to read aloud the names from the list, his voice echoing off the ancient walls. "Senators Ocratius, Plancius, Tiberianus, Valerius, Fannius, and...Piso." His gaze fixed intently on Senator Piso as he concluded, singling him out from the rest. "You are all to depart immediately. You stand accused of crimes against the state, and your seats in this Senate are hereby revoked." The declaration was stark and unequivocal, leaving no room for dissent as Claudius imposed his will.

The bold declaration echoed off the ancient walls, marking a stark and formidable beginning to Claudius's rule and leaving a Senate divided in fear and awe.

"This is an outrage!" Senator Piso bellowed, his face flushed with anger. He gazed down at Senator Didius, who shrugged hopelessly at being able to offer any aid.

"I would never betray Rome!" Senator Fannius echoed defiantly.

"Seize them and take them to the Tullianum if another word escapes their mouths," Claudius commanded sternly, his voice cutting through the tension like a sword.

Beside him, Junius watched the unfolding scene with disbelief. He had known Claudius to be a leader of determination, yet the unyielding harshness was startling even to him. The Tullianum—Rome's most notorious prison—was a fate few could endure. As the chamber descended into an eerie silence, Junius exchanged a glance with Senator Fabius, both men silently acknowledging the drastic shift they were witnessing.

General Aurelian aided the guards in ushering the named senators out of the room. The heavy doors clanged shut, the lock echoing ominously through the hall, trapping the remaining senators inside.

Claudius then started pacing before the assembled senators like a general addressing his men. "Senators, I know many of you are here by virtue of noble birth, while others have earned their place through merit. Regardless of your path to these seats, I now demand your unwavering loyalty. I will ask only once—is there any man here who objects to my leadership of our empire?"

He halted and surveyed the room, his gaze piercing each senator. The response was a profound silence. The senators merely shook their heads, none daring to voice dissent, resembling children too terrified to speak out of turn.

"Excellent. I shall issue my initial decrees immediately, and I expect each of you to implement them without question," Claudius declared, his voice brooking no opposition. "I have appointed Senator Junius as consul and the new princeps senatus. Senator Paternus, you will be stepping down permanently from that role."

At this, Senator Paternus's eyes widened in shock as he quickly processed the full weight of the transition and all of Senator Junius's covert schemes.

"From here forward, Senator Junius will oversee the execution of my orders within the Senate, and you shall extend to him the same respect afforded to me. Understood?"

The chamber met Claudius's command with resigned acceptance and cautious agreement. The senators, still reeling from the stern dismissal of their colleagues, nodded almost mechanically.

"First, we shall engage our adversaries with renewed and strategic vigor, beginning with the recapture of Mediolanum and the defense against the Germanic tribes and Goths."

Claudius's words struck a chord, eliciting some nods of approval from the assembly.

"Though strength alone is insufficient," he continued, his voice firm. "We will initiate administrative reforms to stabilize our economy, quell the unrest of civil discord, and restore prosperity to our streets."

"Agreed!" a senior senator suddenly called out, his voice carrying across the silent room.

Junius acknowledged the support with a nod, mirroring Claudius's slight gesture of approval.

"And henceforth, my visage will grace our coinage, symbolizing the courage and unity of our people," Claudius proclaimed.

"Rightly so," another senator affirmed, his voice adding to the growing consensus.

"And as we restore Rome's prosperity, we must also rid her of the poisons that have infiltrated her very heart." Claudius paused, his gaze sweeping across the room. "The strength of Rome lies not in its military alone—rather, it depends on the loyalty of its people. No traitors will be tolerated, and no threats to the empire will go unchecked. Be it foreign invaders—or dangerous factions that corrupt the minds of our citizens. Christian gatherings will be outlawed, their places of worship shall burn—and their faith shall cease immediately!"

Junius rose, his voice firm. "The Senate will carry out your will, Caesar." His words reverberated through the chamber, as some senators shifted uncomfortably while others stomped their feet in support. Claudius nodded toward Junius, allowing himself a moment of satisfaction as the chamber reacted.

Aurelian observed the subtle interplay between Claudius and Junius with a deepening sense of unease. As Claudius's primary military adviser, he had long held a position of privilege and influence. However, Junius's rise to the role of princeps senatus, thereby obliterating the role of the current consuls, signaled a troubling shift in the dynamics of power.

"Now that I have your full support, it is time for me to address the people of Rome," Claudius declared.

"Ave Imperator!" Junius shouted, rising to his feet and leading the chorus of acclamations as the chamber echoed with the same cry. He then gestured to Senator Fabius, who stepped forward with a purple *paludamentum*, draping it over Claudius's shoulders to officially mark his ascension to power.

With a decisive nod, Claudius quickly exited the Curia Julia, his departure as commanding as his entrance had been. Junius and Aurelian closely followed, flanked by a retinue of guards, as they progressed toward the rostra in the Forum. Behind them, the senators trailed like a flock of subdued sheep, their silent, compliant forms adding gravitas to the procession that moved through the heart of Rome.

"A most commendable speech, Caesar," Junius offered eagerly as they walked.

"Thank you, Junius," Claudius responded. "Now, ensure you do not disappoint me, or you'll be removed from the Curia Julia faster than those senators today."

"I will not disappoint," Junius assured him.

"Have you instructed the empress to await me?"

"Yes, and I believe you will be quite surprised," Junius hinted, a mysterious smile playing on his lips as he gestured ahead to where their path would soon lead them.

As they approached the rostra, citizens from all walks of Roman life packed the area, craning for a view and buzzing with anticipation to hear their new emperor. At the entrance, Claudius spotted a radiant figure—Serena, decadent and dazzling as ever, poised to accompany him to a large platform overlooking the sea of Romans. Their wedding had been a discreet affair, intentionally quiet and without fanfare, not only to avoid drawing attention to Serena's advanced pregnancy but also to align with Claudius's distaste for grandiose celebrations.

A smile broke across Claudius's stoic face as he saw Serena, who no longer bore the pregnancy swell. Standing beside her was Iset, cradling a newborn in her arms. His step quickened with a mix of surprise and eagerness.

"Emperor Claudius," Serena greeted him with a poised nod.

"Empress," he returned the greeting, his smile sharpening into a sly expression.

"Allow me to introduce your daughter... Claudia," Serena's voice carried a blend of pride and formality as she announced the female version of his name.

"Claudia?" he repeated, uncertain he had heard correctly. The announcement of a girl stole his composure. He had been certain his child would be a boy, a son to carry on his legacy. The unexpected revelation left him momentarily speechless, as disappointment, frustration, and a sense of betrayal battled within him.

Iset stepped forward and gently offered the baby girl to him. Claudius hesitated, his hand instinctively reaching forward before pulling back. Instead, he lightly patted the baby's forehead. The soft warmth of Claudia's skin only deepened the reminder of what he had hoped for—and had not received.

He glanced at Serena and replied plainly, "We shall try for another," his tone almost empathetic, as if assuming she shared in his disappointment.

Mortified by Claudius's reaction, Serena's expression turned to horror just as the announcer suddenly cut through the Forum: "All hail, Emperor Claudius and Empress Serena!"

Imperial horns blared above the rhythmic beating of drums, heralding the arrival of the emperor and empress as they moved together toward their thrones. Claudius, seething inside over Serena's failure to provide him with a son, nonetheless projected the unyielding demeanor of a stoic military leader. His firm and commanding gaze concealed his disbelief that any child of his would be anything but a son.

Meanwhile, Serena quickly composed herself. With each graceful and deliberate step, she exuded the elegance and authority of an empress, fully conscious of the heavy responsibilities weighing on her shoulders. She reminded herself that she had done the unthinkable to ensure the safety of herself and her child, and she would not falter now.

THE TRAIL back to Deodatus and Charu's villa from the nearest town was long and arduous. Valentine had chosen to walk that day, opting to savor the simple beauty around him. He planned to return to Rome the following day and had been walking nearly every day to build his strength. As he moved along the familiar path, his thoughts drifted between the excitement of returning to Agatha, the family he had found with Deodatus and Charu, and the teachings they had imparted to him. Agatha would certainly love them and this place as well, he thought. He could already envision Charu sharing her knowledge of herbs with Agatha.

But the serenity of the meadow was suddenly shattered by the unsightly vision of black smoke drifting into the distant air. Valentine's heart began to race as he ran toward the source of the smoke. As he drew nearer, he saw the disturbing orange glow that grew brighter, emanating from the prayerhouse. A surge of urgency abruptly replaced the peacefulness of his walk as he quickened his pace toward the unfolding disaster.

"Oh, no!" Valentine exclaimed, his voice heavy with dread as he dropped the satchel of goods he had purchased in the nearby village.

As he neared the prayerhouse, a chilling sight met his eyes. A group of fifteen Roman soldiers were wreaking havoc—a mobile cavalry unit dispatched at the emperor's bidding. They moved with a terrifying purpose. Before Valentine could get close, half of the soldiers mounted their horses and rode off, one of them dragging Regalus, who kicked and screamed for help.

"Not Regalus!" Valentine exclaimed, though it was too late. The soldiers rode away with the boy, leaving him to watch in horror. He thought of chasing them, but time was slipping away. Silently, he reproached himself for leaving Regalus unprotected as his attention shifted back to the prayerhouse. A single soldier was pointing his sword at Deodatus, backing him into the structure now engulfed in flames. Meanwhile, other soldiers stormed the villa, and some were beginning to set fire to the infirmary.

Seizing the moment, Valentine grabbed a hoe left by the garden beds, improvising it as a weapon. He charged toward the threatening soldier who had left Deodatus inside the burning prayerhouse. As he closed the distance between them, the soldier turned and swung at Valentine, who dodged him with natural agility and the focus of a well-trained warrior.

In a fluid motion, Valentine struck under the soldier's arm with the hoe, knocking the sword away and delivering a forceful blow to the soldier's head. Crumpling to the ground, the soldier fell unconscious as his sword lay sticking in the ground by the entrance.

Valentine burst through the front doors into the prayerhouse, now a hellish tableau with flames consuming the roof and timbers beginning to fall. He navigated the chaos, reaching the altar where he found

Deodatus cradling Charu in his arms. Charu was motionless; a wound marked her abdomen where she was drenched in blood. Deodatus looked up at Valentine with tear-filled eyes.

"You must save Regalus," Deodatus pleaded, his voice breaking with grief.

Kneeling beside them, Valentine perceived the depths of sorrow in Deodatus's eyes as he clung to Charu, unable to relinquish his hold. "She has passed, Deodatus. You must release her," he urged, his voice laden with a poignant mix of compassion and urgency.

Deodatus shook his head—"I cannot"—his resolve unyielding even as a giant crossbeam crashed down behind them, sending a shower of sparks and embers into the air. The light danced menacingly around the altar.

"There is still time! We must depart now!" Valentine implored, tugging gently at Deodatus's arm. It was then he noticed the dark stain of blood seeping through Deodatus's clothing—a lethal wound to the abdomen delivered by the soldier earlier. Deodatus had been stanching the bleeding, clinging to life to savor his final moments with Charu.

With his remaining strength, Deodatus gazed into Valentine's eyes and made a final, heartfelt plea: "Promise me you will watch over our son."

Tears welled in Valentine's eyes as the weight of his promise settled upon him. "I will find him and raise him as my own."

A faint smile graced Deodatus's lips, a sign of peace in his last breath. His head gently fell back against Charu's as his spirit departed.

Valentine placed his hand on Deodatus's and Charu's clasped hands and bowed to offer a silent prayer. Rising, he turned back toward the entrance. There, the sword dropped by the soldier stood planted in the ground, its hilt casting a cross-like shadow encircled by the flickering light from outside. It was as if the Christian God himself was calling Valentine to take to arms, to protect those who could not protect themselves, he thought. This moment of divine symbolism stirred something deep within him, a blend of duty and compassion. This was not just a call to battle but a sacred mission to defend and nurture the bonds of love and faith.

Valentine dashed through the prayerhouse with renewed urgency, dodging falling timbers that threatened to block his path. Flames licked at his heels as he weaved through the destruction, each step a defiance of the fire's intent to claim him.

Reaching the entrance, Valentine grabbed the sword, its metal cool, firm, and familiar to him. With the weapon in hand, he sprinted toward the infirmary, determined to rescue any remaining souls from the relentless advance of the fire.

Along the way, soldiers emerged from Deodatus and Charu's villa, their arms laden with gold coins and silver candelabra. Startled by Valentine's sudden appearance, they quickly dropped their loot and moved to intercept him.

Overwhelmed by rage and grief, Valentine unleashed the warrior within him. Fury consumed him as he faced the soldiers, every move driven by a raw, primal instinct to avenge and protect.

The first soldier met Valentine's wrath head-on. With a savage cry, Valentine blocked an incoming strike and retaliated with a brutal slash to the soldier's leg, dropping him to the ground in a heap of pain and fear. Blood spattered across Valentine's face as he charged forward.

Before the second soldier could react, Valentine's sword plunged deep into his abdomen, the blade slicing through flesh with deadly precision. The soldier's eyes widened in shock as he fell forward, lifeless before he even hit the ground.

Another assailant tried to strike from behind, hoping to catch Valentine off guard. But the grief-stricken warrior in Valentine was relentless, rolling past the attack and swiftly rising to his feet. Then, in one fluid, vicious motion, he snapped the soldier's neck, his hands moving with lethal intent.

The last attacker charged, screaming in rage. Valentine met him with a ferocious roar, their swords clashing with the moment's violence. The battle was brutal but brief; Valentine's sword found the soldier's throat, opening it with a swift, decisive stroke. Blood gushed forth as the soldier collapsed, a final gasp escaping his lips.

Valentine stood amid the carnage, his breathing labored, his sword slick with the blood of murderers. His eyes swept across the soldiers scattered around him—some lifeless, others moaning in agony. A primal scream escaped his lips, resonating with his fury and turmoil. "Why?! They did nothing to you!" he bellowed at the soldiers.

The soldier whose leg he had sliced looked up at Valentine's blood-streaked face and pleaded, "Please, sir, spare my life!"

Valentine pressed his sword against the soldier's throat, his voice a deadly whisper, "Where did they take the boy?"

Terror flickered in the soldier's eyes as he stammered out, "They intend to use him as a servant at their encampment and then sell him as a slave upon returning to Rome."

Valentine's gaze hardened, the veins in his neck stark as he tightened his grip on the sword. The soldier's eyes widened with fear, his words tumbling out in a nervous rush. "Please, sir, they are encamped along the Via Cassia on the road to Rome! The emperor ordered us to burn all Christian sanctuaries!"

"What emperor would do this?"

"Emperor Claudius!"

The name seared into Valentine's mind, igniting a blaze of fury. His heart pounded as he was transported back to that fateful battlefield where Claudius had stripped him and his men of their armor, leading to his severe injury and Scaro's death. Valentine knew he would need reinforcements to retrieve Regalus. Yet, the soldier's plea for mercy tested the limits of his wrath. He heard screams coming from the direction of the infirmary, snapping him out of his fury. Torn between vengeance and duty, he tossed his sword aside and ran back toward the infirmary to rescue any survivors, his mind a storm of grief, anger, and determination.

As he approached the doors of the infirmary, however, he noticed the soldiers had cruelly barricaded them, trapping the patients and others inside. Flames consumed the structure, sending a column of black smoke twisting into the sky, merging with the fiery orange glow.

In a moment of sheer helplessness, Valentine collapsed to his knees. Blood from his enemies streaked his face, mixing with the sweat and heat from the nearby fire. Silently, he lifted his head, tilting it toward the heavens, searching for an answer, a reason why God would allow such atrocities. As he did, his thoughts drifted toward Agatha's well-being. A pang of fear gripped him, but he quickly forced himself to halt the cascade of negative thoughts that threatened to overwhelm him. Instead, his gaze shifted to the horizon, where the silhouette of the soldier he had spared rode away. His solitary act of mercy flickered faintly against the overwhelming darkness of Claudius's war on Christians.

CHAPTER 19

REUNITED

"The wound of love is healed by the same who makes it."
—PUBLILIUS SYRUS

The crisp winter air swept through the streets of Rome as the city reveled in the vibrant and unrestrained celebrations of *Saturnalia*. Along the bustling Viscus Tuscus, vendors adorned their stalls with a dazzling array of colors—from richly dyed fabrics to the shimmering gold of intricate jewelry—showcasing Rome's wealth and splendor.

Musicians, playing the lyre and the flute-like *tibia*, filled the air with melodies that resonated along the stone streets. Both slaves and free citizens danced in the streets, moving with joyful abandon, mixing traditional Roman steps with influences from the far reaches of the empire. The smell of roasting meats and the heady aroma of wine— poured freely without regard to status—drifted through the crowds, epitomizing the spirit of Saturnalia, a time when social hierarchies were temporarily upended, and excess was embraced.

At the heart of the celebrations, Marius, Proculo, Albus, Linus, and

Efebus sat at a sturdy wooden table in a popina. They had been granted special leave by the legion to partake in the festival, and their spirits were high. Empty wine jugs and goblets, stained red from countless refills, littered the table, evidence of their exuberant revelry. Albus, particularly caught up in the wild joy of Saturnalia, laughed heartily as he poured another libation to Saturn, his voice rising above the hum of the festival's noise.

Linus leaned toward Marius with a mischievous spark in his eyes and teased, "So, you haven't bedded Porcia yet?"

Marius responded calmly, "She is not one of your tavern maidens, Linus."

Proculo joined the fray. "Then, what type is she? You've dallied with her for weeks, yet she has not graced your pallet?"

"And I will continue to do so for as long as it takes to win her heart."

The group burst out in mock dismay at Marius's noble stance, jeering playfully. "Ahhh…," they exclaimed, chuckling, as Albus playfully tossed scraps of food in Marius's direction.

"Enough, enough," Marius said with a smile.

Slurring his words, Albus added, "You will lose her. Sooner or later, we lose them all."

Seizing the moment, Linus quipped, "No more wine for Albus."

Albus glared at Linus, his eyes narrowing with anger and blurred by wine. "And what of thee, Linus? Where hides your latest she-wolf?"

Linus smirked, retorting, "Oh, you speak of your mother? Awaiting me at the tavern, I presume!"

Albus lunged at Linus, irrationally driven by the wine and overrun by his raw emotions since his brother's loss. Just as the scuffle threatened to escalate, firm hands grabbed the two by their collars. Adorned in a dark brown cape and sturdy military *calcei*, leather boots, Valentine pulled the two apart, leaving them momentarily stunned.

"Still causing havoc, brothers?" he asked, his voice dripping with amusement.

The atmosphere shifted instantly as the men looked up at Valentine as though he were a ghost miraculously appearing before them.

Proculo muttered, "Valentine?"

Efebus, equally shocked, said, "It cannot be!"

Marius shouted with joy, "It is!"

Albus shrugged off his grasp and sat back down.

Linus, with theatrical grandeur, proclaimed, "He lives! He lives!"

Before Valentine could utter a word, all but Albus surged forward, enveloping him in a collective embrace, hoisting him up like a hero.

"Valentine! Valentine! Valentine!" Efebus initiated the chant, growing in voices, and drawing the attention of nearby onlookers.

Valentine's moment of embarrassment was overshadowed by the love he felt from his men in that moment. The camaraderie they shared was unmatched, a bond forged through the trials of life and death. In addition to thoughts of Agatha, it was a moment of bliss he had dreamed of for months leading up to this reunion.

"Okay, okay, put me down now," Valentine pleaded, then nervously glanced around, wary of any military officers nearby. Once back on the ground, he leaned in and quietly cautioned the group, "The army must not know of my presence here."

"This is true—quiet down, brothers," Marius interjected. "Come, let us find a more private tavern where we may speak more freely about your recovery at Deodatus and Charu's villa," Marius added, while taking inventory of his surroundings and other soldiers on the street.

As they moved to another tavern, Albus quietly followed but kept his distance from Valentine, his expression untouched by the festive atmosphere. As Valentine made his way through heartfelt embraces with each friend, he finally approached Albus. A heavy silence settled between them until Valentine's voice, thick with remorse, filled the air. "I'm sorry about Scaro, Albus."

He looked at him, emotion-filled, and replied, "He loved you, Valentine. He followed all your orders."

Valentine sighed heavily. "And I loved him too, my friend." He placed a comforting hand on Albus's shoulder, but Albus brushed it off as he reached for more wine.

Valentine looked at Albus momentarily confused by his reaction, but his gaze turned away as Marius pulled his attention. "Valentine, it's been months! Tell us more about your recovery. How are Deodatus and Charu? They are remarkable, are they not?"

Valentine settled onto a wooden bench, its frame creaking under their collective weight. He wanted to immediately tell Marius what had happened to Deodatus and Charu, but he held his tongue, waiting for the right moment to share the tragic news, knowing that their deaths would not settle well with his friend. In truth, he questioned whether he would be able to share the news without losing his composure. He was uncomfortable with such a public display of vulnerability and felt guilty that he had not been able to save them.

Marius handed Valentine a half-filled wine cup. "Efebus, more wine!"

Efebus responded eagerly and hurried off.

Marius leaned in with a curious expression and quietly asked, "Are you a Christian now?"

"I am," Valentine replied proudly in a hushed voice.

"Ha!" Marius replied excitedly yet with a quiet voice. "You hear that? I am no longer alone."

At the end of the table, Albus shook his head. It was Valentine's embrace of Christian prayer that had led to his brother's death, a truth that never escaped him. He remained deep in thought as the others chuckled and sipped their wine, enjoying the banter.

Valentine scanned the surroundings cautiously, ensuring their conversation remained private.

"What else did they impart upon you?"

"They taught me many things," Valentine replied quietly. "They were like family to me."

Marius suddenly lowered his wine cup, sensing Valentine's reluctance to share more. "You mean, they *are* like family to you."

Valentine's expression darkened as the lively atmosphere seemed to cool around them. "Marius, the news I bear will not be to your liking." His voice cracked as he recalled witnessing the horrifying scene of Deodatus and Charu dying in the prayerhouse engulfed in flames.

Marius leaned forward, his voice dropping even lower as his heart sank. "Not them."

Valentine hesitated, then revealed with deep sorrow, "They were murdered, Marius."

"Who did this?!"

The group fell silent as the festival sounds faded into a distant murmur. Marius appeared as if the ground had been swept from under him, while Valentine's mind swirled with grief and guilt. He had fought countless battles, faced innumerable enemies, but the loss of Deodatus and Charu in such a senseless act of violence tore at his soul. Sharing this with Marius made the pain even more real, a wound that bled anew with every word.

Just then, Efebus returned with wine jugs, cheerful and unaware of the somber shift. "Wine, anyone?" he asked brightly.

Not wanting to hear more, Albus quickly answered, "Indeed!"

Proculo snapped at him, "Quiet, Albus!"

Marius, meanwhile, seemed to have aged years in mere moments. His eyes blazed with disbelief and fury. "Soldiers?"

Efebus slowly took his seat. "What have I missed?"

"This cannot be!" Marius shouted, his voice echoing the pain of betrayal.

Valentine replied with a heavy heart, "At the emperor's bidding."

Unable to contain his anguish, Marius shot up, pacing restlessly around the gathering. "Caesar goes too far! Murdering priests? Innocent women? For what crime? They treat us as if *we* are the enemy—simply because we worship differently?!"

"Yes!" Albus cut in sharply. "I warned you all of this before our last battle with the Goths!"

"Shut your mouth, Albus, or I shall silence it myself!" Marius snapped, angered by Albus's thoughtlessness.

Valentine remained silent, nodding solemnly.

"We must stop them before they kill others," Marius commanded, his eyes fixed on Valentine, seeking agreement.

"There is more," Valentine added gravely.

"What more?" Marius demanded, his anger flaring anew.

"They captured Regalus and enslaved him at their encampment."

"We must free him!"

"I hoped you would see it that way," Valentine replied, a trace of relief in his voice. "I promised Deodatus and Charu I would care for him."

"We shall *all* care for him," Marius said firmly. "I have kin here where he could stay and be safe. He's only a boy!"

"We stand with you, Valentine," Linus declared.

Valentine took a moment and addressed them earnestly: "Brothers, serving in this emperor's army is no longer my path, though it may still be yours. You must each consider carefully if you wish to join Marius and me from this point forward."

Silence fell upon the table as Marius's gaze shifted to Porcia approaching—her arrival brightening the mood. A smile began to form on Marius's face. "Greetings, Porcia," he announced, his spirits visibly lifting. "Valentine, you remember Porcia, do you not?"

Valentine looked over, his demeanor softening instantly upon recognizing her. "Indeed," he replied, quickly rising to his feet, eager to learn of Agatha's whereabouts.

"Valentine, I thought you were badly wounded in battle?" she said with a blend of concern and unease.

"I was, though I have since recovered. How is—"

Before he could finish, Porcia interrupted, her tone brightening. "Valentine, would you do me the honor?" She grabbed his arm and pulled him toward the crossroad outside where an unusual scene had unfolded—a small group of citizens were dancing about to the music.

Caught off guard by her forwardness, Valentine hesitated. "Well, uh...What are we doing?"

Marius chuckled and pushed Valentine forward with a mischievous grin. "Go on, show her how helpless you are!"

Street musicians played an infectious tune, their instruments jangling with a feverish intensity that filled the night air. At the center of the commotion was a man from Phrygia, a region in Anatolia known for its wild festival dances. His energetic movements, foreign to Roman eyes, coaxed the wine-fueled crowd into an exuberant frenzy. Normally restrained citizens stumbled through unfamiliar steps, laughing as their usual decorum fell away in the chaotic joy of Saturnalia.

Valentine felt out of place among the revelry, his mind still on Agatha. He moved awkwardly, trying to match Porcia's steps but struggling to focus as the clamor of music and drunken laughter swirled around him.

"Porcia, please—how is Agatha? Where is she?" he implored, his voice rising above the din as they weaved through the crowd.

Porcia hesitated, her smile faltering for the briefest moment. The weight of her deceit tugged at her, but she forced herself to answer. "She is well, Valentine," she replied, her tone evasive as she tried to shift the conversation. "Will you be returning to battle soon?"

"Porcia, I must see your sister. Why isn't she here with you?" he pressed, trying to keep up with her erratic movements, his gaze scanning the faces in the crowd.

A shadow flickered across Porcia's face. "I left her closeby," she said, her voice strained as she noticed Valentine's eyes dart anxiously toward the stage.

"I do not see her—where?" he pressed, urgency in his voice.

Porcia abruptly stopped dancing, turning to face him. Her heart raced as she prepared to deliver the final blow. "If you must know, Valentine, Agatha's heart is with another," she said bluntly, hoping to end his persistence. She had convinced herself this lie was necessary, for Agatha's own good. But beneath the words, guilt gnawed at her.

Valentine froze, as if the ground beneath him had shifted. The noise of the festival seemed to fade as her words struck him like a physical blow. "What?!" he exclaimed, his voice trembling with shock, his disbelief etched across his face.

Porcia met his gaze defiantly. "She thought you had fallen!"

"I have not fallen; I am here—very much alive! How could this be? Did Marius not deliver my letter to her? Did she not think to wait?" Valentine unleashed a torrent of questions, his voice fraught with disbelief.

"I'm sorry, Valentine. Agatha waited until you didn't return with the other soldiers. By the time your letter arrived, she had already accepted her suitor's proposal," Porcia replied, intent on keeping them apart to protect her secret.

"She's taken a husband?" Valentine's voice cracked with the question.

"Soon," Porcia replied, her lies spinning further out of control.

Valentine looked as though someone had ripped his heart from his chest. He struggled to comprehend Agatha's decision not to wait for him. All his dreams of a future filled with joy and love evaporated in an instant. He'd lost Deodatus, Charu… *and now Agatha?*

"Please, Valentine, for her sake, do not approach Agatha. I fear this news will be too much for her to bear," Porcia pleaded.

"How can you ask that of me, Porcia? I must hear this from Agatha."

"Then I shall take you to her now if it is her heart you wish to break."

Porcia began to usher him away from the crowd.

"Wait!" As much as he wanted to go to Agatha, he could not cause her pain.

Valentine's stomach churned, he took one last look around the festival, hoping to catch a final glimpse of her. Suddenly, his gaze locked onto a disturbing scene.

In a narrow, dimly lit street near the heart of the celebration, he spotted a large, menacing man forcefully pulling Agatha away. The man was neither Tiber, nor a suitor or friend—he seemed far more dangerous.

"Is that her new suitor dragging her away?!" Valentine asked sharply.

"Where?!" Porcia spun around, her voice tinged with anxiety. She rarely left Agatha unattended, and when she did, she always informed Tiber so he could keep an extra-careful watch, knowing how vulnerable Agatha's blindness made her. But this time, she hadn't checked with Tiber upon seeing Marius, and Tiber had stepped away briefly to use the *latrinae* in a nearby tavern—an oversight that did not go unnoticed by a silent admirer.

"Over there! With her suitor—who looks more like a brute," Valentine pointed out, his agitation mounting.

Porcia followed his gaze, her face paling as she saw the large man dragging Agatha away. Panic gripped her. "No! I don't know that man!"

Valentine dashed through the crowd without waiting for Porcia to act.

. . .

MEANWHILE, in a narrow street, Agatha's situation grew dire. The large man, Hercules, who had escaped from a nearby village jail, was dragging her farther from the crowd. Known for his brutal strength and a past marred by violence, Hercules was not someone you could reason with. As fear overwhelmed her, Agatha managed to scream, hoping for rescue. But Hercules quickly stifled her cries with his thick hand, plunging her into silence.

"Feisty one," he sneered. "Be good now."

"No!" Agatha shouted, though Hercules's grip muffled her voice.

With a swift, brutal motion, Hercules slammed Agatha against the cold, unyielding wall of the narrow alley, his hands clawing at her mantle, ripping it away before grabbing at her tunic. Agatha fought back with a sharp kick, momentarily breaking free from his grip. In their violent struggle, Hercules hurled her onto a low wooden platform piled with bundled linens left out by a washerwoman. The tightly packed fabric cushioned her fall like an improvised bed but left her vulnerable beneath him.

Hercules's voice dripped with malice: "If it is rough you desire, so it will be." He tightened his grip on her neck as he climbed over her.

"No! Help me! Tiber!" Agatha's plea cut sharply through the air, but Tiber was nowhere near.

At that moment, Valentine appeared, fueled by a surge of fury. Seizing Hercules, he ripped him away from Agatha and slammed him against the stone wall of the narrow street.

Though stunned, Hercules quickly recovered and threw a wild punch. Valentine dodged it swiftly and slammed Hercules's head against the brick wall. The thud echoed briefly before silence fell, and Hercules lay motionless on the cobblestones.

Agatha sat shaken on the ground, her tunic disheveled.

"You are safe now, dear one," Valentine assured her as he quickly took a knee beside her.

Agatha froze, thinking that her ears betrayed her.

"Valentine?" she asked in disbelief.

Kneeling beside her, Valentine gently adjusted her tunic and took her hand. "Yes. It is I," he affirmed, his voice offering a quiet comfort.

"Oh, Valentine," Agatha leaned into him, her body relaxing in his embrace as the weight of the world momentarily lifted. "I thought you had perished," she whispered, her voice tinged with sorrow.

"I am here," Valentine replied soothingly. He touched her face gently, brushing away hay and tears, allowing his fingertips to linger on her skin.

Agatha's voice thickened with emotion. "I am so ashamed."

"This was not your fault. You are safe now. I am with you," Valentine reassured her.

Just as the weight of their reunion began to settle, Porcia's sharp voice cut through the stillness. She rushed down the narrow street, pulling Agatha away from Valentine and embracing her tightly. "Agatha, you scared me so! Father will be furious if he finds out! We need to clean you up immediately before Tiber sees you like this!" she exclaimed, her thoughts torn between her sister's well-being and the scolding she and Tiber would face if their father ever found out what had happened.

Agatha shifted back to Valentine. "Wait—Valentine! When will I see you?"

Valentine hesitated, his eyes flickering to Porcia, whose face betrayed guilt, then replied to Agatha, his voice uncertain, "I will await you, though Porcia..."

"You will be together soon." Porcia interjected, "For now, sister, we must clean you before Father sees you like this."

Stepping closer, Valentine whispered in Agatha's ear, "There is something I must attend to first. I will visit in the coming weeks. I promise to return. Please do not marry another before we can speak."

"Marry another?" Agatha asked, confused.

"Enough, you two—come, Agatha, citizens are taking notice. I will explain everything later," Porcia insisted, urgency lining her voice. She then turned to Valentine, her eyes brimming with tears of shame and guilt. "I'm sorry, Valentine... I am grateful." And with that, Porcia wrapped her arm around Agatha's shoulders, guiding her away.

Valentine stood still, his mind overwhelmed with emotions as the news of Agatha's possible marriage to another pierced his heart anew. It couldn't be true, he thought. *But, if it wasn't, why would Porcia want to keep us apart?* he wondered. Doubt gnawed at him, each possibility more painful than the last. His eyes locked on their retreating figures, his face a canvas of relief, confusion, and lingering uncertainty.

As the sisters disappeared into the crowd, he steadied himself and returned to his men. Each step felt heavy, burdened by the fragile hope that their love might survive. The battlefield of his heart was just as tumultuous as the physical ones he had fought on, and the fight for Agatha's love now felt like the most uncertain battle of all.

Chapter 20

Renewed Purpose

"Every lover is a soldier."
—*Ovid*

In the southern reaches of Tuscia, the crisp twilight air chilled the woods, where the bare branches of oak and chestnut trees swayed in the breeze. The low murmur of Roman soldiers drifted through the fading light, carrying a quiet menace. Hidden among the towering trees, Valentine, Marius, Proculo, Linus, Efebus and Albus, cloaked in dark woolen mantles, blended into the shadowed forest floor. They remained motionless, their eyes fixed on a nearby clearing where a mobile cavalry unit had made camp.

Valentine's voice, barely above a whisper, broke the silence: "I count thirty. The emperor is indeed making his presence felt here."

Marius responded with a nod, his voice equally subdued: "Engaging soldiers is no small matter. Are these the same who attacked Deodatus and Charu?"

Valentine, straining his eyes in the faint light, conceded, "It's hard to tell in this darkness, though it seems likely."

Proculo interjected, "There! It's the boy!"

Their attention shifted to a small figure moving toward the campfire. He collected empty wine cups and attended to the soldiers congregating around the flames.

"Indeed, that's Regalus," Valentine confirmed.

Albus was uncertain why he had agreed to accompany them and asked sarcastically, "What now, centurion? Do we take up arms against our own army and brand ourselves outlaws?"

With a stern look, Marius interjected, "What troubles you, Albus? Valentine gave each of us the choice to stay behind. If your heart falters, the road home remains open to you."

"I'll help rescue the lad, yet I see not how this ends without us spilling the blood of our own brothers," Albus countered, his voice tinged with frustration.

Linus quickly interjected, "These soldiers are not our brothers, Albus. They are the emperor's mobile cavalry sent to slaughter the innocent. They're likely the same men who fired upon us on the battlefield—leading to Scaro's death."

Albus turned around, visibly shaken by Linus's reminder of how his brother had died. "Is that so?" Albus muttered under his breath.

"You may stay back and watch over us if you like," Valentine suggested. He knew Albus had not embraced their faith yet. "This isn't your battle, Albus."

"Nay, I think I'll fight, Valentine," Albus replied.

Valentine was moved by Albus's loyalty, though he sensed a trace of something darker in his tone—a need for revenge. "Brothers, our grief must not drive our actions," he said looking at Albus pointedly before continuing. "Our sole aim is to rescue Regalus. We must strive to avoid undue bloodshed."

Albus nodded, yet his expression betrayed a different intent.

"You would show mercy to soldiers who slaughtered your comrades?" Linus interjected sharply.

Maintaining his steady demeanor, Valentine replied, "The Christian faith calls for us to rise above revenge, Linus."

"Some of us here are not Christians," Albus countered sharply.

Marius, increasingly irritated by Albus's outbursts, snapped, "Albus, why not listen to Valentine and follow *his* orders?!"

"Enough, both of you," Valentine interjected firmly. "Our mission is to rescue Regalus, not to kill in cold blood."

Proculo eyed Valentine warily. "And what if they're alerted to our presence? Are we to lay down our lives?"

"No, defend yourselves if you must," Valentine explained calmly. "Though avoid slaying them. These are not inherently evil people; they are only driven to be so by the emperor's bidding."

Proculo, still skeptical, pushed back, "They made the choice to obey orders. Does that not implicate them?"

Valentine met his gaze firmly, his face filled with resolve: "It's not our role to pass judgment, Proculo. We act mercifully, demonstrating that compassion prevails even in the darkest times."

Marius's tone softened as he joined the discourse, "Valentine speaks the truth. This is a hard path, brothers, yet we must not descend into vengeance. Before the eyes of God, we must aspire to a nobler conduct."

Valentine continued, "Brothers, overcoming this emperor's wickedness will not be by engaging his entire army at every opportunity."

Efebus, looking for clarity, asked, "So we quietly enter, retrieve Regalus, avoid bloodshed, and withdraw?"

"Yes," Valentine affirmed. "Regalus is one of us. We are to protect each other and resort to violence only if directly attacked—not as instigators."

"Then let us bring Regalus back to us," Marius stated resolutely.

Valentine surveyed his mixed assembly of followers—Romans and Roman Christians united by a shared mission. "Before we proceed, let us pray for Regalus's swift and safe recovery," he proposed. Heads bowed in silent solidarity as Valentine offered a quiet prayer for strength. Yet, when the men lifted their heads, they realized someone was missing.

"Where's Albus?" Marius inquired, his expression twisted with concern.

Valentine grumbled under his breath, his eyes sweeping the surroundings, "What possesses him?"

"Since Scaro's fall, he's been a shadow of his former self," Efebus remarked softly.

"There! Look!" Linus suddenly exclaimed calmly yet urgently, pointing toward a lone figure moving briskly toward the Roman soldiers with his sword drawn.

"Curse this madness," Valentine uttered tersely. "Proculo, Linus—secure the right flank. Marius, Efebus, on me. The rest, hold your position unless the battle is upon us. Remember, subdue—do not slay."

With urgency, the men split into their assigned formations, rushing to intercept Albus, who had already charged into the Roman encampment with a recklessness fueled by his thirst for vengeance. Before the others could properly position themselves, Albus plunged into the midst of the soldiers, catching many of them off guard and half asleep.

Almost immediately, the encampment erupted into chaos as Albus's initial strike met its mark. The anguished cries of his victims tore through the quiet of the night, prompting a lone soldier to shout, "Take arms!"

Sparks flew as steel clashed against steel in the night. Albus, in an emotional onslaught, stabbed one soldier in the gut, slit another's throat, and nearly severed yet another's arm.

"Ahhhh!" The agonized scream of a soldier pierced the air as he clutched his arm, witnessing Albus's rampage through the encampment.

Just as it seemed too late for Albus, with three soldiers bearing down on him simultaneously, Valentine, Marius, and Efebus burst onto the scene with ferocious energy. Valentine's sword flashed through the air, striking down a towering soldier with a deft blow from the hilt that sent the man's head tumbling.

Proculo and Linus joined the fray, engaging several soldiers who raced to join the fight. Suddenly, Regalus burst from a tent, his voice cutting through the chaos: "VALENTINE!" He watched, wide-eyed, as Valentine and the others fought like titans illuminated by the campfire.

All the men, except Albus, subdued their opponents with nonlethal force—using the hilts of their swords for blunt blows to the head or strategic cuts to incapacitate but spare lives. Meanwhile, Albus fought with a raw, unchecked vengeance, his actions marked by deadly intent.

Valentine broke through the chaos and ran to Regalus, pulling him into a protective embrace as if he were his son.

"You came," Regalus whispered, clinging to him.

"Indeed, I did," Valentine reassured him, his voice steady despite the turmoil around them. "Are you hurt? Can you walk?"

"I can manage," Regalus replied. "Valentine, did they...did they kill my parents?"

With a solemn nod, Valentine confirmed the painful truth. "Yes, Regalus, they did."

Tears welled up in Regalus's eyes, reflecting the flickering flames of the nearby campfire.

"Come, I will guard you," Valentine said gently, taking Regalus's hand and leading him away.

As they moved to rejoin the others, Valentine noticed Albus, over-whelmed by his grief, furiously hacking at a fallen soldier's body, his cries echoing into the night.

Valentine acted quickly, his resolve unwavering. He grasped Albus by the shoulder and yanked him back with force. "Enough, Albus!" he thundered, his voice resonating through the tension-filled air.

"Is this not what you wanted, Valentine?!" Albus retorted sarcasti-cally. "After all, we're here because of your beliefs, are we not?!"

Valentine knew Albus was referring to more than the attack on Regalus and his family, "I'm sorry, Albus. I know you are torn over Scaro."

Albus dropped to a knee, his mind racing with images of holding his brother in his arms on the battlefield, dying in his embrace. He took deep breaths, attempting to gather himself and calm his nerves.

Valentine gazed down at him, regretting the pain Albus was endur-ing, and wishing he could somehow alleviate it. "I shall pray for you, brother," Valentine remarked.

Albus remained kneeling, attempting to silence the chaos in his mind.

Valentine stepped back, allowing him space while he surveyed the scene before him—the carnage of the skirmish, with some soldiers lying lifeless and others grimacing in pain, clutching their wounds. He approached one of the injured soldiers who was still conscious. Holding his sword to the soldier's throat, Valentine declared, "Tell the emperor that Christians are no longer his for the taking."

The soldier, trembling, nodded quickly. "I will tell him."

Valentine looked around at the fallen and sighed deeply. "This is not the way." His voice carried a mix of authority and regret.

With that, Valentine, holding Regalus close, led the way back into the woods. Proculo, Marius, Linus, Efebus, and eventually Albus followed silently, their footsteps blending with the rustling leaves.

As the evening sun cast a warm glow over the Suburbium, Horatius and Helvia's modest yet elegantly appointed countryside villa sat nestled within lush gardens, sheltered by a sturdy stone wall. Inside, braziers offered a cozy refuge from the crisp winter air. The triclinium, a formal Roman dining room with three couches arranged around a low table for reclining during meals, was adorned with refined frescoes and tastefully arranged couches, exuding a sense of restrained opulence that blended sophistication with comfort.

Horatius reclined on the central couch, a dignified figure of fifty-two years, his commanding presence tempered by a compassionate gaze. Beside him, his wife, Helvia, of a similar age, bore the marks of the morning's work. Though her hands were clean, the faint calluses and roughness spoke of her own enjoyment in tending to their countryside garden, despite having slaves to assist her. It was a labor she preferred, gathering plants and overseeing the produce that supplied their herbal shop in Rome.

Across from them, Valentine and Marius lay on their lecti—the low couches surrounding the table—finishing their meal, while Linus, Proculo, Efebus, and young Regalus sipped their stew from their reclining positions at the far end of the arrangement.

Valentine began warmly: "Horatius, Helvia, we are thankful for this meal and your hospitality. Through Marius, I feel as though I've become familiar with you both despite today being our first encounter."

"The sentiment is shared, Valentine—you're all most welcome here," Helvia replied warmly, her gaze sweeping across the table.

"Thank you, Uncle Horatius and Aunt Helvia," Marius added. "We have much to share about our recent journeys, yet first, there's a matter concerning the young boy." He nodded toward Regalus, who was intently sipping his stew.

Helvia's gaze settled on Regalus with a gentle curiosity. "He appears quite hungry. To whom does he belong?"

"He's the son of Deodatus and Charu," Marius explained. "We rescued him from soldiers who captured and enslaved him."

Recognition dawned on Helvia's face as she observed Regalus. "Then this must be Raj. It's truly a pleasure to meet you again, young man," she said, her voice carrying a touch of nostalgia.

Regalus looked up, curious. "My name is Regalus."

"Your Roman name is Regalus," Helvia said calmly, her voice steady as the room fell silent. "At birth, your parents named you Raj. When Deodatus and Charu adopted you, they gave you a Roman name to protect you. Much of your Indian heritage remains untold, yet that is a conversation for another time."

Regalus regarded Helvia with quiet curiosity. He had always known he was adopted, though it was rarely discussed with Deodatus and Charu—the only parents he had ever recalled.

Turning to Marius, Helvia's expression grew solemn. "Where are Deodatus and Charu?"

Marius and Valentine exchanged a somber look before Valentine responded, "I am afraid the news we bring is not joyful."

Feeling the gravity of the moment, Horatius and Helvia shifted their full attention to Valentine, who took a deep breath and said, "They were victims of the emperor's latest attacks against Christians, tragically slain by his soldiers."

A pained expression flickered across Helvia's face. Horatius reached for her hand, finding comfort in the quiet connection. Their eyes briefly rested on the fish symbol hanging above the mantel as they offered a swift, silent prayer for the departed.

Turning back to Regalus with profound empathy, Helvia softly said, "I am truly sorry, young man. Your parents were deeply respected in our community."

Regalus gave a silent nod, unable to find words.

"What are your plans now?" Horatius asked gently.

Marius glanced at Valentine, who paused, drawing a deep breath to steady his thoughts. "I have personal matters to settle here first. Afterward, I plan to return to the Arretium region. There, I hope to rebuild the community that Deodatus and Charu once nurtured—providing healing and a sanctuary for Christians. With any fortune, it will remain far from the emperor's reach. Marius and the others have pledged their support and expressed their wish to join me."

Helvia's expression grew contemplative as she considered the broader implications of their plans. "The emperor's actions have indeed cast a long shadow over Rome. We've prayed for Empress Serena to persuade her husband to end these harsh persecutions, yet our prayers seem to go unanswered."

Seizing on a memory from his past, Valentine ventured cautiously, "I once knew a Serena in Rome, married to a magistrate named Tullus. Could this be the same one?"

Horatius and Helvia exchanged a knowing glance.

"Indeed," Horatius confirmed with a nod. "Though, the magistrate met an untimely end last year, falling from the third-story terrace of his house under suspicious circumstances. Not long after his death, the emperor took Serena as his wife, and shortly thereafter, they presented a newborn. The timing of these events stirred considerable rumor and speculation."

"A companion of ours witnessed Emperor Claudius visiting Serena's residence on the day of Tullus's death," Helvia added. "Yet, no investigation was ever made."

Valentine considered the complexities of the political landscape. "Perhaps Empress Serena could be persuaded to soften Caesar's harsh policies against Christians? I recall her being quite influential."

Helvia expressed skepticism: "The empress is under heavy guard. Even if someone managed to speak with her, shifting Caesar's rigid stance on Christians is likely too great of a challenge—even for his own empress."

From across the table, Proculo interjected, "This emperor is mad. He once ordered us to strip off our armor in battle because Marius prayed to the Christian God."

Marius added, "And that order nearly claimed Valentine's life and cost us a companion's life."

Valentine looked around the table. "Still no word of Albus?"

The men shook their heads in unison.

"He'll turn up, Valentine," Efebus reassured him, sensing his concern.

"I wouldn't have survived that day if Marius hadn't taken me to Deodatus and Charu's infirmary for healing," Valentine said.

Helvia leaned forward, her interest piqued. "They healed you?"

"Yes, that's how we met," Valentine replied, pulling down his tunic slightly to reveal the scar from the arrow. "I learned much from them while this wound took its time to heal."

Helvia and Horatius winced at the sight of the scar, imagining the pain it must have caused. Seizing on Valentine's earlier words, Horatius asked, "You spoke of continuing their work in healing and Christian worship. Do you also serve as a healer and unite couples in marriage?"

"I am not a priest," Valentine replied, "though, I am a devout Christian and assisted Deodatus in performing marriages."

"Deodatus was not a priest either," Helvia added, "yet the work he did brought great benefit to the Christians living in their community. Such services would be greatly welcome here as well."

"Do you not have a priest to handle these matters?" Valentine asked.

Helvia smiled slightly. "They fear the emperor too much. As do we all—though many still take great risks in defense of our faith."

"That is truly unfortunate," Valentine said. "I will gladly offer my assistance—though I am a marked man and must remain in hiding."

"You may all stay here. The granary is large enough to shelter you for the night," Helvia offered. "It's far warmer than the forest this time of year—and when you're able, we could use some extra hands around the villa."

Efebus grinned, his large hands raised. "These hands do not shy from labor," he said cheerfully.

"Excellent," Horatius agreed with a nod. "They can start by repairing the stables."

"We'd be pleased to help around the property, Uncle," Marius added gratefully.

Helvia smiled faintly. "Then it's settled. We'll discreetly spread the word of your services, and we'll prepare a space at our shop in Rome, where you can work, Valentine. The wages you earn will support your new life when you return to the Arretium region."

"I am indebted to you both," Valentine replied, then turned to the others. "We can also ensure a secure space for any weddings I may officiate. Isn't that right, men?"

"This is certainly a cause worth fighting for," Proculo affirmed.

Helvia turned her attention to Regalus, who had quietly observed the adults' discussion. Her voice was warm and maternal as she asked, "Would it not be better for Regalus to stay with us at the villa? If there is danger, he will be safer here."

Both Marius and Valentine nodded in agreement.

Regalus spoke up, his voice steady yet respectful. "I want to stay with Valentine."

"Fear not, Regalus," Valentine said gently. "I will not be far. This arrangement is only temporary and for your own protection."

"What other affairs must you attend to before moving to the valley?" Helvia inquired.

Valentine smiled softly before replying: "I am in love with a woman from these parts; her name is Agatha," he revealed, his voice softening further with affection.

Horatius and Helvia exchanged a knowing glance. "The execution-er's daughter—the blind woman," Horatius noted, his eyebrow arching slightly in surprise.

"Yes, you know of her?" Valentine asked, slightly surprised.

Helvia responded, "All the young men from these parts know of Agatha's beauty, though none have dared to court her."

Horatius added, "You are aware that her father tortures and

beheads criminals at the emperor's behest—in addition to his duties as a magistrate in Rome?"

"Yes, I know of him," Valentine acknowledged. "However, nothing will deter me from seeing Agatha again."

Horatius's and Helvia's expressions mingled concern with admiration.

Marius chimed in, a bit hesitantly, "I am interested in courting her sister, Porcia, though we have only met in town a few times for fear of her father's reaction."

"Yes, we are also familiar with Porcia." Helvia nodded in recognition.

"Do they live close?" Valentine interjected, his curiosity piqued.

"Yes, and we can provide you directions to their house," Helvia replied, then cautioned, "Though, there's good reason why men hesitate to pursue these maidens."

"I'm hopeful that once I speak with Agatha alone, she'll agree to move with me to the Arretium region. Afterward, we'll find the proper way to inform her father of our intentions."

Horatius shook his head in disbelief, while Helvia, with a gentle smile, simply replied, "Love is a powerful emotion, is it not?"

Valentine returned the smile. "Indeed it is."

The group gradually dispersed, heading off to inspect their new quarters in the old *horreum*, a sturdy brick building used for storing grain. Meanwhile, Regalus followed Helvia to see his room.

Before retiring, Valentine stepped out into the garden. The brisk night air carried a crisp freshness that sharpened his senses. As he gazed up at the stars, his mind turned to the journey ahead, filled with a sense of purpose and excitement about serving the community. In the tranquility of the night, he reflected on his upcoming visit to Agatha, rehearsing his proposal and the plans he envisioned for their future together.

Chapter 21

Entrapment

"What is freedom, you ask?
It means not living as a slave to any circumstance."
—Seneca

Beneath the soft glow of a crescent moon, the stout brick house of Bruttius stood firm against the crisp winter air. The quiet creak of gravel underfoot and the distant hoot of a little owl were the only sounds that disturbed the stillness. Bare branches of oak trees swayed gently, creating a hushed rustling as the wind swept through the empty landscape, giving the night an eerie yet peaceful calm.

Valentine emerged from the shadows, holding a vivid red helleborus—a winter-blooming flower known for its resilience in the colder months. Its striking color stood out against his dark tunic and fur coat. He looked up at the second level, where one shutter was slightly ajar, letting a warm light of an oil lamp spill into the cold air. Another shutter next to it lay engulfed in darkness. He wondered whether this darker space might be Agatha's or her father's bedroom.

Approaching the house, he observed the ancient grapevine that scaled the façade, its robust branches held up by a sturdy lattice of wood. Standing at the vine's base, he considered the complications a daytime visit would entail, likely drawing Porcia's disapproval and capturing Tiber's watchful eye. An evening visit also carried risks, especially given the stern warnings about Agatha's father's intolerance of suitors. His only viable option appeared to be climbing to Agatha's bedroom window under the veil of night. However, choosing the correct bedroom was paramount if he were to succeed in finding a moment alone with Agatha.

As Valentine secured the bloom between his teeth, his gaze shifted to the robust vine growing alongside the house. He took a deep breath, grasping the vine's sturdy tendrils firmly. His movements were deliberate and calculated, each step taken with precision. Ascending slowly, he remained focused on reaching Agatha's window while striving to make as little noise as possible.

Inside her bedroom, Agatha sat at a modest wooden table, engaged in the soothing rhythm of wool spinning. Though she usually spun during the day, tonight, unable to sleep, she sought to calm her mind through the familiar task. Her hands moved skillfully, deftly twisting fibers into yarn with her trusted drop spindle. As she worked, she softly hummed a childhood melody, the gentle tune blending with the quiet sound of spinning wool. Guided by memory and touch, her fingers danced over the fibers—a technique she had long perfected, undeterred by the darkness around her.

A sudden voice pierced the quiet. "Agatha!" it called out. Her hands stilled on the spindle, and her keen senses strained into the night.

"Valentine?" she ventured, her voice quivering with hope.

"It is I," he responded softly from outside.

Without hesitation, Agatha rose from her seat, approached the small window, and slowly opened the shutters. Their hands met and clasped instantly, and she quickly felt his face, confirming his identity.

"It is you," Agatha exclaimed with a thrill. "Why are you scaling these walls? Porcia could have escorted me to town to meet you."

Valentine, measuring his words carefully, replied, "That has proved more challenging than expected."

"Has it?" Agatha asked suspiciously. "I must speak with Porcia about this. She has been behaving rather strangely since your return."

"That can wait for now. I have brought you something," Valentine said as he handed her the red flower.

Agatha gently ran her fingers over the cup-shaped bloom with five distinct petals. "A helleborus," she murmured as a smile spread.

"Try not to cast its petals into the air this time," Valentine teased.

Agatha's smile grew warmer as she briefly reflected on when they first met. "Why have you been away so long?"

Valentine hesitated, his face shadowed by past ordeals. "My apologies, I came as swiftly as I could."

"I heard of the emperor's soldiers found slain in the forest of Tuscia. Was that your doing?"

Valentine appeared startled. "How did you know of this?"

"I am blind, not deaf. The survivors whispered your name, and my father revealed that Emperor Claudius had decreed your execution."

"Does your father know of us?" Valentine asked with concern.

"No, my father doesn't take kindly to hearing about our courtship."

Valentine's expression hardened. "The emperor's cavalry in Tuscia were murderers, Agatha. They killed innocent friends of mine—Christian healers who cared for me when I was wounded in battle."

"I am sorry for your loss," Agatha replied, her voice gentle yet persistent. "However, the Christian God teaches us to pray for such assailants, not to seek vengeance."

Valentine looked at her, his expression a complex interplay of remorse and admiration: "For someone who lacks sight, you see far more than most."

Her fingers tightened around his, conveying deep affection. "I do not need sight to see you," she declared, her voice rich with emotion.

Valentine edged closer, his voice a soft murmur. "I have yearned to kiss you for what seems an eternity."

Sensing his warm breath against her skin, Agatha whispered, "As have I."

Their eyes closed as their lips met, igniting a surge that radiated through them both. The kiss was slow and exploratory, a tender connection that quickly deepened as pent-up emotions spilled into their embrace. Valentine's hands tenderly cradled Agatha's face, his fingers weaving through her hair, while Agatha's arms encircled his neck, drawing him nearer. Their tongues began to explore, intensifying the kiss, their lips synchronizing in a timeless dance—until suddenly, Valentine's foot lost its hold on the branch beneath him.

"Ah," Valentine blurted as he hastily reached out to grasp the wall for balance.

"Valentine!" Agatha's concern pierced the quiet.

"I stand firm," he reassured quickly, steadying himself as his heart raced.

"Silly boy!" Agatha chided with a laugh.

"I'm not silly!" Valentine instinctually replied as their words dissolved into more laughter.

Meanwhile, Porcia, engrossed in a scroll in the neighboring room, heard their voices drifting through her slightly ajar window. Setting the parchment aside, she picked up her oil lamp and moved toward the window. Opening the shutters, she noticed a man half inside Agatha's window while his feet perched precariously on the vine. A look of shock washed over her face as she turned and cried in alarm, "FATHER!"

At her scream, Bruttius jolted awake. His old warrior's instincts kicked in immediately as he leaped from his bed, seized a giant dagger beside him, and charged into the hallway. A frantic Porcia met him, her voice trembling as she declared, "Someone is breaking into Agatha's room!"

Bursting open her door, Bruttius roared with all the fury of a protective father, "Who dares enter my house?!"

Amid the chaos, Agatha's voice rose, clear and composed: "Father, stay calm, please! I know this man—his name is Valentine." Her tone was a mix of assurance and pleading, trying to stave off misdirected violence.

Valentine had barely begun to speak from outside the window when Bruttius, his expression stern and accusing, pointed his dagger at him and declared, "The deserter who murdered the soldiers!"

In that split second, Valentine understood that Bruttius knew only the distorted truths propagated by Claudius's narrative. Panic flashed across Agatha's face as she stepped forward, her hands outstretched in a desperate plea. "Father—wait!"

Realizing his precarious position, Valentine quickly uttered, "Good night, dear maiden!" and hastily retreated down the vine.

Bruttius bellowed, "He's a dead man!" With a fierce determination, he stormed down the stairs, seizing his sword from beside the door. Barefoot and clad only in his tunic, he charged out the door and collided with Tiber, who had raced toward the house to assist them.

"Out of my way, Tiber!" Bruttius shouted and then continued to run around the house to where Valentine had just reached the ground.

As Valentine landed and turned to face his pursuer, Bruttius swung his sword with all his might. Valentine ducked just as the blade whistled past, narrowly missing his scalp. His heart raced as he rolled forward and bolted into the darkness, relieved to have escaped the near-fatal strike.

Bruttius regained his balance, his features twisted in a mask of fury as he thundered into the night, "Return not to this house!"

From the window above, Agatha's voice pierced the tense silence. "Father! That man is my Valentine!" she cried out, desperation lacing her plea.

"Not anymore!" Bruttius roared back, his words slicing through the night with finality as Porcia watched from her window, her betrayals weighing heavy on her.

As the imperial *carruca*, a covered two-wheeled carriage, made leisurely progress through the verdant outskirts of Tibur toward Villa Adriana, Empress Serena cradled her newborn daughter, Claudia, with a tender touch. The gentle rhythm of the journey lulled the infant into a peaceful slumber, and Serena took a moment to admire her precious newborn. Seated beside her was the wet nurse, who had joined the carriage so that Serena could hold her child for a brief moment before passing her back to the nurse's care.

Across from them, Emperor Claudius muttered the words from the scroll as he read. Though his eyes remained fixed on the text, his expression revealed that his thoughts were burdened by the weight of Rome's affairs rather than the serene beauty of the countryside passing by.

"Observe, my little treasure. We're nearing Villa Adriana," Serena whispered tenderly to baby Claudia, her voice a playful contrast to Claudius's silent absorption. "Soon, we shall stroll through the ancient gardens and listen to the echoes of bygone eras."

As the carriage made its way along the finely paved path, Serena admired the sprawling gardens and statues flanking the road. On either side, marble fountains sent arcs of water into the air, their gentle splashes blending with the distant murmur of the estate.

"One day, my dear," Serena said to Claudia, "you shall grow wise enough to ponder the reflections of poets and philosophers who once found inspiration in these serene surroundings. Isn't that right, husband?" Her gaze turned toward Claudius, inviting him into her whimsical exploration of history. But Claudius merely shifted in his seat, his attention more drawn to the weight of the empire than to the beauty surrounding them.

"I fear your father finds little amusement in our tales today," Serena lightly teased, her eyes briefly meeting Claudius before she redirected her attention to Claudia, whose innocent eyes sparkled with curiosity.

Claudius gazed upon the newborn nestled in Serena's embrace; his features clouded with a subtle shade of disappointment. "She grows more like you each day."

Serena offered a bright smile. "Oh, nonsense, my love, she bears your lips and ears," she retorted playfully.

"Lips and ears," Claudius exclaimed with a feigned shock. "I should hope a child of mine would inherit more significant traits."

"Husband," Serena responded, "without your lips, she would lack the command to lead an empire. And without your ears, she would fail to hear its people's pleas."

Claudius allowed a thin smile to curve his lips. "Your eloquence is ever captivating." Claudius stared intently at baby Claudia. "Still, I hope she will reflect more of us both as she matures."

"Indeed. She is your daughter too."

A pensive silence hung in the air briefly as Claudius contemplated Claudia's youthful visage, his gaze lingering before returning to the scroll in his hand. However, before he resumed reading, he solemnly said, "We shall try for a son while we are here."

Serena merely nodded, her stomach twisting into knots as the unsettling notion crept into her mind—one day, Claudius might uncover the truth. In the stillness of the night, she often lay awake, consumed by fear, the same question haunting her: *What if he realizes she is not his?* Claudius's rage would be unbound, she knew. And even Claudia—sweet, innocent Claudia—would not be spared.

The rhythmic clatter of the carriage wheels ceased abruptly as they rolled to a halt in front of the villa's monumental vestibule entrance. The ornate door swung open, unveiling Iset, who stood ready to receive them gracefully.

"Welcome, Emperor and Empress," Iset greeted them, her smile warm and her bow respectful. With a practiced gentleness, she extended her arms to lift young Claudia from Serena's embrace.

"Oh, Iset, it is truly a delight to see you," Serena exclaimed, her voice infused with relief and joy as she greeted her trusted attendant.

"As you, my lady."

As Serena stepped down from the carriage, her face brightened at the sight of the villa's bustling activity. Slaves hurried forward to assist, helping her and the others from the carriage with swift efficiency. Her gaze swept the surroundings with an eager curiosity. "How do you find the villa, Iset?" she inquired, her voice bubbling with excitement, for she had never seen it before.

"It's magnificent, my lady—I'm certain you will enjoy it," Iset assured her.

"I eagerly await," Serena replied, her smile broadening as she caught sight of Ballavan, her loyal bodyguard, who stood at attention near the entrance. "Greetings, Ballavan. It's good to see you as well," she murmured as she passed him.

"Empress," Ballavan replied as he bowed deeply.

"It seems you two are inseparable now," Serena whispered to Iset, who walked closely beside her, sharing a private moment of lightness amid the formalities of their arrival.

"He's finally come to his senses, my lady," Iset responded with a playful twinkle in her eyes.

"That pleases me," Serena replied, her smile sincere.

The villa seemed to hum with quiet energy as servants, slaves, and Praetorians all positioned with precision to honor the arrival of Emperor Claudius. Yet, amid this orchestrated welcome, Claudius's demeanor starkly contrasted with Serena's warm engagements. With hardly a pause upon disembarking the carriage, he swept past the rows of waiting attendants. His face was a mask of stoic impatience, devoid of any greeting or acknowledgment as he made his way toward the villa's grand entrance, driven by a clear desire to escape the ceremonial reception.

On the other hand, Serena moved among her people with a regal grace that did not diminish her approachability. She exchanged brief but genuine greetings with the staff, each nod and smile weaving a subtle thread of connection and goodwill.

At the grand threshold of the villa, Claudius's impatience surfaced more plainly. His foot tapped against the marble floor. "Empress, make haste," he called out, his voice firm with command.

"As you wish," Serena replied, quickening her step as she entered the glorious, marble-clad expanse of the vestibule, leaving the gathered servants behind. The echoes of her footsteps mingled with the opulence of the ancient hall.

Claudius's gaze swept over the grand entrance and surrounding quarters, his expression darkening. "Why must we linger here?" he muttered. "The slaves and staff have let this place fall into neglect. The villa is but a shadow of its former glory."

"I had hoped that Emperor Hadrian's architectural triumphs might kindle a spark of inspiration within you," Serena replied, her tone tinged with a hint of disappointment.

"We would have been better served basking in the warmth of Baiae at this season," he countered sharply, his gaze sweeping dismissively over the villa's faded upkeep.

"The Gulf of Naples shall welcome us in the summer," Serena

replied smoothly. "It is fitting to visit both the new and those places honored by time, would you not agree?"

"Hardly."

"Perhaps you might order the Senate to allocate funds for the villa's restoration," Serena suggested.

"Why would I waste funds on a private imperial villa when there is so much else to fix in the empire? You appear to disregard the fact that we are at conflict on nearly every frontier, and our treasury groans under the weight of our struggling economy," Claudius countered, his voice reflecting the weight of his concerns.

"Nevertheless, I find the respite from the demands of the capital to be invigorating," Serena confessed, her gaze drifting appreciatively across the architectural marvels before her. "It seems fitting to mark this occasion with celebration."

Claudius appeared unfazed by Serena's excitement.

As they proceeded deeper into Villa Adriana, their path led them through a majestic corridor, where columns soared toward the sky, and the floor boasted mosaics of exquisite intricacy. On either side, grand arches offered fleeting vistas of the meticulously sculpted gardens beyond, each view a splendid canvas of nature's artistry, orchestrated by human hands.

Upon their arrival at the primary residence, a cadre of servants stood in silent attention, their posture respectful amid the grandeur of ornate tapestries that graced the walls. Clea, a middle-aged Greek slave of dignified bearing, met them at the entrance to their chambers. Her olive skin and dark, braided hair, streaked with silver, reflected her heritage. Though a slave, she carried herself with quiet grace. Clea had journeyed ahead of their arrival to meticulously prepare their private chambers and vestments.

"Greetings, Emperor and Empress."

"Greetings, Clea," Serena responded, her voice warm.

"I will show you to your quarters. I trust your journey was pleasant?"

"It was, thank you, Clea," Serena answered gracefully as Claudius's eyes roved critically over the villa's evident signs of neglect.

"Splendid to hear, Empress," Clea replied, leading them with a flourish through the grand doors that opened into their private sanctuary.

These chambers radiated opulence: the marble floors gleamed, and intricately woven wall hangings adorned the walls. Richly hued draperies fell in graceful cascades. The furnishings, crafted from the finest woods and bronze, struck a perfect balance between extravagance and elegance, all converging to highlight the room's centerpiece —a luxurious lectus, draped in silken sheets and layered with soft cushions and pillows.

"It's marvelous," Serena declared, her voice breaking the hush that had fallen over the room. She turned to Claudius, seeking his approval. "Wouldn't you agree, Caesar?"

"It will suffice," Claudius intoned, his gaze drifting to the expansive vistas beyond the window—sculpted pathways, quiet fountains, and trees stripped of their leaves. Despite the beauty of Villa Adriana, unease gnawed at him. He was accustomed to commanding from afar, but this time felt different. Among other troubles with foreign adversaries, Valentine's recent defiance—the slaughter of his mobile cavalry —hung over him like a storm. Claudius vowed not to rest until the Christian who had dared to challenge his authority was dealt with once and for all.

As Clea made to withdraw, Serena observed a change in her demeanor; her walk was brisker, and her posture was more upright. "Clea! Your back appears healed," Serena remarked.

Turning with brightness in her eyes, Clea responded, "Thank you, Empress, a healer has worked wonders upon me."

"That's splendid to hear! Might I inquire as to his name? Perhaps we might also benefit from his services."

"His name is Valentine," Clea answered fondly. "He's a remarkable healer who has recently commenced his practice in Rome."

Claudius turned sharply, his expression suddenly stormy, thoughts racing. "Valentine?" he echoed, his tone sharp, addressing Clea for the first time.

Clea, visibly deflated, replied, "Yes, *Dominus*."

Serena's expression betrayed a blend of emotions—surprise, dread, uncertainty, and even a hint of nostalgia—as she instinctively covered her mouth, endeavoring to restrain the secrets that threatened to spill forth.

"How does he appear?" Claudius demanded, his voice firm as he closed the gap between himself and the servant.

Clea paused, a fleeting moment of hesitation crossing her features before she responded. "He is a man of striking appearance, Dominus," she began cautiously. "Tall and robust, with dark locks—a true embodiment of the stature of a past hero."

"Guards!" Claudius shouted, slicing through the tense air.

In moments, two imposing Praetorian Guards materialized from outside the room. Clea, her face drained of color, nearly crumpled in fright.

"Yes, Dominus," the lead guard responded with military precision.

"Remove this servant; investigate every facet of her acquaintance with her healer friend named Valentine. Then, dispatch men to apprehend this man in Rome immediately," Claudius ordered.

"Yes, Dominus." They secured a firm hold on Clea, who cast an apologetic look toward Serena as they led her away.

"It's all right, Clea," Serena called out softly as she vanished out the doors.

A wry smile curled the corners of Claudius's lips. "And I feared this respite would be drab. What a delightful turn of events."

"Was that necessary? You frightened her," Serena reproached.

"Servant!" Claudius called out, ignoring Serena's concerns with a stern command.

A young male servant, his movements tentative, crossed the threshold, his dark eyes flickering nervously between the emperor and empress. "You called, Dominus," he managed.

"See that the cook prepares the roasted pork this evening and ensure it is presented so that live doves emerge from its belly upon being sliced open. I am told it is quite the spectacle in these parts," Claudius instructed, his voice rich with anticipation. "The empress is right—there is indeed cause for celebration!" His words carried a rare note of excitement.

"Very well, Dominus, I will notify the kitchen immediately," the servant responded, retreating as he shut the heavy doors behind him.

Claudius then turned his piercing gaze upon Serena and commanded, "Now, disrobe, and I shall sire a son upon you," his voice unwavering, leaving no room for objection as he began to undress.

A profound wave of regret washed over Serena as she met the emperor's cold, unyielding gaze and began to disrobe, feeling more like a common slave than the empress she had become. For a fleeting moment, her thoughts drifted back to the raw, unbridled passion she had once shared with Valentine, where she had commanded every moment, reaching peaks of ecstasy again and again. Despite having risen to the highest rank a woman could attain in the empire, the stark realization hit her—she was Claudius's captive, ensnared in the intricate web of deceit she had woven, far removed from the passionate love she had once known.

Chapter 22

Turmoil in the Emporium

"Every new beginning comes from some other beginning's end."
—SENECA

The *caldarium*, the hottest chamber of the Baths of Caracalla, showcased the brilliance of Roman engineering. Its vast dome, soaring over thirty meters high, allowed steam to rise and circulate, creating a space that was both grand and intimate. Several baths, each set around the perimeter of the room, were filled with hot water, their surfaces rippling in the misty air. The walls, clad in richly colored marble, gleamed in the soft light of the oil lamps. Towering arched windows, which normally flooded the room with daylight, now loomed as darkened silhouettes as night crept in.

Beneath the marble floors, the hypocaust system radiated steady warmth, heating the air and the baths. The heated pools offered secluded retreats for those seeking privacy. Slaves moved quietly, tending to the flickering lamps that signaled the final moments of indulgence.

Most of the patrons had departed before darkness settled fully, but in one of the secluded pools, Senators Junius and Fabius lingered, their bodies immersed in the soothing warmth of the water. To a casual observer, they appeared as two noblemen enjoying the comforts of their rank, tucked away in a quiet corner. Yet, to the discerning eye, there was something more between them—the tenderness in their glances, the subtle closeness of their bodies. Beneath the rising mist, they were not just colleagues but lovers, their intimacy hidden like the baths themselves as night fell.

"When shall we expect Caesar to return from Villa Adriana?" Fabius inquired, his voice floating gently over the steam.

"Within the coming week," Junius responded.

"You must be pleased by Claudius's trust in your stewardship during his absence."

"Our efforts are far from fruition, my beloved," Junius admitted with a hint of gravity. "Yet, it is indeed gratifying to hold Caesar's ear."

"You are executing your duties most commendably," Fabius remarked as he emerged from the bath, water droplets glistening on his skin in the dim light.

"Thank you, Fabius," Junius replied, a note of genuine appreciation in his tone.

"Shall I leave you to your solitude?"

"Just a few moments longer," Junius requested, cherishing the brief respite.

"Very well, I shall await you in the *apodyterium*. Take your time, *princeps senatus*," Fabius said with a mix of respect and playful admiration, stepping out of the bath and retrieving his towel and *strigil*, which he had placed nearby.

Junius's gaze lingered on Fabius's slight frame and the delicate curve of his backside as he walked away. A small smile tugged at his lips. Alone in the warm embrace of the caldarium, he allowed the image of Fabius's graceful departure to remain in his thoughts.

The caldarium, now enveloped in an eerie stillness as evening settled in, felt unnervingly quiet. Flickering oil lamps along the walls cast long, dancing shadows that stretched across the misty air. From the dim recesses of a neighboring pool, a deep voice broke the silence: "It surprises me to see you prefer the companionship of a fellow senator rather than that of a slave." The words cut through the darkness with razor-sharp precision, unsettling the heavy air.

Junius rose from the bath, his gaze sweeping the vast room, searching through the veils of steam and darkness. Yet the figure remained an elusive silhouette, hidden within the shrouded shadows.

"Who speaks there?" Junius demanded.

"Nor did I envision Senator Fabius to be one to play the lesser role."

Suddenly, Junius felt exposed. The secret of his love affair with Fabius, which he had guarded so closely, now seemed dangerously close to the surface, leaving him uncomfortably vulnerable.

"General Aurelian?" Junius queried, a note of disbelief while recognizing the voice as he began to move toward him.

"At your service, princeps senatus," came the measured reply from an adjacent bath.

Regaining his composure, Junius began, "I assure you, General, Senator Fabius and I share nothing beyond a professional—"

"Dispense with the formalities. You stand before no tribunal here, Junius. As for me, the love between men bears no mark of guilt," Aurelian interjected smoothly and reassuringly.

Compelled by a mixture of gratitude and curiosity, Junius stepped out of his bath, the warmth of the water trailing behind him as he moved toward the sound of the general's voice.

The mist shifted, revealing Aurelian seated on the edge of his bath on his towel, his muscular form pressed against the marble walls, steam rising from his skin. The general, a living embodiment of Roman martial prowess, was a figure deserving of both whispered admiration and awe. Junius's gaze lingered, betraying a momentary fascination with the general's generous manhood.

Aurelian caught the flicker of astonishment in his expression and, with a self-satisfied grin, remarked, "The gods were kind."

"Indeed they were," Junius murmured, his gaze shifting away to conceal the rush of color to his cheeks, brought on by him getting caught admiring the general.

"Do you know of the story of my lineage?" Aurelian inquired, his tone gentle yet unmistakable in the room's quiet.

"I do not, yet I—" Junius's words caught in his throat, his stance awkward and exposed as he stood naked before the general, feeling more vulnerable than ever beneath the man's penetrating gaze.

"Ease your worries, Junius," the general assured him, gesturing for him to sit across from him at the bath's edge. "May I confide in you a secret of my own?" The general's voice, unexpectedly warm, softened the tension in the air.

"Certainly, General," Junius replied, his voice steadying with new resolve as he quickly sat down, facing him—all of him.

"My father—a man of war and worship to the old gods—taught me to stand firm in the face of Rome's enemies. Yet, my mother taught me the resilience of the concealed heart. She found her faith not in our ancestors' pantheon but rather in the Christians' clandestine gatherings."

Junius's breath caught in his throat. He was aware of the stakes of such a revelation. It was a dangerous confession in a time when the mere whisper of the word *Christian* could spell doom.

Unfazed and uncharacteristically calm, the general proceeded: "She was a woman of profound belief—and it was her conviction that ultimately led to her recent persecution," Aurelian shared as his eyes met Junius's.

Suddenly, Junius's heart hammered in his chest. The implications were clear, the threat delicately veiled behind the recounting of a personal tragedy. "General, surely you wouldn't lay blame for your mother's passing at the feet of my advice—" Junius began, only for Aurelian to silence him with a measured raise of his hand.

"Junius—blame is a peculiar beast," Aurelian mused thoughtfully, his voice calm and reflective. "It assumes we control our fates. Perhaps the gods are the ones shaping our paths."

"Precisely!" Junius exclaimed, quickly seizing the opportunity to deflect any potential blame for Aurelian's mother's persecution from himself. "The responsibility ultimately lies with the divine and Caesar himself."

An awkward grin appeared on the general's face as he looked at Junius almost patronizingly, much as one might regard a naive child. "And how, do you suppose, would the gods view our mortal desires?"

he inquired, his gaze drifting from himself to Junius. The sexual under-tone of his question was subtle yet unmistakably intentional, master-fully steering the conversation away from peril while drawing Junius into a more intimate discourse.

Taken aback by the unexpected shift in their conversation, Junius momentarily lost his composure. Now charged with a sudden inten-sity, the air between them stirred unfamiliar emotions within him. Previously, Aurelian's commanding presence had been a source of mild apprehension for Junius, but it now sparked a thrilling, novel desire. Always used to being in control, Junius found himself venturing into the exhilarating, uncharted territory of vulnerability and anticipation.

"The gods," Junius ventured, his voice steadier than he felt, "are vast in their understanding. They look upon the desires of men with a knowing eye," he continued, his gaze inadvertently drawn to the general's imposing figure. "Love in all its forms is a divine expression."

"Celebrated by all true Romans," the general added, his voice reso-nant with a hint of mischief.

"Indeed," Junius replied, offering a knowing smile. "The hot bath-water would provide a more private setting. Wouldn't you agree, General?"

Aurelian's response was a nearly imperceptible nod, yet it conveyed everything. Together, they rose from their seats, and stepped deeper into the general's bath—the surrounding steam swirling and parting as they entered.

Junius, leading.

Aurelian, towering behind him.

As they descended into the hot waters, Aurelian casually removed his towel beneath him, and with a deft movement, wrapped it around Junius's neck. The gesture was gentle as he pulled Junius's backside toward him, their bodies drawing closely together in the secluded corner of the bath.

Empowered, Junius reached behind to touch Aurelian. "I did not take you for a man who would—" But before he could finish, the towel around Junius's neck tightened unexpectedly. Aurelian drew him in even closer, his grip firm, transforming the earlier gesture of closeness into one of control.

"I have yet to conclude my tale, Senator," Aurelian whispered directly into Junius's ear. His tone was soft yet menacing, and the warmth of his breath contrasted sharply with the tightening towel now constricting Junius's throat. Panic fluttered in Junius's chest as he grasped at the towel, his earlier confidence dissolving into a struggle for composure under Aurelian's powerful hold.

"General, your grip—" Junius's voice was tinged with panic as Aurelian tightened the noose.

A sudden, terrifying clarity washed over Junius as he understood the true nature of Aurelian's intentions. He attempted to break free, but Aurelian's hold, masked by the simplicity of a towel, turned into an unyielding vice, cutting off Junius's breath and trapping him in a desperate, silent battle for air.

"The problem with you, Senator—" Aurelian spoke with a chilling calmness as Junius flailed, his hands clawing futilely at the towel behind him, his face turning a deep shade of purple, "—is that you were never truly cleansed by baptism." With that, Aurelian brutally submerged Junius's head underwater, drowning and suffocating him.

Junius struggled under the water for agonizing moments until his movements abruptly ceased. Aurelian then loosened his grip, allowing his lifeless body to float freely in the warm embrace of the caldarium's waters. Junius's arms spread out, hauntingly reminiscent of a crucifixion, as his body lay submerged and face down.

Aurelian gazed down at the still form and murmured, "Though I walk through the valley of the shadow of death, I will fear no evil." With calm precision, he unraveled his towel, draped it over his head, and exited the bath as quietly and eerily as he had entered.

Hidden behind the grandeur of a nearby marble pillar, Senator Fabius, now cloaked in the solemn dignity of his tunic, collapsed to the ground. Tears streamed down his cheeks as he stifled his sobs, a silent witness to the brutal end of his lover and the unbearable betrayal he had just witnessed.

HORATIUS's herbal shop stood nestled along the bustling streets near the Emporium, Rome's busy port along the Tiber River. Merchant vessels from Ostia regularly unloaded treasures from the farthest reaches of the empire, including the herbs and oils that lined the shop's shelves. At the rear of this aromatic enclave was a modest chamber, where the scents of exotic spices and healing ointments mingled with the earthy air from the nearby river. Though the area was far from quiet, the constant flow of goods ensured that Horatius's shop was always well-stocked with the rarest ingredients.

In this secluded room, Valentine administered his treatments, employing the ancient art of qigong, passed down to him by his mentor, Charu. Prisca, a young and attractive maiden with dark locks pinned up, reclined on a stark wooden table, receiving the gentle warmth of Valentine's hands as they hovered just above her skin, guiding energy and a profound sense of relaxation toward her aching joints.

As the session drew to a close, Prisca eased herself upright. The fluidity of her motions now starkly contrasted the rigidity with which she had entered the shop. As she turned toward Valentine, her eyes mirrored a blend of relief and astonishment. "I feel...renewed. You are truly a miracle worker," she whispered.

Valentine, feeling the lingering warmth from the healing session in his hands, offered a modest smile. "You're too kind. I simply follow in the revered footsteps of those who came before me."

Beside them, Antonius, Prisca's fiancé, watched the transformation with astonishment and admiration. His attire was modest and weathered. His hands were rough, bearing cuts and abrasions from countless hours of labor. "We are indebted to you, Valentine," Antonius said, acknowledging the remarkable change in Prisca.

"The pleasure is truly mine," Valentine responded warmly. "Come, let us attend to your wounds now," he suggested, motioning toward a water-filled basin. He carefully washed Antonius's battered hands, then treated them with a soothing mixture of swine fat and olive oil. After cleansing, Valentine reached for a small clay jar perched on a nearby shelf, unveiling its contents—a rich blend of honey, olive oil, and myrrh that glistened like liquid gold in the soft light. He mixed the salve with a wooden spatula, then tenderly applied a generous amount to the farmer's hands, gently working it into every abrasion and cut with precise, healing movements.

"The honey will help keep the flesh from rotting," Valentine began to explain in a calm voice. "The olive oil will keep your skin from becoming dry, and the myrrh will reduce swelling."

Antonius watched intently, nodding in understanding. The golden salve worked into his skin, immediately easing his discomfort. He slowly flexed his hands, marveling at the sudden absence of pain that had long been a relentless companion after his trying days in the fields.

As the treatment neared its end, Prisca leaned closer and whispered, "Valentine, rumors suggest you're also uniting couples in marriage. Is this true?"

Valentine cautiously asked, "Are you a Christian?"

Prisca looked toward Antonius for approval, who nodded back at her.

"We are," she confirmed quietly. "And we do not want a traditional Roman ceremony but rather our own."

A warm smile broke across Valentine's face as he nodded. "Then, yes, the rumors are true. I am uniting couples in marriage, though I have not been ordained as a priest."

Prisca exchanged a hopeful glance with Antonius, their expressions bright with excitement. "Would you marry us then?" she asked tentatively.

Valentine's smile widened. "It would be my honor," he replied warmly. "When would you like the ceremony held?"

"As soon as possible," Prisca responded, urgency clear in her voice. "We've waited long enough, and we do not want to spend another moment apart."

"Very well, how about in three days' time? We can conduct the ceremony in the forest, away from prying eyes," Valentine proposed, fully understanding the need for discretion and swiftness.

"How much would this cost us?" Antonius asked, his tone reflecting concern for their modest means.

Valentine raised his hand in a calming gesture. "There is no set fee for such a blessing. Whatever you can donate will be gratefully accepted."

Prisca's face lit up with excitement. "We will share news of your kindness and services with those we trust."

"Thank you."

As they prepared to leave, Valentine escorted them toward the front of the store. There, young Regalus meticulously sorted through a pile of roots and leaves, his efforts in sync with Horatius's, who was busy organizing the shelves brimming with herbal remedies.

"Regalus, would you gather honey, olive oil, and myrrh for these good people?" Valentine called out.

Regalus looked up, his eyes alight with the weight of the responsibility now placed upon him. "Yes, Valentine."

Horatius watched the young apprentice with a smile, his pride in the boy's diligence and eagerness palpable in the warm ambience of the herbal shop.

"It's a remarkable change since you've arrived, Valentine. The shop has never felt so vibrant."

"It's a mutual blessing, Horatius," Valentine replied, his voice rich with gratitude.

Marius's entrance at the front of the shop softly interrupted their exchange. "Valentine, there are visitors outside waiting to see you."

Caught off guard, Valentine excused himself, his curiosity aroused. As he stepped out from the tranquil confines of the herbal shop, he greeted the warm glow of the late afternoon sun. On the cobblestone street before him stood the sisters—Agatha, poised with her usual serene composure, and Porcia, visibly tense, her hands clasped tightly in front of her.

"Porcia... Agatha!" Valentine called out, his voice warm and welcoming as he approached them.

"Greetings, Valentine," Agatha said warmly, then nudged her sister to speak up.

Porcia inhaled deeply, her eyes meeting Valentine's, shimmering with tears she was fighting to hold back. "Valentine, there are deeds I have committed and words I have uttered that weigh heavily upon me," she confessed, her voice quivering with emotion. "I am truly sorry for them."

Valentine listened intently, reflecting not only on her lies at the festival but also on his last near-deathly encounter with Agatha's father, prompted by Porcia's midnight scream for help. For a moment, he wanted to chastise her. Yet, sensing her inner turmoil, his expression softened with understanding and empathy, and he replied, "We all have moments we wish we could rewrite, Porcia. Thank you for bringing Agatha here today."

Marius, a quiet observer a few steps back, stepped forward to place a comforting hand on Porcia's shoulder. "Let us afford them some time," he suggested quietly, leading Porcia away. "We won't be far," he assured them.

Valentine then turned back to Agatha, his expression lighting up with a smile. "Where is Tiber?"

"And what makes you think that I need *him* today?" Agatha teased playfully.

Valentine's smile widened. "Then, alone at last," he murmured.

"I must apologize for my father's behavior the other evening. I fear his protectiveness can be a bit overbearing at times."

"A bit, indeed," Valentine replied lightheartedly, eliciting a smile from Agatha.

"Are you going to invite me in?" she asked, her playful tone underscored with sincerity.

"Most certainly," Valentine responded warmly as he gently took her arm and guided her into Horatius's shop. "Come, allow me to show you around."

They strolled through the store, filled with a variety of herbs and remedies. Valentine described the surroundings to Agatha as they moved, his words painting vivid images for her. She picked up on the rich scents of dried flowers and spices, the rustle of leaves, and the soft creak of wooden shelves, creating a sensory tapestry that brought the shop to life in her mind. Soon, they approached Horatius, whose eyes twinkled with wisdom upon meeting her. Nearby, Regalus, engrossed in organizing a collection of botanicals, looked up and greeted Agatha with a look of recognition, his expression revealing his familiarity with the renowned tales of her, before he returned to his diligent work.

Eventually, they reached the quiet room at the back of the shop, where Valentine had set up his space for healing. He showed Agatha the area, explaining how it had become a retreat for those in need of care. The door to the back of the shop stood slightly ajar, allowing the soft sound of the Tiber River's unusually calm flow to drift in.

Agatha stepped closer to the door, feeling the sunlight gently touch her skin. She stood still, sensing the gentle breeze and the quiet calm that filled the space, fully absorbed in the moment, as if the world outside had faded into the background.

"I have a confession to make," Valentine began, his voice carrying a mix of anticipation and vulnerability.

"I am listening," Agatha replied, her heart quickening.

"I returned to Rome solely for you, Agatha. I dream of a life where we can love without bounds. I could see us building a new beginning near Arretium, yet..." His voice trailed off, the depth of his feelings halting his words.

"What troubles you?" she asked gently, sensing the hesitation in his voice and the shift in his presence.

"I fear our fate is tangled in the web of my past and the dangers it brings," Valentine admitted, his voice low.

"You're afraid?" Agatha asked, extending her hand to search for his, offering solidarity.

"Yes, I suppose I am," he acknowledged, his fingers finding hers and intertwining with a gentle squeeze.

"When I lost my sight, it was terrifying. The all-encompassing darkness—it's beyond words. I felt utterly lost. Yet, fear kindled a courage within me I never knew I possessed. If you truly believe in this path, and if it's a just one, then you must not turn away from it," Agatha encouraged, her voice steady and reassuring.

Valentine, deeply moved by her resilience and support, found the courage to confess, "I could not imagine embarking on this journey without you by my side."

Agatha's smile radiated warmth, her voice filled with affection.

"Bear, do you think I would ever let you wander the forests near Arretium without me by your side?"

Valentine's heart swelled with hope as he whispered, his voice barely audible, "Then you will join me?"

"I will," Agatha affirmed, her voice rich with emotion. "Together, we shall face whatever comes."

Agatha pulled him toward her before Valentine could navigate the whirlwind of thoughts. Their lips met in a gentle kiss, brimming with unspoken yearnings and suppressed desires. Agatha's fingers roamed over Valentine's chest and arms, feeling his muscles tense under the fabric of his tunic, his pulse racing beneath her touch. As the intensity of their connection deepened, their kisses grew more urgent and desperate.

The growing heat between them caused them to stumble up against the wall, the urgency of their movements toppling cups of botanicals from the shelves. The sound of ceramics shattering faintly registered beyond the rush of their breaths and the thud of their hearts. The shop around them seemed to vanish at that moment, leaving them lost in a world charged with raw tension and desire. Each touch and each kiss pulled them further away from reality into a vortex of passion that was as overwhelming as it was exhilarating.

However, their intimate moment shattered as Marius's faint shout echoed from the shop entrance: "Valentine—Caesar's Praetorians are coming!"

Reality penetrated their passionate enclave as they parted, their breaths mingling in the sudden chill of looming danger. "This cannot be," Valentine muttered, disbelief and frustration crossing his face.

Marius burst into the room, urgency etched on his features. "You must leave now! Out the back!" he directed, pointing toward the cracked door.

Valentine cast an uncertain glance at Agatha. Sensing his hesitation, she said, "Make haste, my love. I will await you."

The thought of leaving her was unbearable. "Marius, you must keep her safe." Valentine's words had hardly left his mouth when chaos erupted at the front of the shop. Praetorians burst through the door.

"They're here! Run!" Marius bellowed, his voice echoing through the clamor.

Valentine shook his head in resignation and hastened his exit as the soldiers barged into the room just as he departed. They found Marius standing nonchalantly by Agatha, who appeared calm.

"Where is he?" one of the soldiers demanded as his eyes scanned the room fiercely.

"Who?" Marius replied with feigned ignorance.

Frustrated, the Praetorian rushed to the back door, flung it open, and caught a glimpse of Valentine making his escape. "There he goes!" he shouted to his comrades. "Down the river!" The alert began a frantic chase as Claudius's soldiers poured out in pursuit.

Valentine sprinted through the busy streets near the Emporium, vaulting over crates and dodging stacks of shipping goods as the pursuit intensified. He darted across barges moored along the riverbank, his feet skimming precariously over the wooden decks. The shouts of guards echoed in the air, urging him onward as he made his way past the massive Porticus Aemilia storehouses, the smell of trade and cargo thick in the air.

With soldiers closing in, Valentine weaved through the tight alleyways near the Horrea Galbae, barely managing to slip past merchants and workers hauling goods. His heart pounded in rhythm with his feet, exhaustion creeping closer with every step.

Just as he thought he would be overwhelmed, a familiar shout cut through the chaos. Marius, mounted on a sturdy horse, charged through the narrow streets, scattering Caesar's soldiers like startled leaves in a storm. "Grab hold!" he called, extending a hand.

Valentine, with a final surge of energy, clasped Marius's hand and swung himself up onto the horse's back. Together, they galloped away from the docks and warehouses, the rhythmic pounding of hooves on cobblestones echoing through the air. As the soldiers' shouts faded behind them, they disappeared into the winding streets, leaving the escalating turmoil in the Emporium behind.

Chapter 23

Emperor's Briefing

"In war, events of importance are the result of trivial causes."
—Julius Caesar

The Curia Julia loomed with an air of ancient power, its marbled walls witnessing Rome's triumphs and tragedies. As Emperor Claudius strode into the chamber, having recently returned from Villa Adriana, the senators could feel the palpable tension that clung to his robes like the dust of the roads. His eyes, usually a calm sea of authority, now burned with the fire of betrayal and anger over the assassination of his trusted princeps senatus, Junius.

Whispers fluttered around the chamber like startled sparrows, but as Claudius's gaze swept across the gathered men, the murmurs died, leaving only the heavy silence of anticipation.

"Senators," Claudius began, his voice resonating against the high ceilings, "the blood of my princeps senatus demands justice! Who will step forward and shed light on this dark deed?"

The senators shifted uncomfortably, their eyes darting to one another, yet no voice rose to meet the emperor's call.

Finally, Senator Didius pierced the heavy silence. He addressed Claudius with a measured calm that belied the gravity of the situation. "Caesar, the loss of Senator Junius is a wound to the heart of Rome herself. The details surrounding his death are as obscured as the Tiber on a stormy day. We, your loyal Senate, are shaken to our core, struggling to fathom the depths of such a vile deed."

Claudius responded sharply: "So, none among you have heard a whisper as to who might commit such a foul act?"

Senator Paternus interjected, "Caesar, the baths are a labyrinth of secrets, and this tragedy seems only to add a new layer of enigma to their already mysterious depths. Rumors have long circulated about the changing room slaves, many believed to be complicit in regular robberies. Perhaps this incident is linked to such schemes."

Claudius's scowl intensified. "Labyrinth of secrets… These are the musings of poets, not the language of justice. I demand answers, not riddles shrouded in flowery speech!"

A heavy silence fell over the Senate as Paternus sat back down. None dared to meet the emperor's penetrating gaze, each senator internally questioning whether suspicion might soon fall upon him.

Emperor Claudius's voice then dropped to a menacing growl. "It is just as I suspected. A conspiracy of silence grips this Senate. Let it be known—I will find the man behind this, and their punishment will be severe! An assault on my princeps senatus is an assault on me!"

Subdued nods and murmurs of agreement rippled through the assembly, though no one ventured any tangible information or accusation.

Continuing, Claudius turned toward his consuls, "Senators Didius, Paternus, your experience is evident, though only one of you may be my new princeps senatus. Therefore, I appoint you, Senator Paternus."

Senator Didius offered a quick nod in acceptance as Senator Paternus rose, his toga falling in neat folds as he commanded the floor again. "It would be my honor to serve at your side, Caesar," he declared, his voice echoing with practiced gravitas.

From the back row, Senator Ostorius, one of the few bold enough to speak openly, raised his voice, "Should it please Caesar, let us revive the tradition of old—those aspiring to also be consuls may present their candidacy for consideration."

The Senate chamber erupted into a storm of voices. Senators, emboldened by Senator Ostorius's suggestion—an idea not entertained since the height of the Imperial period—voiced their ambitions fervently. Each vied to outshine the others with grand displays of loyalty and competence, all aimed at winning the favor of Emperor Claudius.

"Silence!" Claudius's roar cut through the chamber, sharp and decisive, like a sword slicing through silk. "I will not allow Junius's memory to be tarnished by this unseemly scramble for power. If I choose to change the consuls, that decision will be mine alone—and I will inform you all when I see fit."

The chamber fell silent at once, senators quickly acquiescing to Claudius's stern directive.

Suddenly, a single, unexpected voice shattered the room's stillness: "It was the Christians!" Senator Fabius exclaimed, his declaration reverberating through the chamber like thunder.

All eyes swiftly turned to Fabius, a senator typically noted for his reticence rather than for such audacious claims. A profound silence ensued.

Claudius peered at Fabius with an intense, inquisitive stare. "Explain yourself, Senator."

Feeling the weight of every stare upon him, Fabius stood unsteadily, "I was there, at the bathhouse."

A wave of stunned expressions swept through the senators, leaving the chamber steeped in silence.

"And..." Claudius prompted, leaning slightly forward from his imperial seat.

"Upon my departure, I observed two individuals entering the bathhouse. They wore hoods over their heads, shadowing their features, and—"

"And how do you know these men were Christians, let alone responsible for Junius's murder?" Claudius interjected, his tone laced with skepticism.

Fabius felt a lump in his throat but stood firm. "A confidant disclosed to me that he witnessed these two men marking the bathhouse's exterior with a red fish symbol, using animal blood, right after the discovery of Junius's body."

The revelation sent a murmur of disbelief and horror rippling through the Senate.

"Why have you remained silent until now?!"

"My apologies, Caesar—it was a grave oversight on my part. Yet, I am now committed to revealing the truth," Fabius stated, his voice unwavering.

At this point, General Aurelian, who had been quietly observing from the shadows of the room, emerged into the open. His face revealed a mix of apprehension and outrage as he grappled with the unfolding events. Aware of the fabrication in Fabius's testimony, Aurelian felt a growing unease about where the situation was headed and, more alarmingly, about whether he would be accused.

"How can we be certain these assailants murdered Junius?" Claudius queried, standing upright at his throne, his voice resonating with authority.

"My confidant identified them. They were the same Christians who evaded capture at the Emporium," Fabius proclaimed.

"Valentine Romanus?!" Claudius questioned.

The chamber buzzed with whispered speculation, senators exchanging looks of shock and disbelief.

"The *Christians* who slayed Junius," Fabius declared, igniting the final spark that set the chamber ablaze with tension.

Chaos ensued in the Senate, with accusations flying and voices raised in vigorous debate. One senator cried out, "They're poisoning the blood of Rome!" while others vehemently denied any religious motive.

Aurelian observed the mayhem, struggling to comprehend why Fabius would sow such discord. *He must have been present in the bathhouse,* Aurelian surmised with a pang of fear. Yet, Fabius laid the blame upon all Christians for Junius's murder. *Why?* Aurelian's mind raced with questions as the chamber's clamor drowned out his thoughts.

Claudius's anger flared, his fists clenching in fury. "Christians will not defy the might of Rome! They will pay for their insolence! Aurelian!"

"Yes, Caesar!" Aurelian snapped out of his whirlwind of confusion, stepping forward to heed the emperor's command.

"Convene our newly arrived soldiers and meet me at the palace!" commanded Claudius. With those final words, the emperor exited the chamber with determined steps.

The Senate erupted into a flurry of motion, with senators departing in a chaotic rush. A blend of alarm and confusion marked their faces as they digested the gravity of their sovereign's decree.

Aurelian's figure loomed in the corridor just beyond the Curia Julia. He awaited Fabius, whom he spotted and, with a viselike grip on the senator's arm, ushered him around a corner into a secluded alcove. Dispensing with all pretenses of formality or civility, Aurelian made his voice rumble menacingly as he pinned the senator against the wall. "Explain yourself, Senator Fabius!"

Fabius jerked his arm away, fury distorting his features. "How dare you accuse me? I saw you in the bathhouse! You're the one who murdered Junius, and yet you dare to confront *me*?!"

Aurelian quickly scanned their surroundings to ensure no one was within earshot or sight. He then pressed his forearm against Fabius's neck, the tension escalating rapidly. Unexpectedly, Fabius drew a dagger, halting it mere inches from Aurelian's throat. The corridor, typically quiet with respectful murmurs and the soft footsteps of toga-clad figures, now transformed into a stage for an outpouring of grief and fury.

"Do not presume me foolish enough to have safeguarded my life without a contingency," Fabius hissed venomously. "Should I meet an untimely end, a confidant is poised to reveal your disloyalty to Caesar and adherence to Christianity."

At this revelation, Aurelian's grip loosened slightly. "Then why not report me now? It would be my word against yours," he pressed, his tone challenging.

"And I can only imagine how I might fare in such a trial—my assertions weighed against Caesar's most favored general," Fabius countered. "No, Aurelian. I have crafted Junius into a martyr—his legacy will haunt you beyond this life. Now, you alone will bear the weight of further Christian persecutions on your shoulders."

A shadow fell over Aurelian's features. "You play a dangerous game, Fabius. Why would you see innocent lives lost for your vendetta?"

"Junius was innocent! And your anguish is the chorus to which I will dance."

Aurelian's body tensed as he swiftly disarmed Fabius of the knife and tightened his grip once again. His instincts screamed for him to silence Fabius forever.

"Strike now, Aurelian! I do not fear you," Fabius taunted, his voice cracking under his emotions. "With Junius gone, my purpose has narrowed to vengeance alone!"

The threat hung between them. Aurelian's rage battled with his duty, the muscle in his jaw twitching with restraint. He could end Fabius's threat with a single blow, but the risk of discovery and betrayal bore down upon him with crushing force.

"General Aurelian, Caesar awaits!" The urgent shout of a Praetorian Guard echoed from around the corner, breaking the intense standoff as Aurelian reluctantly stepped back, his gaze locked on Fabius, ablaze with anger.

"Proceed then—flee, General!" Fabius goaded with a sneer.

"This matter is far from concluded," Aurelian promised, his voice low and menacing.

"Indeed, it is not! It is merely the dawn of our conflict!" Fabius retorted, his smile twisted with malice.

Now laced with urgency, the officer called out again, "General Aurelian!"

Casting a final, piercing look at Fabius, Aurelian pivoted sharply and strode off.

"Be swift, General! The truth is swifter than you!" Fabius called after him, his voice echoing mockingly in the empty hallway.

WITHIN THE PALACE, Claudius's council chamber was a grand hall, designed with the meticulous craftsmanship expected of the imperial residence. The floors, made of polished white marble and inlaid with intricate geometric patterns of black and gold stone, shimmered in the daylight. Sunlight filtered through towering, arched windows, casting a soft glow over the room, which was built to reflect the emperor's power and the opulence of the Roman state.

At his side, several Praetorian Guards stood in stoic vigilance. Clad in armor that gleamed like polished mirrors, each member had been handpicked for their unwavering loyalty and martial prowess.

The echoing footfalls of leather calcei against the marble floor announced the arrival of a select group of Claudius's Praetorians. Fresh from their search, still clad in the full panoply of battle, their armor gleamed in the low light. They filled the chamber, the soft clatter of their armor reverberating in the hallowed silence.

At the forefront of this assembly, the praetorian centurion addressed the emperor with deference, "Ave, Imperator!"

"Rise! What news of Valentine and his band of insurgents?" Claudius demanded.

The centurion's face tightened. "Caesar, our efforts have thus far been in vain. Valentine and his followers remain elusive."

A palpable tension gripped the chamber as Claudius processed this news. His movements were deliberate as he traversed the expanse of the war council chamber, his countenance twisted with anger. "How can this be? Have I not provided you with abundant means to capture this Christian insurgent?" ·

"His loyalists conceal him skillfully, Caesar. They're quite cunning."

"Quite cunning?!" Claudius repeated, somewhat entertained.

"Yes, Caesar—it is as if they have anticipated our every move," the centurion replied.

"I see."

The soldiers remained silent, their eyes fixed upon Claudius as he politely seized a javelin from the grasp of a nearby Praetorian Guard. With a gesture, he directed the weapon toward the officer, his gaze piercing with indignation.

"Caesar, with time and perseverance, we shall triumph," the centurion added nervously, observing as Claudius cocked the spear back and forth with deliberate slowness as if practicing its use.

"Caesar, I'm certain..." the centurion began, but Claudius, consumed by the searing storm of his frustrations, heard nothing more. Fueled by the anguish of his princeps senatus having been slain and the bitter failure of his cavalry's pursuit of Valentine, he hurled the javelin with a primal roar. It tore through the centurion's throat with brutal precision, ending his life in a heartbeat. The ghastly sight sent shockwaves of horror rippling through the chamber as the centurion collapsed to the ground, the javelin lodged in his neck like a boar speared in a hunt.

Claudius remained unnervingly composed, resuming his measured pacing as if nothing had transpired. The soldiers stood frozen, their faces pale beneath their helmets, watching in stunned silence as the blood from their commander's lifeless body pooled across the marble floor, creeping toward them like a rising tide.

Claudius fixed his piercing gaze upon them, his voice cutting through the tense silence like a blade. "Would anybody else here care to tell me how 'cunning' Valentine and his allies are?"

The question hung in the air as none of the soldiers dared speak.

"You, soldier, what is your name?" Claudius asked the most prominent soldier in the group.

"Maximus, Caesar!" the soldier shouted back.

"Well, Maximus, have you searched every hidden nook? Under bridges—amid the foliage, among the underbrush, along all the winding paths?"

"No, Caesar!" Maximus swiftly responded.

"Then, I suggest you do not return to Rome until you do so!"

"Yes, Caesar!" Maximus snapped in response.

"Maximus, you will replace command over this cavalry—do not disappoint me as your predecessor did," Claudius cautioned as he gazed at the speared centurion laying on the floor.

"Yes, Caesar," Maximus replied nervously.

"You are my shadow warriors! Excellence is your duty!" Claudius shouted at them.

The soldiers, much like trapped beasts, stood wide-eyed and trembling.

"Arrest anyone seen with Valentine! Double the bounty to one hundred *aurei*, deploy twice the usual number of soldiers, and return only when this *Christian* is captured!"

The soldiers stood still until Claudius's booming voice shook them into action. "Go!" he bellowed.

"Yes, Caesar!" they chorused, springing to their feet and sprinting away.

As they vanished from sight, General Aurelian emerged from the shadows near the grand doors, with a soldier shrouded in the shadows beside him.

"May I approach, Caesar?" Aurelian inquired formally, his demeanor still bearing the weight of the earlier proceedings.

Claudius's fury dissolved as he turned to his loyal subordinate. "Of course, Aurelian. Speak."

"I have brought you someone who claims familiarity with Valentine."

The words hovered between them, charged with anticipation.

"Excellent. Bring this loyal citizen forth," Claudius commanded as Aurelian revealed Albus from the shadows.

Chapter 24

Rebels of Rome

Downstream from the ancient town of Tivoli, the Aniene River roared past a secluded meadow, chosen as the serene setting for a Christian wedding. The sun's rays pierced the late-morning mist, warming the crisp air. Leaves whispered in gentle concord, complementing the hushed tones of guests arriving in anticipation. Clad in wool and leather, the wedding party trod softly over the dew-fresh grass, their faces alight with the joy and solemnity of the occasion. Fallen logs, arranged in a semicircle, faced a simple arrangement of stones that served as an altar, transforming the area into a sacred grove.

The guests had arrived from Rome and the surrounding countryside by modest carriages and horseback, having endured the rugged terrain to participate in this secret ceremony. Horatius and his wife, Helvia, dressed in understated elegance, took prominent seats among the nearly thirty attendees. Seated next to them, Regalus watched the children play by the river, their laughter blending with the sound of the flowing water. On the outskirts, Marius kept a careful watch, his eyes constantly scanning the horizon for any signs of unwanted visitors.

At the center of the gathering, the bride and groom, Prisca and Antonius, greeted their guests with warm smiles and gentle gestures. Prisca wore a long *tunica recta* tied with a cingulum belt, its natural color enhanced by wildflowers intertwined in her yellow hairnet, which shimmered subtly with each movement. She wore a yellow-red veil, called a *flammeum*, cascading elegantly over her shoulders, blending seamlessly with the dappled sunlight of the forest. Beside her, Antonius stood, dressed in a *toga virilis*, radiating quiet strength and anticipation.

Valentine stood at the forefront of the gathered congregation, exuding both authority and kindness. Dressed in simple layered garments suitable for the cold, his cloak draped over his shoulders for warmth, he surveyed the assembly with the quiet confidence of a shepherd tending to his flock.

"Dear friends," Valentine began, his voice warm as his gaze swept across the crowd. "Today, we witness the union of two hearts, united by love and faith, and honoring the traditions of our time. Although I am not a priest, Prisca and Antonius have entrusted me with the privilege of guiding them in this sacred union."

He paused, letting his words settle among the guests before turning his attention to the couple. "I met Prisca and Antonius not long ago. And though we are newly acquainted, a profound kinship binds us, as it does all of us here today. We are united by a faith rooted in love and peace. While we must conceal our worship from public view, we stand firm in practicing our belief quietly and among those we trust. Overseeing this ceremony is deeply meaningful for me, as I am keenly aware of the trials one faces in finding a true partner."

Soft laughter rippled through the crowd, many familiar with the rumors of Valentine's narrow escape from Bruttius and his menacing sword.

"So, when Prisca and Antonius asked me to marry them, my heart was warmed by their request. And thus, we stand united—not in defiance of tradition but in celebration of our faith and this union, as rebels of love," Valentine said with a smile, his words drawing soft laughter and easing the solemn air.

Meanwhile, Proculo, Efebus, and Linus remained vigilant on the outskirts of the meadow, strategically positioned within the sheltering woods. From their elevated vantage point, they kept a sharp lookout for any signs of intrusion, their duty interspersed with lighthearted discussions about future dreams.

"Imagine the vineyards we could cultivate in Arretium," Proculo mused, his eyes never straying from the distant tree line. "Acres of grapes thriving under the sun..."

Efebus chuckled, adjusting his position on the forest floor. "I'm partial to olive trees, myself. Think of the rich golden oil we could produce."

Linus smirked, entering the friendly debate. "Both of you cast your sights too narrowly. We ought to raise goats! Cheese and milk would grace our table at every meal!"

Their chuckles and light banter were suddenly cut short by the distant thunder of hooves—an all-too-familiar, chilling sound. Proculo spotted the rising dust cloud behind the crest of a nearby hill. "Soldiers!" he hissed urgently.

Efebus and Linus immediately tensed, their playful demeanor instantly forgotten as they focused intently on the horizon. "How did they find us?" Efebus muttered in disbelief.

"I know not, yet they are directly upon our path," Proculo replied firmly, rising to his feet and fixing his gaze on the advancing threat.

"We need to warn the others," Linus asserted as they sprang into action.

At the ceremony, Valentine noticed the three men racing toward them, their urgent shouts breaking the peaceful air: "Soldiers—soldiers approach!"

Valentine's heart tightened at their warning, spurring him into swift action to protect the guests. The tranquil ceremony quickly transformed into a scene of calm urgency and quick movements. Valentine's commanding voice cut through the chaos: "To the bridge!"

Confusion morphed into fear on the guests' faces as they corralled children and older people toward the prearranged escape route.

"Swiftly and with order—adhere to the plan," Valentine commanded in his authoritative yet calming voice as the guests hastened toward a nearby footbridge over the river. He then convened with his men to formulate their defense strategy.

"How many are they?"

"At least thirty, approaching from the west," Proculo responded, gasping for breath.

"The Praetorians," Marius added grimly, just joining them.

"Lord, have mercy," Valentine muttered, aware of the soldiers' formidable capabilities. "We shall make our stand at the bridge. Efebus and Marius, cross first and prepare to sever the lines at my command. Proculo and Linus, stand steadfast with me," Valentine ordered as he discarded his cloak, reached for his sword, and braced for the imminent confrontation.

The narrow footbridge, a makeshift structure, hung precariously over the rushing waters, which had surged in force and volume after days of unrelenting rain. Flanked by steep banks, the current churned around sizable boulders below. Constructed of basic ropes and worn planks, it swayed uneasily under the weight of the guests cautiously making their way across to where carriages and horses awaited. This temporary bridge was hastily erected after the original, a sturdy Roman construct, had been damaged by a recent flood, leaving a vital crossing in disrepair. Horatius, Helvia, and Regalus pushed toward the unstable crossing, descending the small hill before it; however, as they hurried down the slope, Helvia's foot snagged on a hidden root, causing her to twist her ankle and fall.

"Ahh!" she cried, clutching her injured ankle.

Horatius swiftly knelt beside her. "Are you well, my love?"

"My ankle!"

Valentine and the others hurried to Helvia's side as the thundering of hooves grew closer.

"Efebus, carry Helvia and assist her across the bridge," Valentine ordered.

"Clear a path," Efebus commanded, swiftly scooping Helvia into his massive arms. Horatius and Regalus followed closely as Efebus carried Helvia toward the bridge, trailing the other guests. Regalus lingered behind them. When it was his turn to cross, his gaze drifted downward to the churning river below, swollen from recent rainfall. Clutching the rope tightly, he felt a surge of fear as the bridge swayed under the weight of the guests.

"Press forward, Regalus—stand strong," Marius encouraged, who followed closely behind Regalus and sensed his apprehension.

Suddenly, Regalus slipped as a cry of terror escaped his lips, and he teetered on the brink of death. But Marius acted swiftly, grasping his arm and hauling him back onto the bridge's safety.

"Grab hold!" Marius shouted as Regalus regained his footing, his relief palpable.

Emerging from the forest, however, the thundering hooves of the Roman cavalry led by Maximus shattered the tranquility. The soldiers' armor gleamed coldly in the wintry sunlight as the men peered down at the congregation escaping across the footbridge, while Valentine, Proculo, and Linus remained, swords drawn.

Maximus raised his sword and bellowed, "Halt their advance! Do not permit them to cross that bridge!"

Three of his men swiftly dismounted their horses and raced down the small hill, spearheading the attack. Valentine's, Proculo's, and Linus's gazes hardened as they formed a human barrier defending the bridge.

As the soldiers attacked, each man engaged in combat with a counterpart. Valentine's movements flowed like a graceful dance, the clang of swords ringing out as he struck first. Proculo and Linus confronted the next wave of soldiers, their actions harmonizing with the chorus of clashing steel as they swiftly dispatched their opponents. However, their victory was short-lived as a fresh onslaught of soldiers descended upon them, led by Maximus himself.

Before Proculo and Linus could confront the oncoming soldiers, Valentine urgently ordered, "Cross the bridge! I will follow after you!" Without hesitation, they obeyed, darting toward safety as Valentine grappled with his adversary, hurling him over the cliff and into the raging river below.

Valentine leaped onto the bridge last as Maximus's sword swiftly clashed with his own. Maximus advanced, driving Valentine toward the middle of the footbridge, where the rapids roared below, leaving only enough space for a one-on-one duel. Maximus attacked with fierce venom, each swing of his sword matching Valentine's skill and power.

Behind Maximus, the remaining soldiers arrived at the footbridge, their swords drawn and shouts of "Kill the Christian!" echoing from their ranks. On the opposite side, Marius, Proculo, Linus, and Efebus shouted words of encouragement, urging Valentine to emerge victorious.

The bridge's wooden planks groaned under the combatants' strain, each step and clash of their boots threatening to send them plummeting into the roiling river below. Locked in their fierce duel, they seemed oblivious to the dangerous abyss beneath them as the bridge swayed with their every movement, its rope-bound structure appearing very unstable.

Suddenly, Valentine caught the edge of one of the planks and stumbled backward, landing hard on his backside and sending his sword tumbling into the raging river below. Maximus lashed out with his blade, aiming to strike him down. Valentine evaded the attack with quick reflexes, twisting his body to avoid the lethal blow. He delivered a powerful kick to Maximus's leg in a swift countermove, causing him to lose his balance and stagger backward. Valentine regained his footing but now found himself unarmed.

"Sever the rope!" Valentine's urgent cry pierced the air before Maximus could strike.

"You'll perish with him!" Marius warned.

"Do it now!"

Wide-eyed, Maximus now grasped Valentine's daring plan to bring the bridge crashing upon them. "Retreat!" he ordered at his men, who had marched out behind him, their forces nearly extending across the bridge.

Without hesitation, Efebus and Marius unleashed their swords on one of the ropes, swinging repetitively until one of the ropes frayed and snapped. Valentine and Maximus clung desperately to the remaining rope, the bridge buckling and twisting beneath them. Maximus lost his footing in the chaos, his sword tumbling into the river below, while two other soldiers slipped off the bridge into the river.

Seizing the opportunity, Valentine swiftly sidestepped the remaining short distance to safety, joining the rest of his men. As soon as he cleared the bridge, Efebus and Marius hacked down on the remaining ropes with determined strokes. With a groan of protest, the bridge gave way, sending Maximus and a handful of soldiers plummeting into the rapids before they could retreat safely to their side. Their screams of dread echoed through the ravine as they were violently swept downstream by the frigid, raging waters.

As the remaining Roman soldiers stood helplessly on their side, shouts of confusion and frustration erupted. Suddenly, one soldier emerged and walked to the cliff's edge, his Roman armor gleaming in the sun. His expression registered awe at the entire scene and Valentine's narrow escape. It seemed unimaginable, but after fighting side by side for years, they could not mistake this soldier for another.

"Albus, you traitor!" Marius's accusation rang out. The weight of his mistake now bore down on him as he realized he had unknowingly betrayed Valentine by trusting Albus with their location.

"Greetings, Christian!" Albus sneered. "I trust you won't mind that I've brought some new acquaintances to join the festivities."

"I will have your head for this, Albus!" Marius roared in fury.

Valentine gripped Marius's arm firmly and shook his head, "Leave him," he said, urging restraint in the face of betrayal.

"It's *your* head the emperor seeks, Valentine! Surrender yourself, and this ends now—or who knows, next time it could be Agatha!" Albus's voice echoed menacingly across the clearing.

Valentine turned, visibly furious and affected by this threat.

"Do not be swayed by him, Valentine," Proculo urged, pulling him away. "He seeks to provoke you where the wound is deepest. Surrender is not an option."

Valentine paused, his eyes reflecting a turmoil of thoughts. "Nonetheless, he speaks truly," he conceded softly. "The emperor's wrath does seem personal."

"Indeed, it's personal! When we rescued Regalus from the emperor's last cavalry, Albus shouted your name loudly enough for every surviving soldier to hear," Marius interjected bitterly.

"Your growing popularity as a Christian priest cannot be pleasing to the emperor either," Linus added sarcastically.

"I'm not a priest," Valentine retorted, his frustration evident.

"Tell that to this emperor!" Linus shot back.

Valentine paused, reflecting for a moment. "Linus, you have a cousin who serves among the Praetorian Guard, do you not?"

"Aye, though he knew not of this attack today. Why do you ask?"

"Perhaps Horatius and Helvia spoke the truth—maybe the best way to influence the emperor is through the empress," Valentine pondered aloud.

"I think you may have taken a few too many blows to the head," Marius replied, half-jesting but with concern.

"Fear not; I don't expect any of you to accompany me on this mission," Valentine assured them, his gaze sweeping over his friends. "I've already asked far too much of you."

"Wait a moment—are you suggesting infiltrating the Imperial Palace?" Marius asked incredulously.

"I am."

"Are you mad?!" Marius exclaimed, his eyes wide with disbelief. "The palace has hundreds of soldiers trained to stop an army—let alone one man!"

"I understand the risks," Valentine replied calmly.

"I'm not certain you do, Valentine," Linus interjected. "Marius speaks the truth. Nobody has ever breached the Imperial Palace. It's the most guarded structure in the empire—impregnable!"

"A mission of certain death," Proculo said gravely.

"They speak the truth, Valentine," Efebus added.

Valentine surveyed his friend's concern and replied, "If I ever hope to build a life with Agatha, I must find a way to convince the emperor to end his persecution of Christians—otherwise, the safety of all Christians will remain in jeopardy. While I may not be well acquainted with the empress, I trust she will lend an ear to my plea."

"Oh, you're quite familiar with her—you bedded her! Another

reason the emperor may want your head!" Marius blurted, frustration evident in his voice.

Valentine waved him off dismissively and began to walk away. "I must try, Marius. If she holds the emperor's ear, she may be our only hope."

Marius glanced at the other men, their faces stunned.

"That's it—he's lost his senses."

CHAPTER 25

SERENA'S CHAMBER

"Love conquers all; therefore let us yield to Love."
—*VIRGIL*

In the dim, flickering light of Horatius and Helvia's barn, Linus guided a blindfolded Praetorian Guard into the midst of Valentine's secret gathering. On the ground, Efebus, Proculo, Marius, and Valentine were intently studying a rudimentary model of the Imperial Palace, constructed from stones, twigs, and other barnyard debris. The group momentarily stiffened at the sight of one of Claudius's trusted Praetorians led into their clandestine meeting. Linus carefully removed the blindfold, revealing the earnest face of a stout young man, barely twenty-two years old. "This is my cousin, Baro," Linus announced.

Valentine stood to greet him. "Apologies for the blindfold, Baro. We must exercise caution in these uncertain times. I'm Valentine," he said.

"You're the most wanted man in the empire; I can't fault you for such precautions," Baro replied, acknowledging him with a nod.

"Thank you for agreeing to meet. Linus tells me you're a Christian?"

"I am, though I rarely admit it these days," Baro acknowledged, his gaze briefly settling on a small silver fish hanging from Valentine's neck—a gift Deodatus had given him.

"All the more reason for this gathering," Valentine replied.

"I hear from my cousin that you plan to breach the palace walls merely to exchange words with the empress," Baro said.

"Indeed."

"Have you not considered sending a scroll instead?" Baro asked, his tone laced with sarcasm.

The room erupted in soft laughter.

"I think I like this one," Marius remarked with a grin.

Valentine countered, "I suppose I'm a bit of a traditionalist." He gestured toward the hay bales. "Please, have a seat."

They gathered closely around the model of the palace, laid out on the ground before them.

Valentine turned his gaze at Baro. "Can you assist me in gaining an audience with her?"

Baro hesitated, choosing his words carefully. "Secretly infiltrating the empress's quarters is not only daring—it borders on madness. The palace is a fortress, designed to thwart any breach. No one, not even an army, has ever succeeded."

Marius shot to his feet. "Exactly what we told him! Excellent meeting. Thank you, Linus's cousin, for coming."

Valentine gestured for Marius to retake his seat, then refocused on Baro. "Forgive him. As you can see, my companions are also wary of this plan," he said, his expression earnest. "Beyond the sheer difficulty of such an undertaking, is it possible?"

Baro took a deep breath before explaining, "For it to work, someone like myself would need to help you gain entry. You'd have to be disguised as a Praetorian. Timing would be crucial—under the cover of night, when our vigilance is lowest. And you'd need to move silently, in and out, without triggering any alarms."

"What kind of alarms?" Efebus interjected.

"At the first sign of a breach, we're ordered to sound the horns," Baro clarified.

"So, it's conceivable?" Valentine pressed.

Baro met his gaze earnestly. "I didn't say that. Why are you willing to take such a risk?"

Valentine responded with firm resolve: "I believe this is our only chance to convince the emperor to cease his persecution of Christians."

"Baro, they murdered Nonius just last month at the emperor's command," Linus added.

Baro nodded. "I heard of our cousin's unfortunate passing. He was a good man, certainly undeserving of the martyrdom he suffered." After reflection, he looked up at Valentine, his determination clear. "What would you require from me?"

"Your knowledge of the palace and assistance with entry is paramount," Valentine said earnestly. "We must plan this meticulously."

"I can devise the plan and help you gain entry, yet beyond that, the responsibility falls solely on you," Baro replied firmly. "And should you be captured and face torture, you must vow never to reveal my involvement."

"Agreed," Valentine acknowledged.

"Very well," Baro concluded.

Marius shook his head in concern, murmuring, "Show us the routes we must navigate to achieve this."

Linus added, "Baro, I built the model. However, I'm uncertain of the most strategic route for all of us to enter."

"Stop there, cousin," Baro interjected firmly. "This mission must be undertaken by Valentine alone. If more than one of you tries to enter, the risk of capture increases dramatically."

"Valentine cannot enter alone. What if he encounters multiple guards?" Proculo chimed in.

"If he's detected, he will most likely be captured," Baro responded bluntly. "Once the alarms sound, the Praetorians will seal all exits and unleash the dogs to track him down."

"Then, how can we help him?" Linus asked.

"Just be prepared to move swiftly if he escapes," Baro answered. "If he does not, the emperor will surely torture and kill him to set a public example."

Proculo shot Valentine a concerned look. "Are you certain about this?"

Valentine ignored him and asked, "Does the empress sleep alone?"

"They have separate chambers. The empress dislikes leaving the baby with the nurse every night, so she sleeps in the same room with the child, while the nurse stays in a nearby chamber," Baro explained. "The emperor's quarters are right next to the empress's, with a private door that allows him to enter her chambers whenever he wishes."

Valentine thought back to his night with Serena and hoped that connection would be enough for her to trust him. "What's the best route to her chambers without triggering any alarms?"

Taking Linus's stick, Baro pointed at the model. "This service gate is your best entry point. It's lightly patrolled during the night."

Valentine studied the model of the palace intently, his mind running through each possible scenario.

"Once you're inside through the service gate, follow this service passage toward the *cubicula* wing. From there, you'll need to scale this section of the wall near the *peristyle*, two levels up. That will bring you close to the empress's chambers through the atrium. Your best way in is through her private balcony, which she usually leaves open at night."

"How's he supposed to manage all of that alone?" Efebus asked, alarmed.

"I will ensure the gates are open and unguarded, yet scaling the wall and slipping past the watchful eyes of the Praetorians will be a challenge. It's possible, though—if you move with care and silence," Baro added.

Valentine nodded. "I will need one of your cloaks to pass unnoticed."

"I'll see to it," Baro answered.

"What about a weapon?" Marius interrupted.

"I wouldn't recommend it," Baro cautioned. "He'll need to move silently while scaling the wall."

"No weapon?!" Marius exclaimed in disbelief.

Undeterred, Valentine asked, "When is the best night for this?"

"Tomorrow," Baro replied. "The Lupercalia festival commences at the week's end, and there will be more guards."

"Then tomorrow it is," Valentine decided.

IN THE STILLNESS of the night, the silence was palpable within Serena's opulent chambers in the Imperial Palace. She lay deep in slumber, nestled in her luxurious bed, its frame carved from rich wood and draped with fine linen and silken sheets. The chamber, adorned with elaborate mosaics on the floor and walls, was bathed in the soft glow of moonlight streaming through the open balcony, where Valentine had quietly entered.

Valentine gazed down at Serena momentarily, recalling their brief encounter with fondness despite their night ending abruptly. He gently clasped his hand over her mouth, jolting her awake. Serena's eyes widened in alarm, the intrusive grip stifling any attempt at a scream. Panic flickered in her gaze until he swiftly reassured her.

"Serena, it is I, Valentine," he whispered. "Please, do not be alarmed."

The tension in Serena's face softened as her eyes caught sight of the small fish necklace, slipping out from beneath his tunic. Dressed in the attire of a Praetorian, Valentine slowly released his hand from her mouth as she sat up abruptly in bed.

"What business do you have here?!" Serena's voice carried a mix of doubt and fear as she whispered, "And how did you get in?"

"I have a favor to ask—and you, of all people, should know that I've had some experience slipping in and out of your private chamber," Valentine quipped, eliciting a brief softening in Serena's expression.

"I see your newfound faith has not dulled your charm," she observed while sweeping aside the strands of her chestnut locks.

"Nor has your new husband robbed you of your beauty," Valentine complimented, aiming to ease their tension.

"Your flattery rivals that of the finest poets," she whispered, a coy smile playing at her lips. "What favor do you speak of?"

"Did you tell him about us?"

Serena looked away. "I had to."

Valentine's expression darkened. "No wonder he fights with such rage."

"I'm sorry, Valentine. I meant no harm to come to you," she said earnestly.

"He's taking innocent lives, Serena. Women, children, priests. Can you reason with him?"

Serena gazed out a window overlooking Rome. She lay in bed, the weight of her decisions pressing heavily on her. This was not the world she wanted her daughter to grow up in. The thought of Claudia inheriting a life filled with deception and danger filled her with dread. She longed for a time when her daughter could be free, when love was not weighed down by fear and hidden truths. Lying there, the bed felt like a prison. Turning back to Valentine, his presence a stark reminder of the love and betrayal that had brought her to this point.

"Reason? He'd sooner see your demise than Rome's greatest enemies. The man who courted his wife, deserted his army, weds Christians in secrecy—he loathes you."

Valentine turned his gaze aside. "Then, perhaps my presence here serves no purpose after all," he murmured.

Serena's expression softened with sorrow. "I'm sorry. I, too, feel as though I am held captive by him," she confessed, her voice tinged with regret. "You do not know what it's like to be with a man like him." Her eyes brimmed with tears.

Valentine tenderly clasped her hands, attempting to comfort her, sensing her sorrow.

Her eyes fixed upon his with a spark of revelation. "Perhaps there is an answer to both of our troubles," she said hopefully.

Valentine leaned closer. "Tell me."

She drew closer, her gaze turning more seductive: "We could arrange for his death."

Valentine quickly recoiled. "I am no murderer, Serena."

"Nor am I," Serena retorted. Her voice was soft yet resolute. "However, should Claudius be removed, we might resume what we once began—you, me, and..." Her eyes drifted toward the dark corner of the room, where the crib lay. Claudia was sleeping soundly within it, but Serena hesitated, leaving the child's name unspoken.

"Serena, we both know our time together was far from love," Valentine quickly interjected.

"It was an unforgettable night—was it not?" she challenged.

"It was… something," Valentine conceded, his words carefully neutral.

"Who's to say what you and I could become if only we were to give *us* a chance?" She leaned in closer, her lips promising more, her eyes searching his for a hint of possibility.

"You flatter me, Empress—though my heart belongs to another," he confessed.

Serena recoiled, her once confident and seductive demeanor crumbling into shock and mortification. Hurt and rage flashed across her eyes as she struggled to process his audacious admission, especially after he had dared to infiltrate her chamber.

"You would leave me, and… my child, to a tyrant who forces himself upon me while you run off with some whore?" she hissed venomously. Her thoughts spiraled into irrationality; in her distress, she saw him not as he saw himself but as the absent father of their daughter.

"You have chosen your path, Serena—and my Agatha is no whore."

"Agatha," she spat with a visceral contempt as if the mere mention of the name repulsed her. Envy gnawed at her, the image of Valentine with another fueling her bitterness. At the same time, she faced the lonely burdens of motherhood, confined within the palace walls, while enduring Claudius's relentless pursuit of a male heir. Anger simmered within her as she stewed in her enforced isolation.

"Please, Serena, I am only here to appeal to your good nature," Valentine implored. "I simply ask that you speak to your husband about changing his intolerance toward Christians."

Her gaze drifted toward the cradle as she muttered, "If only you knew," the pain of abandonment thick in her voice. Then, suddenly, she took a sharp breath and screamed, "GUARDS!" Her voice cracked with hysteria, the desperation and madness palpable as she shrieked for help.

"Have you lost your senses?!" Valentine exclaimed, staring at her in disbelief.

"CLAUDIUS!" she cried again, her voice echoing through the chambers like a dire proclamation, as if she were sealing Valentine's fate.

The chamber doors burst open as two Praetorian guards poured in, their swords glinting ominously in the dim light. Claudius rushed in through his secret door, draped in robes and a face contorted with anger, while baby Claudia's cries instantly pierced the air, sounding a piercing alarm throughout the palace.

"What is the meaning of this?!" Claudius roared as he entered.

"It's Valentine! He seeks your life!" she accused, pointing at the intruder.

Claudius's sharp gaze settled on Valentine, who had already reached the balcony overlooking the atrium. Claudius's eyes filled with fury; his lips twisted into a fierce scowl.

"Then, he shall meet his fate!"

Valentine glanced over the balcony's edge, assessing his only way out as a guard rushed toward him. Quick on his feet, Valentine dodged and capitalized on the guard's momentum, tossing him over the railing. He seized the plummeting man's sword in the chaos as his scream echoed off the walls.

Within moments, Claudius grabbed another guard's sword and ran toward the balcony.

"Get back! He's mine!" Claudius yelled as other Praetorians fanned out, sealing any potential escape routes.

The air soon filled with the fierce cacophony of metal striking metal under the moonlit sky as Claudius and Valentine dueled.

Valentine attempted to strike Claudius's arm, but he retaliated with increased savagery. They moved in a lethal ballet, each strike inching closer to its target.

Meanwhile, Serena watched, her heart pounding, as Claudia's cries echoed from the depths of her chamber. For a moment, she wondered if she had done the right thing. It was possible Valentine could still kill Claudius and she and Claudia could finally escape his grip.

Sweat streamed down Claudius's face as his actions, though slower, remained fierce. In a vicious swipe, Claudius sliced off Valentine's necklace, narrowly missing his throat.

Reacting quickly, Valentine took a daring swing at Claudius's head. The emperor dodged just in time, but as Valentine's blade descended, it slashed across Claudius's leg, slicing it open.

The emperor screamed, collapsing to his knees in agony, blood seeping into the elaborate mosaics of the balcony. Vulnerable and desperate on the ornate floor, Claudius looked up and bellowed with a mix of pain and humiliation, "Kill him!" His command was a visceral roar.

Valentine's heart pounded as he rushed to the balcony's edge. Two floors below, the palace courtyard glowed in the flicker of torchlight, casting long shadows across the stone pathways. Taking a deep breath, he carefully lowered himself over the edge, reaching for the ivy-covered trellis clinging to the wall one floor down, praying it would hold.

As he descended, his weight hit the walled trellis with force, and his fingers clung desperately to the thick vines. The impact made the ancient wood groan and crack beneath him. Suddenly, it gave way, and he plunged downward, crashing through a large canvas canopy. The fabric tore under the strain, slowing his fall just enough to send him tumbling into a decorative fountain below. Cold water enveloped him as he struck the mosaic bottom with a bone-jarring thud. Wincing from the pain, Valentine forced himself out of the fountain. His body ached, but there was no time to waste.

The palace's horns resonated through the grand halls, accompanied by the distant barking of dogs and the shouts of Praetorians. Yet none of these sounds carried the menace of Emperor Claudius's voice, which continued to boom from the balcony above: "Kill him!"

Valentine dashed through the palace, his wet clothes clinging heavily to his limbs. Each step sent jolts of pain through his bruised body, but the fear of being captured pushed him forward. Navigating the opulent corridors, Valentine relied on Baro's familiarity with the palace's layout, which led him back toward the small, hidden gate near the *servus* quarters, his only hope of escape.

As Valentine raced down the final corridor, he caught sight of

Maximus leading ten Praetorians in pursuit. Maximus's scarred face, a reminder of his near-death fall into the river, was twisted in fury as he charged toward Valentine. With no time to hesitate, Valentine sprinted for the hidden service gate and burst through it. Once outside, he shouted to Marius, "Seal the gate!"

Marius acted swiftly. He jammed his sword through the iron handles, locking the door and trapping Maximus and his men inside. Their furious pounding and muffled shouts followed as Valentine and Marius bolted down the steep, narrow stairs winding down Palatine Hill.

The alarms from the palace rang out behind them. Praetorian patrols had already begun sweeping the lower levels of the hill. Valentine and Marius moved as quickly as they dared, keeping to the shadows and hugging the walls of the ancient structures that lined the path. The torches from the guards flickered in the distance, closing in.

When they reached the base of the hill, Efebus, Linus, and Proculo stood ready, holding the reins of the smaller, swift horses suited for the tight Roman streets. The animals were restless, sensing the danger in the air. Without hesitation, Valentine and Marius mounted, casting a final glance back at the palace, which still loomed behind them, ablaze with torches and oil lamps, alive with movement.

The moment they spurred their horses forward, the sound of hooves on the cobblestones rang out, and Praetorians on the walls spotted them instantly. "They're escaping!" one shouted, his voice carried by the night air. Arrows whistled from above, clattering against the stone streets and thudding into the doors of nearby homes. The horses galloped through the narrow streets of Rome, and despite the constant barrage of arrows, Valentine and his companions managed to disappear into the night, narrowly escaping capture.

LATER THAT SAME NIGHT, outside Bruttius's residence, beneath the shadow of an ancient tree, a solitary figure lingered. Valentine, his clothes still damp from falling into the fountain during his earlier duel with Claudius, scanned the second-floor windows of the humble abode. He picked up a smooth pebble and tossed it gently toward a weathered wooden shutter. The pebble struck with a soft thud, and soon, the shutter creaked open, revealing Porcia's anxious face.

"Porcia, it is I, Valentine," he whispered urgently.

"What matter brings you here so late?" Porcia asked, her voice steady but sharp.

"Please, Porcia—bring Agatha down. I must speak with her at once!"

Before Porcia could reply, another face appeared at the neighboring window. "Valentine? Is that truly you?"

"Yes, it is I," he answered, his voice carrying a sigh of relief.

"Wait there," Agatha whispered, her tone urgent yet cautious.

"If Father or Tiber hear us..." Porcia began, her voice heavy with worry.

"Quiet, Porcia—help me reach him," Agatha interrupted sharply, and though reluctant, Porcia obliged.

Moments later, the ancient front door of Bruttius's home creaked open, revealing Porcia's silhouette as she assisted Agatha.

As Valentine emerged from the shadows, the moonlight illuminated his anxious expression. He approached them, his voice barely a whisper, "Agatha."

"Valentine, this is hardly an appropriate time to—" Porcia began.

"Enough, Porcia," Agatha interrupted, her voice calm yet authoritative. "What brings you here at this late hour, my love?" she asked Valentine.

As Valentine's hands gently met Agatha's, Porcia exclaimed alarmingly, "He's wet and has blood on his tunic!"

"Valentine, are you hurt?" Agatha asked urgently.

"No, I am unharmed," he replied, pausing briefly as his gaze shifted to Porcia. "May we speak—alone, for a moment?"

"Agatha, if father—" Porcia started to protest again.

"Porcia!" Agatha cut her off sharply. She turned back to Valentine, her expression softening slightly. "That will be fine."

"May I take your arm?"

"You may," Agatha responded, smiling gently.

"Do not go far," Porcia called after them as Valentine and Agatha walked away.

They approached a clearing bathed in moonlight. The soft illumination filtered through the trees, casting gentle shadows around them. They paused by a giant oak, where Valentine, his voice heavy with emotion, said, "I fear I have come to bid you farewell."

Agatha's voice cracked with frustration: "What? Why must you always depart?"

Valentine's expression was grim as he responded, "The emperor does not share our Christian belief. He slaughters the innocent in his pursuit of me...and I have been forced to take lives again."

"The entire town speaks of your valor by the river," Agatha countered, her voice filled with pride and sorrow. "They tell of how you rescued Christians from the emperor's forces at Prisca and Antonius's wedding. You fought to protect others, not to harm."

Valentine sighed, the weight of his choices evident in his eyes. "Yet, I fear I am becoming the man I promised myself I would never again be. Even one of my brothers has turned against me."

"Then, he is a fool."

"I am putting too many in harm's way," Valentine whispered, the burden of his actions weighing heavily on him.

"And I? Am I in harm's way?" Agatha turned toward him, seeking comfort in his embrace.

"I cannot be certain. Should the emperor learn of you, he would seek your life as swiftly as he seeks mine," Valentine said, his voice trembling with raw vulnerability.

"Then, take me with you," Agatha responded, her voice fierce and determined.

"Agatha, we would need to depart at once and live far from here."

"If that home is with you, then where we live matters not," Agatha replied, her resolve clear.

"Your father would not approve."

"My father would, in time, accept my decision."

"You could be harmed, Agatha—possibly tortured."

"No more than if I were to endure another day without you," Agatha declared, her determination unyielding.

In that moment, time seemed to stand still as the depth of their connection struck Valentine with overwhelming intensity. He had intended to bid her farewell, assuming she would understand his reasoning and reluctantly let him go. Yet, as he stood there, he quickly realized there was no turning away from their love. Gently, he placed Agatha's hand over his heart, allowing the rapid rhythm beneath her fingertips to convey what words could not. Beneath the soft, moonlit sky, he gazed at her with deliberate grace, captivated by the beauty that had entranced him since childhood. His heart raced, and his voice trembled as he summoned the courage to make his deepest request: "Agatha, will you marry me?"

Her sharp intake of breath pierced the stillness of the night. "Yes...with all my heart," she whispered, her eyes glistening with tears that reflected her overwhelming joy and love.

Valentine stood taller than ever, his face breaking into a broad smile as she pulled him close. He gently cradled her chin as she closed her eyes, sensing what would come. Their breaths mingled, their hearts beat in perfect harmony as their lips met, and the world around them seemed to dissolve. As they were illuminated by the moon's glow, their kiss felt like the culmination of their shared history, a perfect union where every moment of their lives had led to this one.

Unbeknownst to them, Porcia, ever watchful and protective, had followed and observed from a vantage close enough to overhear their conversation. Her eyes widened with a mix of envy and surprise. After witnessing their profound connection, she could contain herself no longer and called out to Agatha, her voice cutting through the magical silence.

"Agatha!" Porcia hissed from her hiding spot.

The lovers reluctantly parted, their faces flushed with the heat of their embrace. Valentine leaned in, his voice a soft murmur, "Tomorrow, when the sun is at its peak and your Father is away—have Porcia sneak you away and bring you to the brook bridge, where we met at Lupercalia. From there, we will depart for new beginnings."

"I will be there, my love," Agatha promised, her smile radiant in the moonlight.

"Agatha, we must return!" Porcia called out from behind her tree, urgency in her tone. "Father will punish us both if he wakes!"

"I know, Porcia." Agatha nodded, her voice tinged with amusement at her younger sister's insistent nature. She turned back to Valentine. "Until then, my love."

Valentine's expression turned serious as his voice dropped to a whisper, "Agatha, speak to no one of our plans."

"As you wish."

"I love you, Agatha," Valentine declared, his voice thick with emotion. As he spoke the words, he realized it was the first time he had ever confessed his love to her out loud.

"I love you too," she responded, her voice cracking with emotion.

Valentine then gently steered Agatha back toward Porcia, who was waiting. His broad smile reflected his joy. "I am thankful, Porcia," he said warmly. "Good night, and God bless you both!"

CHAPTER 26

BROOK BRIDGE

"Unless one has loved himself,
he hardly understands the nature of a lover."
—PLAUTUS

At the peak of daylight, ominous clouds gathered on the horizon. The weathered stone pillars and arches of the brook bridge, where Valentine and Agatha had rekindled their love, stood gracefully above the gentle stream. Valentine gently held a single red helleborus in his hand, its vibrant petals defying the winter chill. His eyes drifted to his bloodstained tunic, the two objects stark in their contrast. Contemplating his future, he knew it would be marked by unrelenting adversity, yet like the resilient flower in his grasp, he too would find a way to endure.

Valentine looked downstream to where Marius and the others discreetly hid among the streamside shrubs. His plan was clear: meet Agatha, retrieve Regalus, and they would depart together for Arretium to begin a new life together. There, they could find refuge among friends, and Claudius's men would find it far more difficult to discover them living in such a remote area. As Valentine contemplated the shift from a solitary existence to that of a family man, a profound wave of emotion swept over him. The thought of marrying Agatha, raising Regalus, building a home, reconnecting with his cherished community, and introducing new and old friends to one another filled him with an overwhelming sense of anticipation and excitement.

His gaze shifted toward the direction of Agatha's distant home as the clouds above crept closer. His heart raced, yet a growing worry gnawed at him with each passing moment. She was late, and there was still no sign of her. Closing his eyes, he tilted his head upward, letting the first warmth of the otherwise cool winter season to caress his face, seeking a fleeting moment of calm amid his concerns.

However, the distant sound of horses abruptly shattered this serenity, their hoofbeats breaking the stillness and growing louder, more ominous with each passing moment.

Valentine's eyes snapped open, and a wave of dread washed over him. From nearly every direction, soldiers on horseback began to converge, swiftly encircling his location.

Quickly assessing the options for escape, Valentine realized the only viable route was downstream, where Marius and his men awaited. However, running toward them would undoubtedly lead the soldiers to follow, endangering his friends. They were severely outnumbered, and he knew it. For a moment, he considered taking the risk. But then, he leaped onto the bridge, stood as tall as he could, and with all the force his lungs could muster, shouted: "RIDE!"

Marius jumped to Valentine's command, swiftly mounting his horse as Proculo, Linus, and Efebus followed suit. Once they were all atop their horses, they witnessed over a hundred soldiers materializing around Valentine, rapidly closing in from all directions. The sight was startling.

"Curse the gods!" Marius cursed like a pagan. "He stands surrounded!"

"What shall we do?!" Linus cried out, panic rising in his voice.

"It appears as if they dispatched an entire Praetorian cohort to capture him," observed Proculo.

A few Praetorians noticed them from a distance and began to ride in their direction. Marius hesitated, his heart pounding in his chest, as he locked eyes with Valentine across the distance. In that brief moment, an unspoken conversation passed between them, laden with the weight of a thousand words. He saw the acceptance in Valentine's expression, the steely resolve to face what was to come. His sacrifice was clear. Marius's mind raced—every fiber of his being screamed to rush to Valentine's aid, to defy the overwhelming odds and fight to the death by his best friend's side. Yet he knew that doing so would only squander their lives in a futile gesture.

With a heavy heart, he reluctantly turned his horse away. "We cannot prevail this day," Marius declared, his voice thick with anguish, urging his horse forward with a forceful kick as the others followed.

Valentine released a deep breath as he watched them vanish downstream, the widening gap between them and the pursuing soldiers granting a crucial lead.

"Descend from that bridge!" Maximus commanded, sitting high and imposing on his horse.

Valentine turned to face his captor, surveying the sea of soldiers mounted around him from his elevated position on the bridge. "Oh, Agatha," he whispered, his voice a mix of regret and longing as the circle of soldiers closed in, finally taking him into custody.

AGATHA'S BEDROOM was a silent witness to the turmoil of her emotions. Curled up on the bed, she lay distraught, her body tightly folded, overcome by grief. Broken objects littered the floor around her, remnants of her despair, thrown in moments of anguish. With every cry, she released the deep-seated feelings of deceit and heartbreak.

"How could you?! How could you?!" she sobbed.

Standing near the doorway, Porcia responded with frustration and concern: "It was not my doing! Father reported him!" she exclaimed, her voice trembling.

"*You* told Father! I told you not to tell him!"

"What was I to do, allow my only sister to run off with a criminal and say nothing? Father would have *my* head!" Porcia retorted, her frustration palpable.

"That is precisely what you should have done, Porcia! What about you and Marius? Is it not the same?" Agatha rose from her bed with a sudden burst of energy, her blind eyes glistening with tears and determination. "I trusted you!" she cried, her voice breaking with emotion. "Valentine warned me not to speak of this—what a fool I am!"

"This was for your own protection, Agatha! This is madness—you could be persecuted if caught with Valentine!"

"No, Porcia—this is love! Something I have never experienced! Something I never thought possible! And the moment it appeared, you would have it slain as slowly as it had arrived!" Agatha cried out, her arms swinging wildly in Porcia's direction.

Porcia swiftly sidestepped her frantic assaults, her heart racing with the realization of Agatha's deep pain and fierce passion.

"I hate you! Do you hear me? I hate you and never want to hear your voice again!" she yelled.

"Agatha!" Porcia cried out, shaken.

"I hate you!" Agatha screamed again as Porcia hastily retreated from the room, overwhelmed by Agatha's intense, unrestrained outbursts.

Once outside, Porcia quickly shut the door and, acting on a protective instinct, turned the key to lock it from the outside—a measure only their father had resorted to on rare occasions when they were younger.

As the unmistakable sound of the lock clicked into place, Agatha lunged toward the door, her voice desperate and commanding: "Don't you dare lock me in here! Don't you dare!" But her plea was met only by the fading sound of Porcia's footsteps descending the stairs.

The room seemed to shrink around Agatha, the walls closing in with each breath. Exhausted, she slumped to the floor, her back sliding down the locked bedroom door. Her fingers lingered on the handle as she murmured, "Don't you dare."

CHAPTER 27

DIVINE PRESENCE

"He conquers who endures."
—*PERSIUS*

A heavy silence hung over the *Campus Martius* as the Praetorian Guards led Valentine, shackled at both hands and feet, onto a broad execution platform. The wooden rack, placed at the center of the square, was flanked by instruments of torture, their presence a stark reminder of the emperor's unyielding authority. Once a space for grand civic events, this now urbanized district, filled with temples and monuments, had been transformed into a grim stage for imperial justice. The crowd had gathered in one of the remaining open squares, every eye fixed on the condemned.

The audience was as diverse as the empire itself. Esteemed nobles draped in fine togas stood beside humble farmers in simple tunics. Families with children mingled among bustling merchants, while soldiers on duty kept a watchful eye, ensuring order amid the charged atmosphere. All had come to witness Valentine's execution, a man surrounded by conflicting rumors and seen through many lenses—

hailed as a brave soldier by some, revered as a compassionate healer and priest by others, and regarded by many as a dangerous enigma or threat to imperial power.

As the distant clamor of trumpets heralded Emperor Claudius's approach, Senators Didius and Paternus stood on a raised platform near the execution site, their expressions a mix of resignation and distaste. Didius shifted uncomfortably, his gaze fixed on Valentine, shackled and stoic, awaiting his fate. "Despite my sentiments of Christian believers, this is a mockery of our justice," he murmured to Paternus, his voice barely carrying over the crowd's roar. "Once again, Caesar has bypassed every traditional safeguard our judicial system offers. No trial, no defense—just the will of one man."

Paternus nodded grimly, his eyes scanning the assembly. "And yet, the people accept it. Drawn to the spectacle and blinded by fear."

The two men watched in silent agreement as Claudius ascended to an elevated platform near the stage, each step steadied by a crutch, a necessity after his recent duel with Valentine, which had left him with a deep, festering wound. Though he struggled to maintain his composure, the sheen of sweat on his brow and the subtle tremors in his hands betrayed a worsening sickness that had taken hold of him.

Empress Serena, carrying Claudia in her arms, followed closely behind Claudius, observing every slight falter in his posture with detached interest. She took her seat beside him, her attention on the unfolding event. Meanwhile, their loyal attendants, General Aurelian and Iset stood behind them.

"You appear unwell, husband," Serena observed with measured detachment. "Are you certain our presence is necessary today?"

"There is no force that could keep me from this execution. All of Rome must witness the fate of those who defy our traditions and cling to their dangerous superstition."

"And if Valentine does not renounce his faith?" Serena asked.

"He will," Claudius replied with cold certainty. "Rest assured, we shall all witness the madness and frailty of your former suitor today."

"You could have avoided offending the gods and ordered his execution on the outskirts of Rome," Serena remarked, her tone edged with quiet reproach.

"Our gods will understand, and Romans will be reminded today of the consequences of forsaking our traditions." Claudius retorted, his words punctuated by a sudden, rasping cough.

Serena's eyes flashed with irritation as an officiant, draped in fine robes, ascended the stage and approached the podium.

Unfurling a scroll with the practiced ease of one used to commanding attention, he began: "Fellow Romans, Valentine Romanus stands accused of deserting his ranks and performing religious rites of the Christian God. By decree of Caesar, he is offered a choice: renounce his false god, and he will be granted a swift beheading. Refuse, and he shall face torture until death."

As the officiant's proclamation echoed across the Campus Martius, a mixture of cheers mingled with only a few boos. The event evoked the atmosphere of a gladiatorial contest, drawing the attention of many in attendance simply to partake in the day's entertainment. Cabbage and other vegetables arced through the air, landing with dull thuds against the wooden rack, one on Valentine's head, prompting bursts of laughter from sections of the crowd.

Valentine remained silent, his expression unyielding as the officiant raised his voice, directly addressing him. "Valentine, do you denounce your god?"

His silence prompted the officiant to gesture with deliberate authority toward the back of the stage. At the signal, Bruttius, known to the public as "The Executioner," stepped forward, and a ripple of anticipation swept through the crowd. Normally, such executions were left to slaves, but this was no ordinary event. Summoned by Caesar himself, Bruttius stood not only as the emperor's enforcer but as a father with a deeply personal grudge. Valentine had dared to steal his Agatha without his consent, and now the time had come to unleash a father's wrath. Clad in a simple yet imposing tunic, he gripped the heavy leather whip as the veins in his arms pulsed with anticipation.

Interspersed among the spectators, Marius, Efebus, Proculo, and Linus melded into the crowd near the front, their identities shrouded under voluminous capes. Porcia stood by Marius's side, with Tiber nearby, her emotions a turbulent mix of conflict and regret. Far in the back, another figure lurked even more concealed in deceit—Albus, with the hood of his cape drawn low to hide his face. His recent betrayal was a fresh wound, and to Valentine's watchful friends, he would become a marked target should they uncover his presence.

Onstage, Valentine clasped his hands together and began to pray silently, his lips moving with words meant only for divine ears. A murmur spread through the crowd as they observed his quiet act of devotion.

Claudius furrowed his brow in confusion and annoyance. "What is he doing?"

"He prays to the Christian God," Serena remarked.

"Splendid," Claudius responded, his voice tinged with sarcasm as he suppressed his cough. "Then the people shall see how powerless his god is, after all."

Bruttius drew back his whip and unleashed its fury onto Valentine's back. Each lash landed with a sickening crack that echoed across the square.

The initial strike delivered a sting so intense it defied description. Pain radiated through every limb, every instinct urging Valentine to scream for mercy. Yet, as the whip continued its brutal assault, he anchored himself in his newfound faith. Silently, he recited prayers, each word deepening his connection to the spiritual sanctuary he had cultivated over the past year.

In addition to his prayers, he drew from his qigong teachings. Through disciplined breathing and focused mental control, he entered a meditative state that helped him dissociate from the immediate pain. He visualized the pain as waves crashing against a rock—intense, but ultimately fleeting. This blend of sincere faith and qigong training enabled him to transcend physical suffering, placing him in a state of serene acceptance.

Instead of fueling the crowd's bloodlust, Valentine's resilience brought an unexpected stillness—gradually, the crowd grew silent as Bruttius delivered continued lashes.

Porcia fixed her eyes on the heartbreaking spectacle unfolding before the hushed audience. She had never watched her father torture a man before. The gentle giant to whom she eagerly served dinner each night, the pillar of her existence, had transformed into someone she no longer recognized. Unbeknownst to Bruttius, she had snuck out to watch the execution, naively assuming it would be more of a trial than torture. But this was not what Porcia had expected. With each swing that tore through the fabric of Valentine's tunic and into his back, it felt as if the blows were slicing into her heart. Tears of regret and shame for confiding in her father about Agatha and Valentine's plan to flee streamed down Porcia's cheeks as she witnessed the consequences of her actions.

From Claudius's vantage point, he spat out, "Why does he not beg for his life?" directing his query to Serena, whose eyes brimmed with tears as she cradled Claudia in her arms—now realizing more than ever that her daughter would never grow up to know her true father. She reflected upon her actions in attempting to have Valentine captured. They had been impulsive and reactive, driven by envy and a wounded ego. And as she watched Valentine, deep in prayer and miraculously defying Claudius's lashings, a profound sense of sadness washed over her.

"Serena!" Claudius snapped, jolting her from her moment of reflection. "Don't you dare show pity for him!"

Serena wiped the tears from her eyes, tucking her emotions and hatred for Claudius deep inside—a constant turmoil within her, simmering like a volcano ready to erupt with fury.

Then, unexpectedly, the crowd stirred. From among the sea of onlookers, defiant shouts erupted: "Enough!" cried one voice. "Set him free!" another demanded. "He was a soldier of Rome!" shouted yet another.

Valentine's reputation as a healer, soldier, and pious man began to resonate with the people, igniting a belief that the gods might favor him. As the mob's outcry intensified, the atmosphere crackled with energy, as they became increasingly convinced of his innocence.

Realizing the tide of opinion was turning, Claudius felt a sudden pang of anxiety. "What is the meaning of this?! What are they shouting?" he demanded, his voice laced with confusion and alarm as the cries from the crowd grew louder.

Serena looked on in disbelief. "They demand his release."

"This can't be!" Claudius exclaimed, his cough worsening as sweat dripped from his brow. Neither of them had witnessed the mob steer away from the spectacle of torture before.

Suddenly, a cabbage sailed through the air, aimed at the officiant and Bruttius. Stung by the unexpected backlash, the officiant frantically attempted to restore order. "Good people of Rome," he pleaded, his voice desperate for control, "this man is a criminal!"

"He's a healer!" shouted a woman from the crowd.

"He's a man of faith!" another voice added.

"Enough!" Claudius screamed from his platform, signaling Bruttius to halt the torture. Rising slowly, Claudius began to make his way toward the central execution platform as the blast of royal horns echoed across the Campus Martius. Fifty Praetorian Guards swiftly moved to form a pathway, parting the crowd like a tide.

Aurelian shouted, "Make way for Caesar!"

As Claudius approached the stage, a cloak of regality seemed to envelop him as he hobbled up the steps toward Valentine. The once rowdy mob now sank into a profound silence, hanging on every word as Claudius addressed them directly.

"Fellow Romans, this Christian betrays us by disregarding our law. Today, we offered him a chance to renounce his superstition, yet he refuses!"

Every eye in the square fixed on Claudius as he leaned close to Valentine's ear and whispered, "Denounce your god, and I shall allow you to die gracefully. Why must you defy your Caesar so?"

Valentine opened his eyes, pausing from his mindful prayer, and met Claudius's gaze with unwavering resolve: "You are no Caesar of mine."

"Salt his wounds!" Claudius spat.

The crowd grumbled as no one dared to intervene.

Bruttius's hand clutched the rough edge of a wooden tub, scooping up a handful of coarse salt—the cruel agent of torment. Those watching felt a collective wrenching in their hearts as he poured the salt onto Valentine's bloodstained back, sharply intensifying the pain.

Serena stood, placing her hand over her mouth, barely able to watch the scene unfold. Meanwhile, in the crowd, Porcia, a portrait of anguish, tucked her head into Marius's arms, seeking comfort in his embrace.

"Let him plead to his god for mercy now!" Claudius boomed.

As Bruttius inflicted the cruel sting of salt, Valentine stoically resisted displaying any signs of pain as his silent prayers resonated through the arena. A hushed awe descended upon the crowd until a lone voice broke the silence, declaring, "His prayers hold power!"

In an instant, like a gust of wind igniting a flame, passionate cries echoed through the crowd, chanting in unison: "RELEASE! RELEASE! RELEASE!"

Mortified and humiliated, Claudius suddenly appeared frail, doubling over in a coughing fit as he realized he was losing the mob's favor.

Aurelian swiftly intervened, guiding Claudius away from the escalating chaos. Murmurs concerning Caesar's health rippled through the onlookers, adding another layer of tension to the unfolding events.

As turmoil escalated, the officiant found himself gripped by a moment of uncertainty. As he observed Claudius being led away in a state of weakness and the crowd's anger nearing intolerable levels, he swiftly commanded Bruttius, "Take the prisoner to the jail!"

Bruttius swiftly unshackled Valentine from the wooden rack, his movements decisive as he began to escort him away. Through the cacophony of screams from the crowd and the barrage of vegetables hurled at him, Bruttius also felt the weight of the crowd's condemnation. At that moment, he questioned every belief he had held about the righteousness of turning Valentine in.

The crowd erupted into cheers as Valentine, his body nearly broken but his spirit unyielding, was dragged away.

Amid the crowd, Albus watched in silence. He reached into the pocket of his tunic and retrieved a small bag of coins—the reward he had accepted from Claudius in exchange for betraying Valentine and the trust of those who had once counted him as a friend. Unable to bear the weight of his actions any longer, Albus placed the bag in the hands of a crippled child standing nearby and quietly walked away. Regret washed over him as he reflected on his brother, Scaro, and how he might have judged him on this day if he were still alive.

Haggard and overwhelmed by the public spectacle, Claudius staggered into the dimly lit carriage, his movements betraying the weight of the events.

Aurelian followed swiftly, his concern evident. Inside, Serena held Claudia close, unable to meet her husband's gaze, still reeling from what she had just witnessed.

"Caesar, are you well?" Aurelian inquired, breaking the heavy silence.

Claudius struggled to speak, his voice strained with emotion and weakened by his condition. "Aurelian, they must ensure that Valentine cannot pray to his Christian God! Order Bruttius to hood his head tomorrow and move the execution outside the city's walls—away from the mob! We have indeed angered the gods."

"As you wish."

As the carriage pulled away, Serena gently closed her eyes, cradling Claudia, her turmoil roiling within her—a moment not overlooked by Aurelian.

Chapter 28

A Saintly Man

"There is nothing certain, but the uncertain."
—Pliny the Elder

Within the humble kitchen of Bruttius's home, the flickering oil lamp cast elongated shadows across the room. Porcia paced back and forth, her footsteps resonating on the timeworn wooden floor. Suddenly, the front door groaned open, and Bruttius stepped inside. He appeared disheveled, his tunic marred by stains from the cabbage remnants hurled at him by the angry mob at Valentine's torture earlier that day. Meeting Porcia's accusing gaze, his weary eyes spoke volumes about his tumultuous day.

"How could you?" Porcia's voice quivered.

"Do not take that tone with me, daughter," Bruttius responded, his voice rising defensively. "I am in no mood."

Porcia kept her voice deliberately low, careful not to disturb Agatha, whom she had freed from her locked bedroom just before attending Valentine's execution— and who had now placed herself in self-imposed seclusion. "You promised me that our actions were solely to protect Agatha—to prevent her from leaving us. Never did I presume you would turn Valentine over to the authorities so that you could subject him to your torture! He's a fellow Christian!" Porcia protested, her voice trembling with the weight of betrayal and her own guilt.

"We discussed this, Porcia. He's also a fugitive and deserted his ranks! And I will not stand idly by while a criminal attempts to run off with one of my daughters!"

"You tortured him beyond what any mortal should ever endure!" Porcia exclaimed, her voice breaking as tears brimmed in her eyes.

"Torturing criminals is my duty, Porcia. Decreed by the emperor himself. It is not for me to decide the justice in it."

Suddenly, Agatha's bedroom door swung open as she began her quiet descent of the staircase.

"You do not know Valentine, Father. He's a good—" Porcia began.

"Enough!" Bruttius's voice boomed. "It is not for me to acquaint myself with the men I am required to execute—he's a criminal—and you've shared enough for me to discern his character."

Agatha arrived at the landing, clasping her staff firmly at that moment. "Please continue, sister."

"Agatha," Porcia said, surprised.

"Porcia, when you spoke to Father about Valentine, did you tell him he's the same man who rescued me from being attacked by wolves as a child—and who also saved me from being assaulted at the Saturnalia Festival while you and Tiber left me to fend for myself?" Agatha asked.

"What?!" Bruttius exclaimed, turning to face Porcia. "Is this true?"

Porcia bowed her head, ashamed of the events from that day.

"And did you inform Father that Valentine deserted his post only after being struck by an arrow—friendly fire ordered by the emperor, no less?" Agatha continued, her voice unwavering.

"No," she muttered, her admission barely audible.

"Yet come, sister. You've spun many tales of Valentine, yet you've withheld the true breadth of his deeds. Perhaps Father is familiar with some of the couples Valentine has quietly united here or the sick he has restored to health," Agatha's words were sharp, like arrows aimed precisely at Porcia's heart.

"Enough!" Porcia's voice broke. "If you were to leave with him, what would I do?! Who would I be?!" Tears streamed down her cheeks as she revealed her most profound insecurities. "Forgive me, sister." With those final words, Porcia hurried upstairs, her footsteps echoing in the hall before slamming her door shut.

"By the fates," Bruttius remarked with heavy sarcasm, eyeing the scene before him. "Look what this criminal has wrought upon my daughters."

With a commanding strike, Agatha brought her walking staff crashing down onto the wooden table, producing a resounding thud that made Bruttius jump back in surprise. "I am blind, not foolish, Father! He is no criminal. He is a good man—and his name is Valentine!"

"Agatha," Bruttius murmured, stunned and nearly silenced by the force of her conviction.

She turned to climb the stairs but stopped just short of taking a step: "Never have I felt such shame in you." With those parting words, she resumed her ascent.

Bruttius's heart sank, his eyes brimming with tears as he watched his daughter feel her way back into the darkness of her room, leaving him with a singular, heart-wrenching thought of complete and utter failure as a father.

MEANWHILE, in the emperor's private chambers, a *medicus*, Lucius, a short and slender physician with sharp, intelligent eyes, examined Claudius's leg. The wound inflicted by Valentine upon the emperor had worsened, now swollen and reddened, with pus oozing from its ragged edges, filling the room with a foul odor. Angry red lines radiated from the gash that felt hot to the touch. Despite the gravity of the situation, Lucius's hands remained steady as he applied a poultice of medicinal herbs, known for their healing benefits.

Claudius lay in his bed, wracked with fever, chills, and a persistent cough. Lucius worked diligently, cleaning the wound with wine, trusting in its cleansing properties to keep the injury from worsening. Once satisfied, he applied a mixture of honey and herbs before carefully wrapping the leg in linen, hoping to stave off the spread of the illness.

"I bid you good night, Emperor," Lucius added respectfully before rising and exiting the chamber.

Having silently observed from the corner of the room, Serena followed the physician into the hallway, pulling the heavy door shut behind them. Her eyes flickered with curiosity, concern, and shock at the rapid turn of events.

"Will he recover? Is it serious?"

"I fear the wound has worsened, Empress," Lucius said gravely. "He needs time to recover. Rest assured, I am using the most effective remedies at our disposal."

"He wishes to attend an execution tomorrow. It will be held outside the capital, along the second mile of the Via Flaminia."

"The prisoner you speak of—is it Valentine Romanus?"

"Yes," she replied softly.

A wry smile crossed Lucius's face. "I beg your pardon, my empress; it's just that..."

"It's what? Speak freely." Serena inquired.

"Rumor has it that Valentine was an apprentice to Deodatus, a renowned healer along with his wife, Charu. Both were esteemed figures from Arretium, executed for Christian worship under the emperor's decree."

"How does this concern my husband's condition?"

"For a wound that resists healing like this, I would have sought the wisdom of Deodatus and Charu. With their deaths, however, Valentine alone holds their knowledge and skills."

"Are you suggesting that the same man my husband aims to have executed tomorrow, the one who caused his injury by slicing open his leg, could also be his only hope for recovery?" Serena asked, bewildered.

"The irony is striking, yet that is precisely what I am saying."

"The emperor would sooner perish than accept aid from a foe."

"Let us hope for a less dire outcome," Lucius said, his gaze steely with resolve.

Lucius handed the empress a vial and said, "This medicine must be administered to the emperor three times daily—without it, I fear his condition will worsen. Just a few drops in water or directly onto his tongue—no more, no less."

Serena nodded, cradling the vial in her hand. "I am thankful, Lucius."

"Empress," he replied respectfully, before turning and exiting the room.

Suddenly, the lurking silhouette of General Aurelian, who had been eavesdropping on their conversation from the shadows, emerged. "Empress, you called for me."

"Yes, General," Serena replied. "There is much to discuss."

Aurelian and Serena quietly walked off into the darkness.

THAT SAME NIGHT, Bruttius returned to the prison in Rome, where Valentine was being held, consumed by his emotions. Its walls loomed ominously in the darkness, a formidable symbol of the empire's uncompromising justice.

As Bruttius approached the prison, the scene before him starkly contrasted its grim façade. Thirty somber figures stood in line, illuminated by the flickering torchlight. A small terracotta figurine of a shepherd carrying a lamb was set out, surrounded by a mound of helleborus flowers.

"This can't be," Bruttius muttered under his breath.

A jailor, nearing the end of his watch, approached. "Manius, what are those citizens doing? I thought I told you to be vigilant tonight," Bruttius questioned the jailor.

"They're Christian sympathizers, magistrate. They've been coming by all night to pay homage to Valentine, nothing more. I deemed it harmless, considering his execution is imminent."

"Very well," Bruttius replied, though his gaze lingered on the Christians as they silently laid down red flowers and prayed before the small figure for Valentine's life. The sight stirred something deep within the executioner. What would Camilla, his past wife, think of his actions? How would she judge him? The questions gnawed at him in the quiet of the night.

"General Aurelian left orders that the emperor decreed the execution to be switched to Via Flaminia tomorrow at the peak of daylight," the jailer reported.

"What method?" Bruttius inquired.

"Beheading," the jailer replied. "He desires it to be swift and in secret to avoid any more outburst."

"Very well. Good night, Manius."

From a nearby rooftop, Marius, Linus, Efebus, and Baro quietly observed Bruttius enter the prison. Linus turned to his cousin and asked, "Baro, are you certain there's no alternative entrance to the prison? There are guards everywhere."

"There may be one other route; follow me," he urged as the men swiftly descended from the rooftop.

Inside the prison, Valentine lay asleep, sprawled across a straw bed on the unforgiving stone floor. The harsh scrape of a boot against stone announced Bruttius's approach. He carried an oil lamp, its dim flame flickering against the oppressive darkness of the cramped spaces. The weak light cast wavering shadows on the damp interior, briefly illuminating the ancient iron chains and manacles that adorned the walls.

Gripping another prisoner firmly by the arm, Bruttius led the shackled man toward Valentine. This new arrival, whose figure mirrored Valentine's, had a face carved from granite, marked by a fierce scowl and piercing eyes radiating menace. The oppressive air of the prison seemed to amplify the tension as they approached Valentine.

"Rise!" Bruttius barked, peering down at Valentine while unlocking the door and shoving the shackled prisoner inside.

Startled from sleep, Valentine slowly sat up on his cot and eyed the shackled prisoner, recognition flashing across his face as the brute began to immediately protest: "I'm not sharing a cell with this man. Take me back to my—" But before the prisoner could finish his sentence, Bruttius swiftly swung his club, striking the man down. He crumpled to the ground, his words silenced by the force of the blow.

Valentine abruptly rose to his feet, his expression a mix of confusion and concern, having witnessed Bruttius's sudden and violent assault.

"Help me place him on your pallet," Bruttius commanded firmly.

With Valentine's assistance, Bruttius lifted the prisoner's limp body, maneuvering him onto the cot. Once the prisoner settled, Bruttius straightened up and faced Valentine squarely, his eyes cold and calculating.

"Do you love my daughter?" Bruttius asked, his gaze piercing as he scrutinized Valentine's eyes.

"With every ounce of my being," Valentine replied without hesitation.

"How can you be so certain?"

"What reason do I have to lie to you? You've already tortured me and will behead me tomorrow."

"She told me you rescued her from being violated. Is this true?" Bruttius asked.

"It is—and from the very man you just placed on my pallet," Valentine replied as he looked down at the shackled man. It was Hercules, the same brute Valentine had given a beating to at the Saturnalia festival.

Bruttius's eyes turned fiercely intense as he gazed down at Hercules, now lying unconscious in Valentine's straw bed. "I will tend to *him* later."

"How is Agatha?" Valentine asked, his voice heavy with concern.

"She cries herself to sleep with thoughts of you," Bruttius replied, his tone momentarily softening.

Valentine turned his gaze toward the flickering oil lamp, his expression tinged with sorrow. "Fate has never favored us," he remarked, his voice heavy with sadness.

Bruttius had wrestled with his conflicting loyalties throughout the night. His commitment to the empire was paramount, yet his obligations as a father held a sacred place in his heart. "I will allow you both to bid farewell," Bruttius declared. "Yet, should you seek to flee, the suffering you endured today would pale in comparison to the punishment I would unleash upon you tomorrow. Understood?"

With a solemn nod, Valentine accepted the grave terms set before him. Bruttius extended a worn cloak from the shadows and said, "Cover yourself; it will be no small feat sneaking you out of the city in the dead of night."

At the turn of the midnight hour, they arrived back at Bruttius's home in Suburbium.

Porcia, unaware of her father's absence and unable to sleep, had descended the stairs for a late-night bite. The heavy door creaked open, revealing the executioner, followed by a cloaked figure.

"Father, where have you...?" Porcia's voice trailed off as she recognized the cloaked figure. "Valentine." Her expression transformed with a mixture of astonishment and joy.

"Wake your sister," Bruttius commanded sharply. "And bring her outside."

"Yes, Father," Porcia replied quickly, her steps hastening upstairs.

"Outside," Bruttius directed Valentine, leading him back out the door into the cool night air.

"I am allowing you to bid your farewells, yet do not stray far," Bruttius warned sternly.

"We will not," Valentine responded, his figure silhouetted against the moonlit meadow. The offer from Bruttius to see Agatha was beyond belief. Certain he would never see her again in his lifetime, he had resigned himself to meeting her only in the afterlife.

"Valentine, is it truly you?" Agatha's voice emerged from the shadowed doorway like an angel sent from Heaven.

"Yes, it is I," he replied. Despite his exhaustion and the wounds from the torture Bruttius had inflicted on him, he managed a weary smile and quickly approached her.

Their embrace was tender and poignant.

"May I take your arm?" Valentine asked gently.

"You may," Agatha whispered, her voice thick with emotion.

Behind Agatha, in the doorway, Porcia's eyes shimmered with

tears. Happiness for her sister and sorrow for the fate that awaited Valentine filled her heart with turmoil.

Bruttius, still maintaining his stoic demeanor, "You do not have much time."

"That is a familiar tale for us," Valentine responded, his voice soft as he cradled Agatha's hand. "Come, let us walk."

Together, they stepped into the gentle moonlight, cherishing the fleeting moments they had left.

Moved by her father's unexpected act of kindness, Porcia wrapped her arms around Bruttius in a heartfelt embrace. "Thank you, Father," she murmured.

A short distance away, just beyond earshot, Valentine and Agatha sat atop a grassy knoll, their figures silhouetted against the moonlit sky. Facing each other in quiet solitude, they appeared to be in their own secluded world.

"I did not think we would be together again," Agatha confessed.

"You will always be with me; you must know that," Valentine reassured her warmly.

"Do you fear death?"

"I fear not seeing your beautiful smile," he replied, gently caressing her face.

"I wish I could see your face," Agatha murmured, her voice filled with longing.

Valentine paused while reflecting on an ancient qigong healing technique Charu had once spoken of. "There is something I have long wished to attempt with you," he said thoughtfully.

"What is it?"

"Do you trust me?" he asked softly.

"With all my heart."

"Then, close your eyes and tell me your last memory of sight," Valentine requested gently.

"For what purpose?" Agatha asked, a hint of concern in her voice.

"We shall see," he replied enigmatically.

Agatha closed her eyes, giving a nod of consent. Valentine quickly rubbed his hands together, then carefully placed his palms over her closed eyes.

"Your hands, I sense their warmth," she whispered.

"Look into them without opening your eyes. What do you see?" he urged gently.

"You know I cannot," she exclaimed, her frustration evident.

"Let us pretend that you can. Describe your last memory of sight as if you were reliving it now," he coaxed softly.

"It comes to me like a bad dream," she began, her voice reflecting the memory's distant and haunting nature.

"Know that I am here with you. What do you see?"

Agatha paused, delving deep into her subconscious. Her breaths became measured, her face a canvas of concentration as she journeyed within, searching for that elusive memory.

Suddenly, it began to come to her—a version of herself at the tender age of thirteen, dressed in a simple, faded tunic, her hair a touch unrulier, as she took refuge in a dim corner of the living space in their home.

As she narrated, her voice trembled: "I was hiding from my mother while she prepared supper. My father and Porcia were away." She hesitated momentarily, the weight of the memory pressing on her. "This is difficult for me. Must we do this?"

"Know that I am by your side. What was your mother preparing?"

"She was making bread," she whispered.

"Can you smell the aroma from her kitchen?"

Agatha drew in a deep breath and replied, "Yes, the warm scent of freshly baked bread mingled with the earthy fragrance of dried herbs hanging from the wooden beams. I remember the clatter of iron pans and the gentle bubbling from a clay pot over the fire. The kitchen was filled with the soft sound of her wooden spoon scraping against the earthenware as she mixed the dough." Her demeanor easing somewhat.

"What more do you perceive, feel, or hear? Trust your senses," Valentine encouraged, his voice gentle and guiding.

Suddenly, the scene vividly unfolded in Agatha's mind as if she had been whisked back in time. She could envision her mother clearly in the softly illuminated kitchen, surrounded by the customary decorations indicative of Roman domestic life. She paused upon hearing the voice of Camilla, her mother: "Agatha, where are you hiding?"

From the shadows, the soft, innocent laughter of a younger Agatha echoed softly.

Her mother smiled faintly, kneading the dough with her hands. "I hear you."

But then, a formidable figure burst through their front door, shattering their tranquil evening. Agatha's mother turned in shock and asked the man, "By what right do you intrude upon our home in this manner?! My husband—" her mother began to protest, but the burly man cut her off.

"Your husband murdered my brother—and I will have my revenge!" the man spat, his voice thick with hatred.

"That was Caesar's command! My husband had no choice—it was his duty!" she retorted, shielding Agatha's hiding place from his sight.

"You may tell that to my dead brother…when you see him," the burly man threatened.

Agatha's mother seized a butcher knife, her hands trembling with fear and defiance. "My husband shall see justice served upon you!"

"Not before I have my way with his wife!"

Hidden in the shadows, young Agatha remained silent, a terrified observer of the escalating violence. As her mother lunged forward, attempting to thrust her knife at the intruder, the burly man mercilessly countered with his dagger, sending it deep into Camilla's abdomen. Her piercing scream echoed through the room as she crumpled lifelessly to the cold floor.

Frozen and unable to muster a sound, young Agatha could only bear witness through tear-blurred eyes as the burly man plundered whatever treasures he could lay his hands on before fading into the engulfing shadows of the night.

With tentative steps, her sandaled feet scarcely drew near her stricken mother and settled by her side. Covering her eyes with trembling hands, she surrendered to her sorrow, tears cascading down her cheeks, vowing silently never to unveil her eyes to the world again.

"I cannot endure this—I cannot," Agatha murmured as a solitary tear carved a path down her colorless cheek.

"I am here," Valentine's voice reassured, providing a steady anchor amid the stormy sea of her memories. "Look further. What lies above your mother?"

Young Agatha slowly uncovered her hands from her eyes. The gruesome sight of her mother's visage, the grievous wound, and the ominous pool of dark blood seeping into the floor overwhelmed her senses.

"I cannot," Agatha's voice quivered.

"You can. Look upon her with gentle eyes. What do you see?"

With trepidation, she turned her gaze toward her mother. Suddenly, the room underwent a profound transformation. A mysterious light emanated from above, casting an ethereal glow. Within it, young Agatha observed her mother's luminous and tranquil form, ascending gracefully as her mother's spirit placed her hand over her heart in a gesture of love toward her daughter.

Agatha's voice trembled, laden with emotion: "I see her!"

"What do you see?" Valentine gently prodded, coaxing Agatha to peel back the layers of her memory.

"She sends me her love and ascends toward Heaven," Agatha's voice emerged, tearful yet imbued with a serene acceptance. As her mother's spirit rose, young Agatha mirrored the gesture, placing her hands over her heart.

"We're saying our farewells," Agatha murmured, her voice tinged with sorrow and joy.

"Your mother is at peace. She rests in His embrace. Now, slowly open your eyes, knowing she is safe," Valentine instructed gently. His calm and steadfast voice guided Agatha back to the present, offering her a sense of closure and tranquility.

Tears cascaded down Agatha's cheeks upon the tranquil grassy knoll, glimmering like pearls in the gentle sunlight. Valentine slowly removed his palms from her eyes with tender care, unveiling the world before her. A profound silence enveloped them.

Then, in a voice trembling with apprehension, Agatha whispered, "Something feels different. I'm frightened, Valentine."

"Fear not, dear maiden, God is with you," Valentine murmured soothingly. "Describe to me what you perceive."

As the darkness that had long held Agatha's vision captive dissolved, her world appeared as mere shades of gray. Slowly, these shades took on distinct shapes, and before long, colors started to seep through, vividly repainting her surroundings.

"I can see your face!" Agatha exclaimed, her voice filled with a blend of disbelief and joy. As her eyes adjusted to her newfound sight, she turned to look around.

"Colors dance before me! I can see the radiance of the moon!" Her jubilant cries pierced the tranquility of the night, imbuing the darkness with her newfound joy. "I can see you! I can see!"

Suddenly, Bruttius charged across the grass, his voice heavy with concern. "Agatha! What troubles you? Has he caused you harm?!"

Agatha lunged into her father's arms with the clarity and vibrancy that only the gift of sight could bestow. "Father, Father—behold! I am healed! It's a miracle! I saw Mother! She is safe, Father! Mother is safe!" Her words resounded with triumph as she released her father, spread her arms wide, and cried: "I CAN SEE!"

Bruttius, stunned, struggled to grasp the reality unfolding before him, questioning whether his prayers had been answered at last. He waved his hand quickly in front of his daughter's eyes, skeptical of such a miracle. In a swift motion, Agatha caught his arm midair, confirming the miracle that had come to pass, her smile widening as she affirmed, "I speak the truth, Father!"

Overwhelmed by the enormity of this moment, Bruttius sank to his knees, his voice reduced to a whisper as he gazed up at her and uttered, "Agatha, you can see." Tears carved paths down his weathered cheeks. Agatha knelt beside him, enveloping him in an embrace, and for the first time, she truly saw the pain and worry he had concealed for so long.

Porcia rushed to their side, her voice quivering with emotion. "What has transpired?!" she cried out.

"Valentine has healed me!" Agatha exclaimed, her face alight with radiant joy as she looked up at Porcia and pulled her to their embrace as well.

Struck by the enormity of the revelation, Porcia gazed deeply into her sister's eyes, realizing that they now followed her own.

"Agatha...you *can* see!" Porcia exclaimed, her voice trembling with disbelief. Overwhelmed by the moment, realization washed over her as Porcia joined her tearful father and sister in their embrace.

"I love you all!" Agatha's voice rang out.

Lifting his eyes, Bruttius, the formerly stoic magistrate and executioner turned toward Valentine, wordlessly expressing his heartfelt appreciation.

Valentine sat still, hardly able to believe his own eyes. A miracle had indeed transpired, and he recognized in that moment that he was merely the vessel of a divine act. His heart swelled with a mix of humility and awe.

LATER THAT NIGHT, in the flickering torchlight, Bruttius guided Valentine back through the prison. Upon entering, they discovered Hercules still unconscious and lying on the pallet. With a determined grunt, Bruttius proceeded to drag him away.

Valentine stepped back into the cell.

"It brings me no pleasure to return you here, Valentine," Bruttius admitted somberly.

Valentine's eyes, wearied yet brimming with compassion, met those of Bruttius. "It is the only way, Bruttius. Should you not, Agatha and many other Christians will perish."

"I have carried the burden of Camilla's passing and Agatha's affliction for as long as memory serves," he confessed, his voice heavy with emotion.

Valentine gently placed his hand on Bruttius's shoulder. "At times, we carry the past far longer than we should."

"I lost my faith when Camilla departed," Bruttius muttered. "You have aided me in rediscovering it."

"You lost your path," Valentine reassured him, his tone gentle and understanding. "It's a common affliction."

Bruttius's hands trembled as he hesitated before closing Valentine's cell door. "God will not forgive me for executing you," he murmured, his conscience in turmoil.

Suddenly, another door of the prison burst open, revealing Marius's imposing silhouette. "Marius," Valentine exclaimed in surprise.

"Release him—now!" Marius commanded, pressing a sharp, gleaming sword to Bruttius's neck. "Come, Valentine! We will subdue this beast!"

Linus, Proculo, and Efebus followed, poised for vengeance.

But Valentine's voice rang out: "No, Marius!"

"What did you say?!" Marius responded in disbelief.

"You heard me. Lower your swords—all of you," Valentine ordered.

"This man nearly tortured you to death and will soon kill you!"

"He was under orders, Marius—and he is Agatha and *Porcia's* father."

Marius hesitated, lowering his sword as he realized that killing Porcia's father would not help him win her favor.

"They will execute you, Valentine!" Efebus interjected, his voice filled with concern.

"And if I remain alive, the emperor will continue his pursuit of me and eventually capture and kill all of you...including Agatha," Valentine countered, his resolve unwavering. He stepped backward into his cell, his movements deliberate and resolute. "May this be how I am remembered." His words echoed through the oppressive stillness of the chamber.

A solemn silence enveloped the group, with each member feeling the immense gravity of the moment. Marius approached his friend. "Do not do this," Marius pleaded, but he knew Valentine was right. This was the only way. The emperor would never stop so long as he was alive.

"Promise me you will care for Regalus," Valentine said.

Shaking his head, Marius could barely utter a response. "I will, as if he were my own."

Valentine extended his hand. Their hands clasped. A deep emotion flickered across Marius's face, usually full of jest and laughter, now heavy with the weight of their farewell. His expression, once light-hearted, was transformed by the gravity of the moment.

The others paid their respects individually, leaving Bruttius to approach last. Valentine turned to Bruttius, his voice gentle yet carrying a weight of sincerity: "Bruttius, I have one favor to ask."

"Anything, tell me."

"I would like to write to Agatha. Could you bring me a scroll and stylus before you depart?"

"I will," Bruttius muttered, his voice heavy with emotion.

"And would you ensure that Agatha receives my letter before my execution?"

Bruttius nodded, his mind grappling with the weight of his impending task.

Sensing his anguish, Valentine gently squeezed Bruttius's hand, reassuring him, "Fear not, my friend. Every life, every death, has reason; it is not for us to decide. I am now at peace with what is to come."

His chest tight with sorrow, Bruttius nodded and turned to lead the others out of the prison. His mind churned with conflicting emotions, fueled by two ever-present thoughts that would haunt him throughout the night—*how could he possibly find the strength to execute such a saintly man? And how would Agatha ever forgive him for doing so?*

CHAPTER 29

DEAR AGATHA

"It is not the length of life, but the depth of life."
—SENECA

When Agatha awoke the day after Valentine had visited her during the night, the reality of her restored sight struck her with the joy of a divine gift. It seemed almost inconceivable that she could now discern every detail of her bedroom. As light seeped in through her shutters, she lay still in bed for a moment, marveling at the ceiling where she could see every subtle crack and corner that had previously been beyond her visible grasp.

Sitting up, she took in her familiar yet newly visible surroundings. Her eyes wandered over the sewing station, the clothes folded in the chest, and the wooden floorboards beneath—each detail vibrant and clear, rekindling memories and sensations from the years she had lived without sight. A smile briefly crossed her face as she glanced at her staff, once an indispensable companion, now merely an artifact beside her bed.

Rising with a deep appreciation for her regained sight, she walked to the window and flung the shutters open. Morning light flooded the room, illuminating the meadow where Valentine had laid his healing hands upon her the night before. The world before her blossomed into a kaleidoscope of colors and shapes, a breathtaking mosaic revealed for the first time. Yet, as she absorbed the visual splendors, a grim realization settled upon her. Her miraculous gift of sight came with a cruel price, for on this very day, her beloved Valentine was to be executed at her father's hand, and now, she would witness the event with all her senses.

Agatha quietly entered Porcia's room, where her sister still lay enveloped in the gentle embrace of sleep. Carefully, she nudged open her shutters. As the morning rays graced Porcia's face, she quietly stirred.

"Agatha..." Porcia murmured as she gazed at her sister, her voice soft with sleep.

"Good morning, Porcia," Agatha replied, sitting gently on the bed while taking her sister's hand.

"How is your sight?" Porcia asked, propping herself up against her pillow.

"It is even better today. As if I am seeing the world in a new light," Agatha responded joyfully, her smile warm and sincere.

"Will you ever forgive me?" Porcia's voice carried a somber weight.

Agatha squeezed her hand reassuringly. "It is I who must seek your forgiveness, Porcia. You had reason to be hurt. I often left you behind when we were children. And yet, you never left my side through all my years of darkness. You guided me, ensured my well-being, and protected me—and I will always love you dearly for that."

Porcia's eyes brimmed with tears as the sisters embraced deeply, exchanging an unspoken bond only siblings share. "So, you do not hate me?" Porcia asked as she clung to Agatha.

Pulling back slightly, Agatha looked into her sister's eyes and said firmly, "No, I love you very much."

Porcia smiled softly in relief at Agatha's genuine forgiveness before the day's looming event struck her. "Father is going to execute Valentine today because of me," she said, her voice heavy with guilt.

"No, Porcia," Agatha corrected gently. "Father is going to execute Valentine because we live in an empire ruled by a madman."

Porcia nodded, a silent acknowledgment of the harsh truth.

"Now, I must ask you to be by my side once again," Agatha said as her voice trembled slightly. "For I don't know how I will make it through this day alone."

Porcia embraced Agatha and whispered, "I am here for you, sister —now and forever."

AFTER DRESSING AND WALKING DOWNSTAIRS, Agatha greeted the morning light casting its glow on their wooden dining table, where two letters lay—one open and another sealed, the open one marked with her name. Agatha picked up the open letter, her fingers tracing the familiar shapes of the letters. It had been years since she had last read, and she found herself slowly piecing together the words, reacquainting herself with their forms and meanings.

"What does it say?" Porcia asked, her curiosity piqued as she joined Agatha at the table.

"It's from Father," Agatha replied, her voice steady despite the stirring of her emotions. "They have moved Valentine's execution to the Via Flaminia. We are to inform others in the community who may wish to attend."

Agatha then turned her attention to the sealed letter. The mere sight of it caused her heart to skip a beat.

"Whom is that for?" Porcia inquired.

Agatha hesitated momentarily, the weight of the day pressing down upon her. "It's for me—from Valentine."

"Aren't you going to read it?" Porcia pressed, her eyes locked on her sister's face.

"Father said Valentine gave the letter to him last night—that his words are meant to give me strength today," Agatha explained, her voice a mere whisper.

"Then, open it," Porcia urged, her tone gentle yet insistent.

"Perhaps later," Agatha replied, her heart heavy with anticipation and dread.

"As you wish," Porcia said, wrapping her arm around Agatha's shoulders. "Come, sister, I shall make us breakfast."

ALONGSIDE THE VIA FLAMINIA, the ancient road stretching north from Rome, the atmosphere was charged with eerie anticipation. Dozens of Praetorians had escorted a horse-drawn wagon carrying a caged, hooded prisoner, his hands bound in chains. Far fewer citizens had gathered than the previous day in front of an all-too-familiar site for torture and executions, particularly of Christians.

In the background stood several wooden crosses—temporary structures marred by the stains and frayed ropes that bore witness to their grim purpose. A few crosses still held charred remains, ravaged by scavengers, the flesh torn and bones exposed, a brutal reminder to all who passed. The gruesome display was a stark warning to travelers on this crucial route, threading through both urban and rural territories under Roman rule.

In the somber crowd, Marius concealed his identity under a heavy cape. Fear and sadness marked his face as he stood beside Porcia, who cradled Agatha's arm, her heart pounding furiously within her chest. She clutched the sealed letter—Valentine's last message—in her trembling hands. Though Agatha had not yet summoned the courage to read his final words, she gripped it tightly as if it were the very essence of their love, a beacon amid the engulfing darkness.

Behind them, the burly figures of Efebus, Proculo, and Linus were also draped in cloaks, their eyes darting nervously. Their loyalty to Valentine and the ideals he championed remained steadfast. Yet, on this day, they stood as powerless spectators, their identities shrouded, engulfed in the grim reality of their surroundings.

As the imperial horns echoed, a sudden hush fell over the crowd. Praetorian Guards surged forward, their movements a blend of might and precision, clearing a path through the crowd. Behind them rolled the grand imperial *carpentum*, its opulence starkly contrasting the dismal backdrop of the execution site. Within the carriage, Claudius reclined on a plush, ornate couch, his body frail and ravaged by the unyielding grip of illness. Beside him, Lucius, his faithful physician, leaned in close. "Can you see the stage, Caesar?"

Claudius nodded.

"I thought you chose wisely not to bring your family to the execution today," Lucius added.

"It was not by choice," Claudius wheezed, his breaths shallow and labored.

At that moment, General Aurelian approached the carriage. "Caesar, I have informed Bruttius of your orders. The people will not see Valentine in prayer, and he will be beheaded as you requested."

Gathering his strength, Claudius added, "Aurelian, tell him to burn the body after he severs it in two. The Christians can watch his ashes float up to their god."

"As you wish, Caesar," Aurelian responded obediently.

Onstage, Bruttius dragged the hooded and shackled prisoner out to a wooden block, while Agatha watched helplessly from the crowd. Her eyes widened as her father secured the prisoner's head and neck over the wooden block—a sight nearly unbearable for Agatha to witness. Porcia held her tightly, offering a small measure of comfort as their father returned to retrieve his bloodstained sword—the same one he proudly racked each night in their home like a hunter showcasing his prized weapon.

The crowd appeared eerily quiet this day, starkly contrasting the boisterous, gladiatorial-like spectacle of the day prior. This silence was punctuated only by the distant caws of ravens circling overhead, hoping for another body to pick at before day's end.

On the platform, Bruttius stood with severe formality, unrolling a scroll with solemn precision. He announced in a clear, authoritative voice, "On this fourteenth day of February, according to Roman law, we find you, Valentine, guilty of all charges and sentenced to death by beheading."

As Bruttius's ominous words echoed through the still air, Agatha could bear her feelings no longer. She gently broke the seal and unfolded the letter from Valentine, hoping it would provide her some relief. As she began to read, the surrounding sounds melted away. Time seemed to stand still, the world pausing around her as she immersed herself in the intimate words penned by her lover, each line pulling her inexorably toward what she feared might be their final moments together.

My Dearest Agatha,

May these words provide you comfort in time of need.

As she began to read his words, childhood memories flooded her mind, distracting her—their long walks through the forest, and how he always followed her lead, trusting her implicitly. She recalled his playful laughter and how he listened intently to her endless stories, and the day he rescued her from the wolves, showing courage despite his youthful stature. She replayed each cherished moment until her father's fierce gaze pierced through her reverie, snapping her back to the present.

Bruttius stood over the prisoner's hooded body, blade in hand. Her heart ached as she struggled to find a way to hold on to her love as long as possible. The miraculous events of the previous night seemed to have counted for nothing, replaced now by a nightmarish reality. Desperately, she returned to the letter, clinging to Valentine's final words, hoping to find a connection strong enough to sustain her for the rest of her life without him.

May you help those around you,
who have lost their way,
and forgive others,
never turning love away.

Suddenly, a distant voice rang out: "He's not deserving of this!"

Agatha's eyes snapped back to the stage at the sound of the shout, hoping someone would intervene and end the madness. But all she saw was her father, his bloodstained sword raised high above his head. Every muscle in his body tensed, coiled like a viper ready to strike. With a swift, decisive motion, he swung the blade downward, severing the hooded head cleanly, leaving a visceral red spray and a lifeless corpse in its wake.

Agatha gasped, her legs buckling as she brought a hand to her mouth in utter shock, a tortured cry escaping her lips. Porcia's grip tightened around her, offering what little support she could. Marius, Efebus, and Linus lowered their heads, as though the air had been drawn from their lungs. The crowd fell deathly silent.

Claudius, however, allowed himself a satisfied smile. The execution of Valentine marked his liberation from a long-standing threat. With a gesture, he signaled his guard to retreat to the Imperial Palace, relishing the profound sense of freedom and victory that now surged through him.

Tears streamed down Agatha's cheeks, one landing on Valentine's letter. All that was left of him now, she thought, were these final words, which she read with her fleeting strength:

May you know,
I am with you and love you,
each step you take,
and He will guide you,
in every choice you make.

Perhaps our love
was never fated to be,
yet your spirit,
will always stay with me.

I pray that one day,
we'll meet once again,
surrounded by our forest;
I will await you then.

Forever yours,

Valentine

Chapter 30

Serena's Secret

"Reason requires a certain amount of time to be able to seek the truth."
—Seneca

February 14, 283 AD

Located a day's journey from Rome along the ancient Appian Way stood Serena's villa—her permanent residence and a fitting abode for a former empress. The afternoon sun bathed the central courtyard within the villa. Illuminated by intricate mosaics underfoot and shadows cast by statues of gods guarding its perimeter, the courtyard served as a centerpiece for confessions and activities.

Now in her mid-forties, Serena moved toward the courtyard with a grace that commanded respect. Her robe, rich in color and detailed with subtle woven decorations, draped elegantly around her as she navigated the shaded walkways with a dignified and measured step.

Seated on a bench at the courtyard's edge, Iset wore a colorful garment that complemented her rich, dark skin. Streaks of gray wove through her hair, marking her years. Serena joined her, taking a seat beside her.

"How is she?" Serena asked, her voice layered with a concern that revealed her deep maternal instincts.

"Fearless, like her mother," Iset remarked with pride.

Serena chuckled softly "Perhaps. Yet, her combative instinct is purely from her father."

They fixed their gaze on the vibrant scene unfolding in the court-yard. At its center, a figure in protective armor wearing a helmet skill-fully dodged the lunges of three seasoned soldiers. Armed with wooden training swords, the soldiers swung passionately at a young warrior who danced through their attacks with the grace and swiftness of the wind.

From the courtyard's edge, Ballavan, now Iset's husband and Sere-na's foremost bodyguard, observed the training with unwavering focus. In his traditional Maharashtra garb, he exuded an unmistakable commanding presence. A master of the ancient martial art of Malla-Yuddha, Ballavan had earned Serena's utmost trust and committed himself to mentor the young warrior, carefully shaping each move-ment with a seasoned eye.

Ballavan circled the young warrior, his voice resonating clearly and robustly across the courtyard: "Seek ground—clear path—advance!" Each command carried weight, punctuated by the rhythmic tapping of his walking stick against the cool stone tiles of the courtyard, setting the tempo for the skirmish.

As the trio of soldiers converged, intent on cornering the young warrior, their target responded with fluid grace. The young warrior sidestepped the first soldier and swiftly locked his elbow joint, rendering him temporarily helpless. Then, seizing the soldier's wooden sword, the young warrior struck decisively. The weapon connected, and the first soldier crumpled to the ground.

"Excellent, next!" Ballavan ordered a second soldier into the brawl to attack.

The young warrior deflected the blow and quickly twisted the second soldier's arm behind his back, forcing him to drop his weapon.

The young warrior held a sword to the second soldier's neck, affirming the defeat.

"Attack!" Ballavan instructed the final soldier, a daunting figure twice the size of the young warrior and the most experienced soldier of the trio, who advanced with his sword raised for a decisive strike.

The young warrior quickly avoided the final soldier's initial swing, using the soldier's momentum to take him to the ground. The final soldier fell with a thud, and the young warrior swiftly secured his neck with a leg chokehold. Struggling and with his face turning blue, the final soldier tapped the younger warrior's leg, signaling his defeat at the brink of passing out.

The young warrior rose and quickly removed her helmet. It was Serena's daughter, Claudia, now a formidable and blossoming four-teen-year-old. Her eyes sparkled with triumph as the sun illuminated her face. She raised her hand and yelled, "Victory!"

Ballavan couldn't hide his delight. "Ah-ha! You have listened to Master Ballavan at last—remember, not all victories are won by the sword!"

Embodying the spirit of camaraderie, Claudia extended a hand to the formidable soldier she had nearly choked out. He looked at her with a mix of respect and surprise, clearly in awe that she had bested him this time. Helping him to his feet with a supportive gesture, she acknowledged their shared training with a knowing smile.

Ballavan's dark eyes gleamed with pride as he surveyed the scene, announcing, "That is all for today."

With respect and gratitude toward her master, Claudia brought her hands together, fingers pointing skyward in the *Anjali Mudra*, and bowed deeply. Ballavan reciprocated with a slight bow.

Iset turned to Serena and said, with a hint of jest, "Few men dare challenge her."

Serena smirked, then responded with concern: "As long as there are still a few who will court her."

"Love will find her, Empress; you need not worry," Iset reassured.

"As long as that is all that finds her," Serena replied. "Your husband has trained her well, Iset—yet I fear the time has come to introduce her to society."

"Her father would be proud," Iset said, giving Serena a knowing look.

"Oh, Iset, I fear the news I must share with her today will not sit well."

"She must know, Empress," Iset said gently yet firmly. "It is time."

Serena nodded and replied hesitantly, "I will join you in her chambers after she bathes."

"As you wish, Empress," Iset acknowledged as she moved toward Claudia and Ballavan, ready to guide Claudia away from the training grounds.

As Serena crossed the expanse of her daughter's balcony, the sight of Claudia struck her. The once innocent newborn and carefree young girl who had roamed the Imperial Palace in her childhood had transformed. Her beauty mirrored a younger Serena, a sight to behold. Iset brushed her rich brown hair, which cascaded down her back, catching the light with every brushstroke. Behind them, the view of the hills on the outskirts of Rome stretched as far as the eye could see, providing a breathtaking view illuminated by the afternoon light.

"Thank you, Iset. I will attend to Claudia now," Serena said, her voice steady yet soft.

"As you wish, Empress," Iset replied, her voice respectful as she quietly retreated.

Serena sat beside her daughter and picked up her hairbrush.

"Mother, what is this secret that Iset speaks of? I did not think we kept secrets from each other," Claudia asked, her voice carrying a newfound maturity befitting her growth.

Serena continued the gentle strokes, her thoughts drifting through memories of a bygone era. "Only one, my dear," she murmured, her expression growing intense. Suddenly, she set aside the brush and turned to face her daughter directly. "Claudia, what I tell you now is not to be shared. Understood?"

Claudia nodded, sensing the gravity in her mother's tone. "What is it, Mother?"

Serena took a deep breath before beginning. "When you were a baby, your... Claudius arranged for Valentine's execution," Serena began, her voice steady but filled with the weight of history.

"The man whom many Christians honor each year on this day, remembering him as a saint," Claudia interjected.

"Indeed. Valentine has become quite the martyr since his alleged death," Serena confirmed, a slight tremor betraying her nervousness.

Claudia's mind raced as she connected the dots. "His *alleged* death, Mother?"

Serena cleared her throat, filling the space between them with tension. "Claudius believed Valentine to have died tragically. History recorded it as such. Yet, I will tell you now what few will ever know."

Claudia leaned in, focusing intently on her mother's words.

Serena clutched the brush nervously, her mind drifting into the past. "The night before Valentine was to be executed, I sought out Aurelian and proposed...an alliance. Claudius was growing gravely ill, and I convinced Aurelian that his ascent to Caesar would be inevitable with the support of a formidable noblewoman by his side. He agreed, though I told Aurelian that my consent was contingent upon one condition—Valentine's life was to be spared."

Serena recounted her story to Claudia, detailing the events leading up to Valentine's execution. She began with the night in the Imperial Palace when Claudius's physician, Lucius, handed her the vial of desperately needed medicine for the ailing emperor. There, Aurelian intercepted her, and Serena's mind had raced, setting a daring plan into motion.

Moments after safeguarding Claudius's medicine, Aurelian escorted Serena to her chamber. In a secluded nook, Serena leaned in with her seductive eyes, making her desire for the general known. Passionately kissing—this charged moment set off a cascade of events. In that kiss, Serena bound Aurelian to her, forging a scandalous union in the quiet chaos of the Imperial Palace.

And so, on the morning of Valentine's alleged execution day, Aurelian's footsteps echoed determinedly as he marched into the prison where Valentine awaited his fate. Moving with the urgency of an aspiring Caesar ignited by Serena's spell, he quickly sought out Bruttius and issued his command with regal authority: "Caesar demands that Valentine be hooded and not engaged in Christian prayer when you execute him today," Aurelian commanded.

"Understood, General," Bruttius responded with due reverence. "I was also informed that Caesar wishes for Valentine's execution to be moved outside of Rome today."

"Indeed. And further, I am ordering you to release Valentine into my custody and replace him with another prisoner—one of lesser morals, who will be hooded and executed in his place."

Bruttius's eyes quickly met Aurelian's in disbelief as the chilly dungeon air settled upon them. Seeking clarification, Bruttius asked, "Did Caesar approve of this order, General?"

A tense silence passed as the two formidable men stared at each other, sizing the other up.

General Aurelian finally replied, "No. Caesar shall remain ignorant of my order. Empress Serena has approved of this command."

"You speak of treason, General. I have tortured and killed men for lesser confessions," he stated bluntly.

"And the empress and I shall be in your debt when I ascend to the throne with her by my side," General Aurelian replied, his voice firm and resolute.

The air thickened with tension as Bruttius absorbed the weight of the general's words. Having just returned Valentine to his cell after witnessing the miraculous restoration of Agatha's vision, he was inclined to follow the orders. Yet, the potential repercussions loomed large; if Aurelian did not speak the truth, or his aspirations to ascend to the throne should falter, the consequences would be fatal.

"What assurance do I have that you will take the throne and Claudius will perish?" Bruttius queried.

General Aurelian's voice dropped to a conspiratorial whisper: "Caesar is gravely ill. He requires daily medicine. The empress has been tasked with administering that medicine."

Bruttius's eyes narrowed as the realization hit him. "She means to poison him?" he whispered.

General Aurelian's hand subtly inched toward his sword, prepared for the possibility that Bruttius's allegiance to Claudius might override his discretion.

"Why are you entrusting me with this conspiracy?" Bruttius asked, his gaze hardening at the gravity of being drawn into such a scandal.

"Valentine confessed to the empress that he is in love with a young maiden named Agatha. She is your daughter, is she not?" General Aurelian inquired.

Bruttius paused, now realizing the leverage the general held over him. "She is," he admitted, his voice barely above a whisper.

"Then I presume our secret is safe with you, as yours is with us," Aurelian declared.

Bruttius nodded, sealing their unspoken agreement.

"And what of Quintillus, Claudius's brother?" Bruttius's voice trembled slightly, his concern for the future palpable.

"Nobody has seen Quintillus for some time now. He's rarely in Rome, hardly fit to lead, and the legions will favor me," General Aurelian replied sharply. "And, if he attempted to claim the throne, I can assure you, his time there would be short, if at all."

Bruttius sensed the general's patience dwindling, a delicate tension that held both men on a razor's edge.

"There is no prisoner I would rather set free than Valentine. Yet, I am a loyal servant of Rome and wish no harm to come to myself or my family for this," Bruttius declared firmly.

"You have my word," Aurelian replied, his hand easing away from the hilt of his sword. "Your family shall remain unharmed."

Bruttius nodded. "Come, I will show you to Valentine's cell," he complied, leading General Aurelian deeper into the prison.

Just short of reaching Valentine's cell, Bruttius stopped at another cell. "Wait here," he instructed the general as he opened the door and stepped inside. Shackled and now awake was Hercules—the prisoner Valentine had pointed out to Bruttius the night prior and Agatha's assailant. Bruttius's fists flew through the air with lightning speed, a swift and brutal delivery of justice and the rendering unconscious of a man with lesser morals whom General Aurelian had requested to secure their plan. Bruttius then gagged and hooded Hercules, whose stature closely matched Valentine's and who quickly became the ideal stand-in prisoner to replace Valentine at the execution that day.

As Claudia listened to her mother retell the events, her expression shifted abruptly to shock. "Then, Valentine lived?!" she asked, interrupting Serena's story.

"Yes, he did, Claudia."

"But why, Mother? Why would you have ordered Valentine freed and betrayed my father in the process?" Claudia asked, confused.

Serena's gaze drifted momentarily as her expression softened. "It was for you, Claudia. It was all for you."

"But why, Mother? What truth do you withhold from me?"

"Aurelian fulfilled his vow to me," she continued, "with the condition that I would never see Valentine again and that he would be banished from Rome. As you know, Claudius died shortly after what was believed to be Valentine's execution. When Aurelian ascended the throne, I expected to stand by him as empress. Instead, he chose a younger woman, Empress Ulpia, who was without child… though clearly of lesser standing than I. In the end, however, this was a far better fate for us. We were liberated from the whims of authoritative men, and this countryside villa became our sanctuary, away from the power struggles of the city. Aurelian made me vow never to speak of your true father until you were of age, and after his death, I still thought it best to wait until now."

Claudia interrupted her: "My *true* father?"

Serena reached into her pocket and pulled out the old but well-kept necklace with a silver fish. Valentine had lost it to Claudius during their duel, but Serena had found it on her balcony floor and kept it safe, waiting for this exact moment to share it with her daughter one day.

"This is for you, Claudia. It was your father's."

Serena placed the necklace gently into Claudia's hand.

"I thought my father honored the gods of Rome," Claudia said as she gazed at the fish. "His memory does not serve me well, nor do the tales people speak of his cruelty toward Christians."

Tension hung in the air as Serena summoned her inner strength to finally confess: "Claudius was not your father, Claudia. Your father was a soldier of Rome. He married Christians in secrecy and provided healing to those in need."

Claudia appeared stunned. "You speak of Valentine?"

"Yes—your father," she confirmed.

"Then, if Valentine was my father, and you are my mother, why did you not wed?"

Serena lowered her gaze, her voice heavy with emotion. "Our fate did not lead us to marry, Claudia. Yet, your destiny now unfolds. Tomorrow is Lupercalia, and it is now your time to be introduced to society. And today, many Christians honor the man who truly was your father—and I could not let you grow up believing your father was a tyrant. You deserve to know his true identity."

Claudia's curiosity deepened. "The rumors of him healing a blind lover—are they true?"

"Agatha was her name," Serena confirmed softly.

"What became of them? Did they ever reunite after General Aurelian set my... *father* free?" Claudia asked, eager to learn more.

Serena offered a wry smile, "I was told that when Agatha and your father reunited after his alleged execution, it was as if their prayers had been answered, and the gods themselves had blessed their union."

Her words painted a vivid picture as she transported them both to that moment. Aurelian stood outside of Bruttius's home, near the meadow's edge, where he discreetly delivered Valentine after the execution. His hands were still shackled, but his eyes were alight and hopeful. Across the meadow, Bruttius stood, and beside him, Agatha appeared from their home. Upon seeing Valentine, Agatha gasped with disbelief, having just returned from what she thought to have been her lover's execution mere hours before this moment. Without hesitation, she sprinted across the meadow toward him. Aurelian released the rope that bound Valentine, finally granting him freedom. He raced toward Agatha. As they met, he embraced her passionately as their souls entwined.

"You're alive!" she cried as tears streamed down Agatha's cheeks.

Valentine was speechless, overwhelmed by his emotions. He embraced her more tightly than ever before. The pair seemed to hold each other for an eternity. Eventually, they sank to their knees, locked to each other with steadfast love. At that moment, they were truly united and finally free.

Claudia jolted her mother back to the present with a poignant question: "Wait! Does that mean my father is still alive?"

Serena hesitated as she stared into her daughter's curious eyes.

"Please, Mother, you must tell me! I must know!" Claudia pressed.

In a voice cracked with emotion, Serena answered: "It is rumored that within a valley far from here, there lives an outlaw, quietly and relentlessly pursued by this Caesar, like many Caesars before him, for marrying Christians in secrecy. This man is also believed to be a renowned healer, having saved countless lives, including that of his lover, whose sight, it is said, he miraculously restored long ago. He is said to be well protected by a small army of devoted guardians who have sworn their lives to defend him and spread the message of the Christian God. If these rumors are true, then this man is likely your father, Valentine—who is still alive."

A storm of emotions danced across Claudia's face, each one unfolding as she grasped the significance of her mother's words. "I must find him!" she declared, her voice unwavering.

Serena nodded, tears now brimming in her eyes. "I know," she replied with a heavy heart, having foreseen this moment for years.

A sudden and profound realization struck Claudia as she gazed into Serena's tear-filled eyes. In that moment, she understood why she had insisted on such rigorous training under Master Ballavan all of these years—-knowing that she would inevitably desire to seek her father out, placing herself in tremendous danger when she did. Recognizing the magnitude of her sacrifices and the strength it must have taken to reveal this deeply guarded secret, Claudia wrapped her arms around her and, in an embrace only a daughter could provide, she whispered into her ear: "Thank you, Mother."

Epilogue

Valentine's Day

"Let's live, let's love."
—*Catullus*

One year after Valentine's alleged beheading.

As the much-celebrated death of Claudius still lingered in the air, the populace turned its focus to preparing for the vibrant celebrations of Lupercalia. Yet, far from the clamor of the festivities, a different kind of commemoration unfolded in the foothills near Arretium. Here, among the towering trees, Valentine and Agatha had made their home, where the whispers of their past rustled through the leaves. And on this special day, they returned to the forest for a momentous and long-awaited occasion—their wedding.

This sacred ceremony, woven from the threads of their love and destiny, was notably not officiated by Valentine. Instead, it was Marius who took the honor, now serving under the guidance and blessing of Pope Felix I. The guests, arrayed in their tunics—simple yet elegant, epitomizing the humble grandeur of the moment—were seated upon tree stumps scattered across the forest floor. The soft glow of dozens of oil lamps bathed the congregation and altar in a warm, ethereal light, imbuing the ceremony with a celestial, almost otherworldly quality.

Porcia sat near the front of the assembly, her gaze filled with deep respect and newfound admiration as she looked affectionately toward Marius, now a handsome priest. Beside her sat her father, Bruttius, exceptionally well-dressed in unsullied attire, his face beaming with pride and, if he were honest, relief. Alongside them sat Horatius and Helvia, who had journeyed from Rome, their eyes now fixed on Valentine with a mix of disbelief and wonder, having once been certain he would never survive to see this day.

Valentine stood beside a natural altar, crafted from an artful arrangement of helleborus flowers and branches—symbols of perseverance, thriving even in the harshness of winter, much like the resilience they had all come to embody. At Valentine's side stood Regalus, who after hearing more from Helvia about the origins of his birthname, now insisted on being called Raj. He was dressed with care, and his eyes radiated excitement for the day's event.

Valentine's other loyal companions—Proculo, Efebus, and Linus—maintained a respectful silence, forming a perimeter around the intimate gathering of cherished friends and family to stand watch for any uninvited visitors. A score of local friends had gathered from the surrounding area, and the atmosphere buzzed with lively conversation yet was charged with a deep reverence that reflected the significance of the ceremony.

"Welcome, all," Marius intoned, his voice carrying the weight of the moment. "Let us begin." As he spoke, the familiar musicians who had once played with Agatha in Rome began to softly strum the psaltery and cithara, their delicate melodies intertwining with the gentle voices rising from the crowd. The harmonious blend of strings and singing created a deeply reverent atmosphere, perfectly suited for the ceremony about to unfold. Marius's gaze briefly met Agatha's, signaling for her to approach the altar—an unconventional gesture for such a ceremony, but their love was anything but ordinary.

As the guests turned their attention toward the bride, Agatha appeared more radiant than ever, the soft glow of the oil lamps illuminating her in the heart of the forest. She was adorned in a tunica recta, a long, off-white tunic woven from wool, believed to bring good luck and fertility. Draped over her tunic was a *flammeum*, a large, brightly colored veil in beautiful yellow, thought to symbolize fire and designed to ward off evil spirits.

Porcia had styled Agatha's locks into a six-part *tutulus*, and atop her head sat a vibrant headpiece made of myrtus, crowning her like a princess. Petals strewn along a small path toward Valentine vividly symbolized their unfolding love story. The forest seemed to hold its breath as Agatha began her measured approach toward him, her steps careful and considered in the leather ankle boots designed by a friend for this very day.

In that moment, it was as if time itself had paused for just them. As Agatha moved toward Valentine, guests on either side of the natural aisle gently released petals from the helleborus flower, allowing them to drift down like blessings from above. Agatha had chosen this ritual with care, each petal symbolizing pivotal moments in her and Valentine's journey together. As the petals floated toward the earth, both of their hearts stirred with memories—of joy, but also of loss and longing.

As the couple gazed into each other's eyes, they felt a deep and holy connection, as if God Himself was drawing them closer, binding their hearts and souls in a union blessed by divine grace. Valentine watched, captivated, as each of Agatha's steps felt like her final return after having left him as a child, so long ago. Once Agatha was standing before him, the space felt charged with their love and the silent recognition of all they had overcome.

Marius began the ceremony, offering a warm welcome to the guests and invoking blessings upon the couple, honoring the sacred traditions of the early Christian community. Then, in a testament to their deep affection, Valentine and Agatha, ever the romantics, recited vows they had composed themselves, a ritual of their own making, yet even this carried an undertone of the fragility of life and the ever-present shadow of fate.

"My Dear Maiden," Valentine began as his voice wavered with emotion. "I've traveled a lifetime to be with you at last. The path was neither straight nor without fault—I've made more mistakes than I care to remember. Yet, one misstep I will never regret was when I stumbled into your arms in Rome. In that moment, it was not only your striking beauty that held me; it was the purity of your voice and the sweet harmony that stirred my soul. Agatha, you have been my guiding star on the darkest of nights. Your vision, your voice, and your spirit have brought me back time and again from the brink of despair. Your strength and faith have been an anchor to my unsettled heart. And today, as I stand before you, I promise to cherish and honor you in this life and forever."

Agatha's eyes brimmed with love and gratitude as she helped wipe a tear from Valentine's face. Gathering herself, she took a breath, then began to speak with a soft, tenderness-laden voice. "Bear, my heart has always felt at home in your presence. You have saved my life—first when we met, and again today by taking me as your wife. When I lived as a blind woman..." Agatha's voice began to crack as she thought about her subsequent words. "I feared I would never be worthy of a husband's love, let alone a man as gentle and caring as you. Now that you have aided in restoring my vision, I realize I did not need my sight to know the depths of my love for you. Valentine, you accepted me unconditionally. You put your own life in harm's way for me time and time again. I have never known another man like you. You are truly my hero."

Valentine smiled, remembering how he had once boldly declared as a child that he would one day be a hero. Now, hearing Agatha's words, he realized he had become exactly that—but in a way he had never imagined.

Overcome by love, gratitude, relief, and awe, Agatha took a deep breath before saying, "I vow to always journey beside you and be the pillar upon which you can forever lean."

Valentine lifted his hand, gently wiping away her tears as they smiled at one another. Clasping hands, they could feel a divine warmth flowing through their arms. They each took a deep breath as flashes of all they had gone through to arrive at this moment flooded their minds.

Marius broke in. "In the presence of our Christian God, I unite you both in sacred matrimony. May His grace be upon you," he declared with solemn joy, binding the couple together in their holy union finally and forever.

The newlyweds inched closer, their lips joining in a kiss that embodied a myriad of dreams—transcending time and space, a seal of their eternal bond yet also a silent promise to always hold on to love no matter what challenges might lay ahead.

The air erupted with jubilant cheers from the guests, with hardly a dry eye among them. Most notably, Porcia embraced their father, Bruttius, who was so overcome with joy that he lowered his head, disguising his emotions with his hand, as he finally realized that the burden of Agatha's survival was no longer his alone to bear—the torch had been passed.

In a heartfelt moment, Valentine and Agatha reached over and included Raj in their embrace. Having been orphaned and thrust into a world that had taken so much from him, he had become their adopted son, a meaningful yet bittersweet addition to their new life together.

Surrounded by the timeless beauty of the forest, they stood as lovers, partners, parents, and family, bound by the most sacred of vows. In that moment, the essence of what the world would come to celebrate as Valentine's Day was born—a celebration not merely of romance but of love's triumph over adversity.

Author's Note

Thank you for joining me on this journey through *The Legend of Valentine*—a story that intertwines the strands of legend, history, and imagination. As I delved into Valentine's life, I attempted to carefully balance the rich tapestry of myth with fragments of historical evidence while weaving in the creative elements needed to bring this tale to life. That being said, it is important to recognize that this work is ultimately a piece of fiction. While I strove to remain true to the spirit of the past, certain creative liberties were necessary to fill in the gaps and make the story resonate compellingly.

I hope that *The Legend of Valentine* not only entertained you but also inspired curiosity about the intersection of history and legend. For those interested in the historical foundations of this narrative, I have included a section at the end of the book detailing some of the sources that guided my work. Additionally, readers will find historical blogs on my website. While visiting, you will also find links to the audio-book I directed and updates on my future works.

Independent authors gain traction through honest reviews from readers on sites like Amazon and Goodreads. If you have a moment, I would greatly appreciate it if you could take the time to leave a review, as your feedback is what truly helps stories like this reach a wider audience.

Otherwise, I look forward to continuing the conversation online. Please connect with me on my social media channels, which can be found on my website.

Warm regards,

Sheldon Collins

Join my mailing list and stay updated on my future work at:
www.SheldonCollins.com

Glossary of Characters

Agatha: A blind woman whose close relationship with Valentine shapes much of his life.

Albus: Scaro's older brother, a Roman soldier and trusted ally of Valentine.

Antonius: A Roman who seeks to marry Prisca.

Aureolus: One of Emperor Gallienus' most trusted and high-ranking generals.

Aurelian: A prominent Roman general and the right hand to General Claudius.

Ballavan: The loyal protector and enslaved servant of Serena.

Baro: Linus' cousin and a member of the Praetorian Guard.

Bear: The nickname given to Valentine by Rose (young Agatha) in his youth.

Bruttius: The magistrate of the jail in Rome and a feared executioner, known for his rare yet significant role in carrying out justice. He is also the father of Porcia and Agatha.

Camilla: Bruttius' late wife, whose memory lingers and impacts his decisions.

Charu: The wife of Deodatus, mother of Regalus, and an ancient healer.

Claudia: Serena's daughter.

Clea: A lead servant to the Emperor and Empress.

Claudius: A Roman general with a childhood scar, whose military prowess and personal vendettas shape much of the conflict.

Decimus: A thief who roams the valley near Deodatus and Charu's villa with Felix and Spurius.

Deodatus: A Christian physician who runs a healing sanctuary with his wife, Charu, near the town of Arretium.

Didius: A consul to the Emperor with a significant role in the political workings of Rome.

Efebus: A Roman soldier and trusted ally of Valentine, known for his prominent size.

Fabius: A Roman senator involved in a secret love affair with Junius.

Fannius: A senator who oversteps his bounds.

Felix: A thief who roams the valley near Deodatus and Charu's villa with Decimus and Spurius.

Firmus: A noble who married Lucia.

Gallienus: The reigning emperor, grappling with political and military challenges.

Helvia: The co-owner of an herbal shop in Rome, working alongside her husband, Horatius.

Hercules: A physically imposing figure involved in moments of conflict.

Horatius: The co-owner of an herbal shop in Rome, working with his wife, Helvia.

Iset: Serena's most trusted and loyal slave.

Junius: An ambitious young senator who plays a key role in the political machinations of Rome.

Linus: A Roman soldier and trusted ally of Valentine, known for his antics.

Luca: A young and eager Roman soldier, serving under Valentine.

Lucia: A past childhood lover of Valentine's.

Lucius: A Roman physician involved in the health and well-being of the Emperor.

Magistrate: The father of Vibia and organizer of the Saturnalia festival in the Suburbium.

Marius: A Roman Christian soldier and Valentine's closest ally.

Maximus: One of Claudius' commanding officers.

Novius: A man who walks with a limp, a friend of Porcia, and works in a fish stall.

Ostorius: A senator and proponent of reviving an old tradition.

Paternus: A consul to the Emperor and one of the most seasoned senators in Rome.

Piso: An older senator who experiences the wrath of the emperor.

Porcia: The daughter of Bruttius and sister of Agatha.

Postumus: A usurper and self-proclaimed emperor of the Gallic Empire, who betrayed Emperor Gallienus by seizing control of the Western provinces.

Prisca: A Roman woman seeking a Christian ceremony with Antonius.

Proculo: A Roman soldier known for his philosophical depth.

Regalus (Raj): The son of Deodatus and Charu.

Remmius: A young soldier serving under Valentine.

Rose: A nickname that young Agatha uses during her youth with young Valentine (Bear).

Scaro: A Roman soldier and trusted ally of Valentine, younger brother to Albus, known for his laid-back approach to life.

Serena: A woman of high social standing in Rome, who seduces her way into trouble. She is also Claudia's mother.

Spurius: A thief who worked alongside Decimus and Felix.

Tiber: A slave who serves Bruttius and looks after his daughters, Agatha and Porcia.

Tullus: Married to Serena and a magistrate in Rome.

Valentine: A Roman soldier whose deep love for his childhood sweetheart defines much of his journey.

Vibia: The daughter of the magistrate who shares a dance with Valentine.

Zeno: One of Serena's slaves, skilled in reading and writing.

HISTORICAL SOURCES

(PARTIAL LIST)

SAINT VALENTINE

De Sanctis Martyribus Maris, Martha, Audifax, Abachum, in *Acta Sanctorum, Ianuarii,* tomo II, edited by Bolland, Jean – Henschen Godefroid, Anversa, 1643, pp. 217-219

De S. Valentino Presbytero Martyre Romae via Flaminia, in *Acta Sanctorum*, Februarii, tomo II, edited by Bolland, Jean – Henschen Godefroid, Anversa, 1658, pp. 751-754;

De S. Valentino Episcopo, in *Acta Sanctorum*, Februarii, tomo II, edited by Bolland, Jean – Henschen Godefroid, Anversa, 1658, pp. 754-757

L. JACOBILLI, *Vite de' santi e beati dell'Umbria, e di quelli, i corpi dei quali riposano in essa prouincia,* 1647-1661

LITERATURE

Edoardo D'Angelo, *La Passio sancti Valentini martyris (BHL 8460-8460b). Un "martirio occulto" d'età postcostantiniana?, in San Valentino e il suo culto tra Medioevo ed età contemporanea: uno status quaestionis, Atti delle Giornate di studio Terni,* 2010, edited by M. Bassetti ed E. Menestò, Fondazione Centro italiano di studi sull'alto medioevo, 2012, pp. 179-222.

RELIGION AND PRIESTHOOD

Stefan Heid, *Celibacy in the Early Church_ The Beginnings of Obligatory Continence for Clerics in East and West,* 2000

Paul F. Bradshaw, *Ordination Rites of the Ancient Churches of East and West,* Publisher: New York: Pueblo Pub. Co., 1990

Paul F. Bradshaw, *The search for the origins of Christian worship: sources and methods for the study of early liturgy,* 2002

Landon, Edward H, *A manual of councils of the Holy Catholic Church,* 1909

CHRISTIAN MARRIAGE AND WOMEN

David G. Hunter: *Marriage and Sexuality in Early Christianity,* Ad Fontes: Sources of Early Christian Thought, Minneapolis (Fortress Press) 2018

Landon, Edward H, *A manual of councils of the Holy Catholic church*, 1909

Karen Armstrong, *The Gospel According to Women*, London, 1986

VV.AA, *Storia del cristianesimo*. L' età antica (secoli I-VII) (Vol. 1)

Balch, David L., and Carolyn Osiek, editors. *Early Christian Families in Context: An Interdisciplinary Dialogue*. Wm. B. Eerdmans Publishing, 2003.

SYMBOLS AND RITES

Baudry, Gérard-Henry. *Simboli cristiani delle origini. I-VII secolo*. Jaca Book, 2016.

Zorzi, M. Benedetta. *L'allegoria alla vita cristiana della vox strumentalis nelle Enarrationes in Psalmos di S. Agostino*. Reportata, 2007.

"PAGAN" WORD

Il paganesimo. identita e alterita come paradigmi dell'eta costantiniana - Enciclopedia - Treccani

https://www.oed.com/dictionary/pagan_n?tab=etymology

POLITICS AND LAW

Mommsen, Theodor. *Römisches Staatsrecht*. 3 volumi, S. Hirzel, 1871-1888.

Echols, Edward. "The Roman City Police: Origin and Development." *Classical Journal*, vol. 53, no. 5, 1958, pp. 377-384.

Cascione, Cosimo. *Tresviri Capitales: Storia di una Magistratura Minore*. Editoriale Scientifica, 1999.

Serges, Giuliano. "La tortura giudiziaria: Evoluzione e fortuna di uno strumento d'imperio." In *Momenti di storia della giustizia. Materiali di un seminario*, edited by Leonardo Pace, Simone Santucci e Giuliano Serges, Aracne editrice, 2011, pp. 213-320.

Russo, Alfonsina, and Patrizia Fortini. "*Carcer Tullianum. Il Mamertino al Foro Romano*." Parco archeologico del Colosseo, 2022, colosseo.it/pubblicazioni/carcer-tullianum-il-mamertino-al-foro-romano/.

MAGISTRATES AND SENATE

Jones, A.H.M., J.R. Martindale, and J. Morris, editors. *The Prosopography of the Later Roman Empire*. Cambridge University Press, 1971-1992.

Russell, A. G. "The Procedure of the Senate." *Greece & Rome*, vol. 2, no. 5, Feb. 1933, pp. 112-121. Cambridge University Press on behalf of The Classical Association.

Consular Feasts 509 BC - AD 354 (Chronography of 354 AD. Part 8). Monumenta Germaniae Historica, Chronica Minora I, 1892, pp. 50-61

EMPEROR AND PROTOCOL

Avery, William T. "The 'Adoratio Purpurae' and the Importance of the Imperial Purple in the Fourth Century of the Christian Era." *Memoirs of the American Academy in Rome*, vol. 17, 1940, pp. 66-80.

Panella, Clementina, ed. *I segni del potere. Realtà e immaginario della sovranità nella Roma imperiale*. Edipuglia, 2011.

Avery, William T. "The Adoratio Purpurae and the Importance of the Imperial Purple in the Fourth Century of the Christian Era." *Memoirs of the American Academy in Rome*, vol. 17, 1940, pp. 66-80.

Panella, Clementina. *I segni del potere. Realtà e immaginario della sovranità nella Roma imperiale*. L'Erma di Bretschneider, 2011.

Tantillo, Ilaria. *Le orme dell'imperatore: La proscinesi tra immaginario retorico e pratiche cerimoniali*. Edizioni Quasar, 2015.

Tantillo, Ilaria. *I cerimoniali di corte in età tardoromana (284-395 D.C.)*. Edizioni Quasar, 2018.

Arena, Patrizia. "Imperator Salutatus Est: Rapporti tra Salutationes Imperatoriae e Cerimonie da Caligola a Nerone." In *Il Princeps Romano: Autocrate o Magistrato? Fattori Giuridici e Fattori Sociali del Potere Imperiale da Augusto a Commodo*, edited by Jean-Louis Ferrary e John Scheid, IUSS Press, 2015, pp. 139-183.

Mangiameli, Rita. *Tra Duces e Milites: Forme di Comunicazione Politica al Tramonto della Repubblica*. EUT Edizioni Università di Trieste, 2012.

Scrittori della Storia Augusta (Historia Augusta), edited by Leopoldo Agnes, Utet, 1960.

WARFARE

Goldsworthy, Adrian. *The Complete Roman Army*. Thames & Hudson, 2003.

Cascarino, Giuseppe. *L'esercito romano. Armamento e organizzazione. Dal III secolo alla fine dell'impero romano d'Occidente*. Il Cerchio, 2009.

Bishop, M.C., and J.C. Coulston. *Roman Military Equipment: From the Punic Wars to the Fall of Rome*. 2nd ed., Oxbow Books, 2009

Le Bohec, Yann. *The Encyclopedia of the Roman Army*. Wiley-Blackwell, 2015

Le Bohec, Yann. *The Imperial Roman Army*. B.T. Batsford, 1994

Sumner, Graham. *Roman Military Clothing: AD 200-400*. Vol. 2, Osprey Publishing, 2003

SOCIETY AND DAILY LIFE

Lançon, Bertrand. *La vita quotidiana a Roma nel tardo impero*. 2018.

Corbeill, Anthony. *Nature Embodied: Gesture in Ancient Rome*. Princeton University Press, 2004.

Sittl, Carl. *Die Gebärden der Griechen und Römer*. 1890.

Canali, Luca, e Guglielmo Cavallo, curatori. *Graffiti latini*. Biblioteca Universale Rizzoli, 1999.

NAMES

Klebs, Elimar, Paul von Rohden, and Hermann Dessau, editors. *Prosopographia Imperii Romani*. De Gruyter, 1897-2015.

Pauly, August Friedrich von, et al., editors. *Paulys Realencyclopädie der classischen Altertumswissenschaft*. J.B. Metzler, 1894-1980.

CLOTHING

Croom, Alexandra. *Roman Clothing and Fashion*. Amberley, 2010.

Sebesta, Judith Lynn, and Larissa Bonfante, editors. *The World of Roman Costume*. University of Wisconsin Press, 1994.

TRANSPORT AND TRAVEL

Pisani Sartorio, Giuseppina. *Mezzi di trasporto e traffico*. Edizioni Quasar, 1988.

Stanford University. "*ORBIS: The Stanford Geospatial Network Model of the Roman World.*" Stanford Libraries, 2024, orbis.stanford.edu/.

COINS

Federico Barello, *Archeologia della moneta. Produzione e utilizzo nell'antichità*, 2006

ROME, URBANISTICS AND ARCHITECTURE

Steinby, Eva Margareta, editor. *Lexicon Topographicum Urbis Romae*. Edizioni Quasar, 1993-2000.

Carandini, Andrea, editor. *Atlante di Roma antica*. Mondadori Electa, 2012.

Grimaldi Bernardi, Grazia. *Botteghe romane. L'arredamento*. Edizioni Quasar, 2005.

Adam, Jean-Pierre. *L'arte di costruire presso i romani: Materiali e tecniche*. Tradotto da M. P. Guidobaldi, Longanesi, 1994.

Nissinen, Laura. "Cubicula diurna, nocturna – Revisiting Roman Cubicula and Sleeping Arrangements." *Arctos*, vol. 43, 2009, pp. 85-107.

Samuel Ball Platner, *A Topographical Dictionary of Ancient Rome,* London: Oxford University Press, 1929

VARIOUS

Smith, William, ed. *A Dictionary of Greek and Roman Antiquities*. Revised by William Wayte and G. E. Marindin, John Murray, 1890.

Goldsworthy, Adrian. *The Fall of the West: The Slow Death of the Roman Superpower*. Phoenix, 2010.

Acknowledgments

I owe my deepest gratitude to the many people who supported me in writing this book. Presenting these acknowledgments chronologically reflects my journey in bringing this novel to life.

In 1997, my dear Italian friend Giuseppe Carella introduced me to Rome, guiding me through the *caput mundi*. This experience ignited my love for Italian history, its people, and its culture. I am forever thankful for our friendship and for Giuseppe's introduction to this beautiful ancient civilization.

In 2006, Lee Holden shared his *Saint Valentine* screenplay with me. With the support of my Italian investor friend, Maurizio Manno, we purchased the rights and significantly developed Lee's script, forming the foundation for parts of this novel. Although, the screenplay version of this novel has not yet been produced, I deeply appreciate the unwavering support of both Lee and Maurizio, without whom the wheels of this story never would have been set into motion.

In 2023, after stepping away from the entertainment industry for about a decade, I wanted to return to storytelling. I enrolled in master writing courses offered by the BBC and listened to lectures from Ken Follett, Lee Child, Jojo Moyes, whose insights and wisdom helped me refine my skills as a novelist.

In 2024, after months of research and writing, I completed the first draft of *The Legend of Valentine*. As anticipated, the story had evolved significantly from the screenplay version. The adaptation process pushed me to explore my characters, storyline, and historical research more deeply. It was at this time, I was fortunate to meet my incredible editor, Laurie Chittenden, whose decades of experience with the Big Five publishing companies were instrumental in elevating the story.

I also enlisted the expertise of historians specializing in ancient Rome to fact-check my research. Professor Kira Jones from Emory University and Chiara Torrisi, an accomplished Italian historian and archaeology scholar from the University of Turin, were invaluable resources. I am thankful for both of their hard work and dedication.

Ellen Tarlin copyedited my novel, catching mistakes that often slip through the cracks. Her meticulous attention to detail and ability to encourage deeper exploration of my characters were essential.

Shaun Loftus and her amazing team at Book Whisperer, based in Italy, guided me through the self-publishing journey. Their support during the editorial and publishing process was invaluable, and I am grateful for their patience with all my questions about the publishing world, especially Rachel Curran for proofreading my novel before publication.

Filip Sersik from the Czech Republic dedicated weeks to meticulously recreating the Roman map you'll find enclosed. I appreciate his artistry and attention to detail.

Tracy Lyn devoted countless hours to crafting my book cover and trailer, researching images and footage to create a compelling introduction that draws readers into the story.

Rocket Expansion in South Africa designed my author site, ensuring the layout and aesthetics matched the feel of my story.

Directing the audiobook with my incredibly talented co-director, Becky Parker, was an absolute thrill. With the invaluable guidance of our insightful casting director, Samantha Cooper, we had the privilege of selecting eighteen exceptional voice-over actors from around the world to bring this production to life. This international collaboration gave voice to my characters, further enriching the story, and I am deeply grateful to David Sweeney-Bear, who served as the Main Narrator; Ryan Haugen as Valentine; Katrina Michaels as Agatha; Scott Allen as Claudius; Kitty Kelly as Serena; John York as Marius; Lesley Dessalles as Porcia and Claudia; Nicholas Corda as Bruttius and Junius; Wayne LeGette as Emperor Gallienus; Tom Mumford as Maximus; Jez Jameson as General Aurelian; Benson Simmonds as Senator Fabius; Manish Dongardive as Deodatus and Master Ballavan; Elias Khalil as Senator Didius and Lucius; Ken Teutsch as Horatius;

Chris Coxon as Scaro and Baro; Sakshi Sharma as Charu; and Becky Parker as Iset and Helvia. This production would not have been possible without the outstanding post-production and behind-the-scenes efforts of Jerrilee Geist, who served as Project Manager; Ken Teutsch, who adapted the manuscript; Carlos Bolivar, who evaluated audio samples; Tristan Wright, who assisted with narrator audio setup; Dave Young, who handled editing, mixing, and mastering; and Elias Khalil, who managed submissions for audiobook distribution. Together, their collective talent and dedication made this project a reality.

Along this journey, my friends and family have kept me grounded with their encouragement and support, for which I am very thankful. A handful even agreed to be beta readers, and I greatly appreciated their thoughtful notes.

Finally, to my readers, thank you for being the best part of *The Legend of Valentine*. I hope you are moved to share this ancient love story with others. Together, let's help the over one billion people who celebrate Valentine's Day worldwide gain a deeper understanding of the holiday's origins, spirit, and history.

About the Author

Sheldon Collins is a distinguished storyteller whose career began in Hollywood as a screenwriter and director. His films, known for their compelling narratives and rich character development, have been featured on premium television and showcased in numerous film festivals, earning critical acclaim and a host of awards.

Collins' debut novel, *The Legend of Valentine*, marks the beginning of an exciting trilogy. This work delves into themes of adventure, love, and redemption, reflecting Collins' passion for intricate storytelling and vivid world-building.

He received his undergraduate degree in Rhetoric from UC Berkeley and a master's in Directing Film from the prestigious American Film Institute. His background in film greatly influences his writing, bringing a cinematic quality to his novels.

Residing in California with his wife and daughter, Collins finds inspiration in the natural beauty of the great outdoors. When not writing, he enjoys spending quality time with his family and friends, hiking, and exploring new landscapes.

With a blend of cinematic flair and literary depth, Collins continues to captivate audiences with his storytelling prowess.

facebook.com/authorsheldoncollins

instagram.com/sheldon_collins_author